DEAD END

GLOBE PUBLISHING GROUP
P.O. Box 27386
Lansing, Michigan 48909-7386

Correspondence regarding sales to individuals and book resellers within the continental USA should be directed to Globe Publishing, Lansing, Michigan.

USA Library of Congress information is available from Globe Publishing.

Front cover photo: Courtesy of Globe Marketing Group, Lansing, Michigan
Back cover photo of author: Steve Dean Photography, Lansing, Michigan

Note for Librarians: A cataloguing record for this book is available from Library and Archives Canada at www.collectionscanada.ca/amicus/index-e.html
ISBN 1-4120-8520-9

Book sales for North America and international:
Trafford Publishing, 6E-2333 Government St.,
Victoria, BC V8T 4P4 CANADA
phone 250 383 6864 (toll-free 1 888 232 4444)
fax 250 383 6804; email to orders@trafford.com
Book sales in Europe:
Trafford Publishing (UK) Limited, 9 Park End Street, 2nd Floor
Oxford, UK OX1 1HH UNITED KINGDOM
phone 44 (0) 1865 722 113 (local rate 0845 230 9601)
facsimile 44 (0) 1865 722 868; info.uk@trafford.com
Order online at:
trafford.com/06-275

10 9 8 7 6 5 4 3 2

DEAD END

James J. Pecora

TRAFFORD PUBLISHING
CANADA
&
GLOBE PUBLISHING GROUP
USA

DEDICATION

To my wife Gloria, and all my children and their spouses whose encouragement instilled within me the desire to complete this novel.

IN REMEMBRANCE

The Richard C. Robison Family.

PREFACE

DEAD END is a fictional novel based on a mass murder of a prominent Detroit, Michigan advertising executive and his entire family in June of 1968. The murders at this point in time remain unsolved. The names of persons, places and certain events have been changed in order to protect the innocent.

—The Author

CHAPTER 1

September - 1999
10:00 a.m.
Ottawa County, Michigan

Ray Randall sat comfortably behind the steering wheel of the late model Oldsmobile as he guided it along the winding, two-lane, county blacktop road. The leaves of the large oak and maple trees were just beginning to turn into their fall colors and lined the roadway that would lead him to his scheduled appointment. The mid-morning sun, surrounded by a pale blue sky highlighted the autumn colors that dotted the landscape. To his right, a split-rail wooden fence separated the roadway from the now harvested acres of blueberry bushes. The man who tended that blueberry orchard was the reason for Ray Randall's visit from Lansing. Randall's thoughts about the meeting concentrated on reasons far more important than the growing of blueberries. He lifted his foot off the accelerator and turned the steering wheel slowly guiding the sedan on to the gravel driveway. The driveway curved easily towards a large, white Victorian farmhouse that sat prominently on a hilltop a hundred yards in front of him. The farmhouse had recently been painted and the slim, dark green shutters appeared to squeeze the long narrow windows that were common to this type of structure built in the 1880's. The farmhouse stood in stark contrast to the updated, big red barn nearby which housed the farm equipment and other implements needed to make this land a prosperous and viable producer of blueberries.

Frank Stevens sat in his cane-backed rocking chair, gently moving it back and forth on the covered front porch of the farmhouse. A muted, creaking sound from the aged floorboards cut through the morning stillness as the rockers crossed over them. His steel-blue eyes watched the white car as it approached the house, finally coming to a stop. Stevens leaned forward in his rocker trying to get a better look at his expected visitor, but the bright sunlight reflected intently off the car windshield and prevented him from seeing the person inside. He rose slowly out of the rocker and the shadows of the porch into the sunlit area. His face was weathered, with bushy eyebrows that arched over a pair of gray eyes that were separated by a narrow, straight nose. His thin lips led to a firm, square jaw that filled out a pleasant looking face. Streaks of silver at his temples blended naturally with the crop of chestnut brown hair that covered his head. He pulled a red bandanna from the rear of his bib overalls and casually wiped away the small beads of perspiration that dotted his forehead. He reached for a pair of wire-rimmed glasses from his breast pocket and put them on. He let his eyes focus on the young man with rumpled and unruly dark hair sitting behind the steering wheel of the Oldsmobile. Randall cut the ignition and exited the car.

Stevens watched intently as the young man began to survey the vastness of the property that was spread out before him. The sunlight forced him to shield his eyes in order to get a better view. The casual style shirt, blue jeans and tennis shoes made him look more like a college student than a professional journalist. He turned towards Stevens who now stood at the edge of the porch and spoke. "Mr. Stevens, I presume?"

"That's right young man." Stevens answered. "You must be Ray Randall of the Lansing Journal."

"Yes sir, that's me," Randall answered as he slowly made his way towards the steps of the porch. "You have quite a place here," he added as he continued to look around.

"It's more than enough when the berries are in," Stevens replied.

Randall quickly moved up the porch steps and greeted his host with a firm handshake.

Stevens motioned for Randall to sit in the matching rocking chair next to his, as both of them sat down and began to easily move the chairs into a rocking motion.

"Thanks," Randall said as he settled himself into the seat. "I'm sure grateful to you for taking the time to discuss this murder case with me. When I told my editor that I was coming over to talk to you about it, he was more than skeptical about the whole thing. But, after I'd shown him some of the research that I've been working on, he thought that it might be a good idea to talk with you about it. If you had turned me down, I'm afraid that he would've told me to forget about the story and I really didn't want that to happen. So this interview means a lot to me."

Stevens looked at the young man carefully and smiled. "It's been such a long time, I'm not sure that I can recall all the details surrounding that case. Hell, I'm not sure that I can remember half of the people involved in it. I've put a lot of that stuff out of my mind since I left the State Police. But, I'll be happy to help you if I can."

"That's all I ask Mr. Stevens. I'd appreciate anything that you can tell me about the Rawlings case."

"I'll do my best."

"I really love your home, especially this porch setup you have," Randall continued as his eyes gave the freshly painted house a once over.

"Thank you," Stevens answered, "It's something that my wife Molly and I had dreamed about when I was working all those long hours with the State Police. Eventually, when I retired in 1980, both of us had saved enough money to make a pretty good down payment on this place. We've worked hard to develop the blueberry crop and our efforts have been rewarded every year since we've been here."

"Is your wife here?" Randall asked, looking over his shoulder towards the doorway that led into the house.

"No. I'm afraid not. She decided to go to Indiana to visit my son and daughter-in-law for the weekend. She said that the two of us should have the day to ourselves to discuss the case. I have to leave early tomorrow morning and head up to Ludington and do some fishing with a couple of friends of mine."

"That's fine, Mr. Stevens. I have a tape recorder in the car, along with a list of questions and some notes regarding specific areas of the case in order to save time. I think that will help us keep on target. If you'll excuse me, I'll go and get those things from the car." Randall rose from the rocker and walked quickly down the porch steps to the car.

"When you get all your stuff together, come right into the house," Stevens yelled out as he rose from his rocker. "It'll be more comfortable inside. How about a beer?"

"That sounds great Mr. Stevens. I'll be right in," Randall shouted back.

"Let's get rid of the formalities. You call me Frank and I'll call you Ray, all right?"

"You got it," Randall answered.

Stevens opened the screen door, went inside walking directly to the kitchen. He pulled open the refrigerator door and took out a couple of cold cans of Budweiser beer and set them on the kitchen table. Casually, he reached into the nearby cupboard and grabbed two small, clear glasses and set them down on the table. He sat himself into one of the sixties styled chrome-leg chairs and opened the tab from the top of one of the cans and poured the golden brew into his glass.

The sound of the screen door banging against the door jam made Stevens aware that Randall had entered the house. A moment later, Randall walked into the kitchen and placed a small tape recorder and extra blank tapes on the table.

He sat down in the chair at the opposite end of the table directly across from Stevens. "The woodwork in this house is fantastic Frank. How did you find such a place?" he asked, looking closely at the molding and trim work around the kitchen.

Stevens pushed a glass and can towards his guest. "About a year after I was stationed at the Grand Haven Post, I would pass by this area when I was on patrol. One day I saw a For Sale sign staked out on the front lawn. That night, I told Molly about it and we decided to make an offer as quickly as we could. We drove over here the next day, gave the owner our offer and he accepted it. Later he told us that his wife had died about six months before. He said he just had to leave this house. I guess there were too many memories for him here. He went to live with his daughter in California."

"It was kind of a lucky break for you and your wife," Randall said, sipping slowly on his beer from the can, pushing the glass aside.

"It sure was. Molly and I started right in cleaning up the place. I spent a lot of evenings refinishing the woodwork. Molly did the decorating. We had a professional guy come in to remodel the kitchen. This is where we spend most of our time, right here at this table."

"It's a beautiful view from here," Randall said, his dark eyes looking out through the kitchen's big bay window next to him. The landscape revealed numerous rows of blueberry vines that were dormant, but would produce fruit the following spring.

"You bet. Fruits gone now. Had a good year."

Both men gazed out the window looking at the vines and tall trees in the distance that separated the land from the horizon.

"I guess we'd better get down to business Frank, or I may have to go fishing with you in order to finish this project," Randall said jokingly.

"I think your right. I'm ready when you are." Stevens answered, pouring more beer into his glass.

Randall moved the tape recorder closer to Stevens as he removed a small bundle of 3x5 cards from his shirt pocket. " When you're ready Frank, I'll just push the start button and you can start talking about the Rawlings murder case."

"That's fine with me" Stevens answered.

Randall inserted a tape into the recorder. "First, let me provide an introduction. When I'm finished, I'll point to you. Just start at the beginning with as much detail as you can recall."

Stevens waited patiently as the reporter marked the tape with his introduction, then Randall pointed at Stevens to begin. The tape wound slowly, from spool to spool.

Frank Stevens pushed back the fog of time and closed his eyes. Little by little, he began to recall the famous Rawlings murder case that happened over thirty years before. The year was 1968.

CHAPTER 2

June, 1968
Detroit, Michigan

The State of Michigan, like the rest of America in the summer of 1968 was a smoldering tinderbox of unrest, racial turmoil and discontentment. The City of Detroit seemed to reflect much of the nation as a whole. The city had become a war ground for different political ideas, racial equality, white and black supremacy groups and a multitude of other social and political issues. The forces of good and evil had invaded both major political camps. The constant notes of discord, from politicians to the everyday working man and woman made it difficult to resolve important problems that had been tearing at America's soul for a long time.

The Vietnam War was the birthplace of that discord. It was America's first 'Television War' and the pictures it produced created distinct divisions among many groups in America. Adults distrusted the youth. Students distrusted everyone and everything. People of different ethnic and racial backgrounds were at odds over their status in society. The professional white-collar worker and the traditional blue-collar worker appeared to be worlds apart on what was "true patriotism." Every political decision, regardless of ones party affiliation, was fodder for the masses. The smallest incident could explode into a full-scale confrontation between citizens and law enforcement. Riots were commonplace in many of the large metropolitan centers of the United States. In many cases, the riots were so severe that the National Guard had to be called out in order to guarantee 'domestic tranquility' and to secure the safety and well being for the majority of American citizens.

Michigan wasn't any different than the rest of the country and Detroit was a city in constant chaos. No one in the public arena appeared to have a solution to counteract this type of internal disrespect breeding within our nation. Riots and confrontations were a brand new concept to political and educational institutions. Detroit's future would be forever marred because of what the rest of America saw on its nightly television news programs. While buildings burned, snipers on rooftops would shoot at the police and fire personnel who were trying to preserve or protect those buildings. Many cities had sections or neighborhoods that resembled Berlin Germany at the end of World War II.

It was out of place for America. A nation that had provided immigrants from every part of the globe an opportunity to live the American dream was now under siege by the very children of these immigrants. The sons and daughters of slaves had reached an impasse with the American promise of equality and hope for a better future. Turmoil and hatred, like waves of an untamed sea, pounded at all of the traditional establishments and institutions. Civil discourse and other standard codes of conduct were abandoned. These conditions would eventually tear apart the very fabric of the nation.

In its place would be created many different and volatile segments of American society and in the end, this disorder would erode the basic foundations for a number of established and honored institutions. Many, would never recover.

On April 4, 1968 Martin Luther King, Jr., while taking a leisurely walk with some friends and other civil rights associates on the balcony of a second-rate motel in Memphis, Tennessee, was gunned down by a white supremacist named James Earl Ray.

Two months later, on June 6, 1968 as millions of people watched on television, Senator Robert F. Kennedy was shot in the head and killed by an Arab extremist named Sirhan-Sirhan in the kitchen of the Sheridan Hotel in Los Angeles, California. Just minutes before, Mr. Kennedy had been voted the winner in that state's Democratic Presidential primary. Now he lay dead in a pool of blood in the hotel kitchen. Many Americans believed that the United States of America was spinning out of control and had finally 'gone to hell in a hand basket.' No one seemed to know how or when it would end. Most Americans thought this great country was headed towards total destruction.

It was during this Age of Aquarius, that one of the most brutal and despicable crimes of the century was about to occur. It would be far from big city lights and not about famous people. It was about a family, who, on the surface appeared to be the all-American family. It turned out not to be true.

CHAPTER 3

June 25, 1968
7: 30 p.m.
Thunder Point, Michigan

Winding its way northward out of the summer resort village of Harbor Springs, a black asphalt road named M-31 weaves its way towards another resort area called Thunder Point. The road is shadowed by an abundant number of tall pine, maple and birch trees that line both sides of the narrow, two-lane highway.

The State of Michigan has rightly designated it as a scenic route for travelers headed to the famous Mackinac Bridge that connects the lower and upper peninsulas of Michigan.

Thunder Point is nestled along the northwestern coastal edge of Lake Michigan and is a quiet, out-of-the way summer vacation area, announced only by a weather beaten wood sign. Each year, it provides a number of well-to-do families from the Midwest, a convenient getaway from the hot and muggy days of July and August. The families come mainly from big cities like Detroit, Chicago and Cleveland to enjoy the cool breezes and fresh air that are part of the northern Michigan mystique. Shortly after World War II, many people of wealth and influence came to the area during the summer to find rest and relaxation. Eventually, many became convinced that building a cabin or cottage would be their way of securing a place for their retirement years. With each succeeding year, construction of the cottages began to cover the rolling hillsides and sandy bluffs that overlooked the turquoise waters of Lake Michigan.

A half-mile beyond the village limit sign, sits the only significant landmark in the village. Located on the west side of the road, an old-fashion general store, painted a bright, fire engine red with white trim acts like a large magnet in order to serve the summer residents with a variety of food items and other merchandise. It is a convenient way for the area inhabitants to survive in this out of the way vacation spot. The store also acts as a postal substation and is the main center of activity from Memorial Day through late September.

A stones throw away, to the north of the general store, is a partially hidden dirt road that connects the blacktop highway to another gravel road known as Lakeshore Drive. Lakeshore Drive is the main access road to the cabins and cottages located along the Lake Michigan beachfront. A long plateau of solid land, perched slightly above the lake's shoreline, allows a number of cottages to exist, each one well hidden from the other by cluster's of birch, pine and aspen trees that surround them.

Northern Michigan has always been an area of legend and mystery. Long before the missionary zeal of Jesuit priests who came to the upper regions of the Great Lakes to expand the word of Christianity, native tribes had a variety of traditions that interfered with the missionary objectives of the priests sent to convert the native population to Catholicism. This expansion of ideas and worship by men of the cloth created new conflicts between different Indian tribes and the continued immigration of white settlers.

The spilling of blood was a natural result of the strain caused by those who had already established themselves in this wilderness and by those who came to teach them the words of Christianity and carve out a space for themselves. This was not a land for the squeamish, but for men and women of vision, skill and toughness that would help them survive in America's eventual march westward.

Gray, overcast clouds produced a thin mist of rain as daylight lingered on the horizon refusing to let nightfall overtake it. In the midst of this gloomy twilight, at the north end of Lakeshore Drive, a picturesque and well-built log cabin style cottage was nestled among a variety of tall timbers. A manicured lawn, with newly planted flowers, surrounded the fairy tale type abode and it reflected the care and pride of its owners.

Inside the cabin, each of the six members of the Richard C. Rawlings family sat patiently reading, writing, playing cards or listening to records. In the next few minutes, their world and the world of those close to them would change forever.

A gentle breeze pushed its way inland along the beach and wooded shoreline. The rustling of the needles in the pine trees and stirring of the small leaves on the nearby birch trees made brushing and slapping sounds against the trunk and limbs of the trees. In the distance, the loud knocking of a woodpecker's beak on the hollow trunk of a dead hardwood tree echoed throughout the wooded area.

In the dense, wooded area north of the Rawlings cottage, the muffled sound of human footsteps crushed the small twigs and leaves lying on the forest floor. The animals in the forest were the first to hear and smell the intruder and their natural instinct for survival made them scatter deeper into the woodlands.

A human figure moves towards the small clearing adjacent to the Rawlings cottage. He circles the clearing and moves forward keeping his body low and close to the ground, while an observant pair of dark eyes pierce the holes of his pullover wool hood. The camouflaged design of his military fatigues permit his body to blend with the natural surroundings of the terrain making him invisible to the untrained eye. Wearing tight deerskin gloves, the long fingers of his right hand hold firmly to a .22-caliber Armalite, semi-automatic rifle. Gently, he presses the safety mechanism of the rifle to the off position making it ready to fire its deadly clip of 12 rounds.

The fading light of day makes the stalker apprehensive as his eyes search intensely for any movement that would interfere with his intended objective. He sees none. The green leaves of a nearby Poplar tree begin to dance like little summer fans as heavy gusts of wind challenge the new spring growth of leaves on the tree branches. The figure stops behind a mature oak tree rooted next to a waist-high honeysuckle bush in front of the Rawlings cottage. The natural cover provides him the best location for what he is about to do. Quietly and quickly he settles himself into position directly behind the oak tree and kneels down on his right knee. He inhales deeply the damp, muggy air in an attempt to steady and calm his nerves.

The misty rain is a minor nuisance as he wipes his eyes with the back of one of his gloved hands. From this spot, he can see each of the targets inside the Rawlings cottage. Mentally, he tells himself that he needs to be patient. His mind whispers that he must be calm and confident before he can rise up and begin to spew death from the open end of the small rifle. He needs only to pull the trigger to make it happen.

The interior of the cottage is well lit by three standing floor lamps placed throughout the small living area. The bright lights offset the natural darkness created by the dense forest outside, and the thickness of the overcast and darkening clouds.

Richard C. Rawlings Sr. is a forty-two year old, distinguished looking man with chiseled, but refined facial features. He sits quietly in his leather lounge chair in the southwest corner of the family cottage. He is the owner of a successful advertising agency in Detroit, but is best known for publishing a monthly entertainment and arts magazine called 'The Director.' The magazine serves the high society set in the metropolitan Detroit area and is considered a successful and popular publication. It features stories about Detroit actors, artists and other theater professionals who have made an impact within the local arts community or who have been fortunate enough to go on to the bright lights of New York and Hollywood. The magazine staff is very professional and the articles are well written. Mr. Rawlings uses the forum to write editorial viewpoints that are mainly conservative and are directed toward Detroit's political governing bodies. As the creator and publisher of this prominent magazine, he is extremely proud of its acceptance among the Motor City elite. The magazine's wide circulation allows him to rub elbows with some of the most powerful movers and shakers in the business and social community, while at the same time, fulfilling a deep personal need for notoriety among the established intellectual set.

On this day however, within the comfort of his vacation cottage, he sits quietly in the large lounge chair, studiously calculating different sets of numbers on a legal pad. Ben Franklin style glasses are perched on the end of his nose as he continues to add and subtract the numbers on the pad. Mr. Rawlings, who is an accomplished artist by profession, would have been more comfortable sketching a face or a human figure, but now his thoughts are centered on wealth and long-term financial security. Briefly, his blue eyes glance to his left in order to look out the big picture window and view the beach and the grandeur of Lake Michigan. The lake is in a turbulent, restless mood and the agitation of the early summer cold water, produces a deep, blue-green color with frothing whitecaps. The tremendous force of the rolling waves crash against the large boulders that extend out from the sandy shoreline and send water spraying in all directions along the beach. Mr. Rawlings is content with his life and returns to the pad and continues to work on the numbers he has carefully jotted down. From time to time, he looks up and stares at the open doorway at the opposite end of the cottage. It is obvious that Mr. Rawlings is expecting someone to arrive at any moment. That particular doorway is the main entrance to the cabin from Lakeshore Drive.

The gravel drive is just fifty feet from the front of the cottage doorway and passes within a few feet of where the silhouette of a human figure kneels silently.

A wood framed, screen door protects the family from the spring crop of black files swirling outside, while the late afternoon rain, together with the lingering mist, has created a humid stuffiness within the cottage.

In order to relieve the humidity, Mr. Rawlings's has elected to open the jalousie windows above the kitchen sink located at the backend of the cottage. The window is approximately twelve feet to the left of where he is sitting.

This form of ventilation allows the air from the lake to filter through the cottage under a controlled condition and exit normally through the screened main doorway. Earlier in the day, Mr. Rawlings had made the decision not to open the kitchen door along the back wall of the cottage because the cross draft generated by the gusting winds would be too strong to control and would blow over anything in its path within the cottage.

The hands of the wall clock over the fireplace show the time to be 8:07 p.m. Mr. Rawling's glances at his Rolex watch to confirm the time.

The interior lights create a soft, warm glow within the connected and open living areas of the cottage. Mr. Rawlings looks to his immediate left and observes his nineteen-year old son, Richard Jr., the oldest child, playing double solitaire with his seventeen-year old brother Gary. They are sitting at the wood, picnic style kitchen table a few feet away. Gary is sitting across from his older brother, looking at the cards being dealt.

To Mr. Rawlings immediate right and kneeling on the floor next to him, is his twelve-year old son Randy, the youngest of the three boys. Randy's current interest is music and he is studiously looking at a number of LP record albums that he is holding in his arms, trying to determine which one appeals to him. He wants to put a few albums in the stereo unit console in front of him. The modern stereo unit is set against the wall and next to the floor to ceiling stone fireplace.

An unmistakable look of pride and affection appears on Mr. Rawlings face as he looks diagonally across the room at his daughter Susan. She is sitting comfortably and quietly on a futon type sofa that has been positioned along a paneled wall. Susan Rawlings is eight years old and is the pride and joy of her father. She is the only daughter in this male dominated household. Her brown hair is cut in bangs, reflecting the style of the day, while her round, innocent looking face is dotted with two, large brown eyes, separated by a pert nose. The smooth skin is scattered with a face full of freckles and accent her toothless smile of her missing two front teeth. She plays intently with a new toy doll and looks comfortable and happy. A new yellow dress and shiny black patent leather shoes that cover her delicate white stockings are part of a new wardrobe. Her spit-polished appearance suggests that she is dressed to go somewhere important.

Directly across from Susan, near the main doorway, sits Shirley Rawlings. Mrs. Rawlings is forty years old and a dedicated wife and mother. She is sitting quietly in an overstuffed rocker, which glides back and forth as she flips the pages of a current issue of Better Homes and Garden's magazine. She appears to be trying to visualize some new ideas for decorating the summer cottage. Her fine and delicate features reveal the look of a once startling and beautiful high school beauty queen. Unlike her opinionated husband, she is a reserved and soft-spoken person who does everything in her power to avoid controversy. She is a woman of confidence and intelligence, who for the most part has accepted at this point in her life, to be a supporting wife and full-time mother to four beautiful children.

Mr. Rawlings jots down another figure on his pad, then pauses. His eyes narrow as he pushes the pair of Ben Franklin glasses closer to his eyes. He attempts to focus on the fuzzy outline of a shadowy figure that appears beyond the screen door, to be rising out of the honeysuckle bush in the front yard. The outline is that of a human figure, but the mist conceals its true identity.

Richard Rawlings tilts his head back slightly so that he can look directly through the top part of his glasses. He wants to see who the shadowy figure outside might be. He may have heard the sound of the first shot as it hit him just above his heart and below the collarbone.

Chapter 4

8:30 p.m.
The Killings

The assassin moves swiftly from his spot behind the tree, skirting the honeysuckle bush and approaches the cottage. He stops. He's about twenty feet in front of and slightly to the right of the main doorway. A sidelight of one-foot square glass panels to the right of the doorway has allowed the killer an expanded view of the movements by the people inside the cottage. He knows that his first shot has hit its mark and has left a small hole in one of the glass panels. Again, he takes aim and pulls the trigger a second time. The shouting inside the cabin muffles the plinking sound of glass being penetrated by another projectile. The second shot passes over Mr. Rawlings left shoulder and burrows into the soft padding of the lounge chair.

Randy Rawlings, reacting to the sounds of both the first and second shots, and the painful groans of his father, stands up from his kneeling position on the rug in front of the stereo. The LP records tumble from his hands and fall to the floor. His instincts move him in the direction of his wounded father. As he does so, a third bullet has left the barrel of the rifle and unknowingly, Randy Rawlings moves directly into the killer's line of fire. Randy takes the third shot meant for his father in his upper back, just to the left of his spine. His last vision on earth is the sight of blood covering his father's chest and turning the white polo shirt, crimson. He falls limp to the hardwood floor. Noise and confusion rings out within the cottage walls.

Little Susan, who had been sitting patiently on the sofa, playing with her toy dolls, bolts towards her mother immediately after the second shot. The third shot that will penetrate Randy's back passes over Susan's head as she momentarily stops in the middle of the room. The quick report of a fourth shot grazes the top of her skull as the bullet speeds onward and rips into the floorboard at the feet of her injured and immovable father. Susan tumbles to the floor as blood trickles from her scalp. She is not dead, but wounded and unconscious.

Shirley Rawlings at the sound of the first shot had looked up from her magazine and turned her head towards her husband. His painful groan brought her to a full state of anxiety. Her initial instincts suggested that her husband was having trouble breathing as she watched the legal pad drop to the floor and both his hands grab at his chest. She rose quickly from her rocker, then hears the second shot whistle past her and hit the back of her husband's chair. She does not see her daughter Susan coming towards her, but hears the third shot ring out and watches with disbelief as Randy falls to the floor. She moves hastily forward to help her husband when she hears the fourth shot and turns to see Susan fall to the floor.

In the blink of an eye, what had been a warm and tranquil scene within the cottage is now one of distraught and incomprehension. Shirley Rawlings becomes paralyzed by uncertainty. Her body shuts down and her appearance becomes like a statue and she cannot move.

When the sound of the second shot had echoed within the cottage, the two older boys, Richard Jr. and Gary realized that their father was hurt and in a great deal of pain. They reacted quickly, bolting from the kitchen table towards their father. The playing cards they had been using for the game of double-solitaire, fall haphazardly on the table and to the floor.

Young Richard sees blood on his father's shirt and hears the sound of the third shot as both he and Gary turn to see Randy fall to the floor.

When the fourth shot had tumbled Susan's body near Randy on the living room floor, Young Richard appears to comprehend more than the others as to what is happening and possibly why. His eyes reflect that he knows that the family is under attack. Instinctively, he tries to bring some type of control to the situation. It has been less than a minute from the time that the initial shot had been fired.

Young Richard yells at Gary to get the .22 caliber rifle from their parent's bedroom at the back of the cottage. In the bedlam, Gary reacts slowly. His eyes reflect his fear and uncertainty about what is happening around him. He sees blood pooling beside the body of his younger brother Randy, while his sister is sprawled, motionless on the floor. A dark red liquid covers her brown hair, turning it into a matted clump. His brain registers his older brother's command, but he is petrified and his legs feel like two pillars, unable to move. Anticipating that the next bullet is for him, his body has shut down from terror!

A thick, rising mist outside the cabin doorway provides an additional veil for the assassin as a fifth shot whistles past young Richard's ear. The bullet pierces the knotty pine paneling at the back wall directly behind his father's chair. The oldest son of the Rawlings family knows that they are in a life and death struggle as he watches his mother try to regain her composure.

Mrs. Rawlings has knelt down beside Randy and Susan and tries to comfort them in whatever way that she can.

Young Richard screams a second time at Gary to get moving and go for the rifle. Gary reluctantly obeys and cautiously moves forward. His legs brush against the front of the futon sofa along the wall where his sister had been playing with her dolls. There are different body parts of the dolls scattered across the floor. Quickly, he turns left through an open archway and moves down the short, narrow hallway. The hallway leads to his parent's bedroom at the back corner of the cottage. His objective is the .22 caliber rifle tucked away in a corner of the bedroom clothes closet.

Richard Jr. remembers the handgun that his father owns and keeps in his bedroom dresser. He shouts to Gary. "Get dad's Beretta too! It's in the dresser!"

In the surreal moment of this assault on the Rawlings family, the killer stands poised outside the cabin. The rifle is raised to his shoulder and pressed hard against his right cheek, but he does not move. He is like an ornamental statue, composed and ready to shoot at anything that might move within the cabin. For some unknown reason he remains stationary and stops shooting.

Shirley Rawlings, seeing blood and death around her, has become more confused as to what is happening and why. She cannot find a way to stop the flow of blood coming from these two young bodies she once gave life to. Her heart is desperate and her mind is frantic!

Young Richard quickly understands that he can't do any more for his father and moves swiftly along the same path that Gary had taken to get to the back bedroom. He mumbles some words of encouragement to his mother as he passes by her, his hand touching her shoulder. He moves quickly down the hallway towards the back bedroom. He prays to God for help, while at the same time hoping that Gary has found and loaded the guns. As he arrives at the bedroom doorway, he sees Gary fumbling around through the mass of hanging clothes in the closet, trying to get at the rifle. Cold sweat begins to overtake Richard's hands and brow. Momentarily, he ponders as to why the figure outside has not entered the cottage and the shooting has stopped. He tries to think clearly and put his mind in order. He wishes he were stronger.

In the initial attack, no one remembers to close and lock the front door! It is a fatal mistake. The only thing between the remaining Rawlings family members and a cold-blooded killer is a wood framed, summer screen door. And it is neither locked nor latched!

Outside, the killer sheds his temporary slumber and realizes that he must move rapidly before some form of retaliation can be directed at him from inside the cottage. He had observed Richard Jr. heading towards the front screen door, before turning and going down the hallway. He had paused his assault, thinking that the young man was coming for him and may have had his own weapon. He regains his composure and rushes forward towards the unlocked screen door. His large hand grabs the door handle and pulls it open. He enters the cottage knowing that he must kill all of them before they have a chance to identify or eliminate him!

Shirley Rawlings is kneeling on the floor still trying to help little Susan and Randy as they lay bleeding and dying. Incantations to the Almighty seem to be coming from her lips when she hears the sound of a stretching, screen door spring. She looks up and turns her head to the right. The outline of a human figure appears inside the cabin. It's him! She has no time to ask why or for mercy. He raises his rifle quickly and pulls the trigger. The bullet hits her in the right side of the skull, just in back and above the right ear. She slumps slowly downward and settles next to Susan and Randy. She dies instantly.

Out of the corner of his right eye, the killer sees movement at the end of the dark hallway. The filtered light of dusk has permeated the corner bedroom windows and in turn has outlined the body of Richard Jr. standing at the end of the hallway.

It's a target the killer cannot miss. He raises his rifle and takes aim down the barrel through the peep sight. His finger slowly squeezes the trigger.

Richard Rawlings, Jr. when he arrived at the bedroom straddled the doorway as he talked to Gary, leaving his back partially exposed to the main living room. He yells again at Gary to hurry.

A sudden silence fills the cottage. A split second later, he hears the sound of the screen door slam against the door jam and another rifle shot rings out! His heart stops! He knows the killer is inside the cottage. Under his breath, he mumbles some form of prayer begging for just a few more moments of time! He turns his head to look back down the hallway towards the living room. He has exposed the right side of his face and sees the shadowy outline of a human figure and the orange flash. The hourglass of time has run out for Richard Rawlings Jr. The .22-caliber; hollow-point bullet enters the right temple of Richard's skull and his body turns as his knees buckle, then drops headfirst into his parent's bedroom. His feet and legs extend out into the hallway as his torso rests just inside the bedroom door archway.

The rapport of the shot makes Gary look towards the doorway as he continues to fumble through the clothing to find the rifle. He sees his older brother drop into the bedroom, blood gushing from the head wound. Gary becomes even more terrified and his nerves are shattered! He rushes from the closet to the dresser hoping to get the Beretta pistol and load it before the killer comes for him. He pulls open the top dresser drawer and spots the Beretta and the ammo clip. His hands are shaking so much that he cannot load the pistol properly. His mind is racing. He must hurry! He throws the pistol and clip on the bed and rushes back to the closet to find the rifle. He pushes the remaining hanging clothes away. He hopes the rifle is loaded, but he is not sure. He sees the rifle in the corner and grabs it. The magazine clip is missing! It's not loaded! He sees the loaded clip on the edge of the shelf above him. He holds the rifle by the barrel and extends his right arm out to grab the clip and load the rifle. For a split second, his mind prays that this is all a bad dream.

In the darken hallway, the killer, moves slowly and cautiously along the knotty pine wall. He sees Richard's body lying still on the floor and moves closer towards the bedroom doorway.

Gary's senses are tuned to an ultimate pitch. The soft sounds of the killer's cautious footsteps are coming closer! Then silence!

The killer and Gary appear to move in slow motion. Gary looks over his right shoulder at the doorway behind him as he tries to insert the magazine clip into the open chamber of the rifle. It's too late!

The shadowy figure of death swings his body into the bedroom, raises his rifle and fires in the same motion. The bullet hits Gary in the middle of his back and spins his body around to face his executioner. In the thunderbolt of eternity, Gary thinks he recognizes the assassin! The pullover mask cannot conceal his identity from him, but before Gary can curse or yell out to condemn his attacker to eternal damnation, the orange flash erupts from the barrel of the killer's rifle. The long, silver projectile penetrates Gary's cheekbone and explodes in his brain. He falls backward and lifelessly to the floor.

Gary Rawlings, his short life of seventeen years is over. His inanimate body is stretched out on the bloody carpet of the bedroom. The glazed stare in his eyes and the bloodied face reflect the horrible death that has consumed his youthful body.

The killer moves gradually towards Gary's lifeless body and glances at the rifle lying on the floor beside his victim. He lets it stay there. His eyes notice the .25-caliber Beretta on the bed with the ammo clip. He stuffs them both into the pocket of his military fatigues and walks out of the bedroom. As he steps over Richard's body, he fails to notice the footprint he leaves in the blood soaked carpet. He proceeds back down the hallway to the main living area.

Pools of blood are accumulating on the hardwood floor from the assaulted bodies. The killer ignores it. His ears pick up a slight, but pitiful moan. It's coming from Mr. Rawlings Sr. He is motionless and slumped over sideways in his chair. The new white polo shirt and silk gray slack are completely soaked with blood. The killer looks at him. The dark eyes behind the mask reveal the venom of hatred that is in him. He is overcome with an uncontrollable rage. He notices a carpenters hammer near the fireplace on top of a small pile of firewood. The wood has been stacked neatly against the side of the stone hearth. The killer calmly walks over to the woodpile and picks up the clawed tool.

The handsome and prosperous advertising executive from Detroit, who, only minutes before had been content and satisfied with his life and surroundings, was somehow clinging to the last thread of life. Whatever plans he had been contemplating for himself and the future of his family were slowly fading away, like the life ebbing from his body. The lids of his eyes narrowed as they tried to discern again, the foggy outline of the bestial human figure moving towards him. It made no difference.

The backhand motion by the killer drives the cold steel hammer into the right side of Rawlings temple and rocks his skull. Blood splatters against the walls and on the picture window as the lake's waves pound against the beach below. The killer's anger becomes more violent as he swings the hammer again, in a forehand motion that smashes against the left eye socket of the mutilated figure before him. Blood engulfs the hammer's head and sprays over the stone fireplace. The killer flips the hammer on the floor near the legs of the picnic-style kitchen table. Blood drips on the playing cards as the handle of the hammer rests against the backdoor. This savage is the devil in human form as he walks over to the three bodies spread out before him on the living room floor.

Little Susan begins to stir; the concussion of the bullet that had grazed her scalp is starting to wear off. Like a hunter who sees a reptile at his feet, the killer uses the butt of his rifle to give her a forceful blow to the forehead. It leaves a half-moon cut in the soft white flesh. The force of the blow cracks her skull. It is not enough for this marauder. He shoots her between the eyes.

He pauses to take a deep breath, then surveys the death he has inflicted upon this family. A sense of power falsely fortifies his body. Instinctively, his mind becomes sharp with tactical thoughts. Like a panther moving silently and swiftly, his movements now become quick and deliberate.

At the entrance to the hallway that leads to the back bedrooms, the killer looks into the first bedroom on his right. From the doorway, he can see an open suitcase half-full of young men's clothing with a camera sitting on top of it. It doesn't interest him and he continues down the hallway a second time. He feels the small compact Italian-made pistol in his pocket. He approaches the back bedroom where Richard and Gary are lying prone in their own pools of blood. Again, he steps over the body of Richard and pulls the small handgun out of his pocket. It is a powerful and deadly weapon. He checks the gun's chamber and the clip. He racks the Beretta so it's ready to fire. There are nine bullets, eight in the clip and one in the chamber. It is more than enough to complete his morbid task. He moves towards the lifeless body of Gary near the closet, the motionless blue eyes looking straight up towards the ceiling.

The killer reaches down and fires the first round into Gary's forehead. The body lurches slightly then lies completely still. He moves over to Richard Jr. and fires a round into the back of the skull of an already lifeless body. He pauses for a moment, takes a deep breath and closes his eyes.

The bloody scene reminds him of an earlier time, but he cannot recall exactly when. He walks down the hallway and returns to the main living area when suddenly he sees Randy Rawlings trying to raise his upper body from the floor. He is alive and trying to lift himself up! The killer moves quickly into position directly over the arched body and aims the sight at the end of the polished barrel of the Beretta at the back of Randy's head, then pulls the trigger. The young body falls gently to the floor and his second chance at life has been denied. The last and youngest of the Rawlings sons is dead.

The killer realizes that he must confirm that everyone is dead before he leaves the cottage. He looks at Mrs. Rawlings, then at little Susan. He has seen death many times before and discerns that they are beyond any human help. He moves again towards the lifeless body of Richard Rawlings, Sr. and for some diabolical reason doesn't trust the motionless body before him. He is not confident that the bullet to the chest and the two crushing blows to the skull have ended the life in that body. He grabs Mr. Rawlings by the wrists and pulls him forward off the chair, dragging the body over to the hallway that leads to the back bedrooms. Pulling the Beretta out of his pocket, the killer places the barrel against Mr. Rawlings right temple and pulls the trigger. To his ears, the sound of gunfire is like a distant echo. The smell of gunpowder enters his nostrils and burns the back of his throat. The cordite taste in his mouth brings him back to reality.

The small, round hole just above the right ear of Mr. Rawlings is barely visible because of the curly, salt and pepper hair surrounding it. It brings a slight smile to the face of this madman! Outside, total darkness is quickly approaching. The killer turns off the interior lights, except for the small lamp sitting on a corner table, behind the rocker where Mrs. Rawlings had been reading.

Overcast clouds begin to part and a golden hue emerges along the lake's horizon. The light filters through the large picture window that faces the lake and fills the cottage with its unrestrained glow. Nature's final evening performance commences as the rim of the sun hangs onto the horizon and leaves a sparkling hue on the choppy, blue waters of Lake Michigan.

Ink type reflections begin to dance inside the cabin and small, black silhouettes swirl on its walls. The stillness of the forest provides a silence that seems unnatural. To the unknowing ear it appears to be another quiet evening along Michigan's northern shoreline.

The terrible truth of what has happened within these walls is hidden from the outside world. The executioner ignores the carnage that surrounds him. He is totally alone with his thoughts and deeds, but he has no sense of remorse or sorrow for what has taken place.

The constant sound of the waves crashing on the beach brings the killer back to reality from the shadows of the massacre he has just committed. The lake has become more restless, producing a foaming wash that cleans the sandy beach. Inside the cottage, scarlet trails of blood zigzag across the wooden floor. It is a red roadmap of death.

The sparkle of a two-carat diamond ring on the ring finger of Mrs. Rawlings attracts the killer's curiosity. He looks at her youthful body lying still and peaceful next to her daughter. A small pool of blood separates them. He reaches down and slips the ring from her finger and puts it into his pocket but leaves her wedding band in place.

Suddenly, he hears human voices outside the cabin. They're muffled, but close enough for him to hear a mixture of words and other sounds. He pauses and keeps his body still. The voices sound as if they are coming closer to the cottage. He squats down and moves closer to the window near the rocking chair and avoiding the light of the lamp as much as he can. Cautiously, he moves the curtain slightly aside in order to leave a narrow opening that allows him to peer out the window at the yard where only moments before, he had commenced his rampage and slaughter of the Rawlings family. The pores on his forehead push out small beads of sweat, but are absorbed by the pullover mask. He reaches up with his left hand and with one quick motion removes the mask and stuffs it into the pocket of his military field jacket. He remains still as the cool air pushes against his uncovered face. He moves into the corner and crouches down just below the windowsill. His eyes search for the cause of the commotion being made outside. The corner darkness helps keep his face concealed as he moves the curtain aside even more, in an effort to observe the people who are carrying on the conversation a short distance from the cabin. He cannot see them. Just as quickly as the voices had arrived, they now fade away. He moves slowly towards the screen door entrance and quietly closes the interior door. He ponders for a moment, realizing that if one of the members of the Rawlings family had closed that door immediately after the first or second shots, he would have been doomed. He would never have had access to the cottage and would have had to retreat back into the forest. He would have been the target of a concentrated manhunt by the police and probably caught.

For the first time he realizes that he had allowed the interior door to remain open during the entire period of his assault on the family. The thought makes his nerves fragile and he begins to feel sick to his stomach. He begins to take slow, deep breaths and it quickly passes. He knows that he must conceal the bodies. He stops to think where he can dispose of them. He cannot take them out into the woods or drag them down to the beach and dump them in the lake. If he attempts to do that and someone sees him, he would be forced to kill again. He moves deliberately from room to room grabbing at the drapes and pulling them shut.

The jalousie window over the kitchen sink and the picture window that was next to Mr. Rawlings chair do not have any drapes or curtains. Because those windows face the lake and the beach, the killer doesn't feel threatened and leaves them uncovered, but closes the jealousy window. Briefly he pauses in the middle of the living room and notices a slight bulge in the back, pants pocket of Mr. Rawlings. He walks over to the lifeless body and reaches down and pulls out a brown leather wallet containing a little over $700 dollars in cash. He shoves the money in his own pants pocket and throws the wallet down on top of the body. He turns back into the living room and notices another suitcase next to the wall near the kitchen. The suitcase is full sized and is closed. It matches the one in the front bedroom sitting on the bed. He decides he will take this one and open it later. He wants to leave the cabin immediately, but he must do whatever he can to cover up his hideous crime. He grabs Randy's arms and drags his body from the middle of the living room area into the bedroom hallway. He piles him on top of his dead father. Next, he grabs little Susan by her wrists and pulls her along the floor, eventually dumping her next to her battered and dead father.

The new, brightly colored yellow dress is crumpled, soaked and smeared with blood. The brand new white anklet stockings and black patent shoes are also covered with blood. It is a cruel reminder of the trip she was going to take with the rest of her family. Now that trip would be eternal. The killer leaves her lying face up.

The only body left in the open room is that of Mrs. Rawlings. She lays rigid on her left side with her cheek touching the floor. In this position, she has inadvertently trapped the blood from her head wound and it has coagulated on the wooden floor. Some of the blood on the right side of her face has trickled down past her ear and wrapped itself around her pale, white throat like a scarlet necklace. The killer grabs her ankles and pulls her towards the front corner of the cottage near the rocking chair. As he moves her body towards the chair, her skirt rises slowly upward. He continues to pull her towards the front corner of the cottage. With the bottom half of her body uncovered, the killer sees the delicate lace undergarments and the smooth white flesh of Mrs. Rawlings' shapely body. One of the beige colored, high-heeled shoes has fallen off her right foot onto the floor. He picks it up and tosses it onto the nearby lounge chair.

The killer removes one of his deerskin gloves and feels the warm flesh. The sight of her partially naked body begins to arouse sexual emotions within him. The sight of her silk white panties and tight-fitting girdle pushes his evil mind to even more bizarre thoughts and perversions. He wants to have sex with the woman he has just shot and killed! His mind rationalizes how easy it would be. There would be no resistance. It would be different. Yes. He will do it! His arousal starts to peak! He pulls the folded sports knife from his back pocket, opens it and let's the saw-tooth blade easily cut through the elastic straps that hold her nylon stockings. Gently, he rolls the stockings down around her ankles.

He can feel the softness of her flesh. He pulls the girdle and white panties down slowly, letting them rest just above the nylons. His excitement grows as he looks at the half-naked figure in front of him. She cannot resist him now, or can she? He stares at her again. The initial excitement gives way to an internal fear. It's the fear of losing his power. He's afraid that by violating this dead woman's body, it will drain from him, his precious bodily fluids. The sudden fear of losing his manhood and making him weak and confused makes him retreat. He swiftly turns away and mentally pushes his evil desires back into the darker recesses of his mind. He moves quickly away from the naked body.

The final shade of daylight is a brushstroke of pink against a light blue sky. Death shadows begin to surround the killer's spirit. He feels his own legs losing their rigidity and suspects that the spirit of Mrs. Rawlings dead body is tugging at his ankles.

Darkness has engulfed the area and the killer needs to make sure that nothing of his is left behind that could identify him. He becomes more apprehensive that someone outside may see the light from the corner table lamp, but he must leave it on to see what he is doing. He hopes that the heavy drapes will conceal both his movements and the light from the corner lamp. The harsh light from the lamp produces jagged, outlined forms and shadows while at the same time creating eerie silhouettes on the ceiling and walls of the cottage. Without warning, the sound of the refrigerator motor comes on, quickly followed by the furnace motor and fan. The sudden noise of the two appliances' startles him and then becomes a deafening roar to his ears as the sounds continue. The once silent cottage has come to life on it's own.

For an instant, the fear of being caught begins to overcome his mind and body. He must leave now! His breathing becomes heavier and his lungs gasp for air. He inhales as much air as his lungs will allow, but the weight of what he has done begins to make his limbs feel like anvils and his movements become slow and deliberate. He is convinced that the dead bodies piled up in the bedroom hallway are consuming all of the vital oxygen he needs to survive! The aroma of blood starts to burn in the back of his throat. His mouth is dry and feels like cotton as he turns and lifts the blood spattered, fireplace rug and haphazardly throws it over Randy's body in the hallway. He finds another throw rug and covers Mrs. Rawlings, leaving the calves of her legs exposed, along with the panties around her ankles. He reaches with his right hand to check his own pockets to be certain that he still has the money, the diamond ring and some keys. On the kitchen counter, he notices a handwritten message on a piece of paper towel and stops to read it:

"Will be back 7-10, the Rawlings."

He pauses, then reaches for a small dispenser of Scotch tape next to the note. He picks up the note and puts the tape into his pocket. He makes a final surveillance of the kitchen and living room areas. He snatches his semi-automatic rifle, pats the side of his pants pocket to confirm that the .25 caliber Beretta is there and steps toward the suitcase near the wall. He wraps his glove hand around the handle and moves quietly towards the same door that less than an hour before had permitted him to enter the cottage to commit these terrible crimes.

He sees a padlock hanging on a hook near the front door and grabs it. He will use it to secure the hasp lock on the cottage door when he leaves. He moves cautiously towards the front window and moves the edge of the drape edge aside. The black of night limits his visibility and he can only see the areas where the soft moonlight has filtered through the trees and revealed the outline of the surrounding forest. He does not see anyone, but is still concerned that someone might unexpectedly be walking along the access road and see him. He doesn't want to create a situation where he will have to justify his presence there. His mind recalls the voices he heard just a short time earlier.

In military fashion, he slides his right arm and shoulder through the sling of the rifle and lets it rest across his back. He opens the interior door and pushes the screen door outward. With his foot, he pushes the suitcase against the screen door to hold it; then closes and padlocks the interior door with the hasp and staple locking mechanism. Again, using his foot, he moves the suitcase out of the way and gently closes the screen door.

Removing the handwritten note from his pocket, he places it over the side panel window that has the four bullet holes in it that he created earlier. Using the Scotch tape he removed from the cottage, he tapes the top and bottom of the note to the window panel, covering the bullet holes. A dark cloud causes a temporary loss of moonlight and the killer fails to see the single bullet hole in a window panel next to the one he has just covered. He puts the tape dispenser back into his pocket.

The earlier heavy mist has dissipated and in its place, a cool, crisp breeze brushes against the killer's face. A faint, yellow stream of light from the lamp inside the cottage has sliced it's way through an open edge of the closed drape, but he ignores it and grabs the handle of the suitcase picking it up. He turns towards the wooded area and moves quickly in that direction.

A full moon, with a scattering of stars creates a soft blanket of iridescent moonlight that acts like a soft spotlight, guiding the killer through the dense forest maze.

Like the silent and mystical shadows of Indian folklore that mysteriously move among the tall pines and hills in the land of the Sleeping Bear, the killer vanishes amid the foliage that surrounds him. He body moves quickly towards a narrow trail that leads to the spirits of the Old Indian Burial Grounds, less than a mile away.

CHAPTER 5

Summer Springs Resort
July 22, 1968
Thunder Point, Michigan

Mrs. Gladys Mitchell of Coldwater, Michigan was busy trying to get ready for her annual bridge party as she approached her husband Russell who was finishing his assigned chore of raking leaves, twigs and other debris from the flowerbeds that surrounded their cottage. Mrs. Mitchell wanted the outside appearance of the cottage to match the cleanliness that she had worked so hard to make possible inside. It was very important that the cottage be presentable to the invited guests scheduled to visit during the upcoming weekend.

Russ Mitchell let his eyes focus for a moment on the Rawlings cottage that occupied the lot about a hundred feet to the south from where he was standing. He could still see the two Rawlings cars parked in the yard, side by side, each one facing in the opposite direction. The cars had not been moved since the Mitchells came up to the resort on the 29th of June and a mountain of dusk had accumulated on them. He and Gladys had heard that the Rawlings family had gone south for a visit and didn't think too much about the cars not being moved. Besides, everything appeared to be peaceful and quiet around their cottage. However, from time to time, a strange odor would cut through the air when the wind was right and each time that a southerly breeze pushed its way towards the Mitchell cottage, Russell could expect his wife Gladys to yell at him to go and tell Monty Barr, the caretaker about the strange odor.

Today was no different. Mrs. Mitchell wanted her husband to talk to Monty and have that odor checked out. She wanted to know what that terrible smell was and where it was coming from. She was certain it originated from inside the Rawlings cottage and at this point she couldn't stand it any longer. She had finished setting up the card table in the yard and was covering it with a tablecloth, intending to have a picnic lunch with her husband that afternoon, but the pungent odor was so bad that she had interrupted his raking. "Russ, please go over and tell Barr and that Indian helper of his about that smell. It's just terrible. As the caretaker around here, he should be able to find out what it is. I mean, how many times do we have to tell him and his father about it?"

Russ Mitchell knew from the tone of his wife's voice that to object would mean another argument and besides, she was right about the smell. He placed the rake against the side of the cottage and headed down the path, directly towards Monty Barr and his Indian helper, Steve Lightfoot.

Russ wondered if he should remind them about the bullet holes that he and Gladys had seen when they had gone up to the Rawlings cottage last week to check on the odor for themselves. This would be the third time this spring that he and his wife had come up to begin the process of opening their cottage. Each time they had gone to Monty or his father and requested that something be done about the terrible smell. And each time, one of the Barrs would tell Russ or Gladys that they would go to the Rawlings cottage and check it out. It was obvious to Russ Mitchell, that neither one of the Barrs had done anything about it.

Monty Barr and Steve Lightfoot were busy building another cottage as Russ Mitchell slowly walked towards them.

Monty Barr, together with his father Carlton, had started the Silver Springs Resort development and also acted as caretakers for the cottage residents when they left in the fall and again in the spring before they returned. Monty did most of the work, while his father, who was pushing close to ninety was unable to contribute in any physical way. Monty, even at fifty years of age, maintained an average build with thin facial features that highlighted his sharp beak of a nose. He and his wife, Edith had recently lost their only child, Billy a week earlier. Billy Barr was eighteen years old and had recently graduated from high school in early June. On that tragic night, he was riding his motorcycle returning from a friend's house up the road at Sturgeon Bay. It was 2 a.m. when Billy missed one of the many sharp curves along the twisting, two-lane road and hit a large tree. He died instantly.

Monty was the only son of Carlton Barr who was the owner of the land through a family inheritance. Monty and his father were the main investors and developers of the cottages and the resort area.

All of the residents of Summer Springs Resort affectionately called the senior Mr. Barr, 'Pops.' Pops was always walking through the resort area or down by the beach, talking and telling stories to anyone who would listen. He was a true believer of the Great Lakes Indian tales and folklore.

Monty and Pops had started the resort development in early 1949 when Pops Barr, who was sixty-four years old at the time, had come up with the idea of building a special type of log cabin to accommodate the many tourists and vacationers who plodded their way north each summer in search of solitude and relaxation. The simple design and construction of the buildings proved to be a commercial success. After the first model was built, the demand was so great they couldn't build them fast enough.

The process started by using the abundant amount of hardwood trees native to the area to cut logs in half, lengthwise. Then they would peel the bark away and square the logs. Next they would create specific notches in the logs in order to provide for the joining of each log into a solidly constructed cottage.

The cottages were similar to the homes of early pioneers only more modern looking and weather resistant due to the tight fit of the square logs resting on a layer of thick mortar and the addition of polyurethane coating to seal the construction. A generous application of the polyurethane liquid also protected the logs natural color and sealed it against the different seasonal elements. The dark, foreboding look of the western style log cabin gave way to a light, cream colored, building that was designed to be functional as well as sturdy with a pleasing appearance. This simple and efficient summer home was just what vacationers were looking for. The design and building method produced cottages quickly and at a reasonable cost.

In the early 1950s, with the advent of Michigan's modern freeway system, natives as well as tourists could travel effortlessly and view it's unspoiled beauty from May through October. The Post World War II generation had exploded the population of the Great Lakes State with thousands of men and women crossing the Mason–Dixon Line from the south to work in the automobile industry and other related manufacturing plants in Detroit, Flint and Lansing. The work was hard, but the pay was good. The prosperity of the times provided many people like the Rawlings and Mitchell families to purchase their own cottages and enjoy them.

The Barr family with astute foresight and imagination reaped the rewards from their decision to develop their farmland along the Lake Michigan shoreline. Instead of growing wheat and corn, they built cottages.

Russ Mitchell approached Monty Barr and Steve Lightfoot as the two men were cutting some floorboards for the cottage they were working on. Barr, hearing footsteps along the trail, looked up and saw Mitchell coming towards him. He turned and looked at Lightfoot with a slight look of disgust. It was a signal to his Indian helper that he was not happy to see Mitchell at this moment. Barr put his handsaw down on the sawhorse next to him and stepped towards the oncoming Mitchell.

"Howdy Russ" Barr said, wiping his hands with a rag, and extending it. Mitchell took Barr's hand and pumped it. "Hi Monty. How's the cottage coming along?

"We're doing all right Russ. What can I do for you?" Barr asked. The tone of his voice was short and curt.

"Gosh, I'm sorry to bother you guys, but Gladys is getting pretty upset again about that odor coming from the Rawlings place," Russ answered, pointing towards the Rawlings cottage. "Her bridge group is coming up this weekend and she's worried that if that smell continues to linger, it's going to cause some problems. You know how Gladys can be." Mitchell's eyes averted Barr's look. He was a little embarrassed to ask for the same favor another time.

"Yes, yes, I know," Barr replied quickly. He'd heard the request enough lately from more people than just Gladys Mitchell. "Tell Gladys that I'll check around the cottage again later this afternoon. I haven't found anything yet from the previous times I've been there," Barr said, stuffing a rag in his back pocket and picking up the saw.

"You do smell the odor, don't you Monty?" Mitchell asked, hoping to elicit a confirmation of his own senses.

"Sure I do Russ, but not all the time. It's just when the wind is blowing right. I spoke to Pops about it the other day and he told me that he has looked around the area too. He said he thought it was a dead animal but couldn't find anything. As I said, I'll have another look later today. Maybe we can find out what the hell it is. It's starting to bother Steve and I when the weather gets warm, especially when the breeze is just right."

Barr's answer was good enough to satisfy Mitchell. At least he would have something to tell Gladys. "Thanks, I appreciate it," He answered. "By the way Monty, did you notice the hole in the window panel? It looks to me like a bullet hole."

"No, I can't say that I have," Monty responded. "Steve and I have been so damn busy with this cottage, hell, some days I haven't had time to take a leak."

Russ Mitchell nodded. He understood the pressure that Barr was under to finish the cottage before the end of the summer. The buyer from Detroit was not an easy person to do business with. It was something that the Barr family did not count on when they had started their land development project. The ability to please ambitious and professional people who wanted things done yesterday was not exactly the way they liked to do business. They preferred the unhurried method, not the instant results insisted upon by urban workaholics.

The pressure of meeting construction deadlines was an unknown requirement to the Barr family and the threats of legal action posed by 'outsiders' and 'downstaters,' as they were called, made the father and son team more than upset, it made them angry.

The midday sun reached high in the deep blue sky as an occasional cool breeze rolled inland from Lake Michigan. Eventually it would push its way past the tall pines and cool the sweating bodies of Monty Barr and his Indian helper, Steve.

Steven Joseph Lightfoot concealed his sixty years well. His bare, hairless chest revealed a muscular body, with strong-arms and callused hands. It spoke of a man who came from the manual labor class of working people. His Indian roots made him a quiet person. Slow to speak about anything unless prodded. And then he would only talk to close friends, of which he had but a few. He had worked for the Barr family for the past year as a carpenter's helper and became a dependable part of the cottage building operation. Before that, it was rumored that Steve Lightfoot had been in prison for a time, somewhere out west. No one really knew for sure. Everyone talked about his heroic war record, yet few people ever knew exactly what had happened. His reputation was that when he came to work, he would work hard and efficiently. The trick was making sure that he came to work at all. Steve Lightfoot liked his liquor.

When Monty Barr lost his son Billy, Steve Lightfoot helped his friend and employer get through the loss with consoling patience and a manly closeness. On the other hand, Steve Lightfoot always had trouble solving his own problems. Most weekends, Lightfoot would get so drunk, his wife Nora, would have other members of the tribe search the areas of the nearby state parks to try and locate him. Many times she wondered why she put up with it. More than once she suffered severe beatings that he gave her after his brother tribesmen would bring him home from his drunken excursions.

On this hot day however, he was more than willing to help Monty Barr locate the source of the strong, putrid odor coming from the Rawlings cottage. It was so rancid that it even made his usually strong constitution weak.

At noon, shortly after Monty Barr and Lightfoot finished their lunch, Barr explained that he was going up to the Rawlings place by way of the beach in order to check out the grounds in front of the cottage. After that, he would proceed around to the other side of the building and check that out too. He asked Lightfoot if he wanted to come along, but Lightfoot politely declined and elected to remain with the tools at the building site. Barr set out toward the Rawlings cottage.

Thirty minutes later, Barr returned and informed Lightfoot that he thought something may have spoiled in the cottage refrigerator and they would have to quit work early in the afternoon in order to have enough time to check it out. He wanted to find the cause of the bad smell and get rid of it.

At three o'clock, Barr asks Lightfoot to get a cardboard box and a shovel from a nearby storage shed while he runs over to his house and get his set of master keys that he has in case of an emergency in one of the resort residences. Barr arrives at his house and walks slowly up the steep wooden stairway to his own home on the bluff. His house overlooks the development below and the Lake Michigan waters beyond. Grabbing the keys for the Rawlings cottage from the key box in the utility room he heads back toward the beach area. When he arrives at the Rawlings cottage, he decides to wait for Lightfoot before starting his search. A few minutes later, Lightfoot arrives carrying an old cardboard box and a shovel.

Barr decides that both of them should take another walk around the cottage before he unlocks the padlock on the hasp that secures the cottage's entrance door. He tells Lightfoot that he prefers not to enter the cottage unless it's absolutely necessary. Lightfoot nods in agreement and starts in the opposite direction from Barr.

Barr starts by rechecking the back door to the cottage. He finds it secure with no sign of a forced entry. As he moves away from the back door, he never looks into the picture window to see if he can observe anything inside.

Lightfoot makes his half-circle around the front of the cottage but does not see any noticeable damage to the main windows, except for the hole in one of the side panel windows. Everything else appears to be in order.

Barr decides they should walk around a second time. Again, both men find nothing suspicious or out of place. Returning to a spot next to the front door on the eastside of the cottage, Barr squats down and removes a square panel, wood door that leads to a crawl space under the cottage floor. He crawls in through the small cubicle and a moment later he yells out to Lightfoot. "I can't see anything through this vent, but the smell is awful."

A few seconds later, Barr emerges from underneath the cabin and stands up, dusting himself off. "The smell is even worse under there. I'm going to have to open the door and check inside and see what the hell is rotting in there."

Barr opens the screen door and secures it from closing by using a horseshoe shape piece of iron and sticks it into the ground. He unlocks the padlock on the main door and hands it to Lightfoot.

Barr searches for the rawhide drawstring that should be coming through a small hole in the door. It's not there. He needs that cord in order to raise the inside steel interlocking drop bolt that secures the door. There's only a small, empty round hole where the rawhide cord should be. He turns to Lightfoot. "Steve, get me a screwdriver from my toolbox."

Lightfoot runs over to the pickup truck and grabs a large screwdriver and returns. He watches intently, as his boss pries the door jam loose with the screwdriver, peeling it off slowly. Barr slides the end of the big screwdriver upward along the opening, removing it easily. At the base of the door, he sees the rawhide cord through the opening and pulls it towards him with the end of the screwdriver. Grabbing it with his fingers, he pulls the cord upward and immediately feels the bolt slide out of the hole in the concrete floor behind the door. The door swings easily inward. A rush of foul air drives both men back and they nearly fall over one another as a swarm of black flies jettison their way out through the newly open passageway.

As the thick black cloud of flying insects erupts out of the cabin's interior, Barr and Lightfoot wave their hands frantically in front of them.

Barr quickly attempts to close the door, but has to be careful not to let the bolt drop back into the floor latch hole. Lightfoot falls to the ground and covers his head in order to avoid the assault from the flying creatures. Within seconds, the black flies have dissipated. Barr regains his composure and leans his upper body forward, slowly pushing the door inward. Holding onto the door handle in case he has to close it quickly, he covers his nose with his other hand and looks inside.

On the floor to his left he can see the legs of a woman protruding from under a rug. The rancid smell is strong and it starts to burn his eyes. "Jesus," he exclaims, "this is terrible." He turns around to get some fresh air.

Lightfoot tries to catch a quick glance of the cottage's interior, but Barr pushes him away. "You don't want to see what's in there Steve. I'd better go and call the Sheriff. "

Both men walk over to the pickup truck and Monty Barr drives Lightfoot back to the cottage where they'd been working. "You'd better stay here until I come back. I'll go up to the house and call the Sheriff."

CHAPTER 6

Sands County Sheriff's Office
3:30 p.m.
Petoskey, Michigan

The late afternoon sun made the water in Little Traverse Bay shine like white gold, while refractions of light from it filtered through the windows of the Sands County Sheriff Department. The building was located at the edge of the Petoskey City limits, twenty miles south of Thunder Point and the Summer Springs Resort area.

Deputy Sheriff Clifford Fillion sat quietly at his desk filling out routine traffic reports when the sound of a phone ringing in the dispatcher's room a few feet away made him stop writing and look towards the doorway.

A few seconds later, a short, stocky deputy entered the room holding a small note in his hand. "Cliff, I just got a call from Monty Barr. He says that there may be some trouble over at the Rawlings cottage on Lakeshore Drive. He thinks there's a woman's body laying under a rug on the floor of the living room and he believes she's dead." He hands the note to Fillion.

Fillion glances at the note, grabs his jacket and moves quickly out of the office and heads for his black and white police cruiser parked outside. He slips his six-foot, two-inch frame behind the steering wheel and turns on the ignition. In a quick motion with his other hand, he flips the switch for the overhead flashing lights and siren. He presses his foot down hard on the accelerator and the high horse-powered Plymouth cruiser swerves out of the parking lot onto highway M–31, in the direction of Summer Springs resort.

The siren and red flashing lights clear away the small amount of traffic along the road, but it will still take the deputy a good twenty minutes to reach his destination.

Highway M-31 with its narrow, two-lane scenic drive snakes along the western shoreline of Lake Michigan. It is a tree-lined, twisting black ribbon of a road, with sharp curves that have taken the lives of many careless drivers. Deputy Fillion is experienced enough not to push his powerful cruiser to top speed. Instead, he maintains a speed that meets the conditions of the road. The road could be unforgiving and deadly to those who tempted it.

Fillion knew Monty Barr and the rest of the Barr family well. Monty Barr was a Designated Deputy of the department because of his long-standing presence in the community and his knowledge of the area. He was given the Deputy status in order to save the county money by cleaning and maintaining the beach area that ran along the Lake Michigan shoreline in front of his family's development. He also cared for the county park beach house just south of the development property line.

In addition, Pops Barr had been the local township supervisor for ten years before retiring just two years before. The Barr name was well known and respected throughout the county.

Fillion's instincts told him that Barr's phone call was from someone who knew what to do in an emergency and not from an excited tourist. His mind began to wonder what could have happened at the Rawlings house. What he could not have known at the time was that he would never be able to accurately describe it to anyone else. It would be too brutal for him to put into words.

Anticipating that he would need assistance, he reached for the two-way radio microphone mounted on the dashboard and contacted his fellow deputy, L.C. Caster.

Deputy Caster was on patrol in another part of the county when Fillion's voice broke over his speaker. Fillion tells Caster about the information he has received from Monty Barr and asks him to meet up with him at the Rawlings place on Lakeshore Drive. Caster gives him a ten-four, turns on his siren and lights and moves in the direction of Lakeshore Drive and the crime scene.

Fillion thinks again about the call from Barr. If it was a murder scene, he knows that he must follow proper procedure. Only a few days before, his boss, Sheriff Harland Zack and his family had left Petoskey and were headed out west on their vacation. He should be somewhere in Colorado but had not contacted the office to give them a number where he could be reached.

Suddenly, Fillion realizes that he will be in charge of a potential major investigation for the first time in his eight-year career with the department. What he didn't know was that this would be the last time that he would enjoy his quiet, peaceful life as a law enforcement officer. Halfway to the Rawlings cottage, Fillion decides to call the dispatcher at the office, and have him notify other members of the sheriff's department. He instructs the dispatcher to call the Prosecuting Attorney and inform him of the Barr message.

At 4:10 p.m., Fillion drives past the general store and turns left down the dirt road that connects the blacktop road with Lakeshore Drive. He spots the

Lakeshore Drive sign and makes a right turn. He notices the diamond-shaped, "Dead End" sign mounted on an old post next to the roadway and senses the irony.

Within moments he stops the cruiser in front of the cottage and turns off the siren and flashing lights. He exits the vehicle slowly, putting his hand on his Colt .38 revolver and looks around. Surprisingly, none of the neighbors have reacted to the noise or exited their cottages. Fillion spots Monty Barr coming around the corner of the cottage, with his helper Steve Lightfoot following closely behind.

Barr motions for Fillion to come toward him and meet him at the front door of the cottage. The long-legged deputy cautiously walks along the cut stone path until he reaches Barr and Lightfoot. They greet each other with firm handshakes as the sound of other patrol cars arriving at the scene fills the quiet area with flashing red lights and sirens droning to a silence.

The one-lane gravel drive that runs in front of the Rawlings cottage turns into a small cul-de-sac at the end of the road and inadvertently becomes a parking lot for numerous police cruisers as they arrive on the scene. As each officer exits his vehicle, a group begins to congregate. Slowly and cautiously they start walking up the flagstone pathway toward the trio standing at the front door of the Rawlings cottage. Fillion puts his hand up directing them to stop. He does not want them to come closer to the crime scene. They obey the silent command and stand fast.

Lightfoot quietly steps around the group of law enforcement people who are asking each other, "What happened here?" He finds a front fender of a patrol car to lean against and lights up a cigarette.

Monty Barr decides that he needs to speak with Fillion in a more private setting and gently takes his arm and guides him off to a clearing about fifty feet away and tells the deputy what he has observed inside the cottage. He explains what has transpired from the time Russ Mitchell spoke with him in the morning until he called the Sheriff's office. When Barr finishes, Fillion jots down the last of his notes and returns to the other deputies who have been waiting patiently for directions.

He instructs them to carefully inspect the grounds for any evidence that could have been left after the murders. He is particularly interested in finding shell casing, clothing or footprint impressions. He insists that if they find anything, they are to mark it and holler out, so that it can be verified and photographed. He instructs them explicitly not to touch anything they find.

Steve Lightfoot takes a deep drag on his cigarette and watches the increase in activity by the officers as they bend, kneel and even lay down on the ground in order to try and locate any evidence.

Within a few minutes a black sedan arrives and stops behind the line of police cars. Prosecuting Attorney Bill Walker exits the car and looks over the scene being played out before him. He walks slowly toward the cabin, waving and nodding at the officers as he passes. As he approaches Fillion and Barr, a man with a camera bag hanging from his left shoulder and a newspaper style flash camera in his right hand, hurriedly moves between the parked cars and rushes toward the gathering trio.

"Hey Bill, what have we got here?" he shouts to the prosecutor.

Fred Lowrey of the Petoskey Press had heard the police call over the police scanner at the newspaper office and had driven directly to the Rawlings cottage. He was there to cover whatever story might be waiting for him.

"Don't know yet Fred, I just got here," Walker said. "I need to talk to Deputy Fillion here. Sheriff Zack is on vacation and Fillion is handling this right now."

Lowrey moves off in the direction of Lightfoot and the parked police cars and places his camera on the hood of a police car. He too lights up a cigarette and asks Lightfoot what he knows. Lightfoot shakes his head denoting that he doesn't know anything. Lowrey moves among the other officers to try and find out what he can.

Deputy L.C. Caster has arrived without ceremony. He parked his cruiser a hundred yards south of the cottage, near the State Park area and had been looking for any clues or evidence that could have been left by someone who may have used the park before or after leaving the Rawlings cottage. Only after checking the beach area and the bathhouse and finding nothing of importance, did he proceed toward the cottage area and the other officers.

By this time, Fillion and Barr have brought the prosecutor up to date on what they know. Fillion tells the prosecutor that he is reluctant to enter the cottage unless the prosecutor gives him approval to do so.

"Bill," Fillion asks. "Do you want us to go inside and look around? What are we going to do about the person under the rug?"

Bill Walker pauses a moment and ponders the situation and then replies. "If what Barr is telling us is accurate, then I think we'll need to call the State Police on this one. But we won't know what to tell them until we go in. Try to avoid touching or moving anything. I realize that you may have to, but try to do as little as possible, okay?" Walker pleads as he gets his first whiff of the odor from inside the cottage. "God Almighty. What the hell is that smell?" The answer to his question came quickly.

Fillion nods to Barr to open the door so that they can re-enter the cottage. Barr pushes open the door and another blast of foul smelling air and black flies emerge from the cottage.

The prosecutor tells one of the officers to call headquarters and to request gas masks be brought to the scene immediately.

Fillion, along with two other deputies enter the cottage using handkerchiefs to cover their nostrils in an attempt avoid the stench of death that engulfs them. The stunned looks on their faces tell more than just finding the dead body of Mrs. Rawlings.

Unexpectedly and without permission, Fred Lowrey walks into the cottage right behind the deputies, camera in hand. No one says anything to him as he begins to take pictures of the murder scene. The smell of death doesn't appear to bother him.

Fillion reaches down and pulls back the blanket that has been covering the body of Shirley Rawlings for almost a month.

The sight of Mrs. Rawlings half decomposed body makes his stomach wretch. Black flies are everywhere. The live ones head for the open doorway and into the forest.

Deputy Caster enters the cottage and stands quietly near the stack of bodies blocking the hallway. He uses his powerful flashlight to look down the dark hallway that leads to the back bedrooms. He sees the legs of another body on the floor at the end of the hallway. He yells to Fillion, "Cliff, I don't want to crawl over these bodies here, but the only way to see what is at the end of this hallway is to go outside and get in through one of the bedroom windows."

"Check with Walker," Fillion answers.

Caster retreats from the hallway in order to locate the prosecutor and seek his permission to enter the cottage through one of the back bedroom windows. Fillion walks over to inspect the pile of bodies, stacked like a cord of wood in the hallway. The smell of death is getting to be too much for him to take. He exits the cabin and walks over to Prosecutor Walker who is standing and talking to another group of deputies. The discussion is about the magnitude of the crime scene. No one there has ever dealt with anything like it before. Some of these lawmen had been in the military and seen death. They find the murder scene hard to look at.

Prosecutor Walker speaks to Fillion, who is wiping sweat from his brow with a large, white handkerchief. "Cliff, I gave Caster permission to break through one of the bedroom windows to gain access to the hallway area. With this many dead bodies, we'd better call the State Police and have them get over here right away." The prosecutor shakes his head at the thought of so many dead people, slaughtered like cattle, lying just a few feet away from him.

At 4:52 p.m. on July 22, 1968, complaint # 78-785-68 is filed with Michigan State Police, Post #78 in Petoskey, Michigan. Deputy Fillion requests that the State Police Crime Lab team come to the scene of a mass homicide as quickly as possible.

Corporal John Lawton and Trooper Edward Hyde are the first State Police personnel to arrive. What they find does not please them. Over a dozen people have invaded the crime scene. There is no doubt that some of the evidence has been compromised.

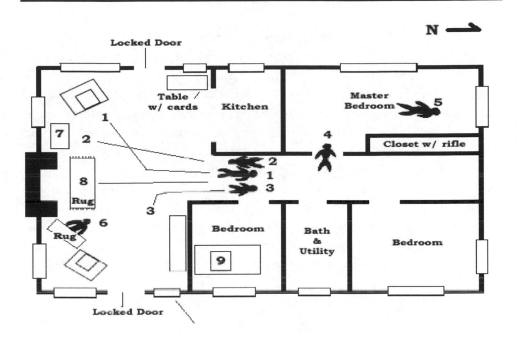

Where Bodies were found: Mr. Rawlings (1); Randy (2); and Susan (3). All were shot in the living room area and their bodies dragged into the hallway. Mrs. Rawlings body (6) partially covered with a rug. Richard Jr. (4) and Gary (5) found in the back bedroom. Record player (7); Throw rug (8) used in an attempt to cover the three bodies in the hallway and the suitcase with clothes and camera (9) in the front bedroom.

MURDER SCENE:

Initial Report submitted by: Troopers Lawton and Hyde

The cottage is of log construction and has an attached small tool shed on its north side. The eastside of the cottage has a screen door opened outward, held by an iron horseshoe stake. The inner main door is opened inward. The door jam has been removed in order to gain access to the cottage. The north side of the building has two ground floor windows that lead to two bedrooms. Each of the windows has two 10"x 12" panes of glass that have been broken out. The inside mounted screens have been removed. The northeast window screen is on the floor. The northwest window screen is lying on top of a bed. In the northwest corner bedroom, there are two bodies, which can be observed on the floor from outside of the building. One of the bodies is lying with the head to the North; the other body is also laying on the floor with the head to the west. The legs of the last body are protruding out through the bedroom doorway into a hallway. Both of the bodies are in a very decomposed stage and are dressed in men's clothing.

On the outside of the west side of the cottage, which faces the lake, there are two crank type windows, which are open to the fullest extent. The inside mounted screens are in place.

A west side main door is opened in, with the west side screen door closed. We were notified that the doors and windows were opened after the arrival of the sheriff's deputies in order to air out the building.

On the south side of the building, there are two windows, one on each side of a stone and mortar-constructed fireplace. They appear to be intact and in a closed position.

The cottage itself is of a one and a half story construction. The upper level does not appear to be anything other than a normal loft area. As we approach the entranceway on the eastside of the cottage, a very strong odor is coming from inside the building and the visible interior floor is covered with dead flies. Live flies are in masses around and near the bodies.

The eastside main door entranceway has a double sidelight window panel on the north side that runs from the top of the door jam to the floor with 10"x 12" panes, placed side by side. There are what appear to be four holes in one of the windowpanes and one hole in the pane beside it.

The holes are of the type made by a bullet and not a shotgun blast. The holes are located from 36" to 42" from the base of the window. The one pane with the single bullet hole has a piece of paper, which appears to be either a paper towel or napkin type and is affixed to the window pane with a Scotch brand type of tape and covers the bullet hole.

In the center of this paper, the following is printed in ink: "WILL BE BACK 7-10" signed (written) Rawlings. Penciled on top of the inked message are the words: "GOODMANS WERE HERE" or something as to the GOODMANS being there. A heavy drape is closed on the interior of this window with no apparent holes in the drape. There are no electric lights or artificial lights on in the cottage.

A motor can be heard to come on at times and it is believed to be the furnace. A telephone ring can be heard at certain times. The ring is one solid ring and it would ring several times as if the party called would not answer. Subsequent information revealed that the Rawlings rings were a double or two short rings because this was a party line area.

Deputy Fillion has confirmed that on instructions from the prosecutor, one of his deputies was directed to forcefully break the two bedroom windowpanes in order to gain access to the cottage and to verify the disposition of the two bodies that were in the northwest bedroom. He also stated that the prosecutor and the medical examiner directed him to obtain the hammer that had blood on it which was found near the kitchen table. It is noted that if any latent prints would have been on the hammer's handle they have been smudged from the indiscriminate handling of that piece of evidence. It is doubtful that any print evidence can be obtained from it.

The wallet that was near one of the bodies was also recovered and is being sent to the Crime Lab Identification Unit. The identification tag in the wallet was that of RICHARD C. RAWLINGS. There was no money in the wallet. This ends the preliminary report.

The activity surrounding the cottage increased significantly with the arrival of the gas masks. Neighbors having heard the sirens and commotion at the Rawlings place begin to approach the area, some individually, while others in groups of two and three. Sheriff deputies roped off the immediate area around the cottage to keep the crowd back. The evening mosquito population also does a good job of crowd control.

Trooper Hyde seeks out witnesses from the crowd that has gathered and takes statements as quickly as he can. A call on his car radio prompts him to notify Fillion and Prosecutor Walker that it will take State Police lab experts coming from Lansing about five to six hours to reach the crime scene and it will be nightfall by the time they arrive. He requests that high power, night lighting be obtained from whatever source is available because the lab team will work through the night.

Trooper Hyde locates Monty Barr and begins to question him about his activities prior to and subsequent to his appearance on the scene. Barr is more than cooperative and appears to be pleased with the attention. He commences by providing his own theories as to how the crimes may have been committed.

Hyde requests that Barr stay with the facts and to avoid any personal evaluations or speculations as to what might have happened. Barr appears to be offended but complies with Hyde's request.

Barr informs Hyde that beginning on Friday, July 19th, Mrs. Russell Mitchell owner of the cottage directly south of the Rawlings cottage called him to complain of a 'foul odor in the area.' Barr said he didn't check the area because he thought it was a dead animal. However, his father, Carlton did check the cottage, including the crawl space under the cottage floor through the trap door. Barr explained that neither he nor his father felt it was right to check the interior without one of the Rawlings family members being present. He admitted that he could smell the odor, from time to time, but was unable to locate it. So, today, after Russ Mitchell had come to talk to him about the smell, he walked down to the beach area around noon, approaching from the south, because both he and Steve Lightfoot had been working on the Watkins cottage and could smell the odor, on and off. He thought maybe something had gone sour in the refrigerator.

Hyde continues to make notes as Barr presses on with his story. He explained that he didn't have his master key to the cottage and he told Lightfoot that later in the afternoon, he would get the key and open up the Rawlings cottage and remove and bury whatever bad stuff was making that smell. Later, he went to his house, got the key and came back to the Rawlings place. Barr first went into the crawl space under the floor and had Lightfoot wait at the entranceway. The smell was very bad, so then he went to the front door and removed the padlock to enter the cottage"

"And then what?" Hyde asks as he and Barr move over to Hyde's patrol car. Barr lighting a cigarette continued his story. "I couldn't enter because the interior latch drawstring had been pushed back through the access hole in the door and

I couldn't lift the special type bar latch from the outside. I asked Lightfoot to get me a screwdriver so I could remove the door jam and lift up on the bar. As the door opened, I was hit with a strong odor and swarms of flies. As I was ducking away from the flies, I could see the legs of a woman protruding from underneath a rug or blanket that covered the upper part of her body. It was then I asked Lightfoot to go back and stay at the worksite and to wait there while I went and phoned the sheriff."

Hyde asks, "when was the last time you saw Mr. Rawlings or any of the other family alive?"

"Mr. Rawlings had stopped by my house on June 24th, the day after my son Billy had been killed in a motorcycle accident. The accident occurred at night on M-31 between Thunder Point and Sturgeon Bay. Mr. Rawlings had talked with my wife and left $20.00 for funeral flowers and told her that he and his family were going to Kentucky and then on to Florida and would not be able to attend the funeral. That's why I didn't think it was odd that the cars were left in the yard. They do a lot of flying and I figured that someone had picked them up."

Hyde inspects the two vehicles parked in the Rawlings front yard. One was a 1967 Chrysler, Newport, four-door sedan and the second, a 1968 Ford LTD four-door hardtop. Both were locked and Hyde made no attempt to open the doors or look inside at that time. He tagged the cars for identification purposes and they were removed to the State Police Post in Petoskey. The forensic team would not find anything unusual or revealing about the contents of the cars.

Hyde proceeds to inspect the locking mechanism that is attached to the cottage front door. It is a simple, but effective way to lock the exterior door of the cottage temporarily. The lock consists of a steel bar bolted to the bottom inside of the door. A leather strap is attached to this steel bar. The strap then goes through a hole in the door about 12 inches above the bolt. This steel bar can then be lifted with the strap and the weight of the bar will be able to be dropped into a notched piece of flat iron that is securely fixed to the door casing. If the rawhide strap is left protruding through the hole and resting on the outside, the door will open by pulling on the strap. However, if the occupants wish to keep someone from entering the cottage while they are inside, they can just pull the strap through the hole in the door, and it cannot be opened without a great deal of force or by removing of the entire doorjamb. When that mechanism is employed, it would be necessary for someone to break the door down to gain access to the cottage. There were no marks on the door that would indicate that force had been used to gain entry to the cottage during the time of the crime.

The last lingering daylight of July 22, 1968 faded quickly as more law enforcement people arrived at the murder scene. Different pieces of lighting equipment had been setup to alleviate the difficult task of trying to recover and locate any evidence from the bushy and wooded areas around the cottage.

Deputy Fillion is informed that the lab team from the Michigan State Police Post in East Lansing had departed for the crime scene and will be escorted by additional State Police vehicles. The estimated time of arrival is between 9:00 and 9:30 p.m. Many different law enforcement officials come and go while waiting for the lab team to arrive.

Detective Sgt. Paul Bozung and Detective Donald Hartman of the State Police crime lab arrive from East Lansing at 9:30 p.m. They discuss the initial findings at the crime scene with deputy Fillion and trooper Hyde. As requested, all the portable lighting that had been available in the area was set up inside and outside of the cottage. The inside of the cottage was sealed off and secured so that the crime lab detectives could start their forensic work. Bozung and Hartman are not happy about the numerous people who have been permitted to enter the crime scene. They forge ahead, in an attempt to compile the pieces of this gruesome puzzle.

CHAPTER 7

July 23, 1968
9:00 a.m.
Headquarters, Michigan State Police
East Lansing, Michigan

The Michigan State Constabulary was the forerunner of the Michigan State Police and was created by the Michigan Legislature on April 10, 1917. It was intended to be a small paramilitary unit, a special police force that could be speedily dispatched anywhere in the state and was modeled after the Northwest Canadian Mounties.

In recent times, the MSP became one of the most efficient law enforcement agencies in the nation. They led the fight against the notorious gangland mobsters that tried to run their "bootlegging" operations through Michigan during prohibition. Michigan's long, unguarded coastline bordering Canada made the state susceptible to all types of illegal activities. The State Police grew under many fine directors, and continues to be recognized as one of the nations finest state police agencies.

In 1968, the Michigan State Police Headquarters was located in East Lansing, Michigan directly opposite the Michigan State University Campus at the corner of Harrison Rd. and Kalamazoo St. The brick brownstone buildings contained different divisions of the MSP and were spread over a ten-acre site. The green lawns that surrounded the buildings made it look more like a campus study hall than the state's premiere law enforcement center.

A large sign with gold letters superimposed on a dark blue background with the department's official seal identified it as the Michigan State Police complex.

The morning sun rose quietly in the eastern sky, its light filtering through the office windows of Colonel Frederick A. Darrens, the commander of the Michigan State Police. His tall frame sat erect in the high back desk chair as he looked directly across the large mahogany desk at Captain Ray McCarthy, his supervisor of detectives.

Col. Darrens sported a thin mustache that accented a handsome face and a lean, hard body. He reflected the kind of officer that the MSP nurtured and promoted into positions of leadership. He had over two decades of service in law enforcement and had earned the respect of his peers from across the country. More importantly, he had the loyalty and respect of the men under his command.

The crime scene reports that had come in from the Petoskey Post held both political and economic concerns for the entire state. Governor George W. Romney had made it clear to the Colonel that he wanted this crime solved quickly and with as little fanfare as possible. The brutality of the murders and the need to apprehend the killer or killers was of paramount importance.

An astute man of principal and political savvy, the governor realized the public relations costs of such a dastardly crime happening within the state.

The cost would be measured in terms of tourist dollars that could be lost if vacationers and other potential visitors to Michigan thought that a mass murderer could be on the loose somewhere in one of the state's prime vacation areas. Michigan had already suffered from the riots that had occurred in Detroit during the prior two years and it did not need another lawless incident to further exacerbate the situation.

Colonel Darrens wasted little time in getting to the point with McCarthy. "Ray, we got a hell of a mess up there in Sands County and we need to get a crack team together to start sorting out this situation."

The seriousness in the tone of the Colonel's remarks was not lost on Captain McCarthy. "I understand completely sir. I've already contacted the Second District Post in Detroit and I'm assigning Detective Sergeants, Frank Stevens and John Ford to lead the investigation. They're two of the best we have. As you know, the Rawlings family lived in Towne Village, a suburb of Detroit. The detectives will coordinate with detectives Schafer and Rodgers at the Petoskey Post, but I want Stevens and Ford to be in charge. It's their case and they will be the two people accountable for putting all the evidence together. All of the physical evidence that was at the murder scene will be analyzed at our lab here in East Lansing. Everything else will be done where it's most efficient. In my opinion, Detroit is where we will obtain the type of information that Stevens and Ford will need in order to know more about the Rawlings family and Mr. Rawlings' business connections."

The Colonel stood up and walked over to the large window in his office and looked out at the vast Michigan State University campus that was spread out before him on the other side of Harrison Road. "You might be right about that Ray. But, something tells me that we're not going to have an easy time with this one. The initial reports that I've read indicate that these murders may have been committed over a month ago. Whoever did it has had more than enough time to move on or disappear. They could be out of the state or across the border into Canada or Mexico by now."

In the distance, Colonel Darrens, his gray eyes narrowing, could see the empty football stadium standing like an abandoned concrete coliseum amid the green of summer. The fifty thousand seats contained within the large bowl of the stadium were empty, but by September and October, in those autumn afternoons, they would echo with the shouts of the university's fight song and the roar of the crowd when a MSU player scored a touchdown.

The Colonel turned slowly and looked directly at McCarthy. "At this moment, I'd believe that our chances of finding anyone associated with this crime, would be like trying to find a needle in that stadium over there. Only throw in a Saturday afternoon crowd for good measure. I want some answers Ray, and the sooner the better. Use whatever personnel and equipment we have, but let's move on this."

Ray McCarthy had been around long enough to know that the Colonel was very concerned about how quickly the investigation could produce some results. No one in the department had to be reminded that six members of a well-known Detroit family had been slaughtered in their northern Michigan cottage and that whoever did it was still on the loose. Even more difficult for Captain McCarthy to understand was that for a month, none of the current and living Rawlings family members had seemed concerned that Richard Rawlings and his wife and children had not been heard from.

McCarthy looked directly at the Colonel. "I can't promise any miracles Colonel, however I can promise you that I'll have Stevens and Ford pursue this investigation with vigor and expediency."

McCarthy's words reassured the Colonel only for a few moments. "I'd rather have some miracles Ray. Stevens and Ford are to provide daily reports on all significant matters regarding this case, no exceptions." The Colonel did not want any misunderstandings about his position on pursuing this as quickly as possible.

McCarthy got the message and quickly gathered up the few papers he'd brought with him and headed for the door. As he reached for the doorknob, he glanced back at the Colonel. "You know sir, there's one thing that really bothers me. We've been trying to keep a lid on the turmoil going on in Detroit, where anyone can be shot at or killed without a reason. This family lived as close to Detroit as you can get, but they're all killed in a little cottage, five hours away from the big city. It just doesn't make any sense to me."

"Murder never makes sense Ray, you know that. The magnitude of this one is completely despicable. If it takes miracles, then miracles are what I want!" The Colonel was looking out of his office window towards the stadium.

Captain McCarthy exited the room and quietly closed the door behind him.

CHAPTER 8

July 23, 1968
4:00 p.m.
State Police Post, Second District H.Q.
Detroit, Michigan

The humid heat of summer filled the office of detectives Frank Stevens and John Ford as they prepared to interview the first person on their list. His name was Frederick Marshall. A small ceiling fan labored to circulate fresh air around the room and provide some relief to the detectives.

Frank Stevens was thirty-two years old and stood 5'11", with a stocky build and light sandy hair that sported a butch style crew cut. He had a pair of cold blue eyes that could stare at criminal suspects until they felt like his eyes were hot lasers penetrating their bodies. He loved the outdoors and had a passion for fishing the big lakes that surrounded Michigan. He had served four years in the U.S. Marine Corps, and then joined the Michigan State Police. A ten year veteran of the force, he was respected as a no nonsense detective, who always put his job duties first. Recently married, it gave his wife Marilyn periodic headaches, but she understood his work before she married him and adapted to his varied schedule without complaint.

John Ford was also thirty-two years old, married with two children. He stood 6'-1" with a slim, wiry frame that had made him an outstanding swimmer at his alma mater, Michigan State University. His curly black hair accented his almond brown eyes and dark eyebrows. He had graduated from Michigan State with a degree in criminal justice and then joined the Michigan State Police. A few months later he married his high-school sweetheart Carolyn. Eventually, the couple had two children, a girl, Sandy and a boy Christopher. He was a devoted husband and father and loved his profession as a detective with the Michigan State Police. Early in his career, he was selected by his superiors to attend the highly competitive FBI law enforcement program in Quantico, Virginia. He had graduated with outstanding evaluations and on his return to the MSP, Captain McCarthy teamed him with Frank Stevens. Ford was considered one of the top investigators in the department. As an eight-year veteran of the homicide unit, he was a skillful and tenacious interrogator.

Both detectives liked and respected each other. In previous murder cases, their superiors were impressed with the two men and their detective skills. Their reputation for obtaining quick arrests with solid evidence, led either to convictions or plea bargains that put the criminals behind bars. It moved them up the promotional ladder quickly. Both had exceptional instincts when it came to evaluating clues, murder scenes and suspects. They were a good combination to hunt down the perpetrator of this crime.

Frederick A. Marshall was forty years old, overweight and noticeably uncomfortable as he entered the office. Stevens introduced himself and Ford as he motioned for Mr. Marshall to be seated. Marshall immediately began to fidget and showed signs of nervousness with his hands. He wore a clean but wrinkled suit and his hair was disheveled and uncombed. His overall appearance was that of a person without discipline. It happened that Marshall was a fourth cousin to Richard Rawlings and an employee of the U.S. Customs Agency in the Detroit office.

Ford, as was his custom, remained silent while his partner began the questioning process. He leaned back in his chair and let Stevens proceed with the questioning.

Stevens began, his voice soft, but firm. "Mr. Marshall, in a preliminary statement you gave to Trooper Franklin, you told him that you own a farm up north in Sands County. That farm is not too far from the Rawlings place, correct?

"Yes, that's right. It's just east of the Rawlings cottage."

"And the last time you saw the Rawlings family was on June 23rd in their car on a county road. Is that right?"

"Yes, that's right."

"And how was it you came to see Richard and the family on the 23rd?" Stevens asked.

"It was like this," Marshall responded, tightly closing his hands. "Around five o'clock in the afternoon of June 23rd, I believe it was a Sunday, I was driving along Wormwood Lane, about ten miles east of where Richard and Shirley have their cottage. My youngest daughter Shelly and I, along with her two girl friends decided to go and get some ice cream over at the little red general store. I left my house, piled the kids into the car and headed west along the road toward the store. As you know, the store is located over near the lake on M-31. However, at the intersection of Wormwood Lane and Wilderness Road, I unexpectedly met Richard and his family going in the opposite direction. Richard was driving his

Ford Sedan. We slowed down and pulled our cars next to one another. We must have talked for about five or ten minutes. Richard asked me how long my family and I would be up at the farm. I told him that I wasn't sure. It would depend on the weather."

Marshall adjusted his seating position and continued. "It was still early spring up there and I'd made the weekend trip in order to evaluate how soon I could start to plant some vegetables. I like growing my own stuff. During our conversation, Richard asked me if my wife and I, along with the family, would like to come over to his cottage that evening because he and his family were leaving the following morning on a trip. He didn't say where he was going or for how long. He told me that the family had just been out to eat and they were headed back to the cottage to pack and get ready. The entire family was all dressed up at that time."

"What else?" Stevens asked.

"Richard didn't tell me where he and the family had been, but as a rule they liked to go to the Kenilworth Restaurant in Mackinac City near the railroad tracks. He knew a lot of the people at the restaurant."

"Did you go over to his place that evening?" Stevens asked.

"No. Alice, that's my wife, and I, were tired. Besides, I was busy trying to get some things done at the farm before we had to return to Detroit. Alice wanted to get the kids' stuff ready to pack before we left. And we really don't like staying out late anymore. Richard loved to talk and we would've probably been there all night."

"What else can you tell us about Mr. or Mrs. Rawlings?" Stevens asked.

"I know that Richard owns a Cessna plane and he liked to keep it at Peabody's Flying Service at Harbor Springs when he was at the cottage. He also used the Pellston Airport on some occasions. I never knew Richard or Shirley to drink. They were both active in their church. Richard didn't hunt or fish. I don't believe that he had any guns around the cottage or his house. At least, none that I knew of."

"Anything else?" Stevens asked, still probing for more information.

After a slight hesitation, Marshall continued, "The next day, the twenty-forth, I happened to run into a deputy sheriff over on Van Road and introduced myself. The deputy told me that he was from Pellston and was headed over to the beach on Lake Michigan to investigate a report about a purse that had washed up on the shore. That's basically all I know."

Stevens and Ford thanked Marshall for the information and told him that they would get back to him if something came up that they thought he might be able to help with.

Frederick Marshall said goodbye and made his way out of the office, passing by a man and a woman sitting on a wooden bench outside the office door. He didn't recognize the couple and continued on.

Stevens looked at Ford. "What the hell do you make of that situation?"

"I'm not sure Frank. Obviously, Richard Rawlings didn't keep the family trip a secret. He told Barr and now Mitchell. I'm not sure what to make of it at this point."

"Well maybe our next guests will give us some insight as to what may have been going on."

The guests that Stevens was referring to, were Elaine Finney, the sister of Richard Rawlings, and her husband, Douglas Finney. The Finney's had arrived at the State Police Post during the Marshall interview and had been escorted to the bench outside the detectives office.

Ford, checking his watch moved toward the doorway and looked out. He spotted the Finneys and invited them in.

Mrs. Finney was a mature woman in her early forties, poised and well dressed. Mr. Finney worked for a Michigan Telephone Company and was dressed in his work clothes. He was friendly and outgoing. His early summer tan made him look younger than his forty-three years.

Mrs. Finney began the conversation by indicating that the last time she had seen her brother and the rest of the Rawlings family was on June 1st. She told the detectives that on June 8th, she had spoken with her sister-in-law, Shirley Rawlings and that Shirley had told her that she was getting the family ready to go to the cottage for the summer.

"Would your brother and his family ever take a trip without telling anyone else in his family where they were going?" Stevens asked.

"No. As a rule, my brother would leave an itinerary, on a day-to-day basis as to where they would be. This itinerary would be left with our father, Ross Rawlings. The rest of the family would be kept informed based on their need to know."

Mr. Finney spoke up. "I would like you detectives to know, that today an insurance agent, along with Joe Santino, Richard's publishing assistant and Marvin Fowler, Shirley Rawlings' brother, all left this afternoon by a private plane for Harbor Springs and the Thunder Point area."

Stevens and Ford gave each other a quick glance. All business associates and relatives of the Rawlings family had been advised by the detectives that they were to be notified if anyone had to take any kind of trip, within or outside the state.

"Do you know why they left, Mr. Finney? Was there an emergency?" Stevens asked.

"No. There was no emergency that I'm aware of. Marvin called around lunch time, noon or a little after, while I was at home and left the message for Elaine telling her that they were going. That was all."

Stevens asked the Finneys not to tell any of the three men that the detectives had been told of their trip. They would follow-up on the information later. After a number of general questions and very little information being derived from the interview, the detectives thanked the Finneys for their cooperation and told them they would be in touch.

Ford poured himself a cup of coffee as Stevens looked over some notes. After taking a drink of his coffee, Ford asked Stevens, "Frank, why would Rawlings not provide his family with an itinerary of where he and the family were going or what they were up to this time? It doesn't make sense to me."

Stevens looked up from the notes. "I guess we'll have to wait until we can talk with Richard Rawlings' father and see what he has to say. It doesn't make sense to me either, especially when it seems a lot of people were being told about it."

Ford silently wondered if there had been some type of conflict within the Rawlings family structure that might have been the reason that they were not told.

The detectives were methodical and precise in their work habits, but they had never had a murder case that was more than a month old before they were called in to begin an investigation. In particular, they never had a case where they were starting out more than a month behind in gathering evidence or in interviewing witnesses or suspects. It put them behind the proverbial eight ball. And that wasn't a place they liked to be.

The investigation was less than forty-eight hours old and it felt like half a year had passed by. Stevens poked at his typewriter with both index fingers, filling in the daily information report about the case. Both interviews today left him with very little confidence or satisfaction. He was looking forward to tomorrow, when he and Stevens would have a chance to talk with the late Mrs. Rawlings' mother, Mrs. Aileen Fowler. Perhaps she might be able to come up with a motive. They could only hope. Patience was a word both men disliked, but knew it was part of the job. It was going to be a word that would pursue them throughout this case.

CHAPTER 9

July 24, 1968
10:00 a.m.
Detroit

The weather was like a damp, hot towel trying to smoother the city. It was still early in the day, but the temperature was already above 80 degrees and the humidity was heavy.

A woman with a pleasant face and slightly graying hair entered the State Police Post and asked for Detectives Stevens and Ford. She was escorted by one of the troopers to the detectives' office. She introduced herself to Stevens and Ford as Mrs. Aileen Fowler, the mother of Shirley Rawlings. Mrs. Fowler carried her sixty-four years of age well, but her self-confidence in handling difficult situations had diminished extensively after the loss of her husband four years earlier. No mother could feel adequate enough for the task that had been laid out for her.

Ford invited her to sit down and asked her if she would like something to drink. She opted for a cold glass of water and tried to make herself comfortable in the wooden chair that had been provided.

Ford handed her the glass of water as Stevens asked her if she felt up to taking questions about the tragedy at Thunder Point. His sensitivity to the situation put her at ease.

"Yes. I think I can answer whatever questions that you have detective," she replied quietly. Her face reflected a lack of comprehension as to why, at this particular time in her life she had to endure such a terrible tragedy and the circumstances that had brought her here to this place and this room.

Stevens began. "Mrs. Fowler, we realize that some of the things we are going to ask you are going to be difficult for you to answer. But you must realize that in order for us to try and find out who may be responsible for your daughter's death and that of her family, we have to do things that are unpleasant even for us. However, with your help maybe we can put together enough bits and pieces of information that could lead us to who did this despicable deed. We're not here to pry into any family secrets, but we do need to know how your daughter's family lived their everyday lives."

Mrs. Fowler looked at Stevens for a few seconds "I know that you're right detective, but it's very difficult to think of Shirley and the children in the past tense. I never thought that my life would end after hers, especially like this. Nothing will ever be the same again."

Stevens and Ford did all they could to keep their composure. They could feel the despair in the woman's voice, but they had to push the emotional part aside and press forward.

Stevens spoke up. "We need your help Mrs. Fowler. Detective Ford and I have a job to do. That job is to try and catch whoever committed this crime. And we can only hope to do that with your cooperation. If it's okay with you, we will turn on the tape recorder, so that we can review your answers on a day to day basis if need be, without having to call or bother you again with the same questions. Anytime your ready, you can just start talking. Let's start with the last time you talked with Shirley."

Mrs. Fowler dabbed at the small tears that had welled up in her eyes with the white handkerchief she had taken from her purse. With some ease she began to speak about the last time she had spoken with her daughter. "I received a phone call around 7:00 p.m. on Sunday, June 23rd, from Shirley. She told me that they had just returned from having dinner in Mackinac City and were having a good time, but also told me about Billy Barr being killed on a motorcycle the day before. Shirley was upset a little more than usual because as a mother of three young boys, two of whom were in their teens, she couldn't stop thinking how tragic it was for Billy's mother to have to deal with losing a son like that in an accident. That was the last time I spoke to her in person. On Thursday, June 27th, I received my monthly check from Shirley for $60.00, which I would normally receive on the first of each month or very shortly after. A note with the check said: "Dear Mom: I'm sending this check early – will write more later. Love, Shirley." There was no mention of any trip. On Monday July 8th, my brother, William Belsen passed away. I tried to call Shirley at the cottage in order to tell her about her uncle's death, but there was no answer at the cottage. Then I called Joe Santino at the office, he's Richard's business assistant. Joe told me that Richard and Shirley were on a trip to Kentucky and Florida and would be back the 15th or 20th of July. He told me that he didn't know how to get in touch with them. From July 16th on. I continued to call the cottage until this past Sunday, the 21st, without any success."

Mrs. Fowler stopped for a moment took a sip of water and located some LifeSavers in her purse. She opened the tubular candy container and offered some wintergreen mints to the detectives. They declined and she continued. "Shirley was at her house the last time I saw her in person on June 15th. She had been wearing her two rings, the wedding ring and the anniversary one that Richard had bought for her a couple of months ago. Shirley told me that she had put her other jewelry in the safety deposit box. She would never take those two rings off, even when she washed dishes."

Stevens asked if she knew the cost of the rings.

"I believe that Shirley said that the rings were valued somewhere between nine and twelve thousand dollars."

"Did your daughter ever say anything about taking a trip to the south?" Ford asked.

"No. Shirley didn't mention anything to me about a trip to the south or any other place for that matter. In fact, because of my age and health, Shirley made it a habit to have an itinerary made so in case I had to call someone, we would know where to call."

"It seems awful strange to me, Mrs. Fowler that in this instance, Shirley decided to abandon what had been her past practice of keeping you notified of her whereabouts and didn't mention anything about this trip to Kentucky or Florida."

"Yes. It's strange, all right. I don't have an explanation for it. She was a good daughter. She was always concerned about me. I really don't have a clue as to why her and Richard would make such a plan, and then not say anything to me about it."

"Did Richard ever confide in you about some of the business deals he was involved in, Mrs. Fowler?" Ford asked.

"Oh no! Richard was very private about things like that. It wasn't that he didn't trust me. He would always have these complicated type deals going on and it would always take him hours to try and explain how they worked. Even Shirley would discourage him from trying to talk about them in front of the children. I wasn't told about them, and I really didn't want to know. I'm still having a hard time accepting that they are all gone. It's so unbelievable. Words just don't seem to be enough to tell someone how painful it is. That's about all that I know."

"I want to thank you for coming in today, Mrs. Fowler," Stevens said. "You have been very helpful. I'm sure that we'll probably be talking again. Please accept our condolences. We're here to help, so don't be afraid to call us if you think of anything else."

Ford assisted Mrs. Fowler from the chair and walked with her to the doorway. Turning slowly, she looked at both of the detectives. "You both have been so nice. I hope and pray that you will be able to find whoever did this to Shirley, Richard and the children. There was nothing that they could have done to warrant this."

"We are going to do our very best, Mrs. Fowler, you can be assured of that," Stevens replied.

Mrs. Fowler said goodbye and left the office.

Stevens and Ford returned to their notes and different pieces of information spread out on their desks. One of the prime questions that concerned the detectives was that Mrs. Fowler could not obtain any information about her daughter or son-in-law from Mr. Rawlings closest business associate, Joe Santino. It didn't make sense that he wasn't able to tell her where her daughter and the rest of the Rawlings family were. It didn't seem reasonable to them that Santino wouldn't know the whereabouts of his business partner. Stevens wrote that question in red on his notepad and drew a circle around it.

"Frank, we need to fly up to Thunder Point tomorrow morning and look over the murder scene. I'll put in a call to the airport to have the department plane ready at eight o'clock."

"That's fine John. The sooner we get up there and look things over the better I'm going to feel. I see we still have a few people scheduled to come in later this afternoon."

"They're all employees from the Rawlings firm. When I spoke to some of them this morning I got the impression that they won't have much to say, but you never know what may pop out of the hat."

It was four o'clock in the afternoon when four individuals showed up at the Post asking for Stevens and Ford. First, there was Leo Sears, a production manager with the Director magazine. Glenda Saunders, his executive secretary accompanied him. Also included were Earnest Gladden, an editorial writer and Theodore G. Schmidt, the executive editor of the magazine.

Ford and Stevens spent less than ten minutes with each one of them. They had little information about Rawlings' personal life, but they all agreed in one way or another, that Richard C. Rawlings had been a hard man to work for. It was evident from the interviews that Rawlings had a violent temper and lofty expectations for the work that was produced by his employees. On the other hand, he could also be very generous person at the most unexpected times.

The only one of the four that sparked the curiosity of Stevens and Ford was

Glenda Saunders. Her answers sounded rehearsed and sometimes evasive. She was twenty-five years old, attractive and single. She had been Mr. Rawlings' personal secretary for the past three years. She claimed that she knew very little about any of Mr. Rawlings' business dealings and insisted that most of her work time was devoted to the magazine part of the company and not with the advertising agency section. The advertising section, according to Miss Saunders was where most of Mr. Rawlings' business ventures originated. She told the detectives that Mr. Rawlings' business dealings where always conducted in private, with only Mr. Santino being part of those discussions.

Ford and Stevens were suspicious that this striking and shapely woman couldn't provide them with more information about Mr. Rawlings' business practices. She didn't look as if she would have been kept in a closet about anything that went on within the structure of Rawlings' businesses. They dismissed the four employees after the brief interviews, but made a special notation about Ms. Saunders.

It was Joseph Santino, Rawlings' business assistant that Stevens and Ford wanted to question. He was at the top of their list. For now, the detectives would concentrate on going north to Thunder Point in the morning. Joseph Santino would have to wait until they got back.

CHAPTER 10

July 25, 1968
10:00 a.m.
Petoskey, Michigan

The white Cessna 270 airplane with MSP markings, banked sharply into a left turn, then rolled to a level position as the pilot, watching his instrument panel closely, lined up the nose of the aircraft to correspond to the long concrete ribbon of runway below. The Harbor Springs Airport was always busy this time of year. Commercial carriers did not operate out of this airport. However, the airport was crowded with private planes of every description. Many of these adult toys belonged to business magnates or tycoons from Detroit, Chicago, Cleveland and Milwaukee. They used them to reach their summer retreats quickly and to avoid the long drives that would otherwise be necessary.

The detectives moved quickly from the plane to a waiting patrol car that would take them directly to the Petoskey Post, less than a mile from the airport. As they settled themselves into the back seat of the police car, their assigned driver accelerated and the cruiser moved quickly through an exit gate and onto the main road.

At the Post they were greeted by the Post commander, Major, Stanford B. Patten, "Welcome to Petoskey, gentleman," he said proudly. Major Patten was a 30-year veteran officer with the Michigan State Police. He was a man of average build, with a crop of gray hair, ruddy complexion and soft blue eyes. His reputation was of a man known for his fairness with subordinates but with an absolute rule of discipline within the ranks. He was proud of the troopers under his command and a stickler for following the proper polices and procedures of the department.

"Thank you, Major," Detective Ford replied. "We're glad to be here."

The Major told Stevens and Ford that an unmarked patrol car was available for their use. He offered his regrets that he could not stay with them longer, but he had a previous meeting to attend in Traverse City. He hoped that he could return from the meeting before they had to return to Detroit. Stevens and Ford thanked him for his hospitality and assistance as the Major departed.

The detectives went to work by reviewing written reports submitted by different troopers relative to the crime scene. An hour and a half later, they had finished and left the Post in the unmarked car. Their first stop would be the little, red general store at Thunder Point. Along the way, Stevens quickly learned that he couldn't drive the same way he did in Detroit. After a couple of close calls navigating the twisting curves, he slowed the cruiser down to a respectable speed. It made his partner extremely happy.

Forty-five minutes later, they entered the general store and introduced themselves to the owner and the purpose of their visit.

The owner was unable to recall anything specific or strange around the time period that the murders had occurred. He told the detectives that the store closed at six in the evening and he went directly home which was located behind the store.

When the conversation ended, the storeowner stepped outside with the detectives in order to show them where they could access the dirt road that would lead them to Lakeshore Drive and the Rawlings cottage.

Ford took the wheel of the patrol car and drove it to the roadway entrance. He followed the directions and located the hidden dirt road that led them to Lakeshore Drive. Ford guided the car past the Dead End sign until he saw the ribbons of yellow police tape surrounding the Rawlings property.

A couple of young boys were headed to the beach area in their swimming trunks, with beach towels wrapped around their necks as they walked past the slow moving patrol car. They gazed curiously at the two detectives without speaking, but waved to them.

Ford and Stevens were intrigued by the quiet and peaceful nature of the location. It was hard, even for them who had witnessed almost every kind of brutality, to imagine the tragedy that had occurred in this picturesque and quiet area.

The sound of voices could be heard somewhere along the beach area, but the people making them could not be seen from any spot near the cottage. The tall trees and abundant shrubs surrounding the grounds, provided the ultimate privacy.

Stevens unlocked the padlock that secured the door of the Rawlings cottage with a set of keys he had obtained from the State Police Post. The unexpected rush of foul air made both men turn away, coughing to clear their throats. The stench burned their nostrils as they stepped back to draw in fresh air and clear their lungs.

Black flies were still swirling inside the cottage, and Stevens had provided them with an escape path to the outside world. Cautiously, both detectives entered the small building and immediately observed the blood patterns on the floor. The streaks of crimson had dried to a light brown, but they could still see how three of the bodies had been dragged to the nearby hallway. The detectives surmised the killings had been quick and ruthless.

Ford made notations on a diagram pad as to the location of the bullet holes implanted in the interior back wall, the floor area and lounge chair. He gave special attention to the glass side panels adjacent to the door. He observed the placement of furniture and the view from the picture window, looking out at the lake and the beach area below. Continuing, Ford took measurements with his tape measure and stepped-off different areas of the cottage to gather distance points.

Stevens inspected the bedrooms and the blood patterns on the hardwood floor. Streaks of dried blood covered the hardwood floor area of the cottage and could also be seen on the soiled carpet that ran down the hallway towards the two back bedrooms.

When both men had finished their inspections, they padlocked the door and took an extended walk around the cottage. Immediately, they could see how easy it must have been for the assassin to get within a short distance of the cottage, keeping hidden while sighting in his intended targets. They walked over to the birch tree and stood behind the cover of a honeysuckle bush.

"I don't think the killer would have much trouble firing into the cottage from this position, Frank," Ford said looking at his partner.

"Especially, if it was dark and the lights were on inside the cabin," Stevens replied.

"You know Frank, just looking around at the area, it would be easy for anyone to hide in the brush or trees without being seen by anyone else from any of the other cottages, unless they happened to be walking directly along this roadway behind us."

"I agree," Stevens answered. "On the other hand, how many people would risk killing that many people without being heard or noticed, unless they knew this area or had checked it out more than one or two times? And why was it necessary to do it from outside?"

"That's a big question Frank. A hired killer would want to know exactly what kind of activity would be in the area at that time. He'd have to know who was in the other cottages, their daily movements, and a lot of other intangibles. The sound of a weapon repeatedly being fired would definitely arouse attention and suspicion. It's inconceivable to me that an outsider would know all of those things."

Stevens and Ford studied the area for another hour and then returned to the Petoskey Post. They met briefly with Major Patten, who had returned from his meeting in Traverse City and filled him in on their initial inspection of the crime scene. They congratulated him on his pending retirement in a few weeks, after noticing the announcement on the bulletin board. They said goodbye, headed for the airport and boarded the MSP plane. It was an easy flight back to Detroit.

The duo stopped briefly at their office to pickup some notes about next day's scheduled appointment. The appointment calendar showed a 9:30 a.m. appointment with their prime suspect, Joseph Santino.

As they left the building, both men wondered what kind of person Mr. Santino would be. They wouldn't be disappointed.

CHAPTER 11

July 26, 1968
9:30 a.m.
Detroit

The first thing anyone would notice about Joseph Santino was his height and the broadness of his shoulders. His dark brown hair was almost black and was cut in a neat and fashionable style. It accented an unblemished, almost ivory colored face. The delicate texture of his skin had more of a feminine smoothness to it than a masculine ruggedness. Santino was thirty years old, six-feet, four inches tall and weighed a little over two hundred pounds. He strolled confidently into the State Police Post, stopping momentarily to ask the trooper at the desk for directions, then proceeded directly up the steps to the second floor and his scheduled appointment with Stevens and Ford.

As Santino made his way up the steps, the trooper picked up the phone and informed the detectives that Santino had arrived and was on his way up to their office.

A few moments later Stevens and Ford greeted Santino cordially when he entered their office.

"Good morning," Santino said pleasantly, extending his right hand. The horned-rimmed glasses encircled coal black eyes that revealed little, if anything about the man. His tailored silk suit fit perfectly, and his overall appearance was that of a Madison Avenue advertising executive. Mr. Santino thought himself an ivy-league type and wanted to make that impression with everyone he met. Unfortunately for Santino, he was no ivy-league graduate at all. He had completed only one year of college before enlisting in the U.S. Army. After his enlistment, he served two tours of duty stateside in Washington D.C. and worked primarily in the intelligence section of the Pentagon. His responsibilities had included dispensing confidential information to many different military offices throughout the world. The highest rank he obtained after eight years of service was that of a corporal.

Stevens felt that it odd that a person who had served in the intelligence service for that length of time would only rise to the rank of corporal. It indicated to Stevens that Santino must have lacked promotional qualities or character flaws.

He made a mental note to dig deeper into Santino's military record.

Current information showed that Santino had obtained his honorable discharge in the summer of 1965, and was hired immediately by Richard Rawlings to become his Assistant. He was second in command at Rawlings and Associates, the advertising wing of the company. His starting salary had been $300.00 dollars a week. However, since May 1st of 1968, his salary suddenly increased to $1,000.00 per week, plus bonuses and an expense account. According to one rumor within the Detroit business community, Richard Rawlings had been very pleased with his associate's progress, and more importantly, Santino had made very positive impressions on current clients as well as prospective ones.

Joe Santino believed it was necessary for him to promote his image as a successful advertising professional and part of that image included his clean-cut appearance and fashionable suits and shoes. It was common knowledge amoung the employees at Rawlings and Associates that Mr. Santino was very 'tight' with Richard Rawlings.

That impression had been conveyed to all of the agency's clients. On many occasions, the self-assured Mr. Rawlings had introduced Joe Santino as "My right hand man." With that anointment by Richard Rawlings, Stevens and Ford believed that if anyone in the company should have known what Rawlings was doing, it should have been Joe Santino. That was what Stevens and Ford wanted to find out with this meeting.

Stevens motioned for Santino to be seated in one of the wood chairs that occupied the detective's office. It certainly wasn't the leather high back chair that Santino was accustomed to, but he sat down and attempted to make himself comfortable. He sat erect with both feet planted firmly on the floor and his arms folded across his chest. He stared at the detectives waiting for them to begin their questioning.

Stevens started the interview in a friendly tone, trying to relieve any apprehensions Santino may have had.

"First, I want to thank you for coming in today Mr. Santino. Detective Ford and I both realize that you have some very important responsibilities to take care of since Mr. Rawlings' death. I'm not sure what it takes to run an advertising and magazine business, but I believe that it takes a considerable amount of time."

"Thank you." Santino responded, "I'll do whatever I can to help." His eyes darted back and forth between the two detectives.

"Thank you. We appreciate that. Now, Mr. Santino, can you tell us when it was that you last spoke to or saw Richard Rawlings?" Stevens asked.

Santino leaned back easily in the chair as he took a deep breath, then looked directly into Stevens' eyes. His voice contained little emotion, and he spoke in a matter–of–fact tone. "The last time I saw Richard Rawlings was on Saturday, June 15th, around 10:30 a.m. Richard had called me at home and told me he was at the Metropolitan Airport Hotel and to come and pick him up. I drove out to the airport, picked him up and then dropped him off at his home."

"How come he called you? Didn't he have his own car there?" Stevens asked.

"No, he didn't. It's a long story and I can tell you if you think it's necessary."

Stevens responded quickly. "At this point Mr. Santino, everything and anything someone can tell us about Mr. Rawlings or members of his family is necessary."

Recovering from his casual attitude toward the interview process, Santino continued. "I'm sorry, I didn't mean to make it sound trivial. Anyway, here's what happened. On Wednesday, June 12th, around two o'clock in the morning, I drove Mr. Rawlings to the airport so he could catch an 8:00 a.m. flight out for a business trip. Mr. Rawlings didn't want to divulge the nature of the trip, or where he was going. He did tell me that he would be gone about a week. From June 12th through the 15th, I received several phone calls from Mr. Rawlings, telling me that he was back at the Metropolitan airport and was between flights. On two or three occasions, he had me return his calls at the airport. On one of those days, June 13th, a Thursday, Mr. Rawlings asked me to come to the airport and have lunch with him. I met him in the airport restaurant and we had lunch. Mr. Rawlings was alone at the time and we didn't discuss the nature of his trips. His manner was that whatever business project he was working on, he preferred not to discuss it. Prior to the start of these trips, Mr. Rawlings had mentioned to me that he was attempting to get national circulation for his Director magazine. I assumed that this was what he was trying to do."

"And you never directly asked Mr. Rawlings what the trips were about?" Stevens asked.

"No." Santino responded quickly. "All of us in the company respected Mr. Rawlings privacy with business matters. If he wanted us to know something he would tell us. However, it was not something you would question him about."

"Really?" Ford interjected. "Does driving your boss to the Metropolitan Airport at two o'clock in the morning seem a normal business practice to you, Mr. Santino?"

"The answer is yes, Mr. Ford, especially if you worked for Richard Rawlings," Santino answered.

"Are you telling us sir, that you weren't curious enough to ask what the reason was as to why he was asking you to take him to the airport at two o'clock in the morning for an eight o'clock flight?"

Santino looked directly at Ford and tried to explain. "I can understand why you might think that is unusual behavior, but if you'd known Mr. Rawlings, you wouldn't have thought it to be strange behavior for him. Again, I will tell you that when it came to business deals, Mr. Rawlings would seem to act strange at times."

Ford continued. "And when he asked you to come to the airport to have lunch with him, what did he want to discuss with you then?"

Santino shifted his body slightly in the chair. "We discussed the day-to-day operations at the agency. Mostly, he wanted me to follow the operational procedures that were in place and not to deviate from them. He was a strict taskmaster about keeping things in an orderly manner where his business was concerned."

Ford had made his way to the hot plate where the coffee was brewing. He made a gesture to Santino if he would like a cup. Santino waved it off.

Stevens moved his chair closer to Santino. In a level and matter-of-fact tone, he asked Santino. "Joe, was Richard Rawlings seeing another woman? "

Joe Santino squirmed a little more in his chair and showed some discomfort with the question. "I don't know what you're talking about," he replied, his tone indignant.

"Just so we understand each other, Mr. Santino, what you're asking Detective Ford and I to believe, is that on one occasion you drove Mr. Rawlings out to the airport at two o'clock in the morning so that he could catch a plane that's going to take off at eight o'clock. Then on another occasion you meet with him for lunch at the same airport and you don't even ask what the hell was going on. That's pretty hard for us to swallow Joe."

Santino remained silent as Stevens and Ford stared at him. Finally, he spoke, "That's the truth. It's exactly what happened. I'm telling you the truth."

Stevens continued. "Okay, at the time when you met Rawlings for lunch, what did you discuss with him as to what was going on at the agency?"

Santino stared at the floor for a few seconds before answering. "Richard would call the office periodically and speak with me about advertising contracts, advertiser complaints and other business dealings. Sometimes he would be in St. Louis, or Los Angeles or San Francisco. When I met him at the airport, it was more of a personal update by me to him. He was a man who just wanted to know that everything was going smoothly back at the office. Nothing revolutionary."

Santino, feeling more confident now continued. "Then on Saturday, June 15ᵗʰ, I picked up Richard at the airport and drove him home. The following day, Richard, his wife and the rest of the family left for their cottage at Summer Springs Resort."

"Did you stay in touch with Mr. Rawlings after he had gone up to the cottage?" Ford asked.

"Yes. I made some business phone calls to him at the cottage and Mr. Rawlings called me on numerous occasions. I was also responsible for keeping an eye on his house in Towne Village by going over and checking on it while they were on these trips." Santino answered.

"Do you recall the last time you spoke with Mr. Rawlings?" Stevens pressed.

"Yes. I called him on Tuesday, June 25ᵗʰ, around ten in the morning. It had been raining very hard here in Detroit and I went over to his house to check for any water leaks in the basement. Mr. Rawlings had asked me to look after the house, especially the basement when we had those kind of rains because sometimes the basement would get water in it."

"What did you find?" Ford asked.

"There was some water and I knew that I'd have to call Richard and tell him. So that's what I did."

"What did Mr. Rawlings say or tell you to do?"

"Well, I told him about the water and that nothing seemed to be damaged. I reassured him that I would have it taken care of and he approved."

"Did you talk about anything else?" Stevens asked.

"I think it was at this time that Mr. Rawlings told me that he and the entire family were going to take a trip to Kentucky and Florida. He mentioned something about horses and a condo and that they were going to fly down there from either Pellston or Harbor Springs."

"Did he mention any names?" Ford asked.

"No. I don't recall him ever mentioning any names." Santino replied.

"And of course, you didn't ask?"

"That's right."

"Did you talk about anything else?" Stevens asked.

"Yes. Richard asked me if I had received a package of signed, blank business checks in the mail. I told him that I had not received them. He told me he would call the bank and stop payment on them. After our phone conversation, I went to the Post Office and picked up the mail. The package containing the checks was with the rest of the mail. I believe it was around noon when I returned to the office and called Richard back. I told him that the checks did arrive with today's mail. Richard said he would call the bank again and have them remove the 'stop payment' order. Then he told me in very explicit terms, that if anyone called or inquired about him, to tell them he would be back on September 1st. He made it clear that he and his family would not be at the cottage but would return to Summer Springs around July 15th. And that he would call me when he got back."

"Anything else?" Stevens persisted, while handing Santino a cup of water.

Santino took a long drink and crushed the paper cup in his hands, and continued. "That same day, the 25th, I attended the plumbing convention at Cobo Hall in the afternoon. That was shortly after I'd spoken with Richard. I wanted to check up on some of our clients and see how the convention was going. After I'd made my rounds, I went home. The next day, my wife and I, along with my young son, Joe Jr., headed for Indianapolis. My fraternity was holding a convention at the time and I wanted to attend it with my family. All of us returned on the 29th." Santino seemed a little agitated at this point and was hoping the questioning would come to an end soon. It didn't. He asked for another cup of water. Ford gave him one and Santino took a sip then sat it down on the desk next to him.

"Do you own any guns, Mr. Santino?" Ford asked rather casually as he picked up some file cards resting on the desk.

"Yes, I own a .25 caliber Beretta, automatic."

"Would you mind if we have ballistics run a test on it?"

"No. Not at all." Santino appeared unconcerned.

"How long have you had this .25 caliber automatic?" Ford continued.

"Since January or February of this year. Richard asked me to find him a pistol and I did."

"How come Mr. Rawlings asked you to get him a pistol? Why didn't he just go out and buy one himself?"

Santino shifted slightly in the chair. "Well, Richard knew that I had this friend in the firearms business by the name of Bill Hathaway. Bill is a licensed gun dealer over in Waterford Township and we've been friends for a long time. Anyway, I went over to Bill's place and told him that I was looking for a good pistol for protection purposes. Bill recommended the .25-caliber Beretta automatic. I liked it so much that I ordered one for myself."

"Was Rawlings pleased with your selection?" Stevens asked.

"Yes he was. Then I went over to the Birmingham Police Department where they fingerprinted me and issued me two purchase permits. I was able to pick up the pistols a week later along with 400 rounds of ammunition. I registered both guns in my name and brought everything to the office. Richard took one of them and all of the ammunition."

"Why did you register both guns in your name? Why didn't Mr. Rawlings want to register the Beretta he had in his name?" Stevens pressed.

"It's like this detective. Richard's public position was that he was anti-gun. But the past couple of years, with all the rioting and violence in Detroit, he felt it would be prudent to have a gun in order to protect himself and his family. He attended a lot of late night functions in downtown Detroit as part of his business and one never knew who you could run into during those late hours."

"You still haven't answered the question Mr. Santino." Stevens demanded. "Why didn't he want the Beretta registered in his name?"

"It was because a few years ago, Richard had written some editorial comments in his magazine regarding guns and how he was opposed to the uncontrolled distribution of them and that he felt there were too many out on the streets. I'm sure that Richard believed that if he were to have a handgun registered in his name, and someone found out, it might appear to his readers anyway, that Mr. Rawlings was a charlatan or hypocrite."

"Interesting," Ford said, pouring himself another cup of coffee. "You said you purchased 400 rounds of ammo. Is that 100 rounds to a box? Why so much?"

"That's right, a hundred to a box and it was because that was the amount Richard suggested I buy."

Joe Santino was feeling very uncomfortable in the wooden chair. It seemed to become harder as the questioning continued. It was bad enough he had to account for his own actions, he was not thrilled that now he had to rationalize the actions of his deceased boss.

"Mr. Santino, what exactly was your relationship with Mr. Rawlings and what kind of boss was he?" Ford asked.

"He was a brilliant and energetic man. He liked people with initiative, but he didn't like to be countermanded by any of his subordinates. He could be very generous or he could be a bastard. He could praise lavishly or he could demean cruelly. It depended on the mood he was in. He was an artist by profession and a businessman by necessity. He was good at deal making because he was always thinking about it."

"Do you think he made any enemies by doing some of these business deals you've mentioned?" Ford continued.

"I was about as close to Richard Rawlings and the business operation as anyone could have been. Often, when he spoke with clients or other business acquaintances, he would refer to me as 'my brother' or 'my right hand man.'

We were very compatible. I took care of the office, while he had free rein to be creative and do the kinds of business promotions he liked to do. I've been running the office since April of this year. That's when Richard took his family to Hawaii for two weeks."

"Did you also handle the payroll?" Stevens asked.

"I made out the checks, filled in the blanks, but Richard never liked to give up control, so they were always signed by him before they went out."

"Can you think of any reason why someone would want to kill Mr. Rawlings, or members of his family?" Stevens asked as he poured himself a glass of water.

Santino paused then shook his head. "No. I really can't think of any reason why someone would do such a terrible thing."

Stevens and Ford didn't like the vibes they were getting from Santino. There was something about this man and his causal manner that disturbed them.

Ford, sipping the last of his coffee spoke up. "We'll give you a call and tell you what time to bring in the Beretta for ballistics testing, Mr. Santino. But, before we finish, there is one more thing that I need to clear up. When Shirley Rawlings' mother, Mrs. Fowler called your office to try and locate Shirley because her uncle had died, she said that you told her that Richard and the family had gone on a trip to the south and you didn't have any idea how to get in touch with them. Is that true?"

"Yes. That's what I told her. It was true." Santino replied.

"Then explain to us why Rawlings would refer to you as 'my brother' or 'my right-hand man' if he didn't even trust you to even know his whereabouts or what he was doing, even in a family emergency situation. It doesn't sound to me like he trusted you very much Mr. Santino."

 Ford looked directly at Santino for an answer.

Santino cleared his throat, and then he replied. "I thought you might ask me that question. The last time I spoke with Richard, he was at the cottage. He explicitly told me that he was not in a position to discuss what he was doing or how he was putting what he called 'a big deal' together. He did tell me that he'd have very 'good news' when he returned. However, for the time being, it was imperative that no one, including me, should know what he was doing. He was the boss and because I trusted him, I agreed to do as he asked. That was the reason that I could not reveal to Mrs. Fowler or anyone else for that matter, where her daughter or the rest of the family were going. I really didn't know exactly when or where they would be myself except they were going south."

Stevens countered. "Why didn't Rawlings think it was necessary that he be contacted in case of an emergency?"

"Richard was paying me to handle those types of things, while he was doing other things for the business," Santino responded confidently.

"And if you couldn't handle something?" Stevens continued.

"The thought never crossed my mind. Besides, I knew that Richard would call the office and check in when he thought it was appropriate."

"Speaking of checking in, there is one last thing, Mr. Santino," Stevens said. "We understand that three days ago, you, Marvin Fowler and an insurance agent by the name of Willis Becker flew up to Thunder Point and went to the cottage. Can you tell us why you didn't notify us first, as we had requested, before making that trip to the cottage?"

Santino knew he had made a mistake by not informing the detectives before he left and his response was less than adequate to satisfy Stevens and Ford. "Marvin called and asked me to go. He told me that the insurance guy was going to fly up there and back the same day and thought I might like to go along. Becker wanted to inspect the property and evaluate the damage for the insurance company. I really didn't think there was any harm in my going and to be candid, I was a little curious to see the place. I'm sorry."

"I appreciate your candor, Mr. Santino, but from now on, if your going to go on any trips, I suggest that you make sure that either detective Ford or I know about it, for your sake more than ours."

There was a long pause and then Ford broke the silence. "For now, I think that's about it, Mr. Santino. Thank you for coming in."

Santino rose from the chair and walked toward the door. "Your welcome. I'll do whatever I can to help." He gave a nod of his head to the detectives, turned and walked down the corridor toward the steps that would take him out of the building. It was 12:30 p.m. Stevens and Ford watched Santino from their office window as he walked to his car and drive off.

"There's just something about him I don't like." Stevens said as he walked over to the nearby sink and dumped a cup of cold coffee into it.

"Yeah, I think I know what you mean Frank. All that bullshit about buying a pistol for Rawlings and then buying the same kind for himself."

Stevens interrupted his partner. "Did you pick up on the part about Rawlings keeping all the ammo? Does Santino believe that we think he's going to fill a new .25 caliber Beretta with water? He's clever, I'll give him that, but we need to keep an eye on him and apply some pressure at the same time. I think he knows a hell of a lot more than he's telling us."

" We'll have to wait and see Frank. He acts too sure of himself. He didn't appear to be too shaken with our questions. Why did he tell Rawlings that the checks hadn't come in the mail until he had first checked on the post office box? Could Rawlings already have been dead and he's making this up? He may not be in total control, but for the most part he had his answers down pat. It might take a lot a pressure to rattle this guy, even if he is guilty." Ford said.

"Don't worry John, if I have to rattle his cage, it won't be an easy shake. If I think he's our man, I'll make more noise than he can stand."

Ford knew his partner well enough to know that if Santino's actions and statements didn't pan out, he would be in for a hell of an awakening.

"Who's next on our agenda, John?" Stevens asked, putting some folders into the file cabinet.

"I think we better get things cleaned up in here Frank. We have Dr. Roger Fielding and his wife Margaret coming in. Both were very close friends of the Rawlings'. They're scheduled to be here at one thirty."

"Good. Call down to Gino's and have them deliver some burgers, I'm starving," Stevens said as he began to clean up the papers on his desk.

CHAPTER 12

1:30 p.m.
State Police Post
Detroit

Dr. Roger Fielding and his wife Margaret entered the State Police Post and were directed to the second floor office of the detectives.

When the introductions were complete, Ford escorted the couple to a small conference room adjacent to the office area. The conference room's large windows let in the afternoon sunlight and with it, a bright, clean look.

Stevens adjusted the blinds so the sunlight was directed away from Mr. and Mrs. Fielding as they sat across the table from both of the detectives.

Dr. Fielding was forty-five years of age, held together by slim, wiry frame that reached just over six feet. A slight touch of gray marked his temples, giving his tanned face a distinguished but youthful look. His bushy eyebrows, accented the blue eyes that were soft and attentive. Dr. Fielding was the head of the surgical department at the University of Michigan hospital in Ann Arbor. He was fashionably dressed in a conservative dark suit, white shirt and a red tie.

Mrs. Fielding was an attractive looking woman, forty-three years of age, with ivory skin, absent of any telltale age lines, while the striking brown eyes and pretty smile reflected a warmth and charm that could disarm even the most cynical person. She wore a cream colored dress that accented her brunette hair and the well-coifed hairstyle. She was a perfect match for the doctor.

Ford started the conversation. "We know this must be difficult for both of you to come here today and talk about things, maybe even some personal things, that you and Mr. and Mrs. Rawlings may have discussed when being together. Detective Stevens and I will try to avoid subjecting either of you to anything that we do not feel is relevant to the case. I'm sure that you realize that under these special circumstances in which all of the Rawlings family were killed, it may be necessary for us to ask both of you some very intimate questions about your relationship with Mr. and Mrs. Rawlings."

Dr. Fielding gave his wife a quick glance. On the drive over to the State Police Post, they had anticipated just such a direct approach by the detectives and both had agreed that their entire relationship, no matter how private, would be open for discussion.

Dr. Fielding, with a slight clearing of his throat responded. "Do not concern yourselves gentlemen. You can ask us whatever you wish to know. We'll answer everything we can about our relationship with the Rawlings family. They were our close, personal friends for over twelve years and we want to help anyway we can."

Stevens thanked them and then asked them when was the last time they remember being or talking with either Mr. or Mrs. Rawlings.

Dr. Fielding took the lead and answered. " The last time we saw them I believe was on Saturday, June 8th. We had a dinner date, but I know that Margaret spoke with Shirley on numerous occasions between June 8th and June 15th."

Mrs. Fielding confirmed her husband's statement. "Yes that's true. In fact, it was either Friday, the 14th or Saturday the 15th, just before they were to leave to go up north when Shirley called me. She told me that a man was going to be coming to their cottage to spend some time there. She was worried about having everything presentable when he arrived and that Richard had called her long distance and told her his trip was going fine. She mentioned that Richard had put their expected visitor on the phone to talk with her. The man came on the phone and asked her not to make a fuss at the cottage because he knew that they were going up there to relax and not to entertain him. Shirley said that she was surprised when the man asked her if she would make some of those pasties that her husband had told him about."

"Pasties are those meat and potato filled little pastry covered pies that they make up north, especially in the U.P." Dr. Fielding interjected.

"Yes, we know what they are Dr. Fielding. I've had plenty on some of my fishing trips to the Upper Peninsula. I don't dare leave the dock without some," Stevens replied smiling.

During the pause Mrs. Fielding's eyes welled up with tears. She reached in her leather purse and pulled out a handkerchief as Dr. Fielding patted her arm to reassure her that everything was all right.

Stevens poured Mrs. Fielding a glass of water. She took a small sip then continued with her story. "During this same discussion, Shirley told me that the children would be driving up to the cottage with her on Sunday, June 16th, and that Richard would follow a few days later with his guest. Then on the 15th, Shirley called me to tell me that Mr. Rawlings had come home unexpectedly and that there was a change in plans. She said that Richard was going to drive up to the cottage with the rest of the family the next day and that his guest was coming up later. She understood that the guest would be flying in with his own plane."

Ford leaned across the table. "Do you remember if Mrs. Rawlings ever mentioned the name of this guest or where her husband had called from?"

Mrs. Fielding paused, "No. I don't think she ever mentioned his name once or where Richard was when he had called. I'm positive that she never mentioned it to me. I know I would have remembered if she had."

Stevens looked at Dr. Fielding, who began discussing one of the last conversations he had with Mr. Rawlings. "At our dinner date with the Rawlings on Saturday, the 8th, Richard told me he was planning a 'big business deal' of some sort and that we, Margaret and I, shouldn't be surprised at anything we heard about him in the near future."

"What did that mean to you?" Ford asked.

"I took it to mean that Richard may have been working on one of his grandiose business deals that always seemed to be a subject at our dinner dates. He said he couldn't tell us the details, but when it was completed, he wouldn't have to worry about money for the rest of his life. He told us he wanted us to share in his good fortune and that he wanted us to travel with him and Shirley at his expense."

Mrs. Fielding took the opportunity to interrupt her husband to make a point. "Shirley told me that she didn't approve of this business transaction, whatever it was. She believed that her family had all the things they needed in life. She seemed apprehensive about it. In what way, I can't say."

Dr. Fielding looked directly at Stevens. "I will tell you that I was shocked when I learned that Richard had purchased a gun. He was always anti-gun in his political views. In fact, in February of this year, I purchased a handgun for protection while I was going back and forth to the hospital. I remember telling Richard about it and he had no reaction to it, which I thought was strange considering his public position on the subject. I think if Richard was going to buy, or had already bought a gun he would've told me about it."

Ford and Stevens looked at each other, thoughts of Joe Santino crossing their minds.

Stevens pursued the thought. "Do either of you know Mr. Joe Santino?"

Mrs. Fielding answered immediately. "Yes we know Mr. Santino. In fact, I was just about to mention his name. The last time we saw Mr. Santino was when he stopped by our house on Friday, July 19th to drop off an edition of the Director magazine that my husband had told Richard he missed seeing. We had a brief discussion about not hearing from Richard or Shirley since they had left for their cottage up north. I'm positive that he told us that he'd received a phone call from Richard and said that they were headed for Kentucky and that everything was fine. I asked him that question again after the news reports about the death of the Rawlings family and he told me that wasn't what he said. But I know that is what he told us."

Dr. Fielding nodded in agreement with his wife's statement.

Stevens continued. "Doctor, can you think of any reason why Richard Rawlings or any member of his family should have been harmed?"

Roger Fielding paused, thinking deeply before answering. "The only trouble I ever heard about, that Richard was having, was because of the cottage and his property. That was about three or four years ago. It seems that the assessment on his cottage had tripled, while during the same time, the permanent residents homes were left at the same assessment rate. He felt that it was unfair and had gone to the assessor and told him directly, that if it was not corrected, he would go to the State Board and report it. The assessor made an adjustment and it was reduced back to what it had been. However, just recently, Richard told me that the same thing happened again. He was very upset and said that when he got to the cottage this summer, he was going to raise hell with the assessor again. He said that if they gave him any guff, he was going straight to Lansing and file a formal complaint with the Attorney General's office."

"That wouldn't seem like enough to put him on a hit list. I'm sure that a lot of seasonal cottage owners run into that problem." Ford said.

"I agree with you Mr. Ford," Dr. Fielding said, "But Margaret and I have tried to think of anything that would've been out of the ordinary. Since our last meeting with the Rawlings, we can't think of anything that would've led to such a violent action like the one that happened to them. It's such a tragedy. Everyone of them lost."

"We agree with you doctor," Stevens responded. "Is there anymore you can think of?"

Dr. and Mrs. Fielding looked at one another. The doctor answered. "No."

Stevens thanked them for their cooperation and requested that if they did think of anything else, a conversation or some other information, to contact them.

As the Fieldings left the office, Stevens handed the doctor his business card.

The interview ended at approximately 3:30 p.m.

Dr. and Mrs. Fielding left the State Police Post and headed for their home in Bloomfield Hills.

Stevens and Ford had another interview in just one hour.

4:30 p.m.
Detectives Conference Room

Bill Hathaway was a short, robust fellow with a gregarious smile. He liked everybody and most everyone liked him. He was a natural storyteller and could embellish those hunting and fishing stories that made men listen and laugh. The women, on the other hand, who happened to hear him spin his tall yarns, knew a bull-shitter when they heard one. They were not as easily captivated with his oratory skills or his escapades as were his male counterparts.

Bill Hathaway was a talker and he liked to talk. He gingerly made his way up the front steps of the State Police Post and entered the building.

Like the previous visitors, he was given directions to the upstairs office. He was dressed in his normal outfit of blue jeans, plaid shirt and high top leather boots. His lumberjack style boots created the appearance of a miniature Paul Bunyan as they squeaked nosily on the freshly polished floor. His low voice had an almost gutteral tone to it, but occasionally, when he became excited he would produce a momentary high pitch. This condition made him speak slowly and deliberately. He never hit any high notes when he was using an expletive. Those always came in loud and clear. He was a legend in many fishing and hunting lodges across the state as a dedicated storyteller and twister of tales.

"You guys must be Detectives Stevens and Ford," He said as he approached the two men in their office. He held out his fat paw of a hand and squeezed theirs.

"And you must be Mr. Hathaway," Stevens said, grabbing on to the chubby mitt.

"Right. But just call me Bill. Hell, I don't need a handle. I'm just regular people," He replied, letting a big smile slice across the weathered and tanned face.

"Hi Bill. I'm Detective Ford," Ford said as he motioned for Hathaway to have a seat in the same chair that Santino had previously sat in. Hathaway dropped into the straight back wooden chair and watched the two detectives as they took a moment to organize some of their notes and other documents that were on the table.

Hathaway studied his callused hands, with dirty fingernails as he waited for the detectives to start asking him some questions.

Ford began the dialogue. "Bill, as we discussed with you before on the phone, we have an issue regarding the weapons used in the Rawlings murders and we think you might be able to help."

With the nod of his head affirming that he understood, Hathaway remained silent and listened intently, as detective Ford continued. "What can you tell us about either the sale of an Armalite .22-caliber automatic rifle or two .25-caliber Beretta automatic pistols to Joe Santino."

"There is nothing I can tell you about the Armalite .22. I never sold one to him. As far as the .25-caliber Beretta goes, Joe asked me to get two of them for him. He also wanted 100 rounds of ammunition. He told me that his boss, a Mr. Rawlings had asked him to locate a pistol for him. Joe said his boss wanted to have some personal protection."

"Are you sure that Santino said that Mr. Rawlings wanted him to purchase the gun?" Stevens asked.

"Yeah. He said he needed to find a gun for his boss and that he might as well get one too!"

"Why did he choose a .25-caliber?" Stevens continued.

"We talked about the need to conceal it and the number of rounds it should hold in order to make it a good weapon for protection. We both decided that the Beretta fit the bill."

"Did both of you make that decision, or only Santino?" Ford asked.

"I suppose Joe made the final decision, but I agreed with it."

"Okay, then what?" Ford continued.

Hathaway pulled some note cards from his breast pocket and looked them over before giving an answer. "On February 4th, I called the Zackery Gunsight Company over in Bay City and ordered two Beretta pistols. A couple of weeks later they came in and I called Joe. I told him I had the pistols and to come over and pick them up. Joe told me that he was having some kind of delay in obtaining the permit to purchase, but eventually he got it, then came over and picked both of them up."

"When did he pick them up?" Ford asked.

Shuffling his note cards, Hathaway studied one of them for a moment and then answered. "Looks like he came over on April 5th to get them and also purchased 100 rounds of SAKO ammunition."

Stevens face reflected curiosity as he spoke. "Bill. Santino picked up the guns over two months after he ordered them. Did he tell you why he was having trouble getting a permit?"

"No, and I didn't ask. I was glad as hell that I didn't get stuck with two pistols that I didn't need."

"You said SAKO ammo, isn't that a Swedish make?" Ford asked.

"Yup," Bill replied.

Ford made a notation on the notepad he was holding.

"Did he buy more ammunition when he picked up the pistols?" Ford asked, determined to find out why Santino had told them that Rawlings had ordered 400 rounds of ammunition.

"400 rounds? Holy Smokes, that's a lot of ammo to buy unless you were going to spend a lot of time target shooting. But I never sold him 400 rounds of ammo."

"Did you know Richard Rawlings?" Stevens asked.

"Nope. Never laid eyes on 'em. All I ever knew about Rawlings is what Joe told me."

"How did you come to know Joe Santino?" Ford asked.

"Oh, that's a long story. Joe and I go back a little. Primarily we both belong to the State Trapshooting Association and we meet every so often for competitions and contests."

"So Joe Santino is a good shooter then?" Stevens asked.

"Yup, he's a pretty good shot. He likes to shoot and I believe that he goes out on the range quite a bit and takes target practice. Joe knows I have a gun dealer's license and I give him a break on gun pricing and ammo. If he wanted 400 rounds of ammo, he could have come to me."

" In other words, Joe knew that he could get the best deal from you?" Ford asked.

"You betcha. I mean, we're friends and all that, so if he needed something along those lines, I was his man."

Both Stevens and Ford paused, looking directly at Hathaway.

Sensing that he may have said or did something wrong, Hathaway tried to clear away any suspicion for his actions. "Look fellas, this is all legit. I have my license from ATF and I keep good records. I always obey what the law says. I don't do any hanky-panky business where guns are concerned." Hathaway seemed a little agitated and under pressure.

Ford sensed the apprehension and tried to alleviate it. "Don't misunderstand or take our questions too personally Bill. We have an investigation procedure that we need to follow. We have to get a feel of what transpired between you and Joe Santino regarding the purchase of two Beretta pistols. That's all."

"I'm sorry if you think I was out of line. When anyone and I mean anyone appears to question my honesty or integrity regarding the sale of guns, I become a little upset," Hathaway answered.

It was obvious to both Stevens and Ford that this was about the best information that they were going to get from Mr. Hathaway. Their main purpose had been to have Hathaway verify and to acknowledge that he had sold the two handguns to Joe Santino. The bonus was that now the detectives knew about the 300 extra rounds of ammunition that Santino had ordered or obtained from someone other than Hathaway. It was clear that Santino would have to explain his lie about the purchase of it from Hathaway. Santino either had in his possession the 300 rounds or he had used them. Only Joe Santino knew the answer to that question.

The detectives didn't feel there was much more they could gain by pressing Hathaway on that point.

"We understand and appreciate that Bill." Stevens replied. "We just wanted you to verify your association with Santino and the business deal you had with him, that's all."

"Okay. Sorry if I got a little upset."

"That's alright Bill. We appreciate you coming in and confirming the information we had on this. I believe that's all we need for now." Ford concluded.

Stevens led Bill Hathaway to the door. All three men shook hands and Hathaway left.

Ford sat quietly looking at his notes. "You know something Frank? I'm going to have to look over these notes several times in order to get a clearer picture of what we did here the past couple of days. I need to see how it all adds up."

"I know exactly how you feel John," Stevens answered. "Right now, my mind needs some rest. I have a terrific headache and all this information has probably short-circuited my brain nerves to a point that I'm not sure I can find my way home."

Ford stood up, and put on his suit jacket. Stevens grabbed his jacket and draped it over his shoulders as Ford flipped the switch and turned off the office lights. They walked slowly out of the building into the evening fresh air. As they walked toward the parking lot, each one stopped momentarily and looked at one another.

"This is going to be a ball buster Frank, I have a gut feeling about it."

"It could be John, but somewhere there are clues. We just need to find them."

CHAPTER 13

July 27, 1968
9:00 a.m.
Detroit Post

The early morning rain fell softly from an overcast blanket of gray clouds that shrouded the city and suburbs of Detroit. Overnight, the temperature had fallen into the mid-thirties and it felt more like January than July. The weatherman predicted the cold rain would give way to warm and sunny conditions in the afternoon, but in Michigan, it's a throw of the dice with the weather.

Stevens and Ford left the Post in an unmarked car and headed north along Telegraph Road. They had an appointment to speak with Ellsworth Osborn, owner of the Osborn Insurance Agency. He was the insurance agent for the Rawlings family and now the estate.

Stevens sat quietly in the passenger seat and sipped on some hot coffee out of a Styrofoam cup while the heater in the car, set on low, pushed warm air across his feet. He caressed the cup with both hands and let the heat from it relieve the cold in his fingers.

"If there's anything I hate, it's those damn weather forecasters that don't know what the hell they're talking about." Ford said, tightly gripping the steering wheel.

"Yeah. It's a damn good thing there's not a hunting season on them in Michigan. None of them would survive," Stevens mumbled as he took a sip of the hot coffee.

Ford spotted the insurance office and pulled police car into the driveway and parked it in a designated VISITORS spot in front of the small, brick building.

The detectives exited the vehicle and headed for the doorway. Stevens dropped his empty cup into a trash receptacle near the entrance as they entered the building. The sound of a small bell broke the silence as they stepped inside.

Mr. Osborn had consented to meet with the detectives at his office in order to verify the items that were insured by the Rawlings family. Specifically, the detectives wanted to know about the jewelry that had belonged to Mrs. Rawlings. Mr. Osborn emerged from a glass enclosed office area. He was neatly dressed, short in stature, standing five foot five, more slim than rotund as he walked confidently towards the detectives. He approached the waist high barrier that surrounded the secretarial area from the visitors waiting lobby and extended his hand to greet the two men standing before him.

"Good morning," he said quietly. "I'm Ellsworth Osborn and you gentlemen must be from the State Police."

"That's right." Stevens answered, as he held open his badge case to identify himself. "And this is Detective Ford," he said replacing the badge in his pocket.

Mr. Osborn acknowledged the identifications with a nod of his head. "Please come in gentlemen. I'm delighted to be of service."

The detectives followed Osborn's lead as they went through the waist-high, swinging gate and entered his office.

Osborn sat himself behind the large mahogany desk in an overstuffed, leather back swivel chair. The detectives each picked one of the stationary matching chairs on the opposite side of the desk and sat down, facing their host.

The office was pleasing, but small. It contained the standard file cabinets and wooden bookshelves. Each shelf held different volumes of statistical insurance information.

It was a very well organized area and reflected the diligence that Ellsworth Osborn took in administering the insurance needs of his clients. "Our regular office hours are from 10:00 a.m. to 6 p.m., so this will work perfectly," Mr. Osborn said.

"We'll get right to the point then Mr. Osborn," Stevens replied as he began the questioning. "Yesterday, when I called, you indicated that you would be able to provide us with the information that we need regarding the Rawlings family insurance coverage. It's very important for us to know what items of value Mr. and Mrs. Rawlings had insured. We are especially concerned about some jewelry that Mrs. Rawlings owned and that she may have been wearing at the time of the crime. Those would be her rings. What can you tell us about that?"

Mr. Osborn produced a typewritten list from a manila folder on his desk. "I believe this will answer any questions you may have. It's a copy of their policy with the attached rider and list of items that were insured at the time of their deaths."

Stevens took the folder, pulled the insurance form sheets out and looked at them. As he looked at the list of items he asked: "It says here that one of the diamond rings is insured for twelve thousand dollars. Is that correct, Mr. Osborn?"

"Yes, that's correct." Osborn replied immediately. "That ring was an anniversary present to Mrs. Rawlings from Mr. Rawlings. The wedding band was insured for six thousand dollars. That's no small piece of change for those type of items."

"I would agree with you," Stevens replied.

Mr. Osborn sat quietly while the detectives continued to look over the documents. When they had finished, they replaced them in the folder and handed it back to Mr. Osborn.

Mr. Osborn continued. "I've talked with one of the adjusters, a Mr. Becker at American Casualty and he told me that the company will wait for the Probate Court to make a ruling as to value, what is to be divided up and to whom. It is obviously a very unusual string of events and a terrible thing to have happened to that nice family."

"You knew the Rawlings well?" Ford asked.

"Not extremely well. Mr. Rawlings and I met at a luncheon in Detroit for some business seminar when he was first starting his business. He needed insurance coverage and I just happen to have been there. As a rule, he would just call our office, tell us what he had purchased, send me a copy of the invoice and it would be posted in our ledger. I don't believe that either he or his wife were ever in my office more than three or four times in the ten years I knew them."

"Did Mr. Rawlings ever act out of the ordinary about the insurance coverage he wanted for his valuables?" Stevens asked.

"No. He would get upset sometimes when I would tell him how much it would cost of having to insure something he bought, but in the end he always approved of how I was handling his needs. And he always paid his premiums on time."

"I can see from your insurance forms that Mr. Rawlings had all of his family possessions and their life insurance policies with you. Is that correct Mr. Osborn?" Stevens asked.

"That's correct, Mr. Stevens. Mr. Rawlings knew that my office provided him with individual attention, anytime, day or night. That's why I believe he gave us all of his insurance business."

"It looks like you're going to have a pretty big payout on this," Stevens responded.

"Unfortunately, you are correct, Detective Stevens. As I mentioned in my phone conversation with you yesterday, because as Mr. Rawlings agent, I'll have to wait along with the insurance company for the estate to be probated. When that happens, depending on what the court decides, we are here to meet our professional responsibilities. That's the insurance business. I certainly wish that it wasn't necessary, if you know what I mean." Osborn replied.

"I think we do Mr. Osborn," Ford responded, but continued the questioning. "Did Mr. Rawlings, even in the minimum time of your contact with him ever give you reason to believe that he was under some type of pressure either at home or with his business?"

Osborn folded his hands and leaning his forearms forward on his desk answered. "The first day that I heard that this family had been murdered, I tried to think of anything that might have been said by Mr. or Mrs. Rawlings to me. I can't think of a thing that would fall into the category of being unusual or odd. They were both very proper about how they spoke or did business with me. Usually, as an agent, you would notice something like, let's say, when one of the spouses takes a large policy out on the other one. Then if there is some kind of foul play, you have a suspicion about the circumstances. That's obviously not the case here. Everything was in order and has been for the past two years, with the exception of the rings." Osborn paused, shrugged his shoulders and completed his thought, "there's not much one can do when something like this happens."

"We would appreciate it if you could mail us copies of the insurance forms you showed us today so that we can make them part of our file, Mr. Osborn," Ford requested.

"No problem. I will get it done today and have it in the mail by the time we close."

"One more thingMr. Osborn," Steven said. "This Mr. Becker from the insurance company went up to the cottage with a Mr. Fowler and a Mr. Santino. Do you happen to know what that was all about?"

Mr. Osborn hesitated for a moment then answered. " As far as I know, Mr. Becker was the adjuster assigned to this claim and he needed to get a personal look at the cottage and anything that may have been in the cottage or part of it. He called here to get some information and during that conversation I recall him mentioning that he was going to take along a relative of the family to assist him with identifying items at the cottage. The only name I'm familiar with is that of Mr. Santino."

"Why is that?" Ford asked.

"On a few occasions, Mr. Rawlings authorized Mr. Santino to receive some of his personal information that we have in our files. As for the other person, Mr. Fowler, that's the first time I ever heard that name."

"Thank you Mr. Osborn. You've helped a great deal. If something comes up or that you recall something later that you think we should know, please call us" Stevens said shaking Osborn's hand.

The next stop for the detectives would be the branch office of the Commerce Bank of Detroit at Eleven-mile road and Southfield highway.

Stevens eased the cruiser out into the morning traffic and spoke. "Why would Rawlings authorize Santino to have access to that kind of personal information regarding his insurance?"

"Right now Frank, I couldn't even venture a guess," Ford replied.

As Stevens approached the bank's parking lot, he cautiously entered the area that was busy with morning customers trying to find parking spaces, while other drivers were trying to jockey their way into the access lines for the three drive-up window service stalls. The weekend was coming and the weather forecast was for hot and muggy conditions. People needed weekend cash for their trips up north.

Eventually the detectives found a parking spot and pulled into it. As they stepped from the vehicle, the early morning coolness had evaporated and hot, humid air was engulfing the city. They made their way through the revolving doors into the main area of the bank. Long lines of customers were patiently waiting their turn to get the teller windows, most of them enjoying the cool air that flowed from the buildings air conditioning.

As Stevens and Ford entered the bank, the first thing they noticed was a waist high marble railing on their left that surrounded an open area filled by secretarial staff and bank loan officers. This is where the bank's customers could apply for car loans, checking accounts and numerous other services that the bank offered.

The detectives walked over to an attractive woman in a well-pressed business suit, who was sitting at a large desk by the railing, busily typing out a letter. As they approached, they presented their badges for identification. She stopped typing. Her desk was positioned near a swinging brass gate that allowed visitors to enter.

"And what can I do for you gentlemen?" she asked.

Ford politely introduced himself and Stevens and informed her that they had an appointment with Mr. Jessup, the bank manager.

The woman used her intercom to call the manager and inform him that his guests had arrived. A few moments later, a man appeared in an open portal along the back wall that separated the working area from the manger's office. He motioned for the detectives to enter through a swinging brass gate.

Mr. Jessup was a tall, wiry looking individual who moved slowly and deliberately. His lanky frame supported a well-tailored navy blue pinstripe suit, light blue shirt with a matching paisley tie. His wardrobe reflected the conservative environment of the bank. Everything should be orderly in the banking business. That was Roger Jessup's motto.

"Thank you Martha," he said to the young woman. "If you gentlemen will follow me, we can discuss the matters you called about in my office."

Stevens and Ford followed and entered the office as Jessup closed the door behind them.

When everyone had been seated, Stevens spoke first. "Mr. Jessup we appreciate you taking the time to speak with us informally. As I mentioned to you over the phone, Detective Ford and I are in the process of confirming certain movements, transactions and conversations by the Rawlings family prior to their deaths. We would like to know what you know about them either as a customer or personally."

Roger Jessup, in his usual and unruffled manner placed the palms of his hands together, in a prayer fashion. Glancing first at Ford and then looking directly at Stevens. To an outside observer, it appeared as if he were sizing up each of the detectives as if they had applied for a loan.

"Gentleman, I've been the manager at this bank for a little over three years and the Rawlings account was here when I arrived. Mr. Rawlings rarely discussed his business with me. I didn't think that was unusual. I surmised he was just that type of person. He was hard to get acquainted with and I am not the type to push."

"Did you have any conversations with either Mr. or Mrs. Rawlings in late May or early June?" Ford asked.

"Yes. I believe it was in the early part of June," Jessup said as he flicked back the pages of his desk calendar. "Yes, the 13th Mr. Rawlings called me and requested the balance on his checking account. I checked and told him the amount that was showing. It was around twenty-eight thousand dollars as I recall."

"Was that a normal amount for him to have in that account?" Stevens asked.

"Yes. Nothing unusual."

"Did he say anything else after you told him the balance?"

"I believe he said he was on the West Coast or something. He said he was calling long distance, but that he would be home soon. He said something about the need to be at his cottage for the summer."

"Did he ever call you again or come in after that call?" Stevens asked, his eyes studying Jessup's.

Jessup reached again for his desk calendar and flicked through some pages until he found what he had been looking for. "Yes, on the 25th of June. According to my notes, it was shortly before noon when Mr. Rawlings called and asked if a two hundred thousand-dollar deposit had been made to his account. I checked and told him that no such amount had been deposited. His voice seemed irritated and he said: 'It should have been there.' He then told me, 'I'm expecting two million more to be coming in shortly.' He said he would call back the next day."

"Did he mention from whom or where that money was supposed to come from?" Ford asked.

"He said it would be coming from the Bank of America, but didn't give me any more details than that. However, he did ask me to stop payment on his business checks. Then a half an hour later, he called back and told me to remove the stop payment order and to honor all checks from his agency. This is one of the reasons that I documented our conversation on my desk calendar. There was a flurry of activity by Mr. Rawlings regarding his deposits and stop payment orders and I wanted to have some reference in case there was any question in the future if I had acted properly regarding his requests. You can't be too careful in this business."

"Mr. Jessup, did Rawlings ever mention anything about other companies or individuals he was doing business with or going to do business with?" Stevens asked.

"No. Mr. Rawlings never mentioned any particular business or individual to me. He did tell me a couple of months ago when he came in to make a personal deposit, that he was planning a large business deal, but wouldn't tell me what it was at the time. I can tell you that the Bank of America is a western regional bank with its main headquarters in San Francisco. With that amount of money to be transferred, I can assure you that it would come from the main office, not from any branch. You can be certain of that."

Ford made notations in his spiral notepad regarding the information Jessup was providing. When he finished, he asked Jessup, "Can you tell us what the amount of the balance of the Rawlings account is today?"

"Sure." Jessup picked up the phone and dialed an extension number. "Jan, this is Mr. Jessup. I would like the balance of the Rawlings account and any large deposits made since June 1st please. Thank you."

Jessup waited until he received an answer. He wrote down a figure on a piece of paper. "Here you are," he said pushing the paper toward detective Ford. "Twenty-four thousand. As I said before, that's a normal amount for this account.

There have been no large amounts deposited. Internal Revenue has a "lock" on the account and the safety deposit box until probate is settled."

Ford folded and stuffed the paper in his coat pocket.

Jessup continued. "That's about the extent of my knowledge of the Rawlings account. Mr. Rawlings was a good customer, but never outgoing in his relationship with employees here. It was all business with him and I guess that is the way some people want it."

Ford rose from the chair. "We'll get back with you if something comes up regarding these amounts, transfers or the safety deposit box contents. Thank you, Mr. Jessup."

"Your very welcome gentlemen. The bank is here to serve the needs of its customers, both in life and death. Whatever assistance that we can provide to the State Police in this matter is the least we can do to meet our responsibility as good citizens and members of this community."

They shook hands and the detectives left.

As they got into their car, Stevens looked at Ford. "Do you think bank managers have to rehearse all that bullshit, about customers and community when they're talking with us?"

"You're just a cynic Frank. The guy was just doing his job, like us. He's a professional banker. You're a professional cop, okay? Aren't you getting any at home?"

"Your right, John. I guess I'm getting a little frustrated with this case already and it hasn't even been a week. Can you believe that?" "It seems like a year," Stevens countered.

"You'd better relax Frank. I think were going to have a long way to go with this one."

"Yeah. I think that's why I'm getting a little impatient. I know your right, but I keep having this gut feeling that Rawlings was up to no good. I tell you, I can feel it in my bones. Rawlings was dirty. I just want to find out what it is. That's what's really bothering me."

"Whatever Rawlings may have been involved with Frank, it probably cost him and his family their lives. I'm still trying to figure out what kind of mind it takes to slaughter a whole family and walk away from it. What kind of human being can do that without having the need to confess it to someone or ending their own life just to forget about it? It gives me the chills."

"Only animals commit that kind of savagery," Stevens answered.

CHAPTER 14

July 28, 1968
8:00 a.m.
State Police Post-Detroit

The morning temperature was extremely hot and humid. The thermometer showed 75 degrees and it was climbing. Michiganians are used to the juxtaposition of daily weather patterns.

A 1967 black Cadillac pulled into the State Police Post parking lot and came to a stop in one of the visitor's parking areas.

Julius W. Mueller turned off the ignition and exited the vehicle. He walked quickly toward the Post building and entered. The building lacked the refreshing coolness of air conditioning like that of his car. The air in the building was heavy, with little if any breeze to refresh anyone unlucky enough to have to visit or work in the building.

Mueller was an immaculate dresser and never left home without wearing a suit and tie, shined shoes and silk handkerchief. His dress habits reflected the taste of a well-bred gentleman who was accustomed to only the finest. He introduced himself to the trooper at the desk and was given the directions to Stevens' and Ford's office.

A full head of gray hair accented his square jaw and high cheekbones. His face was rough, yet mature and tanned. Julius Mueller's physical appearance made him look older than his forty-six years. He stood 6' 3" with a solid build and looked more like a boxer than a businessman. He had recently retired as a purchasing agent for an international aluminum company and was a neighbor of Richard Rawlings for the past five years. He considered himself a close friend and during the past year, his association with Richard Rawlings had become closer due to mutual business deals. Mueller was single and had never been married.

Mueller entered the detectives' office and came face to face with Stevens. Instinctively, he introduced himself. Noticing Ford nearby, he reached out and shook hands and introduced himself again to the detective.

After some small talk about the weather and the Detroit Tiger's positive season and possible pennant, detective Ford began the questioning. "Mr. Mueller, how did you come to know Richard Rawlings and his family?"

Mueller, having seated himself in the infamous wooden chair, quickly responded to Ford's question. "Well, I first ran into Richard about six years ago at a convention here in Detroit. He was handling an advertising account for a plumbing fixture manufacturer. I was in the aluminum business at the time and was responsible for one of our accounts at the convention. Someone, I can't remember who, introduced us."

"Did you become friends based on that introduction?" Ford continued.

"No, not really. I happened to mention to Richard that I was looking to move from my apartment in downtown Detroit because I didn't like what was going on as far as the race trouble thing was concerned. I told him that I wanted to get away from it. He told me about a house for sale in his neighborhood over in Towne Village and suggested I check it out."

"Is that how you came to be Rawlings neighbor?" Stevens asked.

"Yes. I followed his advice and inspected the area and just fell in love with it. That's when I decided to buy the place. It's a beautiful subdivision and I recommend it highly to anyone who's interested in moving to a better location."

"Do you have any ideas or thoughts as to why someone would want to kill Mr. Rawlings or members of his family?" Ford asked.

Mueller appeared to be taken back by the directness of Ford's question. It took a few seconds for him to answer. "I don't know why anyone would want to kill Mr. Rawlings or anyone in that family. They were wonderful people and I'm terribly saddened and upset by this whole tragedy."

"Did you ever have any business dealings with Mr. Rawlings?" Stevens asked.

"Yes I did. It started about six or eight months ago when I approached Richard with an idea I had and how we could put it together."

"What kind of idea was that?" Ford asked.

"I'd rather not say at this time. It's a pretty large and complex project, but Richard had worked it out. From what I know, he had five backers with him. It was going to take $50 million to start, with an additional $50 million for backup resources."

"That's a lot of cash for any project, Mr. Mueller. What was your cut in all of this?" Stevens asked.

"Richard was going to put me in charge."

"Of what? And when?" Stevens asked.

"Of what, is the project that I told you I would prefer not to discuss. As for when, Richard said that it would be in the near future, this fall, I believe. It all depended on his tying everything down with the investors."

"Did you know who any of the investors were?" Ford asked, making notations in his note pad.

"No. Richard was very secretive about that. I do recall one name that he mentioned at a luncheon meeting we had shortly after I had presented the idea to him. I believe he mentioned the name of a Mr. Roberts or Robiere, something like that. It sounded French to me. They were part of something Richard called the Round Table. There was supposed to be five of them."

"Can you recall anything more about this Roberts person or the others involved in this Round Table?"

"No. It just sounded confusing. I don't think Richard mentioned it more than that one time."

"Are you sure that you wouldn't like to tell us something about that project, Mr. Mueller? It might assist us in finding the murderer of Rawlings and his family."

Mueller thought for a moment. "No sir. I'm sorry, but I can't. I prefer not to discuss it at this time. If it got out, someone else might try to cash in on it. I don't mean that you would say anything, but business ideas have a way of traveling and I would rather not do it at this time. Besides, I don't think the project could have anything to do with the killings. I hope you understand."

Stevens looked disgusted at Mueller's refusal to mention the project and turned away.

Ford responded. "How do you know that this project wouldn't have anything to do with the killings Mr. Mueller?"

Mueller became rigid but held his ground. "I really don't know that one-hundred percent, but I just can't imagine that it would have anything to do with such a terrible crime. I came here voluntarily, without counsel, to help if I could. I don't think that business secrets are part of police work."

Ford knew that to force Mueller at this point would be counter-productive and backed off. "That's okay Mr. Mueller. We understand. However, I hope you know that if we need a court order to subpoena any documents that you might have or that may be pertinent to this case, including any documents related to your little project, we are not going to be very happy about it. That is part of police work."

A concerned looked crossed Mueller's face, but quickly vanished.

Ford replaced the notepad in his breast pocket and cut off the interview.

"Thank you for coming in Mr. Mueller. We'll be in touch if we have any further questions."

As Mueller started to leave, he turned to the detectives and said, "If you think it will help, I'd be prepared to offer a reward of ten or fifteen thousand dollars to try and catch whoever murdered Richard and his family."

Stevens cleared his throat. "That's mighty generous of you Mr. Mueller. We'll let our superiors know about that. I'm sure that they'll contact you if and when they feel it might help. Thank you."

Mueller turned and left without saying another word and disappeared down the hall.

The detectives slumped into their chairs and looked at each other for a long time.

Finally, Stevens broke the silence. "Why the hell would Mueller, out of the blue, cough up ten or fifteen grand reward money for Rawlings and his family?"

Ford was drawing circles on a desk pad. "This must have been some idea he and Rawlings had put together. If it was going to take fifty million dollars to start and then another fifty in reserve, were talking pretty big shooters here, Frank."

"If it's true, yes. If not, it's a lot of bull."

CHAPTER 15

July 29, 1968
9:00 a.m.
New Hudson, Michigan

It was a short drive to the Detroit suburb of New Hudson. Stevens and Ford wanted to check with the owner of the New Hudson Airport about the personal airplane Mr. Rawlings kept there.

The airport owner was a bald-headed man in his late sixties with a bushy gray mustache and wearing a greasy pair of white coveralls. He approached the detectives as they exited the patrol car.

The detectives explained to the man why they were there and without any hesitation, the airport owner pointed to the Quonset style hanger about fifty yards from where they were standing.

The owner excused himself, explaining that he had a lot to do, but told the detectives they could help themselves because the hanger door was unlocked. Hanger #14 was leased by Rawlings to house his Cessna 172 Skyhawk aircraft.

Stevens and Ford approached the closed hanger door and pushed it open. The Cessna sat quietly, its wings showing a little dust, but for the most part it was like the rest of the plane, clean and neat. They searched the cockpit area and the rear seats but did not locate anything of value, possible clues or potential evidence.

A flight log on the passenger seat was the only document in the plane. Stevens picked it up and noted that the last time the plane had been used had been on June 10, 1968. There wasn't any flight plan entered on the log for that date.

The date was two days before Rawlings had requested that Santino take him to the airport for his mysterious meetings. Stevens decided to bring the log with them. They closed the hanger door, gave the airport owner a receipt for the log and thanked him for his cooperation.

Their next destination was about fifteen miles east of the airport, in the city of Birmingham. Birmingham, Michigan is a prosperous community with numerous successful and very wealthy business and professional people among its residents.

The main objective of the visit was for Stevens and Ford to stop at the Larson Jewelry store. Mr. Larson, owner of the store had agreed to meet with the detectives regarding the appraisal of the two rings that Mrs. Rawlings had been wearing at the time of her death. The wedding band had been recovered at the crime scene, but the diamond ring was still missing.

Mr. Larson was a man in his early fifties, slightly bald with a short, squat figure and pudgy face. He told the detectives that he could definitely identify the diamond ring if it were recovered. The ring, according to Mr. Larson, was valued between $9,000.00 and $11,000.00. He gave the detectives a written statement for their file. They left Mr. Larson with his precious stones and bracelets and returned to the Post.

There were still a significant number of people that had to be interviewed and time was passing quickly. The dilemma for Stevens and Ford was that they had a two-prong problem. First, they had to determine a motive for the hideous crime. And second, they needed to account for the actions of the Rawlings family from the time they had left their home in Towne Village until the estimated time of the murders. Each day the clock's hands seemed to move faster around the hourly markers.

The Rawlings, bodies had been discovered less than a week before, but so far, Stevens and Ford had little to show for their work. The important information from the crime lab was taking longer than normal because the bodies had been so badly decomposed. To obtain any evidence from them would be extremely difficult and time consuming.

"John, what's on the appointment calendar for tomorrow?" Stevens asked, looking up from his desk. Two large piles of folders were stacked on top of his desk.

Ford glanced at his calendar; "We need to see Calvin Michaels, Rawlings CPA over in Southfield. Then we're back here to meet with Mr. Ross Rawlings, Richard Rawlings' father."

"Another long day," Stevens said, shutting his eyes for a moment.

"Yup."

Stevens grabbed the folders and began to file them. Ford typed out a report for Captain McCarthy and Director Darrens as his last task of the day. It was seven o'clock and within an hour, evening would take hold of the city. Turning off the lights, Stevens looked at Ford and said sarcastically, "This is a fine mess you've gotten me into."

July 30, 1968
9:30 a.m.
Southfield, Michigan

Stevens and Ford in their unmarked, dark blue Plymouth Fury cruiser headed out of the Post in the direction of the city of Southfield to see Calvin Michaels.

The Michaels CPA firm had been the Rawlings family accountants for the past twenty years. Mr. Michaels had personally maintained the R.C. Rawlings & Associate books for the past ten years, including the payroll and tax functions of the business as well as the family personal tax returns. In past summers, Mr. Michaels had made out the paychecks and sent them to Mr. Rawlings at the cottage for his signature. However, this summer Mr. Rawlings had deviated from that arrangement. The last paychecks that Mr. Michaels had made out for the Rawlings account had been in April of 1968.

Calvin Michaels greeted the officers as they entered the building. He was a tall, string bean of a character, with a protruding "Adam's apple." His skin was sallow and he looked more like a cadaver than a living being. His looks were obviously the result of his heavy smoking, steady drinking and lack of exercise either in- or out-of-doors. His gait was slow and deliberate as he approached the detectives, greeted them and then led them to his antiquated office.

As the three men settled themselves into their chairs, Stevens began the questioning. "As you are aware Mr. Michaels, detective Ford and I are in charge of the criminal investigation into the Rawlings family murders. We hope that you may be able to shed some light on Mr. Rawlings' financial position, either with the business or personal matters. We are looking for any facts about the deceased family that could assist us in the case."

Mr. Michaels responded with a confident tone. "Certainly. I will try to help in any way I can. However, there isn't a whole lot that I can tell you about Mr. Rawlings or even the way he did business?"

"Why not?" Ford asked, expecting that Mr. Rawlings accountant should have a very good insight into his client's habits.

"Because detective Ford, Mr. Rawlings was such a private person. He provided me with the invoices, receivables and other financial data and my firm just processed it. He spoke very little about his business with me. I know that sounds odd, but that's the way Mr. Rawlings operated. What I knew about his business came from my observation of Mr. Rawlings income and expense sheets."

"Did anything out of the ordinary happen within the last six months or year?" Stevens asked.

"No. I don't believe so. He did mention something in May about having to readjust his tax structure for the coming year, but he said he would talk with me about it later, around September as I recall."

"Anything else?" Ford pressed.

"Yes, there is one thing. In the past, Mr. Rawlings always discussed with me who was going to receive raises before he gave them out. However this year, raises were given out, I believe by Mr. Santino. That was before I had a chance to discuss it with Mr. Rawlings."

"Have you said anything to Mr. Santino about that?"

"I certainly did. Just last week I finally caught up with him on the phone and asked why I hadn't been informed of these raises. He told me that Mr. Rawlings had authorized them before he went on vacation and not to worry about it."

"Were you satisfied with his answer?"

"Initially I was concerned, because Mr. Rawlings never trusted anyone near that much money. Frankly, I was not happy about it, but I was not involved with the daily operations of the Rawlings advertising firm. I had no specific reason or authority to question Santino about it."

"Do you think Mr. Rawlings would have approved an action like that without consulting you first?" Ford asked, searching for some concrete evidence that Santino's independent actions were the result of Santino knowing that Rawlings was already dead and unable to countermand the order. He hoped that Michaels could provide an answer.

"It's possible, but in my opinion, not probable," Michaels responded. "Mr. Rawlings liked to watch his money. It's hard for me to believe that he would have allowed someone else to make a decision regarding pay raises without first discussing it with me. He always wanted to know how it would affect him financially. He was always concerned about his tax situation and liability."

"Were there any tax problems with his business?" Stevens asked.

"Not at all. Mr. Rawlings always insisted that he did not want any tax problems and to overpay if there was a questionable item. In fact I'll be doing an audit on the business the day after tomorrow. At that time, I can provide you with more information."

"Did the business have any new expenses or income in the last six months that would seem out of the ordinary to you, Mr. Michaels?" Ford asked.

"No. As I have said before, Mr. Rawlings mentioned some 'big deal' that would require a different tax structure, but that wasn't supposed to happen until this fall. That was it. There was nothing in the way of income or expenses that I was aware of that would have been out of the ordinary."

"Okay. We'll look forward to hearing from you after you're done with that audit Mr. Michaels. Thank you," Ford said extending his hand.

Mr. Michaels watched the detectives leave and then returned to his accounting books.

Ford accelerated and moved the cruiser quickly into the traffic of Southfield Highway. Both men sat quietly thinking about the interview with Michaels.

Ford broke the silence. "Well partner, we just seem to be running into walls. Nothing unusual about Rawlings' business affairs, at least not where his accountant is concerned."

"Maybe. But did you catch that little bit of anger in Michaels' voice when he told us about Santino giving people raises without his permission?"

"Yeah, so?" Ford responded as he eased the cruiser over to an outside lane to avoid the congested traffic and pushed up the speed.

"We both know that Santino may have been overstepping his authority by giving out raises. My question is, would Santino have made that decision if he knew his boss was still alive?" Stevens asked.

"I was thinking of that too, Frank. But, if you recall, Santino's raise came in May when Rawlings was still around. There had to be a reason why Rawlings gave Santino such a large increase in pay. We need to find out what that reason was."

The rising sun glanced off the hood and pierced its way through the windshield directly into Ford's eyes. He reached into his shirt pocket and pulled out his sunglasses and put them on.

Stevens continued. "Santino must have done something for Rawlings or had something on him. You can't explain Rawlings actions any other way. You don't give people raises on a whim, especially if you have an obsession with monetary control, unless something or someone has turned you around 180 degrees."

Ford kept the cruiser at a steady speed and guided it easily through traffic. "I agree with you Frank that there appears to be something screwy about the relationship Rawlings and Santino had, but until we get some concrete facts on Santino, were just flying blind."

Stevens continued to elaborate. "We know that Jessup from the bank received two calls from Rawlings on June 25th. The first call was to check and see if the two hundred thousand dollars had been deposited and to stop payment on the blank checks that Santino told him that he had not received. The second call was to disregard the first call and honor the checks after he had another conversation with Santino. So far, Santino's story matches Jessup's. What doesn't match is Santino's story about the ammunition. And we don't know what other conversations Santino had with Rawlings on the 25th or before that date. All in all, Rawlings doesn't sound like a guy who lets other people go around giving his money away in raises without his approval or that he's afraid of anything."

"Santino said it was approved, but we really don't know what Rawlings said to him."

"There are just too many strange things going on with Santino and his relationship with Rawlings. The deposit, the checks and Santino's reluctance to explain his part in all of it," Stevens answered.

Ford made another quick maneuver and the police cruiser moved past the slower moving traffic. They needed to be on time for their meeting with Mr. Rawlings senior.

July 30, 1968
11:00 a.m.
State Police Post - Detroit

It was going to be another hot July day as the large fan in the corner of the detectives' office continued to move the heavy, warm air around, trying to make the room a little more comfortable. It didn't. It moved the air but that was all it could do. The heat was too much.

Ford moved a large pitcher of ice water to a small table near his desk and set it down, along with a couple of large drinking glasses. As he moved his typewriter stand toward a corner of the room, a small figure of a man, with silver gray hair appeared in the doorway. His seventy-five years were well concealed in the compact and tanned frame. He wore light colored slacks and a flowered shirt. He looked more like a tourist or a sports fan who had lost his way to a Detroit Tigers' game, than someone who could be a source of information in a brutal murder case.

Stevens spoke first. "Mr. Rawlings?" he asked, with a slight hesitation in his voice.

In a quiet tone the man responded, "That's right. Ross Rawlings."

"Come in, come in," Stevens said extending his hand and introducing himself. "Please sit down and make yourself comfortable. We had hoped that the air conditioning budgeted for this year would have been installed by now, but as you can see we'll have to do the best we can with what we've got."

The elder Rawlings gripped Stevens' hand and shook it vigorously. "Thank you." He settled himself into a comfortable, padded chair provided by Ford.

Ford introduced himself as he quickly poured Mr. Rawlings a glass of cold water from the pitcher. After handing the glass of water to Mr. Rawlings, Ford continued. "Mr. Rawlings, we appreciate you coming down here today and please accept our condolences. We realize how difficult this must be for you, but we hope you might have some information about some things that only you would or could know about, regarding Richard and his family."

"I'll try my best. It's been so very hard for my wife and I to accept this tragedy." Mr. Rawlings said, as he pushed back tears that started to fill his eyes.

"We understand Mr. Rawlings. We'll try and be as brief as we can. However there are some things we need to clear up. It's for the record. " Stevens said softly, as he pulled a pen from his breast pocket.

"Yes, I understand detective, and I hope that I can tell you something that will help. I'm ready anytime that you are."

"Let's start from the last time you saw your son. Do you recall what day that was?"

"Yes, It was Saturday, June 15th. Since my retirement from American Motors, I have always stopped by on Saturdays to see Richard or anyone in the family. It makes the week more pleasant, plus I love to see the grandchildren. Most of the time Mrs. Rawlings, my wife, comes along. This time though, she stayed at home to do some baking."

"Was there anything unusual about that visit?" Ford asked.

"No, not at first. Shirley told me that Richard was away on a trip and that she and the children were going to drive up to the cottage the next day and take both of the cars."

"So she didn't know where Richard had gone on his trip?" Stevens questioned.

"No. I asked her about that and she just said that Richard had been very busy working on a business deal and that she'd been busy getting ready to go to the cottage for the summer."

"Did she say how Richard was going to get to the cottage?" Stevens asked.

"Shirley said that she was expecting Richard to be home from the trip on Wednesday, the 19th and would fly up to the cottage with a friend."

"Did she mention this friend's name?"

"No. But about an hour later, Joe brought Richard home."

"Is that Joe Santino?" Ford asked.

"Yes. Everyone was surprised to see Richard. Then the plans were changed for Richard to go to the cottage with the family the next day."

"Did Santino stay around after he dropped off your son?" Stevens asked.

"No. He just poked his head in the door, dropped one of Richard's bags inside, said hello and goodbye at the same time to everybody and then left."

"How did Richard appear to you?" Ford asked.

"He seemed in very good spirits. He asked me into the kitchen and we talked for some time. He told me that a man by the name of Mr. Roberts or Robiere was going to come up to the cottage and spend a few days with him and the family. He told me that this Roberts person was going to fly a jet plane there and would land at Pellston airport when he came up."

"Did Richard ever mention this Roberts first name or where he was from?"

"No he didn't. And I never thought about asking. Richard seemed very excited about this meeting and I was just intent on listening."

"What else did Richard say about this meeting with this Roberts person?"

"Richard said that after Mr. Roberts spent a few days at the cottage, the whole family was going to go with him to Lexington, Kentucky and then on to Naples, Florida. In Lexington, Richard said he was going to buy a horse farm. He said he wanted to do this because little Susan liked horses. Then he told me that when they got to Naples, he was either going to buy or build a villa. He also mentioned something about Spain, but I can't remember now what that was about."

"Did Richard ever mention in this conversation as to how he was going to be able to afford to do all this?" Stevens' curiosity was peaking.

"No. But he did tell me that there was no reason that my wife and I couldn't go to Florida this winter. Then he turned to Shirley and told her that she wouldn't have to do any work at any of the new places as they would be fully staffed."

"He told you that he was going to buy these two places, staff them and then live a life of leisure, is that right, Mr. Rawlings?" Stevens continued.

"Yes. Basically, that's about what Richard said," Mr. Rawlings answered with a tone of certainty.

"And this didn't bring a question to your mind as to how Richard was going to do all of that?" Ford said cutting in.

"No sir, Mr. Ford. Richard was always talking about big deals and usually they came true just like he said they would. So, when he talked like that, it was no surprise to me that he was working on another business deal. It was just his nature."

"Did he say more?" Stevens asked.

"Yes. Richard said that he was at the final stages of winding up this deal, but was keeping it a secret because he didn't want anyone, especially his competitors to learn about it until it was over. He remarked that when the deal was complete, he would be 'a real tycoon.'" Mr. Rawlings paused for a moment as he watched Ford write down his statements on a notepad.

When Ford had finished, Mr. Rawlings continued. "Yes, he told Shirley that she should pack extra suits for the trip. Richard said that they should be gone about three weeks. Then he told me that he was having a pool and two guesthouses built at the cottage and that they should be completed by the time they returned from the trip. He looked right at me and said: "When I get back from the trip, I'll have something big to tell you.""

Stevens walked over to the desk and reached for the water pitcher as Ford finished taking down this last declaration by the elder Rawlings.

"More water, Mr. Rawlings?"

"No. I'm fine. Thank you."

"Was Joe Santino ever mentioned in any of this?" Stevens asked, returning to a chair next to Mr. Rawlings.

"No, not in that talk. However, Richard did tell me that I should contact Joe if I needed anything while he was gone on this trip. Other than our good-byes at the door, those were the last words I remember having with Richard."

"So, you never spoke to Richard after that Mr. Rawlings?"

"That's right."

"Did Mrs. Fowler ever try to contact you about locating her daughter?"

"No. She never did. I knew that she talked with Shirley regularly but since she lost her husband, she's been avoiding a lot of social functions and even some family gatherings. I know it must be a very deep loss for her too."

"Mr. Rawlings, did your son ever indicate to you that he might be involved in something with people, let us say, of a questionable reputation?" Stevens asked.

"No. I knew that Richard had contacts with a lot of people because of his magazine and the advertising business, but I've never heard anything that would make me concerned about him dealing with bad people."

"What is your opinion of Joe Santino?" Ford asked.

"I really don't know the man. That's not bad detective, it's just that I've never had any real dealings with him. Richard thought enough of him to hire him for the company, so I have to assume that he is a capable individual."

"Were there any other individuals that Richard associated with that you had the opportunity to meet or have an opinion about?" Stevens followed.

"No. Since my retirement, I've pretty much kept to myself. Everyone has their own lives to lead and my wife and I are not any different. We're just content to see our grandchildren grow up and be around us when we have the holidays or birthdays, things like that."

"Is there anything else you can tell us about Richard or the family?" Ford asked.

"No. Nothing that I can think of that made an impression on me, Mr. Ford."

"I think that is enough for today, Mr. Rawlings. It's very warm and I think we can continue our conversation another day if we need to." Stevens said.

"I'm sorry I can't give you anymore information, but that's about all I can say about our relationship with Richard and the family," Mr. Rawlings replied.

"We'll try to respect your privacy as much as we can. However, you must know that we sometimes have to ask or do things that might appear to be less than accommodating," Ford explained. "I hope you will understand if that does happen, Mr. Rawlings."

"I certainly will detective. My wife and I are always available to help if we can."

"You've been very helpful today. There are a few things I think we should look into first and then get back with you. Again, thanks for coming in."

Stevens and Ford stood up as Mr. Rawlings rose. He shook their hands, said good-bye and left. Ross Rawlings slowly made his way out of the office doorway and down the hallway to the stairs.

As the detectives watched him leave, they sensed that fate had dealt this broken man a blow from which he would never recover. Stevens and Ford could only wonder what kind of thoughts were going through this father's mind after losing a son, daughter-in-law and four grandchildren in one, swift and tragic moment. Surely, this was a deep price for any parent to pay, especially for a man in the twilight of his life. Stevens and Ford wanted desperately to find the killer or killers and see justice done. They were hopeful that it would be sooner rather than later.

CHAPTER 16

July 31, 1968
8:30 a.m.
State Police Post-Detroit

Gray clouds covered Acacia Park Cemetery and the soft rain now turned into a fine mist. Six silver hearses, each one containing the body of a deceased Rawlings family member was followed by a long procession of black limousines and cars of mourners. They snaked their way through the narrow roadway and lush green mounds of grass that led to the Rawlings' family gravesites. Eventually, they came to a stop in front of a large blue tent that covered the six, rectangular holes neatly cut into the ground. The large crowd of mournful souls exited the vehicles and waited patiently until each of the caskets had been removed from their hearses. The Lutheran minister, garbed in his religious clothing followed the caskets, while a procession of bereaved family members, relatives and friends followed closely behind. The pallbearers struggled with the slippery footing presented by the freshly cut grass, but held firm to deliver the caskets to their proper places and set each of them on their lowering devices.

Stevens and Ford stood quietly under a large maple tree that was perched on a grassy knoll in one of the cemetery sections a short distance away. From their observation point they could see the Reverend Harvey Potter of the Calvary Lutheran Church begin to conduct the funeral prayer service.

The detectives had setup a meeting with the pastor for a later date. It was uncertain how much could be gained from such an interview, but it had to be done. At this moment however, the detectives were looking over the crowd and the grounds for anything out of the ordinary. Their trained eyes scanned the area for any suspicious movements by individuals who were attending the funeral service. This type of surveillance is standard operating procedure in murder cases.

Stevens and Ford remained for almost an hour after the service had ended to see if anyone drove by or walked up to the burial spots after the congregation had left. Only the burial crew showed up to carry out their duties to complete the burial process.

The detectives were soaked from head to foot by the time they returned to the office. They used the Post locker and shower room to clean up and change into a spare set of warm dry clothes. Afterwards, they settled into reviewing the pile of paperwork that covered their desks.

The anticipation of a new clue or evidence is always the driving force with any good detective. Stevens and Ford were no different. Right now, they needed a jump-start.

Outside, the gathering of steel blue clouds produced lightning and thunder as strong winds tore at trees and telephone poles. The swirling clouds covered the city in darkness. The vibrations created by a loud burst of rolling thunder caused the interior walls of the State Police Post to shake. The rain turned to hail and fell hard against the windows, pelting the glass panes as office lights flickered, but remained on. The detectives looked at one another, ignoring the shouts from other officers on the floor who were headed to the basement.

Fellow detectives insisted that Stevens and Ford take cover before it was too late. Tornado warnings had been announced by weather forecasters and the Post had it's own shelter in the basement for exactly this kind of situation. The downpour was exceptionally strong and the windstorm severe enough that most people in the building descended into the caverns below for safety.

Stevens and Ford looked at the pile of reports stacked on their desks. They decided to ride out the storm by staying in their office. When the sounds of large hail began to hit against the windows, the decision to remain didn't appear to have been the correct one.

Yet, amidst the lightning, thunder and hail, they forged ahead, trying the best they could to close their minds to the winds and the rain churning violently outside.

Ford looked at one of the reports that had come from the crime lab. The report stated that the .25-caliber, Beretta automatic handgun that belonged to Joe Santino had been obtained by Trooper William Bowens from Mr. Santino. Trooper Bowens was scheduled to conduct a ballistics test on the weapon the next day. A notation made by Bowens caught Ford's eye. The Beretta was not registered. Not to Santino or Rawlings or any other person. Ford handed the report to Stevens, pointing to the notation.

"It doesn't surprise me," Stevens said.

Another report, confirmed that permission to retrieve mail and documents from the home of Richard Rawlings had been given by the family. However, Joe Santino had been in possession of the keys to the house and had remained in charge of the home and its contents until the surviving members of the Rawlings and Fowler families could make arrangements with the court as to who would assume that responsibility. The court order directed that the confiscated mail should be given to the temporary court-appointed Administrator of the Estate until family attorneys and the Probate Court could determine the proper execution of the Rawlings' will. Any additional mail by court order would be directed to the Administrator.

Ford reviewed another report that confirmed that fingerprints from Joseph Santino and Robert Fowler had been obtained by the Post I.D. section and had been submitted to the crime lab for elimination purposes and then forwarded to the latent print section for evaluation and filing.

Stevens pulled a report from his stack that showed all recently published issues of The Director magazines had been obtained from Mr. Rawlings' business office and were being held at the State Police Post in the evidence vault.

Newspaper articles and stories from across the state about the murders were also being gathered and filed for reference. Requests for telephone records for the Towne Village home, the cottage at Thunder Point and the advertising agency had been completed. Those records would be evaluated when received.

A safety deposit box located at the Commerce Bank of Detroit belonging to Mr. and Mrs. Rawlings had been sealed and would be inspected at a later date with the Estate Administrator and agents from the Internal Revenue Service.

Ford and Stevens continued to read the reports, one by one. Both men realized this case was different in many aspects, but it seemed that there was this mysterious haze that engulfed clues, suspects and leads. This case felt completely out of sync and even strange to both detectives. Those feelings would last for a long time.

A report filed from the Grand Haven Post received special attention. It concerned a fourteen-year-old boy. The report stated that the young man had been helping his father trim trees only fifty yards from the Rawlings cottage on June 24th, the day before the estimated time of the killings.

"Frank, we have a report here from detective Jack Dailey over at the Grand Haven Post about a fourteen-year-old boy, last name of Foster. It says that he was sent up to Petoskey by his mother to visit with his father for the summer. The parents are divorced. Apparently this kid was with his father, Russell Foster, who is a tree trimmer by trade. His ex-wife thinks her former husband is violent enough to have done something like this to the Rawlings family."

Stevens gave Ford a look of skepticism, then replied, "I'll call over there and see if we can set something up with the boy and his mother for Monday. In the meantime, maybe you should call the Petoskey Post and see if they have a file on this Russell Foster."

Ford was on the phone instantly, calling the Petoskey Post. He left a message for Detective Ray Schafer to check out Russell Foster and to get back with him as soon as possible. If anyone in Petoskey knew this Foster person, it certainly would be Detective Sgt. Ray Schafer.

Stevens finished his call to the Grand Haven Post and confirmed a Monday meeting with detective Daily and the young boy.

Ford placed the receiver back in its cradle. "It's all set, Frank. I've left a message for Schafer to check on this Mr. Foster and get back with us."

August 1, 1968
7:00 a.m.
State Police Post-Detroit

The trip from Detroit to East Lansing would take about two hours. Stevens and Ford decided to meet with Capt. McCarthy at the East Lansing Post Headquarters and bring him up to date on the investigation before continuing on to Grand Haven.

The police cruiser moved steadily along Interstate 96 in the direction of East Lansing with Stevens behind the steering wheel. He would periodically glance at the long stretches of farmland and the rows of dark green corn or fields of golden wheat that bordered the highway. It was a pleasant morning and the scenery gave him a feeling of contentment as the car moved easily down the four-lane highway.

Ford, riding shotgun had dozed off within a few minutes after leaving the Detroit Post but was awaken by a small bump in the road.

"You know Frank," Ford began, "I keep trying to think of how the these murders were committed from a tactical standpoint. Forget the motive, at least for a moment. How could it have been done without anyone in the area reacting to it at the time it was happening? "

" I know what you mean, John. It doesn't seem possible that no one was around or close to the cottage when it happened. I'll tell you this though, I believe that we're going to find that Santino was in on it. I believe he knows how it was done, why it was done, and most importantly who did it. But I don't think he's going to tell us anything until we apply some pressure."

" I certainly wouldn't trust him running any company that I owned." Ford replied.

"Damn straight you wouldn't," Stevens added quickly.

"But I'm not convinced that he did it." Why would Santino knock off Rawlings and his family just to get a hold of a business that doesn't appear to be all that successful? We're not talking Las Vegas casinos here. Besides, whatever this big deal was that Rawlings was involved in, I'm sure that Santino could have stolen it if he wanted too."

"You know that people do crazy things for money, John. Hell, even now you can see that Santino is trying to capitalize on the situation. Personally, I don't think he cared all that much for Rawlings. All this brother bullshit and leaving him in charge while Rawlings was on vacation doesn't mean diddley-squat. If that was true, how come Santino had to call Rawlings just about every day when Rawlings was away from the office to get permission to do something? Explain that to me."

"I can't Frank. We know that the weather that day in Detroit was bad, so flying up north would have been very difficult, if not impossible. Besides, that would have meant that flight records would have to have been kept or risk being spotted at an airport. And, it just doesn't make sense to me that Santino would drive a couple of hundred miles up north to kill an entire family, then drive back to Detroit and leave the next morning for Indianapolis. I mean, I can think of a hundred reasons he wouldn't do that. First of all, he could have a flat tire, or be stopped for speeding, or get in an accident. And those things could all happen before or after he had committed the crime. If it was after, he might get caught with stolen property, the rings, the weapons, who knows what else was taken out of there."

Stevens remained unconvinced. "Well, my first instincts tell me that Santino's in on it. I don't know how yet. But I'll find out and you're going to be there when I do," Stevens said firmly.

"I'll be there with you Frank. But I still say at this point, I'm just not convinced Santino actually did the killings. I'm not saying he isn't involved in it, in someway or another. I have a hunch that Santino and Rawlings may have been doing something illegal or under the table and something went wrong. Rawlings and his family paid the price for it."

"That's crossed my mind too John, but, desperate people will do desperate things. And to me, Joe Santino is prime suspect, numero uno until I see some positive evidence that suggests otherwise."

"Okay," Ford said, not wanting the discussion to escalate into an argument.

The detectives remained silent for the rest of the trip as they watched the landscapes of Michigan farms pass by.

It was 10:00 a.m. when they pulled into the Michigan State Police headquarters parking lot in East Lansing. Stevens pulled the car into a parking space adjacent to the Administration building. The mammoth parking lot was filled with numerous police cruisers of every description. They entered the building and stopped at the sign-in desk.

The receptionist announced the detectives arrival to the captain's office and the detectives were allowed to pass through the security checkpoint.

Stevens and Ford climbed the marble staircase to the second floor and entered McCarthy's office. The captain was waiting for them.

"Welcome," the captain said with a broad grin. "How was the trip?"

"Fine, no problems," Stevens answered as he shook the captain's hand.

"Except having to discuss theories and motives with this guy," Ford said nodding towards Stevens as he shook the captain's hand.

"Have a seat and bring me up to date with the Rawlings' case. The Colonel is up at Mackinac Island with the Governor. I told him that I would have an update for him when he returns on Wednesday."

Stevens and Ford relayed all the information they had, including their theories about the crime. They discussed some of the problems associated with trying to move ahead too quickly with the investigation before the forensic evidence was processed. Stevens and Ford made it clear to the captain, that the forensic evidence, because of the condition of the bodies and the crime scene, presented problems that neither detective had been confronted with before in any of their other investigations.

Captain McCarthy was fully aware that his two investigators had been shackled with a thirty-day lag time before the murders were discovered and told them so.

All three men discussed the upcoming interview with the Foster boy. All of them were cognizant of the fact that this fourteen-year-old boy was caught between a set of divorced parents, each one wanting permanent custody rights to their son.

"Personally I think you guys are on the right track considering how everything has come down. I've told the Colonel that you two know what and how to do things, so try not to make me look too bad, Okay?" A slight smile crossed the captain's lips.

"We certainly won't do that sir," Ford replied.

"Good. I appreciate both of you bringing me up to date. The Colonel wanted me to tell you that the daily reports have been excellent and he appreciates them. So keep them coming."

They shook hands and the two detectives left.

Ford took the wheel on this leg of the trip and pulled out of the Post complex and entered the ramp leading to the I-96 highway and headed west.

"John lets stop in Grand Rapids, grab some lunch first then head on over to Grand Haven."

"Sounds good," John replied, stepping on the accelerator.

It would be an hour to Grand Rapids, then another half-hour to forty-five minutes to Grand Haven. It would be around 2 p.m. before they would arrive at the Grand Haven Post.

The City of Grand Haven, Michigan spreads out on the Lake Michigan shoreline and acts like a welcoming beacon for the ships that ply the Great Lakes. Situated at a midpoint on the west side of the Michigan shoreline between Gary, Indiana and the Straits of Mackinac, it is ideally located for tourists, fishermen and boating enthusiasts. The long and winding Grand River empties into Lake Michigan at this point and provides access to the big lake for the variety of boating craft harbored in the nearby marinas.

Grand Haven State Park contains one of Lake Michigan's most famous piers and plays host to thousands of people who visit the long concrete protrusion each year to view the red lighthouse and to do some serious perch and salmon fishing. Men, women and children bring blankets, lawn chairs and other forms of seating so that they can relax while trying to catch one of Lake Michigan's prize fish from the pier. Like most of Michigan's State Parks, people fill the beach on hot days, then climb the sand dunes and party at one of the many watering holes along the shore drive. The State Park is overrun with high school and college students during the summer months, each one trying to soak up as much sun and sand as they can before returning to school in the fall.

The city is the main port for the U.S. Coast Guard's Great Lakes fleet and it maintains its headquarters there. For many years, the town had been a quiet and sleepy vacation spot.

However, city officials during the early 1960's started to notice that members of the younger generation were making their way to the area in greater numbers. The city updated its master plan and decided to capitalize on the tourist market. From that point on, the city grew rapidly.

Stevens, who had taken over the driving after their stop in Grand Rapids now drove across the Grand River drawbridge that separated Grand Haven from another small town nearby, called Spring Lake.

Ford pointed to the right and spoke up. "The Post should be over there on Lake Ave. Frank."

Stevens knew the general direction of the Post, but it had been almost ten years since he had been there and some of the old landmarks had been removed. Partially hidden behind an overgrown shrub, he spotted the blue Michigan State Police Post sign, with the diagonal gold slash and MSP emblem on it. A painted arrow on the sign indicated a right turn at the next intersection. Stevens made the turn and a couple of blocks later they pulled into the Grand Haven Post parking lot.

They entered the building through the main doors and approached the information desk, where they introduced themselves to the trooper on duty, showing their badges and requesting to see detective Dailey .

The trooper buzzed detective Tom Dailey's office, and told him that the two detectives he had been expecting had arrived. A few seconds later, a large, rotund, mountain of a man emerged from the back hallway and greeted his two counterparts.

"If you two are ready, we can go out to the Gaines house and talk with the Foster kid," Dailey said. "The boy's mother took back her maiden name, but the boy wanted to keep his father's name," Dailey quickly explained as the group headed to the parking lot.

Dailey inserted his heavy frame into the back seat of the cruiser and kept up the conversation. "I thought you guys would never get here."

"We had to stop in Lansing for a few minutes to update Captain McCarthy about the case, then we stopped near Grand Rapids for lunch. I think we made good time," Ford answered as Stevens pulled the vehicle out of the parking lot, but stopped before entering into the traffic.

"Okay. Where the hell are we going?" Stevens asked.

"Sorry Frank. We need to go over to Spring Lake. That's back across the bridge, same way you guys came in."

"Okay, I know where that is." Frank answered.

" The boy's mother, Donna Gaines will be with him. They live at 1471 Moore Rd. She and the boy are expecting us."

"Good. I hope we can get some positive info out of it," Ford said.

A few minutes later, Frank Stevens was pulling into the gravel driveway of a small bungalow home in Spring Lake. On the porch, a frail looking woman, with a full-length, cotton summer dress, draped on a bony frame, stood bare foot, with her hair in disarray. She was sweeping off the last of the sand that had accumulated on her porch. Her face reflected a tough life. Her dark blue eyes appeared deeper in their sockets and lacked the luster of a person who had any contentment or hope with life.

The detectives exited the car and stood for a moment before moving toward the house. Detective Dailey spoke first. "Mrs. Gaines?" he asked politely.

"Yes. You must be the gentlemen from the State Police who want to talk with my son," She said, moving closer to the porch steps. The daylight revealed the deep lines in her face and the wrinkles around her chin. She looked sixty instead of thirty-two.

"Yes we are. This here is detective Stevens and this is detective Ford from Detroit. They're here to talk with Johnny and you. May we come in?"

"Yes. Yes, please do. You all will have to excuse my mess, I've been tryin' to get my cleanin' done before goin' to work later this afternoon. Com'on in." she said, as she motioned with a wave of her hand for the men to follow her inside.

The detectives entered the house and sat themselves at the dining room table. The inside was pleasant and comfortable in direct contrast to the rough condition that marked the exterior of the house.

Mrs. Gaines yelled upstairs for her young son John to come down. She mentioned that the detectives from Detroit were here to speak to him. He shouted back that he would be down "right away."

"May I get you gentlemen somethin' to drink?" she asked.

Stevens and Ford declined while Dailey opted for a glass of water.

Mrs. Gaines filled Dailey's request and placed the glass of water in front of him before sitting down. "John just got home from swimmin' and is gettin' dressed. Maybe I can answer some questions before he comes down."

"That would be fine, Mrs. Gaines," Stevens said respectfully. "As I understand it, you called detective Dailey and told him that you thought your ex-husband, Russell might possibly be involved in the Rawlings family murders. What facts or information do you have that prompted you to call detective Dailey?"

"Well, I'll let young John tell you about his experience while he was up north last month with his father. As for me, Russell is a very mean man. One time, he actually beat me up when I didn't wash out the diapers and put them out to dry like he thought they should've been. Another time, he threatened to shoot Johnny and me, if'n I went through with the divorce. I did go through with the divorce, but just before I did, he drank some poison he got from a drug store. He didn't die, but he blames me for it. The man is nuts. That's why I think he could do something like that."

Mrs. Gaines was becoming agitated and her vindictive nature was coming through. It didn't take long for all three detectives to see what the motivation was behind her report.

"Is Mr. Foster making his child support payments regularly, Mrs. Gaines?" Ford asked.

"Well, he was behind until just recently. I asked the Friend of the Court to get after him and I guess they put the pressure on him. In fact, he increased his payment amounts right after that trouble happened up north."

A young looking, freckled-face John Foster entered the room and spoke. "Hello."

The detectives turned toward the young voice and observed a redheaded youth in jeans, tennis shoes and T-shirt standing at the entranceway of the dining area.

"Come in here and introduce yourself to these gentlemen, John. They're from the State Police and they want to talk to you about your father. You can tell them about the kind of work you did up there when you were with him."

John Foster shook the hands of each of the three detectives. Young Mr. Foster was a mature fourteen years of age and was eagerly looking forward to entering the ninth grade in the fall.

"John, would you like to tell us what happened while you were up north working with your father?" Stevens asked softly.

"Sure." John said eagerly. "On June 21st, that would've been a Friday, mom sent me on a bus from here up to Petoskey to be with my dad for a few weeks."

"Can you tell us what you did while you were there?" Stevens continued.

"Yes sir, I helped him with his tree trimming business. I'd go out with him and another kid named Al. I don't know Al's last name. He lives up there, I guess. Anyway, that's what I did while I was there. I helped trim trees, carry logs, rake and cleaned up the yards of the cottages where we worked."

"Do you remember cutting or trimming any trees around a place called Thunder Point?"

"Yes. I think it was called Thunder Point. There were two places we did some work. One place, no one was home and we cut down a couple of big pine trees. At the other one, there was a family there. There was someone who looked like the dad, with two or three other boys, not sure if they were his sons, and a little girl and an older lady."

Ford pulled a picture of the Rawlings family from the breast pocket of his suit coat and showed it to John. "Are these the people you saw John?"

John looked at the photo studying it for a full minute before answering: "Yep. That's the man all right. I can tell by the silver, wavy hair. And that's the little girl too. She had a lot of freckles. I'm sure the boys are the same ones. They weren't all dressed up like in this picture though. I'm just not sure about this one." John said, pointing at Randy Rawlings in the photograph.

"Where did you see this family, John?" Stevens asked.

"From what I can remember, it was a small cottage with lots of trees around it, but you could see the big lake from the lot. They had a couple of cars parked out in front. When we started working, the family left the cabin and came back sometime later. When they came back, the man with the silver hair asked my dad if he could hook up the telephone wire, which we took down while we were trimming."

"Do you remember what he said to your father?"

"He told my dad that he was expecting a phone call from someone. He also told my dad about having to go on a trip the next day or something like that."

"Then what happened?"

"Well, my dad hooked up the phone line, and the phone in the cottage started ringing. Ringing a lot, like a bunch of calls coming in."

"Did you hear the man with the silver hair or anyone in the house say or call out a name that may have been someone calling on the phone?"

"No. I could hear the phone ring, but I couldn't hear anyone talking."

"What else can you remember about this place or these people?"

"Not much. I know that the man with the silver hair paid my dad before the job was finished. On Tuesday, I stayed at my dad's place, while he and Al went back to the same cabin to finish the trimming job."

"Were you, or your father, or this Al fellow ever inside the log cabin when you were there?"

"Nope."

"Why didn't you go with your father and Al on Tuesday?"

"I was sore from all that trimming work. I could hardly lift my arms. In fact, I'm still sore."

"Does your father own a gun?" Stevens asked.

John looked at his mother. She nodded for him to answer.

"Yes. He owns a .22-caliber rifle. He uses it to shoot rodents and other varmints."

"John, is there anything else that you can remember about those people or the cottage?" Stevens pressed.

"No, not really. I only stayed with my dad for about three weeks after that. I just worked mostly. I mean we didn't even go fishing or swimming or anything like that."

Mrs. Gaines saw an opportunity to reveal her thoughts on the subject. "I can tell you officers that when Russell brought John home, he started arguing with me about having custody of John and wanted him to go back up north with him. I told him no. Young John belongs here with me. Besides, he's going to school, so he can go on to college, not running around up north and maybe get into trouble. When I told him that, he threatened me with a beating and I had to go and get my gun. I told him clear, that if he didn't leave immediately, I was going to call the police or shoot him. It was his choice."

"What did he do when you told him that?" Ford asked.

"I think he realized that if he made a move to hit me, it would be his last time. He just turned around, got in his car and left." Mrs. Gaines turned to John. "John, you'd better get down to work at the Soft-serve. They'll get upset if you're late."

"Sure mom. I'm going right now."

"If it's alright with you gentlemen," Mrs. Gaines asked belatedly.

The detectives looked at one another and decided that they were finished. John Foster was gone in a flash.

Mrs. Gaines continued railing against her husband. "I just thought you people ought to know that Russell has had mental problems. Some doctors committed him to the Traverse City hospital. Also, he had psychiatric treatment while he was in the Army at Fort Sam Houston. Russ enlisted just prior to the Korean War and was in for about a year and a half."

The detectives listened patiently until Mrs. Gaines had vented all she could and then Stevens concluded the interview. He thanked Mrs. Gaines for her cooperation.

As they were leaving, Ford requested that she not discuss this interview with anyone, especially her ex-husband. She reassured him that she wouldn't and that she would be available to answer more questions if needed.

The detectives drove back to the Grand Haven Post to drop off detective Dailey. They asked him to stay in touch with Mrs. Gaines in case there was additional information.

After a short conversation about the status of the case with Dailey, they left for the long return trip back to Detroit.

As the patrol car gained speed on the freeway, Ford spoke. "I'm not sure we made much headway with that kid, Frank. I hope Schafer up at Petoskey was able to check out Russell Foster and interview him."

"Yeah. Knowing Schafer, he may have the information already. We still need to go over some more of those lab reports, bank statements and the Rawlings personal stuff. It's going to be a long week." Stevens said as he watched the white stripes of the highway move quickly past the cruiser. He pushed the pedal down and the big V-8 engine roared and the police cruiser disappeared down the Interstate.

CHAPTER 17

August 3, 1968
8:00 a.m.
State Police Post
Petoskey, Michigan

Detective Ray Schafer, forty-seven years of age was a twenty-two year veteran of the Michigan State Police. There was a slight trace of gray marking his sandy blond hair and his lanky 6'2"frame was hardened by his years of service in both the military and the State Police. He had served in the U.S. Marine Corps during World War II, and had been decorated for bravery for his actions on the islands of Iwo Jima and Tarawa in the Pacific.

With over two decades of service with the Michigan State Police, there wasn't much that he had not seen in the world of crime, including murder. He had just finished a phone conversation with Stevens and Ford and was looking through some crime reports on his desk. The Rawlings case was unlike any he had seen in all his years on the force. He knew the ravages of war and the death of young people fighting for their country, but the massacre he had observed in that small cottage on the shores of Lake Michigan was something he could not push out of his mind.

Sitting next to him was Detective Sgt. William "Big Bill" Rodgers, a twenty year veteran of the Michigan State Police. His six-feet, four-inch height and massive body frame contained two hundred and fifty pounds of solid muscle. He was a no nonsense type of law officer. Rodgers had been on vacation when he heard the news of the Rawlings murders and immediately returned to join his partner on the case.

Ray Schafer was lucky to have Bill Rodgers as a partner, but even more fortunate to have him as a close friend.

"You know Bill, going through some of these suspect names, most of them we know couldn't do something like the Rawlings massacre. Look at Charlie Thomas here. He's been in and out of the State Hospital in Traverse City so many times, that his parents don't even remember where he is. Lucky for them he's still in the hospital," Schafer lamented.

Rodgers looked up from the set of reports he had in front of him and looked at a mug shot photo. "Isn't he the one, who took that fireplace poker to his folks on Christmas Day a few years back and the Sheriff's department people had to track him down in the woods to catch him?"

"Yes, that's him. Or look here," Shafer said, plucking another card from his pile. "Here's Jimmy Dale Stubbs. He's gone AWOL again and the Army thinks he may be in the vicinity because his mom lives over there in Harbor Springs."

"Ray, did you see the forensic report I put in your box about the shoe print they found near the boy's body laying in the doorway? Rodgers asked.

"Yeah, I read it. I can't believe that out of all the shoe stores you checked on that you came up empty."

"Neither could I. I think we're looking for some kind of rubber sole boot. I hope the lab is able to come up with something more definite."

A young trooper poked his head in the office area. "Excuse me Sergeant, but there's a call on line three. A man by the name of Ryan wants to talk to someone handling the Rawlings murders."

Schafer spoke up, "put him through." A few seconds later, the black phone on Schafer's desk rang and he picked up the receiver. "This is Sgt. Schafer."

" Sergeant, my name is Rex Ryan and I'm calling from Toledo, Ohio. I'm going to be up in Petoskey within the next couple of days and I wonder if I might be able to stop in and talk to you about the Rawlings killings. I think I might have some information that could be useful."

" Did you know Mr. Rawlings or someone in his family?" Schafer asked.

"No sir. I used to work for Richard Rawlings," the voice replied.

Schafer informed the caller that the Stevens and Ford were in charge of the case and were at the Detroit Post.

Mr. Ryan explained that he would be taking a plane from Green Bay, Wisconsin for business purposes and it would be easier for him to speak with someone at the Petoskey Post.

Schafer decided he had better make the appointment first, then inform Stevens and Ford about it in case they wanted to be there. In Schafer's eyes it was more important to gain potential information than to lose it. He set the date for August 6th at 9:00 a.m.

Within seconds of hanging up the phone, Schafer called Stevens. Stevens and Ford agreed that it was best to go ahead and conduct the interview without them being there.

Stevens informed Schafer that he and Ford were tied up with other matters in the case and would review the report when it was finished.

Rodgers immediately began a background check on Mr. Rex Ryan. The background check showed that Mr. Ryan had been a Probation Officer for Lenawee County, Michigan just west of Detroit. The information also revealed that Mr. Ryan had been assigned to Circuit Court Judge Reston Marlow at the county courthouse. The personnel information obtained also made the detectives aware that the Judge had continual problems with Mr. Ryan's behavior and had requested that he resign from his position.

The reason Mr. Ryan had been asked to resign or be fired was due to his problem with alcohol. Subsequently it was discovered that Mr. Ryan had lied on his original employment application and was currently going through a divorce with his second wife. Oddly enough, his second wife had been acquired in a wife swapping trade with an attorney in Detroit. Each one got a divorce and remarried the opposite mate. The two detectives could not wait to meet Mr. Ryan.

August 6, 1968
9:00 a.m.
State Police Post-Petoskey

Rex Ryan was a small man, literally and figuratively. He stood about five feet, four inches tall, with black curly hair and a rough complexion. One could tell at first glance that he had his nose broken at some point in his life. One would have picked his profession as a bantamweight boxer. His small feet quickly danced there way up the steps of the Petoskey State Police Post and into the building. He approached the information desk and gave the trooper his name, stating that he had an appointment with detectives Schafer and Rodgers.

He was given directions to their office and went directly to the second floor of the building.

"Good morning, Mr. Ryan," Schafer said as their guest entered the room. "This is detective Rodgers."

The two detectives were like two concrete pillars next to the little guy.

"Nothing like having a couple of bookends, eh?" Ryan said, trying to be funny about the size difference.

The detectives gave a slight smile and Rodgers motioned for Ryan to take a seat.

"So Mr. Ryan." Rodgers started, "you have some information you think might be valuable to us in the Rawlings case? Detective Schafer and I are very interested in hearing what you have to say."

For a big man, Rodgers's voice was soft and pleasant. It was void of any harshness or intimidation. Ryan felt comfortable talking with this giant of a man.

"Yes, I believe that I have some information concerning Mr. Rawlings that you may not know about."

"Keep talking Mr. Ryan," Schafer said easily. "If we don't understand something we'll stop you. By the way, would you mind if we record our conversation? That's so if we miss something, we can double check it from the tape and won't have to disturb you again?"

"No, go right ahead. I don't have anything to hide. Tape all you want."

"Fine," Schafer said, pushing the start button that turned on the tape recorder.

As the tape started, so did Ryan. "I worked for Richard Rawlings starting in 1957 and left in 1965. I had a good relationship with him, but I had a better job offer, so I took it."

"What made you think about calling us?" Schafer asked.

"Well I see this newspaper story a few days ago that said that Rawlings had no enemies. That's not true."

"What's the truth as you know it Mr. Ryan?" Rodgers asked.

"Let me say this. Richard was a person that either liked you and would do anything for you or he disliked you and would do anything to hurt you."

"Can you give us an example, Mr. Ryan?" Schafer asked hoping to see if Mr. Ryan might lead them into a more fertile ground.

"Not exactly. It was just common knowledge around the company that Richard was that way."

"Who else was aware of this?" Rodgers asked.

" You can ask anyone who worked there for at least a year. They would know it. Sometimes Rawlings would suspect that he had spies in his own company or it might be someone outside the company trying to find out what we were doing."

"Can you tell us any thing specific?" Schafer persisted.

"Mr. Rawlings had a very good thing going with the Diamond Faucet Company and their advertising account. Plus, he had this magazine called The Director. Well, that magazine was losing between eighty-five hundred and ten thousand an issue in 1965 and from what I know its still losing money."

"How do you know this?" Rodgers asked in a tone that was more direct.

"I was friends with one of the guys in the office and he would tell me that Richard was always yelling over the phone at the printers. First it was the Anwar

Press people in Saginaw, then the University Press people in Ann Arbor, and finally with Starlight Press down in Kalamazoo."

"Did this person ever tell you what Mr. Rawlings was yelling about when he talked with these people?"

"Yeah, he said that Richard was always late paying his bills and the press people were always calling to get their money."

"Are you suggesting that someone from one of those firms might have been willing to kill Rawlings and his family because of that?" Schafer asked.

"That I don't know. But I do know that he owed some of those people lots of money and they weren't too happy about him not making his payments on time. And it was the way Rawlings talked to them."

Schafer continued, "Mr. Ryan, have you ever heard of a fellow by the name of Joe Santino?"

Rex Ryan's face immediately reddened and it took on the look of contempt. "That big blowhard? He replaced me after I left. He's a lazy, good-for-nothing jackass. He doesn't know anything about running that business. Richard bought himself a show horse. From what I've heard, Santino hasn't brought in one dime of advertising to the agency since he's been there."

"Obviously, you don't like Mr. Santino?" Rodgers quipped, believing that he might squeeze more information out of Mr. Ryan now that he was a little upset.

"Look. Richard once told me, a year or two ago, that if he died, that Joe Santino would have it made."

"Do you know what Mr. Rawlings meant by that? Do you think Santino should be a suspect in killing the Rawlings family?" Rodgers pressed.

Ryan hesitated for a second before answering. " I think Richard meant that Santino would take over the business. As for your second question, I wouldn't put it past him. And another guy who you could say that about would be Harry McFarland, the sales manager from the Diamond Faucet Company."

"Why Harry McFarland?" Schafer asked.

"Because Harry McFarland and Richard hated each another. There was some bad blood there. Harry was trying to take the Diamond advertising account away from Richard and Richard knew it."

"How was this McFarland guy trying to do that? He was the sales manager for Diamond wasn't he?" Rodgers asked.

Ryan pressed on. "It might sound complicated to you guys, but let me tell you that in the advertising business, it's big money were talking about. I know Richard thought that Harry was trying to make him look bad to some of the people at Diamond's main office."

"Why would McFarland want to do that?" Schafer asked.

"So that the guys running the Diamond Company would give the advertising account to some other agency. And if that happened, Richard was sure that Harry was going to get a bigger kickback from the new agency then what Richard was already giving Harry."

"And you think that might be enough for Harry to kill Rawlings and his family?" Schafer was still a little skeptical about this whole theory.

"Yes," Ryan said, without blinking an eye.

Rodgers gave Schafer a quick glance. Both detectives thought it was the right time to let Mr. Ryan know how much they knew about him.

"Mr. Ryan," Rodgers began, "Detective Schafer and I have a little confession to make. When you called us regarding this case, we took the opportunity to do a little background check on you."

Ryan began to shuffle in his chair and his face became pale.

Rodgers continued. "Now, we don't want to get into any personal stuff about your relationships, either with the court in Lenawee County or your divorce situation, but we do have to tell you that we're going to check out this information you gave us today. We hope it's all fact and no fiction."

Ryan ran his fingers through his curly locks and looked straight at Rodgers. "Sure, I've had some problems. I'm not as clean as the wind-driven snow, but what I've told you today is the truth. I think you guys should check out Santino and Harry McFarland."

"We certainly will do that Mr. Ryan. We appreciate your cooperation. If we need anything more, we will contact you. Thank you," Schafer responded.

Rex Ryan shook hands with the detectives and left the building, never looking back.

August 7, 1968
10:00 a.m.
State Police Post-Petoskey

Schafer and Rodgers, beginning at 9:00 a.m. had been checking out different suspect files for modus operandi information. The files contained the usual list of people and were mostly concentrated on the town vagrants arrested for drunk and disorderly conduct or for window peeping. There were a few who had committed felonies, consisting of burglary, assault with a deadly weapon and even murder. Most of the felons listed were eliminated because the individuals were still doing time in a correctional facility in Michigan or elsewhere.

The city of Petoskey, Michigan is not an area where known criminal types hang out. It is an area populated with tourists in summer, fall and winter. It's a close-knit community that can sense trouble right away and has little hesitancy in making their law enforcement people aware of potential trouble.

Rodgers finished the last part of a cold cup of coffee, when the phone on his desk rang loudly. "Rodgers."

"Sergeant, a Miss Winters is on the phone. She claims to know who killed the Rawlings family and wants to talk with you."

"Okay Corporal, put her through."

The female voice on the other end of the line was soft and gentle as she spoke. "Is this Sergeant Rodgers?" she asked.

"Yes, this is Sergeant Rodgers."

"Sergeant, this is Miss Esther Winters. I live at 2245 Barton. I think I know who killed those people in the Rawlings cottage."

"You do Miss Winters?" Rodgers asked, stretching for a pad and pencil and pulling it closer to him. "Don't you think it would be better to come to the Post and talk about it?"

"No, I don't think so. My boys would get very upset if they knew I was talking to you and they would hurt me if they knew I was telling you this stuff."

Rodgers could sense the ring of truth in her voice and decided to continue. "Tell me, Miss Winter, who do you think killed the Rawlings family?"

"I think my son, Skip did it. He's vicious and he was around here at the time it all happened. He's been in the Traverse City mental hospital a lot of times. He and his brother, Marvin, are both on parole from Jackson Prison."

"What makes you think that Skip and Marvin would do such a thing, Miss Winter's?"

"Because they're bad. They have their daddy's blood. They would do that kind of thing for kicks. Marvin, my oldest, he's not all there. A couple of years back, he went on a shooting spree just outside of town, shot the windows out of a house. He was lucky that he didn't kill the girl who was baby-sitting. She was in the house watching TV."

In an instant, Rodgers mind flashed back to the incident Miss Winters was talking about and immediately connected the voice on the phone with the individuals she was describing. Rodgers and Schafer knew the three brothers very well. There was Skip, along with Marvin and Jerry. All had served time in Jackson State Prison. Skip was the most violent of the three and the most dangerous.

"Where are they now, Miss Winters?"

"I think they're down in Detroit. I don't know the address. I know that they've got at least one gun, maybe more. They'll use it if they're cornered, I can guarantee you that."

"Do you know where Marvin, Skip and Jerry were on the night of June 25th?" Rodgers asked.

"I think they went up to Mackinac City. They have some friends that hang out at the bars there. That's where they normally go to raise hell when they come back here. They like to go to Detroit and work in one of the factories there so they can make some good money. Then they quit, come up here, raise the dickens, and call it a good time."

"We'll have some officers at the Detroit Post check it out Miss Winters. Don't worry, we won't tell them that you talked with us. Is there anything else you want to say?"

"No. I just hate to think that my own sons could have something to do with this. But I know those boys and they'd hurt anyone if they thought it would get them a few dollars. It's sad, but it's the truth."

"Thank you Miss Winters. Don't worry yourself too much. If the boys were involved, we'll find out without revealing that you said anything. It's possible that what your doing may save some lives."

"Goodbye sir and thank you," she said as she hung up the phone.

"Goodbye." Rodgers said. He slowly replaced the receiver of his phone into the cradle and leaned back in his chair.

"Ray, I'm going to call Charley Schneider, the Parole Officer and see if he can give us an update on the Winters boys. I'm not quite sure what we're looking for with these fella's, but if their own mother thinks that they could have done it, who the hell am I to argue?"

"Fine. It can't hurt. I'm sure that they would have popped up on our list to check out sooner or later. Their mother just speeded it up," Schafer said as he stuffed some suspect files back into the file cabinet.

Rodgers quickly dialed up Charley Schneider.

" Hi Charley, this is Bill over at the Post. Just wanted to see if you know anything about the Winter boys?"

"You don't have enough ink Bill." Charley responded.

Charley Schneider was half Ottawa Indian and the other half, Norwegian. He had been a Parole Officer for over ten years in Sands County and was familiar with every scoundrel who had been or was currently entrusted to his supervision.

"Which one is it this time?" Charley asked with a tone of disgust in his voice.

"Either Marvin or Skip. Jerry could also be involved but we're not sure yet."

"I can tell you that Marvin and Skip just got out of Jackson Prison in March of this year. Not sure of the exact date, but I can send that stuff over to you if you want."

"That would be great Charley. Appreciate it. What about Jerry?"

"I heard he went down state to Detroit to look for work. I haven't seen or heard of him since the first of this month. In fact, he's on my list of people to locate and get a positive address on."

"Is he overdue?" Rodgers asked, wanting to know if the suspect was in violation of his parole.

"No. He's not. But his two brothers are."

"Thanks Charley. I'll have the Detroit Post pick them up for questioning."

"What's it all about Bill? Is it the Rawlings thing?"

"Yeah. We just need to talk to them to clear some things up."

"When you find them, let me know a.s.a.p. Okay? By the way, tell Ray hello. I'm still waiting for him to go out on the bay to do some fishing with me. I want to know if he can catch something other than criminals."

"I'll pass it along, Bye." Bill said, hanging up the phone.

"Let me guess, Charley wants me to go fishing with him."

Bill just smiled. The only thing Ray could catch fishing was a cold.

That afternoon, Schafer and Rodgers headed over to the Harbor Springs Airport and spoke with the airport manager. The manager told the detectives that Rawlings would fly in several times during the summer months, but that he had not seen him do that this summer. Instead, the manager told the detectives that Mr. Rawlings had stopped by and visited with him about a number of different things, including the activity of the airport. He also confirmed previous reports that when Rawlings did fly in; his wife would always pick him up. There was never a time that he could recall that Rawlings called a cab, or made other transportation arrangements to take him to the cottage.

The detectives thanked the manager and left immediately for the little village of Sturgeon Bay. This tiny fishing village was located about ten miles north of Thunder Point and the Rawlings cottage. It was a locale that was home to many of the native Indians that fished its cold and productive waters.

The day before, Schafer and Rodgers had received a brief phone call from a woman who had known the Rawlings family fifteen years earlier. The woman and her former husband had been friends with Mr. and Mrs. Rawlings when they had lived in St. Clair Shores near Detroit. During that phone conversation, she told the detectives that at the time they lived in the Detroit suburb, she and her ex-husband, a man named Terry Marks, had been very close friends with the Rawlings family. She claimed that their friendship was close because it was at a time when Mr. Rawlings was just starting his own advertising business and he handled the advertising account for the company where Terry worked.

Terry Marks had been part of the management staff at Novo Engine Company. She told the officers that she would often ask Mrs. Rawlings to go to different places with her, such as shopping or visiting museums or art centers. In her opinion, Mrs. Rawlings would always make excuses as to why she couldn't go. Then on one occasion, Mr. Rawlings, in a private conversation told her why Mrs. Rawlings had to be careful about where she went. He claimed that his wife couldn't go out because his wife's previous boy friend had been constantly harassing her. He would do this by telephoning her or he would just happen to show up at places where his wife would go alone. On those occasions he would tell Mrs. Rawlings that she should have married him and not Mr. Rawlings. The woman told the detectives that Mrs. Rawlings had been married for six years at that time and she believes that if the suspect could have harassed her for that length of time, he may have also had a motive to kill her and her family.

The woman stated that the she thought that the man now lived in an area called Sturgeon Bay. His name, she said, was Wallace Silva. She requested that the detectives keep her phone call confidential.

Schafer and Rodgers checked out Mr. Silva. He had retired from his job in Detroit and now lived in Sturgeon Bay. Mr. Silva was a paraplegic. He was paralyzed from the waist down from a boating accident that had occurred two years before. He admitted knowing Shirley Rawlings ten years before when he lived and worked in Detroit, but that he never followed Shirley after she was married, and that when he did see her occasionally at the supermarket or department store, she would always stop and chat. He told the detectives he believed that Mr. Rawlings was a jerk, but he didn't even know that the Rawlings family was living just a short distance away until he read about the murders in the local paper. It had been at least five years since he had seen Mrs. Rawlings in a supermarket back in Detroit. The detectives thanked Mr. Silva and left.

Each day, Schafer and Rodgers checked on other potential leads. First, they began with a greenhouse and a florist shop where Mrs. Rawlings had purchased flowers and plants for the cottage. Another dead end. Next, it was the LP Gas Company. They had not made a delivery to the Rawlings cottage this year. Nothing.

However, as the two detectives made their rounds of the area calling on businesses and potential suspects they noticed a high occurrence of damaged mailboxes and signs north of the murder scene along the M-31 road. Most of the damage was within the first mile north of the murder scene. What made it more odd was that mailboxes and signs south of the murder scene were without such damage. Both detectives thought it might be a good idea to try and retrieve cartridge casings found at those sites and send them to the crime lab in Lansing. They got lucky. In one of the mailboxes, about a quarter of a mile from the murder scene, the detectives found a .22-caliber slug. Just a hundred yards north of the mailbox, they picked up seven .22 caliber cartridge casings. All the items were mailed immediately to the crime lab in Lansing.

August 8, 1968
11:00 a.m.
State Police Post-Petoskey

An inter-office communication alerted Schafer and Rodgers that Marvin and Skip Winters had been apprehended in the Detroit area and were being held in the Oakland County jail.

Stevens told Schafer that he and Ford would immediately conduct the interrogation of the two brothers and that they would call Schafer and Rodgers back when their interviews with the former Jackson Prison inmates had been concluded.

Schafer and Rodgers, had plenty of legwork of their own to do, plus there were a number of pieces of evidence and photographs that had to be looked at and examined for clues. Each piece had to be placed in its proper sequence.

The detectives started to compile and catalogue that information, when the phone rang. The ringing seemed louder than usual. It would be more than a normal conversation.

"Hello, this is Detective Rodgers."

"Detective Rodgers, this is Russ Foster. A detective by the name of Schafer left a message for me to call this number."

"Just a minute." Rodgers handed the phone to Schafer and covering the mouthpiece, whispered, "It's Russell Foster."

Schafer nodded and took the phone. "Mr. Foster, this is detective Schafer. Thank you for returning my call. My partner and I are assisting in the investigation of the Rawlings murders and we understand you were doing some tree work on

Lakeshore drive in June for Mr. Rawlings. Would it be possible for you to come down to the State Police Post and talk to us?"

"Sure, I can do that. My conscience has been bothering me for a while. I would like to come in tomorrow morning and talk to you about it." The tone of Foster's voice was contrite and sorrowful.

Schafer did not know what to make of it, but was quick to set up a time for Foster to come in. "How about 9:30 tomorrow morning, Mr. Foster?"

There was dead silence at the other end, then finally an answer of "Yes. I'll be there at 9:30 sharp."

"Thank you, Mr. Foster. We'll see you in the morning. Goodbye." The line went dead and Schafer hung up the phone. "Can you believe it?" he said to Rodgers. "This guy sounds like he wants to bare his soul and tell all and can't wait to do it."

Rodgers gave a questioned look towards Schafer.

"He's supposed to be here at 9:30 a.m. I hope he shows. If not, we'll have to go and pick him up," Schafer said.

It had been a long day and both men were ready to stop at the local watering hole for a cold beer then head for home. They turned off the lights and left.

August 9, 1968
9:30 a.m.
State Police Post-Petoskey

Russell Dale Foster entered the State Police Post wearing Levi jeans, a jeans jacket that covered an aqua colored shirt and finished off by a pair of old cowboy boots. He was forty years of age, with sun bleached red hair and arched bushy eyebrows that covered stark looking gray eyes. There were wrinkles in his weather beaten face that made him look much older and his manner was that of a Texas cowboy. His movements portrayed a man that was always judging the space around him to see if it was friendly or hostile.

He spoke with the desk officer about his appointment with Schafer and Rodgers and was given directions to their office. He avoided the use of the elevator and climbed up the marble steps, two at a time, until he saw the sign on the office door of the detectives. He knocked on the door.

"Come in." Schafer said as he placed a folder in a file cabinet and closed the drawer. Foster entered slowly. "I'm looking for detective Schafer. Is he here?"

"Yes, that's me" Schafer responded. "Russell Foster?"

"That's right" Foster answered, moving closer and extending his hand.

Detective Rodgers who had been looking at a wall map, turned toward the visitor and moved forward to introduce himself. Schafer motioned for Foster to have a seat in the chair next to his desk. Foster obliged. Rodgers pulled up a chair near Foster as Schafer settled into his seat behind his desk.

Rodgers took the lead in asking the questions. "Mr. Foster, yesterday you spoke with Detective Schafer and told him that you had something on your mind that was bothering you about the Rawlings' killings. What exactly did you mean by that?"

"What I meant was," Foster paused, turning slightly in his chair. "Somewhere around the first part of June, I don't remember which date, but it was well before the 25th,I drove out to the Rawlings cottage and talked with Mr. Rawlings about trimming some trees around his place. He wanted more sunlight to come into the cottage to brighten up the place. We drew up a contract for two days at a cost of a hundred and seventy dollars. Mr. Rawlings told me I could start to work on Monday, June 24th. He said that would be a good day because he and his family would have left for a trip south. However, on Sunday, the 23rd, Mr. Rawlings called and reached my wife, Bonnie. He told her that their trip had been delayed and that I should start the job on Tuesday, June 25th."

"Mr. Foster does your wife recall if Mr. Rawlings mentioned any other names in the conversation with her, when he changed the day?"

"No. She told me that all he told her was to change the date."

"I'm sorry. Go on."

"As I was saying, around 9 a.m. on the 25th, we arrived at the Rawlings cottage. I had my helper, a kid by the name of Allen Eaton, he's 16, and my son, Johnnie who's 14. Johnnie normally lives with his momma down in Grand Haven and was up here for a visit."

Mr. Foster, feeling a little more relaxed, leaned back in the chair and let his story roll out. "When we arrived at the cottage, we saw two cars parked together on the east side of the cottage. The Rawlings family was also there. Mr. Rawlings came up to me and told me that they were waiting for an airplane and that they would probably not leave on their trip until the following day. He also mentioned that he was waiting for a long distance call. He told me that the call would let him know that the plane was in and that they would be leaving for their trip."

"Did you happen to ask him where he was going to catch a plane in all that wilderness near his cottage?"

"No. I never thought it was any of my business. Besides, I figured it had to be either Harbor Springs or Pellston. Those are the only two airports in the area big enough to handle a plane that could take aboard six passengers and a flight crew. A short time after he told me that, I had to disconnect the telephone wires to do some trimming. Then around 1:30 p.m., if my memory is correct, Mr. Rawlings did receive his phone call and came out to tell me that he and his family would be leaving in the morning. He seemed very pleased."

"Did you notice anyone else on the grounds while you were there Mr. Foster?"

"Well, I didn't see the woman or the little girl. I did see Mr. Rawlings, along with his three boys drive off in one of the cars. But they came back about an hour and a half later. The only other person I saw who stopped by the cottage was an old man. Mr. Rawlings introduced me to him only by his last name. It was a Mr. Barr. He was a pretty old guy. I never saw any other people or cars in the area."

"How late did you and boys work that day?" Rodgers asked.

"I think we quit around 5 p.m. Mr. Rawlings came out and paid us the full amount of a hundred and seventy dollars that we had agreed on. He said he was paying me because he could not guarantee that he would be there in the morning. I told him that I would take care of our part of the bargain and not to worry about the trees being trimmed properly. So the next day, that would be the 26th, I returned to the cottage with Allen. Johnnie did not come with us this time. He said he was too tired because of the hard work he did the day before. Johnnie is a city boy. If his mother would let me have custody it would be the best thing for both of us."

"Did you see any members of the Rawlings family at that time?" Schafer asked.

"No. Both cars were still parked where they were the day before when we left, but I didn't see any of the family around. The weather that day was lousy. It was overcast, colder than usual and it rained some. Both Allen and I noticed that a light had been left on inside the cottage. It showed through a window at the southeast corner of the cottage. Allen also called my attention to a piece of paper or cardboard taped over one of the window panels next to the door of the cottage. I went over and took a look. There were other holes in a couple of the panels that run down the side of the door. Personally, I thought they were stone holes and I didn't think much of it at the time. Besides, we worked almost non-stop until maybe four o'clock that afternoon. The note said something about returning in July. Sometime during the day, I think it was in the afternoon a car drove into the driveway of the Mitchell cottage, just south of the Rawlings place. I think it was brown in color, but I don't know what make or model it was. There was a man driving. He had a brown straw hat on. I think it was the old man Barr that I met the day before, but I can't be sure. He pulled into the driveway and then backed out without stopping."

"Mr. Foster," Rodgers interrupted, "When you called us, you said that something was bothering you and that's why you called. "What did you mean by that?"

"I was bothered by the thought that maybe on that first day we were there, Mrs. Rawlings and her daughter could have been held hostage in that cottage. I might have been able to do something about it. I thought about it more and more after I read the papers."

"Your recount of the details Mr. Foster match that of your helper Allen Eaton, only the color of the car is different. He thinks the color may have been blue or green. Last month, Mr. Eaton gave a statement to the Sheriff's office and we received a copy of it this morning," Schafer said, letting the information sink in for Mr. Foster.

"I didn't know that Allen had talked to anyone about this. At least he never mentioned to me that he had, but it doesn't matter. The only thing that keeps bothering me is that I can't stop thinking that I might have been able to help that family in some way when I was there. I guess it wasn't meant to be." Foster said.

The interview ended cordially and Foster left the Post to return to his tree trimming work.

Schafer and Rodgers went back to compiling more information for the investigation. Gun and background checks had been requested for both Russell Dale Foster and young Allen Eaton earlier in the investigation. Both requests were returned stating that there were no criminal records in either man's file.

Later that week, Foster consented to a polygraph test and answered all questions truthfully.

Allen Eaton Sr. had to give his written consent for his son, Allen Jr., to take the same type of polygraph test. He did and the results indicated that he also gave truthful answers.

The detectives' attention now turned more specifically to the father and son team known as the Barr's.

Schafer and Rodgers knew that they would have to tread very carefully with this established and well-known area family. They would have to handle the questioning of both men with a little more tact than would normally be the case. Father and son Barr were more than just the developers of a lakeside community resort. They were both politically and financially connected to the area and had been for decades.

Both Barrs agreed to take the polygraph tests without the need of their lawyers being present. The results confirmed that truthful answers were given while additional checks on both men showed that there were no past criminal records in their files.

Schafer and Rodgers then changed tack in their investigation procedure by expanding their interviewing method. They would locate as many different individuals who heard, observed or came in contact with someone or something at or near the crime scene. The drawback with this method is that it's time consuming and the local press was demanding that all of the law enforcement agencies involved solve this wicked crime sooner than later. But each day the clues and potential witnesses were declining until there was only a trickle of information coming in.

August 13, 1968
9:00 a.m.
Summer Springs Resort
Thunder Point, Michigan

Schafer and Rodgers parked their cruiser in the driveway of Mr. and Mrs. William Foresman. The Foresman's cottage was located about 1500 yards to the north of the Rawlings place. It sat openly on a high, overhead and forested bluff. The detectives were greeted by the couple and invited into the cottage. All of them sat around a dining room table as Mrs. Foresman told the detectives that she and her husband had heard gunshots on the evening of June 25th. Mr. Foresman had been bird watching just below the bluff and Mrs. Foresman had the door open to the lakeside of the cottage while she worked in the kitchen. Between 8:00 and 8:30 p.m. she and her husband heard the shots coming from the direction of the Rawlings cottage. Because the weather was overcast with slight misting rain she thought it was strange that the Rawlings boys might have been shooting at the sea gulls that perch themselves on the large rock formations just off the beach. Mrs. Foresman said she heard a shot, then two or three more within two or three seconds after the first shot. Then she heard about five or six more in rapid succession after that. She also believes that she heard the voice of a woman and some men, excitedly shouting at one another. Concluding that it must be a group of young people participating in some form of target practice or sport shooting she didn't think much of it at the time.

Mr. Foresman said that he didn't see anything out of the ordinary while he was bird watching and confirmed his wife's statement.

As the interview was coming to an end, the sister of Mrs. Foresman, a Mrs. Billington happened to stop at the cottage for a visit. Mrs. Billington and her husband own a cottage next to and north of the Foresman's cottage. She told detectives that she recalled the same events happening on June 25th. However, she was positive she heard a total of eight shots.

Schafer and Rodgers thanked the Foresmans and Mrs. Billington and left.

During the course of the day, the detectives interviewed over 20 different witnesses. Many of them only had tidbits of information. None of which was enough to establish concrete facts as to what may have happened at the Rawlings cottage. Others had no facts at all, just gossip.

Around 4:30 p.m., Captain James Jay of the Petoskey Police Department called the detectives and told them that he believed he had found the identical footwear that was used during the commission of the Rawlings murders. The mysterious footwear turned out to be what was known as a stretch half boot, manufactured by the Tote's Company of Ohio, Stock #97P and sold for $5.95 a pair, primarily in shoe and department stores around the country. Captain Jay told Schafer and Rodgers that he had a pair in his office and that he could put his size 12 shoes inside a pair of those boots marked 8 ½ to 9. In addition, with cooperation of some of the other officers in the department, they had inked the boot and walked on paper. The impression left on the paper looked similar to the print found at the crime scene.

Jay was directed by the detectives to make sure that a clear photograph of the print be made, with copies sent to them and to the Detroit Post for Stevens and Ford. The original was to be placed in the file.

Captain Jay also noted that this type of footwear was not the type used by people in the immediate area and expressed his opinion that it was a "big city" type of footwear.

Later in the day, Schafer received a call from Detective Stevens. Stevens informed Schafer that he and Ford had interviewed the two Winter boys, but nothing was gained from the interview. Stevens also told him that they should be on the lookout for a .25-Caliber Beretta that matched the one that Santino had purchased. He believed that Rawlings must have kept the Beretta with him at the cottage, because the search party could not locate any such weapon at the Rawlings home in Towne Village. Preliminary lab and autopsy reports revealed that this was the weapon and the caliber of ammo used for the coup' de grace on the Rawlings family.

Shafer informed Stevens that he and Rodger had their interview with Mr. Foster and their report would be forthcoming. There was also potential identification made of the shoe sole pattern and that a copy of the report would be sent as soon as it was confirmed.

CHAPTER 18

August 14, 1968
11:00 a.m.
State Police Post -Detroit

Sgt. Len Fellows of the Michigan State Police polygraph section conducted an examination of Joseph C. Santino without an attorney being present. Mr. Santino had agreed to take the test without one. The results of the test indicated deception. Mr. Santino was requested to return for a second testing. A verbal agreement was made by both parties to do another exam on September 24th.

September 13, 1968
10:30 a.m.
State Police Post -Detroit

Ellis Solomon, a 43-year-old businessman, whose 5' 6" frame was slim but solid strolled into the office of Detectives Stevens and Ford. He had been invited down because of his prior association with Mr. Rawlings and Mr. Julius W. Mueller. Mr. Solomon owned a business promotions agency. The same kind of business that Mr. Rawlings had discussed starting up with Santino and Mueller.

Solomon told the detectives, "I hired Julius Mueller in January of 1968. Then in February, Mueller comes to me and tells me that a Mr. Rawlings has spoken to him about starting a business like mine and would like to meet with me. The reason was that Rawlings would like to consider going into a partnership arrangement, only on a much larger scale."

"Were you interested in that kind of arrangement?" Stevens asked.

"I'm always open to looking for different ways to increase my business and I thought Mueller was trying to help me expand the company. I didn't see any reason why I shouldn't at least talk with Rawlings."

"Did you meet with Rawlings?" Ford asked.

"Yeah. On February 16th, Mueller and I met with Santino and Rawlings and another man by the name of Tom Ivey. We all met at Rawlings' office around 9:30 a.m. Mr. Ivey was invited to be a part of the group by Rawlings. Rawlings said it was because of Ivey's knowledge with computers. At the meeting, we discussed this new business venture that was very similar to the one I was already operating."

"Was this meeting cordial?" Stevens asked.

"Yes, for the most part. Rawlings was a little more assertive than I cared for, especially when he told me that Tom Ivey would be in charge of all the computer business and that Ivey's department would be the main center for inventory control, ordering and billing."

"That didn't set well with you?" Ford asked.

"I began to feel a little apprehensive about the whole thing. I really didn't appreciate being told how things were going to be done without a little more discussion or participation on my part."

"Why didn't you leave?" Ford said, pouring himself a cup of coffee.

"I started to, when Rawlings said that he had acquired substantial financial backing for the proposed merger and that an amount of $50 million would be available immediately, with an additional $50 million as backup capital."

"How did Rawlings come up with that figure and why that much?" Stevens asked.

"I don't know. He mentioned something about being able to go international with the business and to be honest about it I was flabbergasted. At first, I thought he must have done some real serious research on this type of business but at the same time, there just seemed to be a lot of bullshit being thrown around. I stayed just to see what kind of proposal he had in mind."

"I assume it got more interesting, right?" Stevens answered.

"It sure did. Out of the blue, Rawlings tells all of us, 'the plans for a merger have been made and that they were ready to move.' The meeting lasted until two in the afternoon. I wasn't happy with the arrangement at all and thought that Rawlings was blowing a lot of smoke and unable to answer some questions as to how it was all going to come together."

"So how did you leave it?" Ford asked.

"I left on good terms, but like I said, for such a big enterprise it looked a little shoddy to me."

"What happened next? " Ford continued.

"On February 20th, I called Tom Ivey and asked him to come over to my house so that I could discuss with him how the use of computers in this type of business would work. I also wanted to know how it would work with my company merging with Rawlings. I paid Ivey a retainer of $100 dollars to give me a diagram of how it would work. A few days later, I think it was the 23rd or 24th, I had another meeting with Mueller, Rawlings and Ivey at Rawlings' office.

The meeting was brief, but Joe Santino would come in and out of the office, drop some papers on Rawlings desk, but didn't participate. Then things got hot. There was not as much cordiality. Rawlings told me that everything was set to go and that I could accept the deal and how it was structured or be left out. I told him to stick it and left.

A week later, Mueller came to me at the office and told me that Rawlings had me 'checked out.' He told me that Rawlings didn't think that I should participate in the deal and that I should step aside so the deal could go through. Mueller said the reason was that Rawlings claimed that the backers would withdraw the financing for the deal if I didn't pull out."

Steven and Ford listen intently to Solomon's narrative as he continued.

" It was the request that I step aside for the 'deal to go through' which indicated to me that Mueller and Rawlings were working in tandem and were out to steal my business and promotional ideas."

"How did that make you feel to have been torpedoed like that?"

"It sure didn't make me happy. I was pissed off about the fact that I had hired Mueller who was an obvious plant by Rawlings to steal my business. I found out later that Rawlings was going to put Mueller in charge of the whole operation."

"How did you find that out?"

"In this business, there aren't many secrets, Mr. Stevens."

"Do you recall if any names were mentioned by Rawlings of his financial backer when you were in these discussions?".

"No. But I suspected that the money might be coming from St. Louis, but I can't be sure of that. It was something said during the discussions, but I don't recall exactly."

"What was your relationship with Mueller after the meeting." Stevens asked.

"I fired the son-of-a-bitch," Solomon replied angrily. "I regret ever going to the meetings. On top of that, I heard that even now, Mueller plans to go ahead with the project."

"What will you do if he goes ahead with that deal?".

"I have contacted my attorney and he's sent Mueller a letter, telling him that if he continues to pursue that course of action, we'll sue his ass."

Stevens and Ford tried to dig deeper into Solomon's relationships with the different parties involved in the deal, but Solomon declined to discuss anything further without legal counsel. He adamantly denied that the discussions that he had with Rawlings at the original meeting were a possible basis for him to kill Rawlings or members of his family.

Solomon suggested that the detectives might want to look into some airport deal that Rawlings was involved in with another person up north.

"What airport deal and with whom?" Stevens pried.

"There are a lot of rumors going on in the business community about Rawlings since his death, and that is just one of them."

"What are some of the others?"

"There's just a lot more. That's all I want to say about it." Solomon replied.

"Why do you think Rawlings and Mueller tried to do something like this to you?" Solomon took the bait but hesitated with his answer. "There was something strange about Mueller and Rawlings. I once saw Mueller with some of those porno magazines that showed men without any clothes on. Also, Mueller asked me five or six times as to what the postal policy was on general delivery to post office boxes? I took that to mean that he was trying to find out how much privacy he would have if he had those types of magazines sent to him. I also believe that Mueller acted as a front man for Rawlings not only with my deal, but also with others. It's just a feeling I got. I think he's doing it for Santino now."

Steven and Ford were not surprised that Solomon had suspected that Mueller was a 'front man' for someone. Background reports, suggested that Mueller was continually with organized crime figures. It was more than probable that Mueller may have borrowed money from an underworld source and needed to repay it as soon as possible.

Rawlings may have had the same problem in order for him to keep his publishing business afloat. However, at this point there were no substantial clues or evidence that could confirm their suspicions.

The detectives warned Solomon that he should be careful and if anything came up to call them immediately. It could be that his life was also in danger.

Solomon didn't seem to be concerned and basically shrugged off their advice. He said goodbye to Stevens and Ford and never looked back as he descended the stairway and out the front door.

September 24, 1968
9:00 a.m.
State Police Post -Detroit

Stevens and Ford attended the polygraph exam of Julius Walter Mueller. When the exam had been completed, the polygraph examiner reported that the examination results were 'not sufficient' to indicate deception by the suspect.

In other words, Mr. Mueller was being borderline truthful. The examiner told detectives that he felt that with another exam he could be more definite about Mr. Mueller's truthfulness. Stevens and Ford said they would think about it.

Joseph Santino was scheduled to take his second polygraph test at 11:30 a.m., which was scheduled immediately after Mueller's exam.

Stevens and Ford learned that Mr. Santino had called the Post during the testing of Mueller and told the desk officer that he was "sick" and unable to make it.

Ford quickly called Santino at his home and spoke with him. An arrangement was made to reschedule the polygraph test for October 8th, at 9:00 a.m. Mr. Santino agreed to meet with the polygraph expert at the Post on that date.

September, 27, 1968
1:00 p.m.
State Police Post -Detroit

Three months had passed since the Rawlings family had been murdered. Stevens and Ford sat quietly in their office looking at mug shots when an inter-office manila envelope was placed in their IN basket. Stevens pulled the paper from inside the envelope and began to read it out loud. The report concerned a man by the name of James Bellman, alias James Bradley. The report had come from Schafer and Rodgers at the Petoskey Post and it indicated that a routine check of the Traverse City State Mental Hospital, confirmed that Mr. Bellman had been a patient there but had been discharged on July 13, 1967. Mr. Bellman's parents had requested the court detain their son in the hospital, but the court dismissed the case. The parents believed that James Bellman was a danger to himself and to society. The report also contained the name of Bellman's attorney, a Mr. Phillip Cardwell.

James Bellman had been the owner of a .25-caliber Beretta and his father Luke had owned a .22-caliber six-shot rifle. Both of the weapons had been turned over to the Attorney, Phillip Cardwell on June 5th, 1968 for safekeeping and were to remain in his office on an order from the court.

When Schafer and Rodgers went to interview the attorney, they found out that Mr. Bellman had been released in May of 1968 and not in July of 1967 as previously reported.

Attorney Cardwell informed detective Rodgers that Mr. Bellman had immediately left the state after being released and was working somewhere in Ohio. But the attorney claimed that he did not know his former client's whereabouts. The attorney provided the detectives with visual proof of both weapons, but could not release them due to the court order.

Schafer made a note to contact the court regarding that issue.

October 8, 1968
9:00 a.m.
State Police Post -Detroit

The polygraph exam for Joseph Santino was canceled again when he failed to show for his appointment. Stevens phoned Santino later in the day and setup another appointment for October 18, at 9:00 a.m. Stevens was not confident that Santino would make this test either, but he would have to wait and see if his hunch was correct.

October 9, 1968
8:30 p.m.
Thunder Point, Michigan

Mrs. Agnes Lightfoot, wife of Steven Lightfoot phoned the State Police Post in Petoskey and requested to have the detectives investigating the Rawlings murders to come out to her house because she needed to speak with them as soon as possible.

Schafer and Rodgers responded immediately and arrived at Mrs. Lightfoot's home just north of the general store in Thunder Point.

Moses Lightfoot, eighty years old and a frail looking figure, was the father of Steven Lightfoot, and was present with his daughter-in-law Agnes during the interview.

Mrs. Lightfoot informed the detectives that on the night of October 4th, her husband Steve came home around eleven thirty and had been drinking. In fact, he had been very drunk. She had locked the doors to the house, believing that he would stay out for a couple of days, like he normally did when he went out to drink. However, he came home that night and found both doors locked. At the backdoor, he proceeded to kick it open and then assaulted her by hitting her about the head and body. During the course of the beating, she said that her husband kept yelling that he was "going to do to her what he did to the others."

Mrs. Lightfoot interpreted the "others" to mean the Rawlings family. Steve's father, Moses who witnessed the beating, confirmed that he heard those remarks made by his son.

When the detectives asked Mrs. Lightfoot where her husband Steve was now, she said she thought he might be over in the Harbor Springs area, probably drunk. She indicated that she had not seen him for five days. She led the two detectives to the back bedroom where they discovered a .22 rifle owned by Steven Lightfoot. The detectives took the rifle and the box of ammunition in order to send it to Lansing for testing at the forensic lab.

Schafer advised Mrs. Lightfoot to call the Sheriff's department or the State Police Post if Steve returned home in an uncontrollable or drunken state and to keep her doors locked. She agreed to do so.

October 10, 1968
9:00 a.m.
Thunder Point, Michigan

The next morning Schafer and Rodgers decided to visit Monty Barr and Steven Lightfoot who were supposed to be working on one of the new cottages. They drove along the winding road out to the building site on Lakeshore Drive. There main purpose was to ask Lightfoot about the remarks he made to his wife on October 4th.

When they arrived at the building site, no one was there and the officers began to look around the construction area. Their curiosity was directed towards the mode of the building construction that Barr had developed, rather than looking for clues to the murders.

As Rodgers studied a corner joint used in putting up an outside wall frame, he spotted some muddy footprints on a newly constructed cottage sub-floor. The prints were similar in size and shape to those found on the bloodstained carpet in the Rawlings cottage. He bent down and measured the size of the print. It was 12-1/2" long.

Schafer retrieved his Leica camera from the patrol car and took several pictures. The roll of film would be sent to the photo lab in Lansing for evaluation.

The detectives continued to search the area for Barr and Lightfoot for almost an hour but could not locate them. They found that strange because the work on the job site looked to have been a work in progress. Besides, there were numerous tools scattered about the site.

They drove back to the Post and called Stevens and Ford to tell them about the footprint and that they had taken photos of it and would send it to the lab for developing.

Meanwhile numerous other tests were being conducted at the weapons lab in Lansing. Among the tests being performed were those of certain rifles and ammunition to determine which one's might be involved in the crime scene. All of the reports came back stating that the test bullets and shells from the rifle submitted, including Mr. Lightfoot's were not identified with the evidence bullets found at the Rawlings crime scene.

The extended labor strike that had involved the two Detroit newspapers earlier in the year had finally been resolved. As these two daily newspapers finally brought themselves up to speed, they began to do more in depth reporting about the sensational murder case of a Detroit family that had occurred while they had been on strike. Because they had missed out on the initial story, they were going to try and make up for lost time by running a series of human-interest articles on the murder victims. One of the major Detroit papers started a 'Secret witness' reward campaign that gained national attention

The reward was for five thousand dollars for information leading to the arrest and conviction of the killer or killers. This of course, brought out every conceivable lunatic who thought they knew how the crime was committed, and in most cases, his or her favorite enemy was the 'one who did them in.'

One positive thing that could be said for the reporters assigned to cover the story was that they appeared to be more adept at digging out information from sources and individuals and turning them into leads faster than the State Police investigation teams. It was not a condemnation of the State Police or its methods, it was just that the newspaper reporters consistently adapted their deadline mentality into searching quickly for potential witnesses and acquaintances of the deceased family. When they found someone, they would bore in on them for the information they needed to write their stories. In many instances, it helped the police open up new territory and run down fresh leads.

One of the secret witness tips uncovered a potential, Mr. Roberts. His full name was Willis Joseph Roberts. He lived in New Buffalo, Michigan and was a salesman who covered Michigan and Indiana for an auto parts manufacturing company. Like Mr. Rawlings, he flew his own plane. Unlike Mr. Rawlings, Mr. Roberts maintained a large gun collection. He traveled the state and did a lot of hunting in the northern Michigan area. From time to time, he attended business meetings in Detroit. After those meeting he would often meet his girlfriend who lived in one of the Detroit suburbs.

Stevens and Ford, using the tip provided by the secret witness program interviewed Mr. Roberts. He told the detectives that the reason for the gun collection was that he was active in a skeet-shooting club and that he had always had an interest in guns. He had never heard of either Richard Rawlings or Joseph Santino. He had no objection to take whatever tests were required in order to clear his name or to prove that he was telling the truth.

Stevens and Ford provided him with that opportunity and set a date for him to come to the Post for fingerprinting and a polygraph test. The detectives took an instant photo of him and placed it on file.

October 18, 1968
8:30 a.m.
State Police Post -Detroit

Joseph Santino called detective Ford to inform him that he was unable to make it at 9:00 a.m. due to a number of business meetings and subsequent appointments throughout the day.

Ford remained composed, but this time decided to bear down on Santino. "Mr. Santino I'm only going to say this once, so listen very carefully. We've made arrangements on more than two different occasions in order to accommodate your schedule. You've put this process off at a great inconvenience to me and to other detectives here at the Post. We'd hate to embarrass you by having to come out to your place of business with a warrant. You should know that the reporters from both the Free Press and the News have been hanging around our offices trying to pickup any little tidbit of information they can. I'm sure that if they knew we were about to serve a warrant on you, it wouldn't be too much of a stretch for them to assume that by dodging us, you might have something to hide. So why don't you be reasonable and tell me what time you are going to come in this morning, alright?"

Santino immediately knew what would happen to the business he was negotiating to purchase from the Rawlings estate if he forced the detectives to bring a pack of reporters with them to serve him with a warrant. His answer was a quick, "I can be there at 10:30 this morning."

A slight smile crossed Ford's lips. "Fine, Joe," he answered quickly avoiding the formal "Mr. Santino," this time around. We'll see you at 10:30 a.m. today. Bye." Ford listened to the click on the other end of the line then hung up.

October 18, 1968
10:30 a.m.
State Police Post - Detroit

At exactly 10:30 a.m. Joseph Santino arrived to take his polygraph test. This time another State Police polygraph expert administered the session. During the test, Santino admitted that he had lied in the previous tests about some of the subjects that were contained in the questions. He claimed that he was not trying to confuse the polygraph tester, but couldn't give a logical explanation for his actions. The new expert questioned Santino for two hours but gained nothing from the interview. Santino had said very little in the interview and appeared to be in a deep state of depression. When the session had ended, Santino was permitted to leave. He went directly back to his office.

Stevens and Ford retreated into their office, knowing that they had reached an impasse with their main suspect. Stevens at that point was convinced that now he knew who had committed the Rawlings murders. It was Santino. He believed that it was only a matter of time before they would have the evidence needed to confirm his suspicion. It was not going to be that easy.

CHAPTER 19

October 30, 1968
11:00 a.m.
State Police Post -Detroit

Laura Lynn Santino had been asked by Stevens and Ford to come to the State Police Post for an interview. Ford wanted to make sure that the discrepancies in her husband's polygraph tests were not the result of some personal or marriage related issues. Ford was looking for any answers as to why Santino would tell lies to the State Police polygraph expert.

Mrs. Santino was an attractive and shapely brunette. She looked younger than her thirty years even with the challenge of raising a four-year old son. She told the detectives, "I started to work shortly after I had graduated from high school. I met Joe at a friends' wedding, fell in love and we got married. I think it's typical of the way things like that happen."

"I will be very direct with you Mrs. Santino," Ford said, his voice firm but gentle. "Your husband, Joe is a prime suspect in the Rawlings family murders."

Mrs. Santino's eyes widen slightly, just enough to reveal her concern but she said nothing. She showed little if any emotion and stared directly at Ford.

"Mrs. Santino is there anything that you can tell us about Joe's behavior regarding this case? He appears detached from the events of June 25th."

Mrs. Santino looked at the newly installed rotating fans on the ceiling. Finally, she spoke, but avoided the direct question. "I recall the 25th of June as a day when the city received some very heavy rains. A lot of things went wrong that day. I remember Joe going to work in the morning, but I don't recall when he came home. I think it was some time after dark."

"Do you recall what time?" Stevens asked.

"No. I was in bed, asleep at the time he came in. I believe it might have been around eleven p.m."

"Do you remember anything else that happened?"

"I remember that Joe was soaking wet because the next day his clothes were still damp where he draped them over the side of the washtub in the laundry room. I vaguely remember him saying something about attending a convention at Cobo Hall and then having to go back to the office to check on some phone calls and finally driving over to the Rawlings house to check on a potential water leak in the basement. That's all I can remember."

"Do you know anything about the two pistols Joe purchased for himself and Rawlings earlier in the year?" Stevens asked.

"Yes. I was with Joe when he purchased the pistols from Bill Hathaway. Joe brought them home. He placed one of them in my vanity drawer and the other one he put in a top drawer of our bedroom dresser. Joe kept all the ammunition in his dresser drawer."

"Do you remember what day it was when you went with your husband to buy these guns?" Ford asked.

"I remember that it was cold out. It probably was in February or March, I think."

"And how long did you keep the guns?" Stevens asked.

"I think the guns stayed at the house until sometime around the beginning of June. I know that by the middle of June, I don't remember the exact date, Joe took one of the guns to the office with him. He told me that he had given that gun to Richard Rawlings."

"What did Joe do with the ammunition?" Stevens asked.

"I don't know. One day it was just gone."

"Are you telling us that there isn't any ammunition left at your place?"

"I don't know. I know that the boxes that Joe used to keep in his own dresser drawer are not there anymore."

"Have you seen the gun Joe left at the house?" Ford asked.

"No, not since June. That was about the same time that the ammunition was gone."

"Mrs. Santino, why do you think that Joe would deliberately lie to us?"

"I don't think he wants to lie to you. He gets very nervous and when he gets that way, he tends to make things up."

"Did you ever meet Mr. Rawlings?"

"Just once. It was shortly after Joe was hired and I stopped by the office to deliver his new briefcase. Mr. Rawlings was there and Joe introduced me to him."

"And what was your impression of him?" Ford asked.

"I didn't like him. It was the way he looked at me. You can tell a lot from a man's eyes you know."

"Did you tell Joe that you didn't like his boss?"

"Yes, I mentioned it after we left the building, but Joe thought I was overreacting. He thought Mr. Rawlings was trying to be cordial and not stuffy."

"Was that the only time you met Mr. Rawlings?"

"Yes."

"Has Joe ever mentioned anything about the murders or any other part of this case with you?"

"Yes, we've talked about it. But he's never told me that he had been called in to take a lie detector test. I was totally surprised when you mentioned he had taken a test on the 18th."

"Were you surprised to learn the circumstances and the results of that test?"

"Yes."

It was obvious to Ford and Stevens that Mrs. Santino was telling them the absolute truth about her husband and her involvement. She certainly did not appear to be covering up for her spouse. On the other hand, she did not seem at all surprised by some of the information that the detectives had told her about Joe.

Ford and Stevens felt that the relationship between the married couple was, to say the least, odd. There didn't appear to be any animosity or jealousy between them, but it was surprising to them that Santino's wife could be so openly honest with law enforcement people who were targeting her husband as a prime suspect in a mass murder. They didn't know too many wives who would be so frank and open at the expense of her mate.

"As soon as I get home, I'll speak with Joe and try to clear up some things about what has been going on. I'll ask him about this purposeful lying business and what he hopes to gain by doing that," she told the detectives forcefully.

The interview ended and the officers said that they would wait to hear from her.

Stevens and Ford knew that a wife could not testify against her husband, so everything she told them would be on the record, but would never be allowed at a trial.

November 1, 1968
11:45 a.m.
Detroit

Mrs. Santino phoned the detectives earlier in the morning and asked them to come to her house. Light snow covered the lawns in the neighborhood but would soon melt under the bright midday sun.

Ford pulled the police cruiser over to the curb in front of the Santino home. The house was a traditional two-story colonial on the northeast side of Detroit. The detectives exited the cruiser and walked slowly up the brick walk to the small porch and ornate front door. Stevens pushed the doorbell. The sound of chimes could be heard inside and a few moments later Mrs. Santino opened the door and invited the officers inside. She explained that she had just put her four-year-old son down for his afternoon nap as she led the two men into a den that was adjacent to the vestibule area. She prompted them to seat themselves in a couple of overstuffed chairs that were opposite her and politely asked the two men if she could get them some refreshments.

Thanking her for the offer, the detectives declined.

Mrs. Santino went directly to the point of her phone call earlier that morning. She informed Stevens and Ford that she had confronted her husband about the inconsistency with his polygraph interviews. She asked him why he would do such a thing. She said that Joe told her,   'I lied' or 'I made mistakes in my answers deliberately.'

Mrs. Santino admitted to the detectives that her husband couldn't give her a logical explanation as to why he had acted that way, or deliberately told lies. In addition, she couldn't give the detectives any answers as to why and how her husband's odd behavior had come about.

"I'm completely baffled about his behavior and to be honest, I've never seen him this way before. I just don't know what to make of it. I know he's been under a lot of pressure and I assumed it was because of his taking over the business and the loss of Richard." she said in an exasperated tone.

Stevens asked her if she had been able to locate any of the ammunition that she had told them about.

"I've looked everywhere, but I can't find anything." She replied.

"Did you ask your husband where those items where?" Stevens prompted.

"Yes I did. He completely ignored my question and left the house."

Steven and Ford stood up and thanked Mrs. Santino for her cooperation, turned and headed for the door. As they did, Stevens noticed a pair of men's oxford shoes placed on the stairway leading to the second floor.

"Are those Joe's shoes?" he asked innocently.

"Yes, they are."

"Would you mind if we took them with us? It would help us eliminate a question we have about another piece of evidence we have in our possession," Stevens said and was certain that Mrs. Santino would refuse. Instead, her answer caught him by surprise.

"Sure. Take them. Do whatever you need to do with them," she said, handing Stevens the shoes without the slightest objection.

Stevens took the shoes being as careful as he could be in order to avoid damaging any potential evidence that might be on them. He placed his hands underneath the shoes and let the soles rest on his palms.

The detectives said a quick goodbye and walked directly to the rear of the cruiser, opened the trunk and placed the shoes in an evidence bag. Ford drove directly to the State Police Post, taking the shoes to the evidence section.

Detective Ted Folle marked the shoes and wrote down other pertinent information relating to the footwear. The notations read: Douglas Brand, Men's size 9, Black oxfords and the owner as Joseph Santino. Folle told the detectives that the footwear was made with a corrugated type of sole and initially appeared to have the same number of grooved lines in the heel as those that were found at the murder scene. He cautioned Stevens and Ford that the shoes would have to be sent to the Lansing crime lab for more testing and that the shoeprint found by Schafer and Rodgers at the crime scene was a 'negative match.'

If Joe Santino's sole print matches the one found at the murder scene, it would be the nail they would need in order to arrest their prime suspect. Both detectives believed that the stone was starting to turn in their favor.

November 8, 1968
9:00 a.m.
State Police Post -Detroit

Stevens and Ford receive a registered letter from Mr. Leland Berger, the accountant for the Hansen and McCardel Communications Company. The letter stated:

> We employed a person by the name of James Robert Bellman during the time frame that the murders were committed. Mr. Bellman had quit his employment with the company on August 12, 1968. Personnel records for the dates of June 24, 25 and 26th, 1968 showed that Mr. Bellman had been assigned to the Brookville, Ohio area and it was very doubtful that another individual would have turned in the payroll card for Bellman. However, there always remains that possibility but that would have been done without their knowledge and

was against company policy... the company is involved in construction projects throughout the Midwest area and it would be very difficult to ascertain if payroll records were falsified or what personnel do with their private time. And there were no construction projects by their company in the Thunder Point area during the time in question.

Stevens and Ford filed the letter.

December 3, 1968
9:30 a.m.
State Police Post -Detroit

Ellis E. Solomon's dislike for Richard Rawlings was not reflected in his polygraph test. The polygraph examiner noted Mr. Solomon's responses as: 'There was no attempt at deception and truthful answers were given to all questions asked.' Stevens and Ford placed Mr. Solomon on the back burner as a suspect.

The holiday season was in full gear and Christmas was only three weeks away. Both detectives continued to update their files and check the daily reports coming in from the forensic lab with a variety of information from ballistics to blood tests. The routine police work continued, but the sense of urgency that had been emphasized in July and August had subsided.

The media was more interested in the new political administration of Richard M. Nixon and how he would handle the war in Asia and the turmoil at home. A brutal mass murder in the woods of northern Michigan became 'old news' to newspaper editors.

The detective's stayed on the trail, continuing to review past reports and files, crosschecking them to see if anything had been missed or overlooked.

The forensic lab in Lansing dropped a lump of coal in their Christmas stocking by giving them a "non-conclusive" status on Joe Santino's oxford shoes. They couldn't find any correlation of the sole patterns with the impression found at the murder scene.

CHAPTER 20

January 4, 1969
8:00 a.m.
State Police Post -Detroit

The beginning of 1969 revealed that the amount of evidence compiled by the State Police Posts in Detroit, Lansing and Petoskey was substantial. Notwithstanding all of the information, there was not one piece of evidence that could positively point to a particular suspect with any degree of certainty. There was a lot of circumstantial evidence that pointed to Santino but not definitive enough for Stevens and Ford to make an arrest. The duo realized from experience, that as time passed by, the process of finding the killer or killers would become more difficult, even impossible.

January 6, 1969
10:00 a.m.
State Police Post-Detroit

Stevens and Ford interviewed a Mr. Robert Lynch. Mr. Lynch was a forty-six year old sales manager for the Diamond Faucet Company and Joseph Santino had used Mr. Lynch as his alibi for the day of the murders. Santino had told detectives that he had been with Mr. Lynch on June 25ᵗʰ, 1968 at the Plumbers' Convention at Cobo Hall. Mr. Lynch was an average built man, very well dressed and groomed. He looked the part of a successful businessman who enjoyed his work.

He sat comfortably in the wooden chair as Stevens started the questioning. "Mr. Lynch, can you tell us what you were doing at Cobo Hall on June 23, 1968?"

" Sure. I was attending the Plumbers' Convention at Cobo Hall. It's an annual event for us. Members of our sales staff attend because it helps with our Midwest distribution."

"Can you tell us how long you stayed here in Detroit?" Stevens continued.

"Yes. I arrived at the Ponchatrain Hotel Sunday, June 23ʳᵈ. I checked in at the front desk, then went to my room and settled in. An hour or so later, I walked over to the Cobo Hall to make sure that our display was being set up properly."

" And how long, if you recall, did this convention last?"

"I attended the convention all three days. June 23, 24 and 25th."

"At anytime did you meet with a man by the name of Joe Santino, from the Rawlings Advertising Agency?"

"Yes I did. There was a hospitality room at the hotel and I met with him during the afternoon on one of those days. I don't recall exactly which day it was."

"Do you remember what the weather was like?" Ford asked.

"I do remember saying to Joe that it was a shame we had to be inside attending a business convention when it was so bright and sunny outside."

"So on the day you met with Joe Santino, it was not raining. Do you remember if it rained at all that day?"

"It didn't rain that day, at all. I remember because I would have preferred to have been out golfing and complained a lot to my other sales people and even to Santino about it."

"Then what did you do?"

"When we finished talking business at the hotel, we walked over to Cobo Hall where the convention was going on. I went directly to our display booth and Joe stopped for a minute or two to see our promotional setup and then walked off in another direction. I believe he visited with some of the other vendors who were at the show."

"Did you see him at all after that meeting?"

"No."

"Do you recall if you saw him on Tuesday, June 25th at anytime during the day?"

"No. I believe that the booths were open in the morning, but at noon I think everyone was starting to tear down their displays. I didn't see Joe. But there was a lot of activity in the building and I could've missed him."

"Do you remember any day in which it rained?"

"Yes, June 25th. I remember having to buy an umbrella in the hotel gift shop because I left mine at home. But even with the umbrella, I got soaked. It was just a miserable day."

"Do you remember if you saw Mr. Santino anytime that day?"

"No. I don't recall seeing him at all. After that first meeting, I don't recall seeing him anywhere in the convention areas."

The interview was concluded.

January 7, 1969
1:30 p.m.
State Police Post -Detroit

Cold winds whipped around the State Police Post building making the Stars and Stripes and State of Michigan Flags sound like snapping bullwhips. Small, white, tornado like funnels swirled about, picking up loose snowflakes and carrying them to all parts of the parking lot.

As he exited his car, the blowing wind and bitter cold made Harry McFarland pull the collar of his cashmere coat up around his neck and move quickly towards the entrance doors to the State Police building. He entered and stopped at the front desk for directions. Obtaining the information, he climbed the steps to the detectives' office.

Stevens and Ford greeted McFarland cordially when he entered and McFarland responded in kind. The men sat down at the conference table, each one taking a hot cup of coffee, that Ford had provided.

Ford started the questioning. "Mr. McFarland, what is your position with the Diamond Faucet Corporation?"

"I'm vice-president in charge of sales."

"And what was your business relationship with Richard Rawlings?"

"Well, Mr. Rawlings owned Richard C. Rawlings and Associates. It's an advertising and publishing firm that had the Diamond Faucet account since 1952."

"So, Mr. Rawlings had the Diamond account for over 16 years?" Ford noted.

"Yes, I guess it would be about 16 years wouldn't it," McFarland repeated. Even he hadn't realized that much time had actually passed by. "As I said, the Rawlings agency has always handled the Diamond account since 1952. It was his first major account and he never let anyone forget it."

"Isn't that a long time for one agency to have an account of that size?" Ford continued.

"Well sir, that's really a yes and no answer. There are other accounts, with other agencies that have been there even longer, but we, that is the committee at our company always felt that Richard, uh, Mr. Rawlings, was loyal to our Diamond brand and we saw no legitimate reason to cancel it."

"But you moved the account to another firm this year."

"Yes we did. That's because of the circumstances. The company was not planning to drop the Rawlings Agency and only came to that decision after the untimely death of Mr. Rawlings."

"Do you recall when that decision was made?" Stevens asked.

"Yes. I believe it was sometime in October of 1968."

"Can you tell us what kind of business person Mr. Rawlings was? Like, was he a reasonable man to do business with? Was he demanding? Things like that" Ford asked.

"He probably was all of them."

"All?" Stevens asked.

"Yes. One day Richard, I'm sorry I always called him Richard. Anyway, he could be very cooperative one day about an advertising idea we might have. Then, another day, if you just mentioned an advertising idea, he would start ranting and raving about how he was the advertising person, and tell me to sell faucets and he would create the advertising. Richard was very protective of his creative side."

"Do you ever recall any incident that was different or unusual from your normal business relationship?"

McFarland paused for a few seconds before answering. "I'm not sure how this all fits in, but in February of 1968, Richard called me and asked if I could pay him the fifty thousand in advance on the account. I had to refuse him. I explained that we did our payments on the first of each month and that for us to deviate from that practice would throw accounting off."

"Did you ask him why he wanted the money in advance?"

"Yes, I did. He told me it was for some business deal he had going and that it would help."

"Did he seem upset that you wouldn't advance him the money?"

"No. He said he understood. He just thought he would ask. One never knows, he said."

"Are you aware that your company paid the Rawlings firm over thirty thousand dollars in July and August of 1968?" Stevens continued.

"I know that we, that is, the company owed the Rawlings Agency money for advertising placements in different publications, but I haven't seen the figures. If you're telling me that's the amount, then I believe you."

"We also understand that you purchased the Rawlings plane from Joe Santino. Is that true?"

"Yes, that's true. The family wanted to get rid of it, so Joe acted as an intermediary on my behalf. The family was going to put it on the market and I thought it was a good deal, so I offered to buy it and they accepted."

"Do you have any idea's as to why the Rawlings family was murdered?" Ford asked.

"You know gentleman, I've had plenty of time to think about that, but for the life of me, I cannot think of one reason. I know that Richard was supposed to have a dark side but I never really saw that. He was all business in his relationship with me. He liked the social side of life and he knew what he wanted for himself and his family. It's just a tragedy that such a thing could've happened to such a nice family like that. I've always wondered if there was some business deal that went bad, or that he got in with the wrong people."

"What do you mean by a dark side and the wrong people Mr. McFarland?" Stevens prodded.

"You probably know more about it than I do. You know, those mobster types. They always seem to have money to loan, especially if you're in business. They hang out at sporting events, or the opera or other big social functions. Richard was a part of that scene with his magazine The Director. You never know what goes on in those circles."

"Do you know if Richard ever associated with members of organized crime?" Ford asked.

"No. I never saw him with any of the ones that I've seen in the papers or heard about. There were these rumors from time to time going around after Richard hired Joe Santino."

"What were the rumors?" Ford asked.

"Well, a lot of business people were talking and spreading rumors that Richard had hired Joe because of his connections. The word 'connections' to Richard meant that there was a source of money for him to tap into. It didn't matter if it came from the Mafia, or the Masons, which he was a member of, or the Knights of Columbus. All it meant to Richard was that there was a ready source of cash, if you knew the right people."

"Do you think that Richard was a con man when it came to money?" Stevens cut in.

"I'll say this, Detective Stevens. Richard was a go-getter. He liked good things. He liked to go first class or he wouldn't go. Sometimes there would be some difficulty in just how to pay for what he wanted to do, but he always seemed to find a way to do it."

"How do you get along with Joe Santino?" Stevens asked.

"I don't."

"You don't care for Joe Santino?"

"I really don't care one way or the other about him or what he does. I'm not sure that I can trust Joe Santino to have the same dedication to Diamond Corporation that Richard had. It's one of the reasons the company pulled the account."

"And the plane deal?"

"A good business deal, besides I paid him a couple of thousand as a commission for putting it together."

"Can you think of anything that might have made Mr. Rawlings do something out of the ordinary which could have led to his death and that of his family?" Ford asked.

"No sir, there's nothing I can think of. If I remember something later, I'll certainly call you." McFarland replied.

"Thank you, Mr. McFarland. We'll stay in touch."

Finished with the interview, McFarland made his way out. It was obvious he didn't much care for police buildings or the people inside them.

Stevens poured himself another cup of coffee, looked at Ford then spoke. "Just doesn't seem as if Mr. Santino is a very popular man among his peers."

Ford shook his head, "Popular or not, other than the polygraph tests, we have nothing on the guy. I think our Mr. McFarland is also up to his eyes in shit. I didn't care too much for his attitude. I think he knows more than he's telling."

"I think you're right. Maybe we should dig a little into Mr. McFarland's past and see what we come up with."

After the interview with Harry McFarland, the investigative process dragged on, just like the gray winter days.

The rest of January and February passed by as slowly as the winter snows melted across the state. Only bits and pieces of information and evidence trickled into the Post. Everything seemed to move at a slower pace.

On the last day of February 1969, without any logical reason or warning, even the small trickle of information stopped. It was as if someone turned off the informational faucet.

There were no phone calls, letters, or even anonymous tips to pursue.

The first part of March seemed like an eternity to Stevens and Ford. Each passing day their information basket remained empty. The case had gone completely cold, just like the zero temperature reading outside. Their eagerness to make an arrest in the case began to wavier for the first time in their lives.

On clear, sunny days, their enthusiasm came back for a brief time, but when the gray clouds and bitter cold returned, so did their gloom and pessimism.

The winter doldrums had covered Detroit like a dirty blanket. As veterans of the force, both men recognized that undulating cycles of information and leads were all part of detective work. It doesn't matter what case it might be. They both knew that it was just a matter of time before things would turn around. It was on one of those bright, sunny days that new information filtered into Stevens' IN basket. It made their detective juices stir again.

It was also a day that Stevens and Ford began to see an undiscovered and raw side of Mr. Richard Rawlings.

March 20, 1969
10:00 a.m.
State Police Post -Detroit

It had been the day after the discovery of the murders that Stevens and Ford had briefly interviewed Miss Glenda Saunders. She had been Mr. Rawlings personal secretary.

The first interview by the detectives had been brief and didn't delve into any personal relationship that Miss Saunders might have had with Mr. Rawlings.

Based on new information through the secret witness program, Stevens and Ford decided to request another interview with Miss Saunders. They needed to have Miss Saunders confirm or deny specific allegations that had been coming into their office on a regular basis. The allegations came from different quarters and claimed that there had been more than just a business relationship between Miss Saunders and Mr. Rawlings. According to the reports, it had been a very intimate relationship.

Miss Saunders had stayed on at the advertising firm as Mr. Santino's secretary after the tragedy. She was very cooperative when Detective Stevens had called her to come to the Post for a second interview. She arrived at the Post without a lawyer and was directed to the office where she had previously talked with detectives.

Stevens began the interview while Ford, after receiving permission from Miss Saunders operated the department's new tape recorder.

"Miss Saunders, in our first interview, you told us that your relationship with Mr. Rawlings was strictly business and of a professional nature, is that correct?"

"Yes, I believe that is what I said or something like that. At the time, I thought that it was the proper thing to say under the circumstances."

"Do you realize that by not telling us the complete truth about your relationship with Mr. Rawlings, you may have interfered with the proper course of this investigation?"

"No, I didn't think about it at the time. But now I realize how important it is to let you know everything and to be as open about our relationship as I can."

"Okay. Just so there's no misunderstanding this time Miss Saunders, for the record, now that the tape is on, I would like you to verbally express your permission to record this conversation and for you to tell us everything about your relationship with Mr. Rawlings. Is that clear and do you approve of the recording?"

"Yes I do approve of the recording and this interview."

"You may begin," Stevens said as he settled himself in a chair.

Miss Saunders hesitated for a brief second then started talking. "From the first day I was employed by Mr. Rawlings, he would on several occasions ask me to stay late and work on some of the different projects that he had to do. Most of the time, he would ask me into his office. He would lock the door, put his arms around me and hold me for a long time."

"How long would he hold you Miss Saunders?" Stevens asked.

"Maybe for a minute or two. Then he would sit on the front edge of his desk and he would ask me to pull up my dress. He would stare at my legs. Sometimes, he would touch them, but he never went any further."

Sensing that the detectives were skeptical about her statement, Miss Saunders decided to reinforce it. "That's the truth. He would rub my legs, or feel them. He never went beyond that."

"Okay. I believe you Miss Saunders." Stevens replied. " Did he ever say anything to you while he was making these advances, or touching you?"

"Yes. One time I remember him saying that he didn't want to kiss me, but that he just got his satisfaction from looking at me. He just wanted to be able to touch my legs."

"Did he ever make advances towards you that indicated that he wanted to have sex with you?"

"No. He did say that he wanted to try and arrange to have me take trips with him so that he could have me stay in a hotel with him."

"And that didn't imply that he wanted to do more than just look at your legs?"

"I know it may sound naïve to both of you, but Mr. Rawlings was an artist. Yes, he wanted us to be able to pose in the nude, but he said that he wanted to paint my portrait first. He thought I would look beautiful on canvas. At least that's what he told me."

"And did you ever pose for Mr. Rawlings?"

"No. I never posed for him, either in the nude or with any clothes on. And he never asked me to take off my clothes."

"Never?"

Miss Saunders paused. "Well, on one occasion, he asked me to pull my dress up around my waist. Then he felt my legs and did loosen my garter belt. But he did not go any further."

Stevens was on the verge of asking her if she would have let Rawlings go on, but decided that would be crossing the line of his questioning. Instead he asked her about how long these encounters lasted with her boss.

"I would say that sometimes they would last as long as an hour. I think that most of the time it was about an hour. Sometimes he would pull out a sketch pad and begin to draw me in pencil, then he would stop, feel my legs or hold me, then return to the drawing."

"You never felt threatened or scared that someone might walk in on you?" Ford asked.

"No. Mr. Rawlings was harmless. He told me he was attracted to me in a different way than when a married man is attracted to another woman. He was never rough or forceful. I never thought much about it either way."

"Did anyone else in the office know or suspect that you had had these after hour meetings with Mr. Rawlings?"

"Yes. I think Joe Santino did. In fact, I wouldn't put it past him if he tried to eavesdrop on our conversations."

"Do you like Mr. Santino, Miss Saunders?" Stevens asked.

"I've stayed at the company for financial reasons, but I will tell you that I don't trust Joe Santino."

"Has he ever made any advances toward you?"

"No. It's just that he's a lot different than Mr. Rawlings. Joe Santino only cares about himself. He doesn't care anything about the people who make that office work. There's just something about him that gives me the creeps."

"Then why did you stay? Why not leave?" Ford asked.

"I'm looking for another job now. You won't tell him, will you?"

"No. Miss Saunders. Everything you tell us stays confidential." Stevens reassured her.

"Thank you," She replied, with a look of relief on her face.

"By the way," Ford asked, "did you happen to bring us that list of names of secretaries that you told us about? The one's who worked for Mr. Rawlings before you were hired?"

"Oh yes. I almost forgot." She dug through her large black purse until she came up with a business size envelope. She handed it to Stevens.

"These are all the women who have worked for Mr. Rawlings. I've heard rumors that some of them were also asked to pose, but that's all I know."

"Is there anything else you can tell us about Mr. Rawlings and your relationship with him?"

"No. My relationship with Richard was different, I know. And some people in the office were jealous of it, I'm sure. But Richard was a nice person and he wanted only the best for me."

"I'm sure he did, Miss Saunders," Stevens responded. The detectives thanked her and Ford called the front desk and requested that one of the troopers escort her to her car.

Stevens and Ford saw a whole new scenario of motives and potential reasons as to why Mr. Rawlings at least, and maybe his family had been murdered. Only time would tell if they had found a new avenue for a murder motive created by Mr. Rawlings.

March 22, 1969
11:30 a.m.
Detroit

Now that the detectives knew Mr. Rawlings had a tendency towards infidelity, or trysts with his female employees, they decided to interview another one of his secretaries. Her name was Mrs. Gail Butler.

The detectives drove out to the northwest side of Detroit and arrived in front of a small, but well-kept bungalow. Fresh white paint with black shutters, surrounded by a small yard made the house look fairly new and inviting.

Gail Butler answered the door and after a brief introduction she let the detectives in. Mrs. Butler was a young and attractive twenty-six year old woman, with strawberry blond hair and deep blue eyes. She was married and pregnant with her first child. After everyone had taken a seat, Mrs. Butler explained to Stevens and Ford that she had worked for Mr. Rawlings from April of 1965 until she quit in July of 1966 to marry her boyfriend and now her husband, Jack Butler. She told detectives that while she had been Rawlings secretary, she had traveled extensively with him on numerous airplane trips to record and take dictation at different conferences and seminars. She said all of the work was related to company business matters but acknowledged that on several occasions, "Mr. Rawlings asked me to stay after work for business discussions."

She told detectives that everything was above board and that Mr. Rawlings made no advances of either a romantic or sexual nature. She revealed that she had on one occasion, heard rumors that Mr. Rawlings was having an affair with a former secretary named Wanda. She couldn't offer the detectives anything specific in the way of details or how and when these indiscretions occurred, but it was common knowledge within the company.

Because of Mrs. Butler's pregnancy and having been recently married, Stevens and Ford thought it would be impossible for Mrs. Butler to reveal any impropriety that she may have had with Mr. Rawlings. They concluded that she couldn't have had any participation in the Rawlings killings and decided not to pursue her employment situation while working for Mr. Rawlings unless something concrete developed.

They gave her their business cards and asked her to call them if she thought of anything that might be useful in their investigation.

March 22, 1969
2:00 p.m.
State Police Post -Detroit

Stevens and Ford had arranged a meeting with three sales representatives of the Diamond Faucet Company who were in town for a sales seminar. John Simons, Norman Allen and Lynn Ross were interviewed regarding the alibi that Joseph Santino gave for the 25th of June 1968. All three men had been at the convention in the Cobo Convention Hall on that date. Two of the individuals were there all day, while Mr. Ross was in and out of the convention area as customer demands required. All three stated that Mr. Santino was not there on the 25th, but all had seen him on the 24th.

On the 24th, two of the sales people definitely remember him being with another man. They did not recognize the other person, but assumed he was also from the advertising agency.

When detectives showed the three men pictures of known associates of Rawlings and Santino, none of the trio could idenetify anyone other than Santino in the photos. All three men stated again they were absolutely certain that Mr. Santino did not appear at the convention on June 25th. They confirmed that the convention started on the 23rd, and ended at noon on the 25th. They told the detectives that the majority of the companies at the convention had cleared their displays and had left by 1:00 p.m. on the 25th. After the men had left the convention center, they went for boat cruise on the Detroit River that afternoon. They confirmed that a very heavy rain fell while they were out on the river and they were drenched by the time they got back to shore and to the hotel.

Mr. Simons told the detectives he had two conversations on the 24th. One with Harry McFarland, vice-president in charge of sales and the other with Robert Lynch, sales manager for the company. McFarland told him, in private, that the company was going to drop the account with the Rawlings Agency. He also believed that McFarland's secretary, Mrs. Helen Howe, knew of this pending change well before the death of Mr. Rawlings.

The detectives thanked the men for their cooperation and the interview was concluded.

March 22, 1969
4:00 p.m.
Detroit

The detectives approached the fashionable and enclosed area of the Woodward Manor Apartments and rang the doorbell of apartment #105.

Helen Howe, a recent widow of six months answered the door. She was an attractive woman with a pleasant face surrounded by auburn hair and bright, blue eyes. Her fifty-five years were well concealed by a shapely, tanned figure. She had lost her husband in an automobile accident the previous October. After the funeral, she went south to Florida to try and resurrect her life and to deal with the future. She did not have children from the marriage, but she displayed the maturity and confidence of woman who knew all about life's ups and downs. She invited the detectives into her home and guided them toward the long, plush sofa in her living room.

The detectives explained the reason for their visit and their concern about Mr. McFarland.

Ms. Howe told them that she had known Mr. Rawlings since 1952 when she started working for Diamond Faucet. She said that Rawlings had phoned frequently to discuss the Diamond Faucet account with her and she believed that she knew the operation of the Rawlings Advertising Agency as well as anyone.

She confirmed to Stevens and Ford that McFarland had told her early in 1968 that he was going to drop the Rawlings Agency at the end of the year when the contract expired. According to her, McFarland said he was not very happy with the way Rawlings was handling the account. Specifically, McFarland would complain regularly about Rawlings not being available to discuss advertising plans with him.

Stevens asked her if she had any business dealings with Mr. Santino. She replied that the first time she had dealt directly with Mr. Santino was in July of 1968. He had called her to obtain the phone number of Mr. George James, Accounting Supervisor for the Diamond Faucet Company. Santino wanted an advance on the advertising budget because he was experiencing a shortage of operating funds due to the fact that he had taken over the company under difficult and unusual circumstances.

She told the detectives that she gave him the number of the main office in Indiana, however, she did not know the amount that Mr. Santino was requesting. It was later that she learned that it was for twenty-five thousand dollars.

It was after the murders that her instincts questioned whether that money went for operating expenses or into Mr. Santino's own pocket. She confirmed to the detectives that the Diamond Faucet Company had cancelled their contract with what was now, Santino's company. That ended the discussion and interview with Mrs. Howe.

Stevens and Ford said goodbye to Mrs. Howe and walked toward their patrol car with a sense of satisfaction about their day's work. Bits and pieces of information were how crime cases were solved. They felt confident that this case had found new legs and hoped it would start to bloom again like the approaching spring.

When they returned to their office at 6:00 p.m., they found a written phone message from a Mr. Joseph Canton. Mr. Canton had left a message to call him at any hour that evening. He had information regarding the Rawlings case. Without hesitating, Stevens picked up the phone and dialed the number. Joe Canton answered the phone and Stevens introduced himself.

Canton told Stevens he had worked for Rawlings as an Art Director in 1965 and 1966 but left the company in late '66 to go to work for another advertising firm in Sterling Heights. In September of 1968, he went back to the agency to work for Joe Santino, because with Rawlings out of the picture, he figured he would give it another try. He told Stevens that when he worked there before, he believed that Rawlings was a schizophrenic and very difficult to understand and work for. He claimed there were constant rumors that Rawlings had made several amorous advances with the secretaries in the office. He knew for a fact that Rawlings recorded phone calls with a tape recorder that he kept in his desk. He believed that some of those tapes could still be there.

Stevens asked him how he knew about that. Canton responded by telling him that a few months ago he had borrowed a tape recorder from Santino to do some recording at home for a project he was working on. There was a tape that had been left in the recorder and he played this tape before recording over it.

On the tape, was a recording of Richard Rawlings talking to another man. According to Canton, Rawlings was screaming into the phone mentioning several names and talking about a trip, but did not mention the exact location.

Canton said that he had recorded over the conversation because he did not see any value in it at the time. He told Stevens that when he saw all the publicity in the Detroit papers about the murders, and that the State Police needed any information from the public about the Rawlings family, he thought he should call with this information.

Stevens asked Canton if he still had the original cassette that he had recorded over. Canton said he returned it to Joe Santino. He couldn't be sure it was still at the advertising office.

Stevens thanked him for the information and told him that he would appreciate it if he could try and find a way to recover that particular tape cassette and get it back to them. Canton promised he would try, but could not guarantee anything.

Stevens called the Voice Print Identification section to see if it might be possible to restore all or part of the taped conversation that had been recorded over. The female technician on the other end of the phone must have had a rough day. She replied, "Sure we can. That's why they call us Voiceprint Identification. The only thing we need is a tape to work with, do you have one?"

Stevens answered somewhat sheepishly, "No."

"Call me back when you get one honey." She hung up.

March 25, 1969
8:00 a.m.
State Police Post -Detroit

Stevens removed his topcoat and jacket and hung them on the pole hanger in the corner. Ford had yet to arrive, so he started to brew a fresh pot of coffee. While the coffee was percolating, he sat at his desk and pulled out a pile of papers and envelopes from his IN basket and set them down in the middle of his desk. A previous request to the County Probate Court to provide the detectives with the disposition of the Rawlings estate had been mailed to them. There didn't appear to be anything unusual regarding the contents. The one thing that caught Stevens' eye was that Joseph Santino had been one of the witnesses for Richard Rawlings last will and testament. Stevens stared at this small bit of information for a long time. Something about it didn't make sense to him. Rawlings was known to keep his business matters very confidential, even to the point of excluding Santino from some of the transactions he was conducting. Why would he turn around and make him a witness to his last will and testament? The obvious question was: "What hold did Santino have on Rawlings? And when did he acquire that hold?"

Ford entered the office and took off his coat and hung it on the pole. He walked over to the coffeepot, grabbed two cups and poured the hot, dark brew into them. Bypassing the sugar and cream, he handed one to Stevens. "Careful, it's hot."

"I hope so. I need to get rid of this body chill I got," Stevens replied. "Take a look at this." He handed Ford the probate materials.

Ford took a long sip from his cup and read the will. "What the hell is this? Santino again? Rawlings' witness?"

"Yeah. Every time we turn around he's in the middle of this mess."

"Do we have anything else from Probate?"

"No. I just opened the Probate mail and thought you should see this about Santino."

Ford had the same questions about Rawlings business behavior with Santino. How could Rawlings out of the blue, make him a witness to his will?

"Here's something else, a bulletin from the Petoskey Post," Stevens said, handing it to his partner. "You're not going to believe this."

Ford sat down in his chair. He wished he hadn't come into the office today. "Now what?" he said, taking the sheet of paper from Stevens.

Stevens continued. "Ray Schafer says he and Rodgers went over to the Rawlings cottage yesterday and found a construction company demolishing the cottage. The foreman told them that the bank handling the estate in Detroit had contacted the company and instructed them to demolish the cottage, remove one foot of topsoil and replace it with new sand."

Ford continued reading the additional information on the sheet to himself. The redness in Ford's neck began to creep up around his white collar, "Did you see this?" he asked with a tone of disgust.

Before Stevens could answer, Ford continued, "The only thing that Schafer and Rodgers were able to salvage was the door jam. The same door jam that Barr ripped out when he gained access to the cottage. How in the hell could this happen? Who's the goddamn prosecutor up there?"

Ford was seething mad. He could accept the fact that the crime scene was nine months old and the desire by family members to move on, but the murder case to this point had been a struggle and this action would just about make it impossible to solve.

"There must have been a better way to save that cottage from destruction and preserve the evidence," Ford said with disgust as he threw the papers back on the desk.

The crime scene was gone forever. Outside of the door jam, the only other things that remained were the forensic and blood evidence that had been collected.

Stevens looked at Ford who had moved out of his chair and started pacing in a circle and scratching his head. "You know John, I'm not sure if the people up there want us to solve this case. I keep having this feeling that the locals didn't much care for Rawlings or his family. Maybe he was too abrasive or too demanding. Maybe it was because of the run in he had with the appraisal board, or something else."

"I don't know about you Frank, but this is horseshit. We're charged with trying to solve this thing and we keep getting the rug pulled out from us. Maybe you're right about the locals, but I know one thing, I'm going to find out who killed those six people, if it takes me the rest of my life."

Stevens looked at his partner. "For now John, I'm going to stay focused on what we need to do, day by day. Besides, I think our friend, Santino will cough it up one of these days, and then we won't care what the hell they did up there."

"We'll see." Ford replied.

CHAPTER 21

April 5, 1969
9:00 a.m.
State Police Post -Detroit

The sun was shining brightly and a warm spring breeze blew softly outside the Post building as Stevens and Ford conducted their interview with Mr. Lyle Holleren. Holleren was the Michigan Bell Telephone supervisor for the Thunder Point area and had made the trip down to Detroit as the phone company's representative to discuss the nuances of the Rawlings' phone being part of an eight party phone system.

The detectives believed that it might have been possible that someone on that party line may have overheard a conversation from one of the calls that Rawlings' received at the cottage between June 17th, and June 25th, 1968. According to the phone records, there had been 29 long distance calls made to or from the Rawlings' cottage during that time period. The time consumed for these calls were six hours and thirty-six minutes. The average time of those calls was about fifteen minutes. It would have given someone who had access to one of the eight phones plenty time to have listened in, accidentally or on purpose.

"Mr. Holleren," Stevens began, "can you tell us the names of the eight parties registered for the phone lines at the time of the murders?"

"Yes I can. Here they are," he said handing the list to Stevens.

All of the names were familiar to Stevens and Ford.

The names on the list were: Richard C. Rawlings, Gladys O. Mitchell, R.F. Mitchell, Richard F. Matthews, Monty A. Barr, Carlton P. Barr, A.E. Lewis and Vincent VanderVort.

"Mr. Holleren, how does that system work?" Ford asked.

"Well first, Detective Ford, the eight phone lines are divided into four groups on the ring system. Two rings would mean it was for the Rawlings cottage. The only other people that would hear that ring would be in the Richard F. Matthews home. The other parties on the line would not hear the Rawlings phone ring."

"What if someone in the other group picked up the phone?"

"In that case, they would hear the conversation, even though it did not ring in their sector." Holleren answered.

"That would mean that anyone of those eight parties might be able to eavesdrop on any of the other conversations, just by picking up the phone to see if anyone was on the line," Stevens said.

"Yes." Holleren replied, "If you are a real snoopy person, you could try and listen in to a lot of different conversations during the day, but you would have to be real careful."

"Why is that?" Ford asked.

"Just the sound of the click alone is hard to disguise. You can do it, but it takes a lot of practice so your not heard. Then you must have absolute silence on your end, because if you don't, it can sometimes be traced back to the person who was listening in."

After giving a few more technical details about the system, Holleren concluded his interview with the detectives.

Stevens decided to call the Matthews residence in Thunder Point while Ford checked some recent additions to the IN basket.

Mrs. Matthews answered the phone and Stevens introduced himself. He explained the situation to her and asked her if she could remember anything unusual about her phone system and if she ever indirectly cut in on someone else's conversation.

She told Stevens that on some occasions she had picked up the phone to place a call and found someone else already on the line. She said she immediately replaced the phone back in its cradle. However, she did recall during one period last summer, when her mother, who was visiting from Detroit, accidentally picked up the phone on the first two rings, which was meant for the Rawlings' phone and that a woman asked for "Dick."

She told Stevens, "because my husband is also named Richard, and is sometimes called Dick she thought it was for him. My mother came into the kitchen and asked me if Richard was around the house. Richard had gone into town and I went in and answered the call. It turned out to be Mrs. Rawlings' mother calling for Shirley. I apologized for the mix-up and that was all that happened."

"Do you happen to recall about what time that was last summer?" Stevens asked.

"I think it was around the fourth of July, either before or after. It was during the time my mother had come up for the holidays. That's the best that I can remember. I can call her if you would like."

"No. There is no need to do that at this point Mrs. Mathews. Thank you and good-bye," Stevens answered, concluding the conversation.

From Mrs. Matthews' statement, the phone call she mentioned, must have been the one that Shirley Rawlings' mother made in order to notify her daughter about her uncle's death on the 8th of July, a few days after the July 4th weekend.

The detectives tried to make other phone calls to different people on the party line, but were told by the area operator that these were summer phone numbers and would not be working until they were hooked up again later in the spring. All of lines had to be operational by May 1st according to the contract. The Barr families were one of the groups wintering in Florida and would not return until the end of the month.

Stevens and Ford made a note to contact the Barr families when they returned to find out if they had overheard any phone conversations that involved the Rawlings family.

By the end of April 1969, much of the information obtained was of an elementary variety or just fill-ins for previous questions that had been left unanswered. As the month ended, another piece of information arrived that made Stevens and Ford take particular notice and interest.

On April 30th, the detectives found an invoice in an evidence box taken from Mr. Rawlings' business office after the murders. It was dated July 1, 1968, and stated that Joseph Santino had purchased a .22-caliber rifle at the Montgomery Wards store located at 12 Mile and Telegraph Rd. in Detroit. The rifle was a Glenfield, model 60, semi-automatic weapon made by the Marlin Arms Company.

"John, answer this for me," Stevens asked. "Why would Santino go out and buy a .22 caliber rifle from Wards on July 1st, almost a week after the Rawlings' massacre? And why from Wards, when he has a friend over at the Zackery Gun Sight Company that could get him discounts on stuff like that?"

"It's odd, Frank, I don't have an answer. Wasn't July 1st when he returned from his trip to Indiana? Could that be a connection? Did something happen down there that made him scared? Enough that he needed another weapon?" Ford shrugged and poured himself another cup of coffee.

Stevens continued, "All his other guns are brand name stuff from Zachery. Why would he buy from a rifle from Wards? He obviously knows that they have to keep good records on purchasers. I'm not really sure about all this, but I don't like it."

"I don't either Frank, just about as much as I don't like those rain clouds headed our way," Ford said, as he looked out the office window. April was coming to an end and a conclusion to this case looked about as promising as the dark clouds moving towards the city.

May 9, 1969
10:00 a.m.
State Police Post-Petoskey

The morning quiet that filled the office of Detectives Schafer and Rodgers was interrupted by a faint knock on the wood molding of the office doorway. Both of the detectives were sitting at their desks flipping through pages of criminal mug shots when they heard the sound. They looked towards the doorway as a moderately attractive woman entered. They rose quickly and Schafer asked if he could be of assistance.

"I'm looking for the detectives who are investigating the Rawling's case." She said softly.

"I'm Detective Schafer and this is Detective Rodgers. We're in charge of the Rawlings' case. Is there something we can help you with?" he asked as he motioned for her to sit down.

She sat her small frame into the wood chair and let her hazel eyes evaluate the two men. "My name is Mary Brinner and I'm a nurse. I work at Little Traverse Hospital in Traverse City."

Schafer and Rodgers knew of the mental institution located seventy miles south of Petoskey and waited intently for the lady seated before them to explain why she was there.

"I was assigned to a Mrs. Ellen Barr's room. She is the wife of Carlton Barr of Thunder Point. I believe he's known as Pops."

"And when were you assigned to Mrs. Barr?" Rodgers asked.

She pulled out a small spiral notebook and began to read from one of the pages. "According to my notes, Mrs. Barr was admitted to the hospital sometime in August of '68. It was just shortly after the Rawlings' murders."

Schafer and Rodgers glanced at each other. "Why was she put in there?" Schafer asked.

"From the best I can determine the family decided that she should be admitted because she would talk continually about the tragedy that took place at the resort. I understand that on some days she would talk about the murders around the clock."

"What exactly would she talk about or say?" Rodgers asked.

"Well, at first she would ramble on that she didn't think Mr. Rawlings made his money honestly. She kept saying that he was involved with a bunch of crooks and that he liked to steal things. Another time, she would talk about her grandson Billy being killed in a motorcycle accident. That was Monty's boy who was killed about a month before the Rawlings murders. She would incant to the walls that Monty and his wife had to go out at five o'clock in the morning to find Billy lying on the side of the road dead and that the Rawlings people wouldn't help."

"Do you have any clue to why she would say that?" Ford asked.

"I can only assume detective, that she meant that her son Monty may have asked Mr. Rawlings and his family to help them look for their son, and maybe Mr. Rawlings wouldn't do it."

"Did she say why she thought Rawlings was involved with a bunch of crooks?" Schafer asked, intrigued by the nurse's revelations.

"No, she never said anything specific or mention any names about that, but I think that if she'd known anything for sure, she would have told me. She did tell me that Mr. Rawlings did not want her grandson Billy to come around the Rawlings' cottage with his motorbike and that Mr. Rawlings would say bad or mean things to her grandson. She really didn't like the way Mr. Rawlings talked to other members of her family at all."

"What do you mean by that Miss Brinner?" Rodgers asked.

"I guess it wasn't so much what Mr. Rawlings said, from what I could make out from Mrs. Barr, it was the way he said it. From what I gather he was very abrasive."

"What was your impression of Mrs. Barr? Do you think she knew something or was she over reacting to Mr. Rawlings behavior?" Schafer asked.

"Personally, I think she, and maybe the rest of her family had a deep hatred of the Rawlings family. She told me that one time Mr. Rawlings ordered her grandson off the Rawlings property and told him to keep off. I had a feeling that one incident might be just the tip of the iceberg of bad feelings between the families."

"And why was that?" Rodgers asked.

"I think it was because Mr. Rawlings was a pushy type of fellow and I don't think the Barr family liked that at all. I got the impression from Mrs. Barr that they were sorry they had sold the cottage to Mr. Rawlings. I believe that she felt Mr. Rawlings didn't have any respect for the Barr family and looked at them as uneducated and dumb people who didn't know what they had or how to use it."

"What was your overall impression of Mrs. Barr, Miss Brinner?" Schafer asked.

"In my opinion, I think that the killings put a heavy burden on Mrs. Barr's conscience and because of it, she would talk all the time about the murders."

"Did anything she say ever make you believe that someone in the Barr family might have something to do with those killings?" Rodgers asked.

" I can't say that definitely, detective."

"Is this the reason that you came here today?" Schafer asked as he placed a glass of water in front of Miss Brinner. She took a sip from the glass and then continued her conversation. "I've followed the case since it was first reported in the newspapers and I haven't seen much about it anymore. I have a suspicion that Mrs. Barr knows a lot more than she's telling about the murders and I thought that maybe this information might help. It may not be anything, but I thought the ramblings of Mrs. Barr were strange in many ways, but had an element of truth to them." She replied.

"Every bit of information we can get, Miss Brinner helps. We will send this report on to the lead detectives at the Detroit Post. If they feel that it's necessary to talk with you, I'm sure that they'll contact you immediately." Schafer reassured her.

"Thank you gentleman. I wasn't really sure if I should come up here from Traverse City or not. I was a little uncomfortable about discussing these things at first, but I feel much better now for having done so."

The detectives thanked her and said goodbye.

Miss Brinner's information arrived in Detroit from Schafer and Rodgers about the same time that Ford and Stevens were wondering what the new Sands County Prosecutor, elected the previous November would do with the Rawlings case. The detectives thought the election had been a deserving punishment for the previous prosecutor. It was especially gratifying since it was he who had permitted the Rawlings cottage to be destroyed.

The big question for Ford and Stevens at this point was what was this new prosecutor going to be like? They would find out very soon.

Diamond Faucet Company
May 14, 1969
9:00 a.m.
Franklin, Indiana

Franklin, Indiana is the home of the Diamond Faucet Company and is located 15 miles south of Indianapolis. It is a small rural community whose richness lies with its hardworking people and the bountiful farmlands that surrounded it.

The Michigan State Police Department plane slowly descended onto the runway of the local airport and came to a stop at the far end of the passenger terminal.

Stevens and Ford exited the aircraft and were met by a neatly dressed chauffeur. The driver opened the door of the Lincoln limo for his passengers and once the detectives had been comfortably seated, put the car in gear and quickly drove to the Diamond Faucet headquarters.

The Diamond headquarters was a large, sandy colored brick building with a half circle, asphalt drive that led to the canopied overhang and the buildings main entrance. The limo pulled to a stop under the canopy and the detectives stepped out into the spring air.

They entered the building, stopping briefly to view the large vestibule area with a working water fountain imbedded in the middle of the tile floor.

A young, vivacious receptionist greeted them from behind a large mahogany desk that sat in front of a large, glass block wall.

Within seconds, an attractive, petite woman with large brown eyes and black hair arrived from behind the glass wall and approached the desk. She was well dressed and very professional in a corporate business way.

"Good afternoon gentlemen, I'm Sandi Epson. I'm Mr. Jordan's secretary. I'm here to escort you to his office."

The detectives followed her closely, the fragrance of seductive perfume cutting the air. Within moments, she had deposited them directly into the office of the company comptroller, Mr. George Jordan. In the office with Mr. Jordan, was Byron Clark, a district sales manager for Diamond Faucet.

As the detectives settled themselves into the two large, leather chairs, George Jordan explained to them that he had been involved with all the financial transactions between Richard Rawlings and the Diamond Faucet Company for the last ten years. He emphasized that for the past two or three years, he believed that the Rawlings Agency was in financial trouble. He added that Rawlings would call at least three or four times a year and ask if the Diamond Company could expedite their invoices and mail the checks for services that had not yet been completed. Jordan also made it clear that there were many times that the Detroit branch office for Diamond Faucet would hold up payments for non-performance by Rawlings.

Jordan and Clark also confirmed that Harry McFarland was the person in charge of approving all payments for that sales district. Sometimes, according to Jordan, McFarland would be out of town, and the payment would be held up until he arrived and could approve it. It was standard operating procedure for the company. McFarland had the authority to hold up payments if he thought that all or a portion of the advertising arrangements had not been met according to the contract.

Stevens asked if Mr. Santino had ever been involved in any of these payments.

"According to my records and notes, Mr. Santino called me on June 17th, 1968 and said that the invoices totaling over twenty-four thousand dollars were in the mail and requested that the money be sent to him in advance as he needed it to operate the business."

"And was that the truth?" Stevens asked.

"Yes and no," Jordan replied. "We sent Mr. Santino the payment, but the invoices arrived several days later than when he told me they would arrive."

"Were you satisfied with Santino's approach regarding the billings?" Ford asked.

"No, but that was the first time that Mr. Santino called to have the money sent in advance of the invoices. After the Rawlings murders became public and Mr. Santino took over the agency, we decided to do an audit of the accounts. From what we've been able to determine, over the past four or five years, we've estimated that we've been overcharged for advertising in excess of one hundred thousand dollars by Rawlings and Santino."

Stevens and Ford were stunned by the amount. They asked if they could have copies of those financial records and any other transactions that had been conducted with the Rawlings Company for the past three years. They were especially interested in the 1968 business year.

Jordan told the detectives that he had anticipated their request and that copies had already been prepared for them. In addition, he could provide them with seven canceled checks that had been paid to the Rawlings agency for requested advertising. The checks were dated from April 10th thru Sept.5th, 1968.

The detectives would give the checks to the Latent Print Section for processing.

Jordan also peaked the interest of the detectives by telling them what Mc Farland had told him regarding Mr. Santino.

"About a month after the news of the murders, McFarland called us here at the main office and asked that we stop payment on any invoices submitted by Mr. Santino until they had been approved by him."

"Did he say why?.

"Yes. McFarland said that he believed that Rawlings, prior to his death, had failed to pay some of the national magazine accounts for advertisements that we had contracted for."

"I find that very interesting," Stevens remarked.

"We also found that intriguing because in addition to checking out Mr. Rawlings and his billing procedures, we decided to look at our own man, McFarland. We wanted to see if he had maintained his responsibilities by using proper oversight business practices."

Lynn Jenks, an assistant to Byron Clark entered the office and was introduced to the detectives as he took a seat at the conference table. The conversation continued.

"Where any of you at the Cobo convention in June?" Stevens asked.

Clark and Jenks stated that they had attended the convention at Cobo Hall from the 23rd, through the 25th. They said that during their stay that they were either at the Diamond Hospitality Room at the Ponchatrain Hotel or at the Cobo Exhibition Hall the entire time during their stay in Detroit. Neither of them could recall seeing Mr. Santino or any other person from the Rawlings Advertising Agency at the convention.

Clark said that he had been in Detroit in March of '68 for a presentation meeting with another advertising agency arranged by McFarland. This other agency was seeking to become the new advertising agency for Diamond Faucet. After that agency had made its presentation, it was generally agreed that the Diamond account should go to them beginning January 1, 1969. Clark said he was not aware if Rawlings had been told of this or not, but it would have been McFarland's responsibility to follow-up with Rawlings and let him know as a matter of professional courtesy. He said it should have been done immediately in order to give Mr. Rawlings enough time to locate another business that might need his services and fill the void Diamond would leave by moving to another agency.

After having lunch in the company cafeteria with the group of Diamond executives, Stevens and Ford thanked them for their cooperation and for the copies of the business transactions with Rawlings and left.

A decision was made to fly back to Lansing instead of Detroit in order to inform their superiors about the conversations they had with the Diamond Faucet people.

A State Trooper met them at the Lansing airport and drove them to the State

Police main headquarters in East Lansing.

They entered the building and went directly to the Latent Print Division and turned over the seven canceled checks that had been given to them by Mr. Jordan. They were told that it would take less than an hour to obtain any prints, if there were some left on the checks.

Patiently, they passed the time by visiting with some of their fellow officers and friends in the building before eventually being told that they could return to the lab for the results. The lab assistant told them that four of the seven checks contained the finger or thumbprints of Joseph Santino. They were not quite sure what that would mean to the investigation until they were able to have an audit done on both the business and personal financial records of Mr. Rawlings.

They visited briefly with Captain McCarthy in order to fill him in on their trip and the evidence they had collected. McCarthy seemed pleased, but sensed that his two prize detectives were burning low on investigative fuel and recommended that they take the weekend off.

May 16, 1969
10:00 a.m.
Southfield, Michigan

Stevens sat quietly behind the steering wheel as he guided the police cruiser easily through the traffic. His thoughts were on their next interview. Ford was flipping through his notepad as the gray concrete wall along the John Lodge Expressway flashed by his window. Their destination was the suburb of Southfield. They had an appointment with Reverend Harvey S. Potter, pastor for the Rawlings family.

Reverend Potter welcomed the detectives into the rectory as he made his way around the large oak desk and sat down. He told them he would answer any questions that they had so long as it didn't broach the pastor and parishioner areas of confidentiality.

The detectives understood and respected his position. Nevertheless, Ford explained to the pastor that what they were looking for was a clearer picture of the Rawlings family as members of the parish. They were looking for people who had been close to them, but were not relatives, business partners or social companions. Ford ended by saying: "Were looking for someone who would be more objective as to the Rawlings family and their lifestyle."

Reverend Potter, having set his own ground rules was content with Ford's explanation.

"Reverend Potter, how long was the Rawlings family, members of this congregation?" Ford began.

"The Rawlings family have been members here since 1957, about four years more than I've been here. I came in 1961."

"Did the family or Mr. Rawlings show any odd or hostile behavior towards anyone in your congregation while you've been pastor?"

"No. There wasn't any odd behavior as you put it. The family was very close. I believe that Mr. and Mrs. Rawlings were strict parents, in the sense that they gave their children rules and expected them to be followed. None of the children seemed to have any rejection of their parents wishes."

"Did Mr. Rawlings specifically, have any conflicts with other parishioners?"

"Mr. Rawlings was a brilliant and determined type of person. He believed that what he proposed for an idea should always be accepted because he believed it to be right. He always wanted to be top man. Unfortunately, that does create some problems in any community, especially a religious one."

"Did he ever have a run-in with any of the members of the congregation?"

"Thank God, no. I was able to keep him away from interfering with group projects by telling him that he was my personal advisor on different issues. That kept him busy and also working solo. He would sometimes disagree with me, but he would temper his remarks. I doubt he would have done that with someone else."

"Mrs. Rawlings? Was she involved with the church?"

" Yes and no. By that I mean not as much as I would have liked. I think she had a very nice personality for the community, but she was more devoted to Richard and her children and that left little time for her to get involved in church activities. She was a very good woman."

"Was anyone in this church close to Rawlings?" Stevens asked.

"Once I introduced my brother Edmund to him. Edmund is from Ohio. He and Rawlings seemed to hit it off very well. That was in March of 1968."

"Is your brother a pastor also?"

"No. He just happened to be up here from Ohio. He was looking to go to work in the automotive industry, but Richard almost talked him into going to work for him."

"Really? Why didn't he?" Ford asked.

"One, I told Edmund that in this case, I thought he should take my advice and not get involved with a church member, especially in business and particularly with Mr. Rawlings."

"Why did you feel that way?"

"Because I knew my brother and I knew Richard Rawlings. The two would not mix well and to be blunt, I didn't want to have to be the referee. I have enough to concentrate on as it is. If you understand what I'm saying."

"Yes sir, I think we do. By the way, what is your brother doing now?" Stevens asked.

"Edmund is a district representative for the Chevrolet Motor Division."

"Were there any other members of your congregation that could have had differences with Mr. Rawlings?" Steven continued.

"I would doubt it very much, Mr. Stevens. Richard knew he had my ear, so to speak. So he didn't waste much time with other members of the congregation."

"Reverend Potter, have you ever heard Mr. Rawlings mention something about a Round Table?"

The cleric hesitated for a moment. "You mean like the Knights of the Round Table, Mr. Ford?"

"Maybe. But in this case it's something more like a group of businessmen who refer to themselves as members of a Round Table?"

"No, I've never heard of anything like that. That's a new one."

"It wouldn't appear that you have any mysterious groups here," Ford said quietly.

"No. Between weddings and funerals, a church, Mr. Ford, doesn't have the vibrant life of business or politics. It's usually very subdued and very plain."

"It would be nice if police work were like that," Stevens answered, as he and Ford rose from their chairs and headed towards the door.

"What a tragic situation," the pastor said moving from behind his desk in order to escort the detectives out.

"Yes it is. It makes me wonder what kind of sick mind would do something like that," Stevens answered.

"Very sick, I believe, Mr. Stevens," replied the Reverend.

"Thank you," Ford said as he and Stevens left the church rectory.

"Goodbye gentleman and God bless you both," Reverend Potter said as he closed the door softly behind them.

On the surface, the detectives thought that very little had been gained from the interview. However, they did believe that it gave them a clearer picture of Mr. Richard Rawlings behavior. They were about to get an even clearer portrait of Richard Rawlings when they returned to the Post.

The detectives entered the Post lobby and walked by the main reception desk. A young trooper stopped them. "There's someone waiting outside your office. He says he needs to talk to the detectives handling the Rawlings' case. His last name is Arnold."

Stevens thanked the trooper and the two detectives made their way up the stairs to their office.

Seated on the long wooden bench outside the office was a middle-aged man, meticulously dressed, looking at his manicured fingernails. The air around him smelled like lilac water. Mr. Robert A. Arnold, a former employee of the Rawlings Agency was waiting to lay a bombshell on the two detectives. As the detectives came closer, he stood up.

"Are you the detectives handling the Rawlings' case?" he asked politely.

"Yes we are," Stevens answered. "Are you Mr. Arnold?"

"Yes, Yes I am. My name is Robert A. Arnold. Everybody calls me Bobby."

Flipping on the light switch, Ford motioned for Mr. Arnold to enter the office and to sit down. "I'm Detective Ford and this is Detective Stevens. How can we help you, Mr. Arnold?" Ford refrained from using his first name of "Bobby."

Mr. Arnold settled himself comfortably into a chair.

"The trooper at the desk said that I should wait here for the both of you so I did. I'm not sure that you can help me as much as I may be able to help you."

"And how would that be, Mr. Arnold?" Stevens asked curiously.

"How? Let me explain Detective Stevens. In 1967, I was working for an advertising firm in Chicago when I was given an assignment here in Detroit. I met Mr. Rawlings at that time and he asked me if I would like to go to work for him. I told him that I was happy with my current job, however, if the right offer came along I was willing to listen to any proposals that would be mutually beneficial. In the spring of 1968, I decided to come back to Michigan and go to work for the Rawlings Agency. A short time after I began working there, I got the feeling that the agency was doing a lot of false billings, especially with the Diamond Faucet account."

"When you say false billings, Mr. Arnold, just exactly what are you talking about?" Stevens asked.

"Specifically, I'm talking about charging a client for advertising that is never placed in a magazine or trade journal that the client thought he was paying for. You can do this very easily if the area representative is working with you on this type of scam."

"Do you know for a fact that Rawlings was doing false billings, Mr. Arnold?"

"Look, I didn't keep any records or make copies of them and I don't have any hard proof that Mr. Rawlings was doing it. But I know this business like the back of my hand, and there's one thing I can tell you, the way the billings were being handled, it was the only explanation as far as I was concerned as to how Rawlings was getting his cash."

"Do you think there was someone else in on this scam as you call it?" Ford asked.

Arnold squirmed in the seat before answering. "Personally, I think that Harry McFarland was in on it. He must have seen the invoices and more importantly, he had to approve them before they were paid."

Stevens and Ford knew this to be a fact.

Stevens continued with his questioning. "From what you are telling us Mr. Arnold, I would have to conclude that you're accusing, or at the least strongly suggesting, that Mr. Rawlings and Mr. McFarland were conspiring to steal money from the Diamond Faucet Company and doing it on a regular basis, is that correct?"

Without any hesitation, Arnold answered, "Yes sir, that's exactly what I believe was happening. As I said, I don't have any hard proof in my hands, but I think if you look into both the Rawlings Agency and Diamond Faucet billing records, you may find what you are looking for. I've been in this business a good while and I know what I'm talking about."

"What's your interest in this case, Mr. Arnold?" Ford asked.

"I've been looking at the papers from time to time and I haven't seen anything about what I've just told you. In my opinion, it could be the basis for the murders. I have no ax to grind if that's what your thinking Detective Ford. I just think the police should have as many facts as they can. That's the only reason I came here today."

Ford and Stevens thanked Mr. Arnold for his information and told him that they would definitely get back with him. Mr. Arnold smiled, shook their hands and left as quietly as they had found him.

The two men sat across from each other, their desks were piled high with reports and logs. They were still trying to digest their interview with Mr. Arnold when the phone rang. Ford picked up the receiver. It was Boyd Zackery, from the Zackery Gunsight Company. He was calling to set up a time to come in and talk with the detectives the next day. Ford set the appointment for 9:00 a.m. Zackery agreed.

"That was Boyd Zackery, Frank. He's coming in at 9 a.m. tomorrow."

Stevens nodded his head that he understood. "Well it seems the plot is thickening doesn't it? Our good friend and religious hypocrite, Mr. Rawlings was not only playing around with his secretaries, he was stealing from his clients. What a guy!"

Ford looked at the pile of papers on his desk. "I'm beginning to believe Rawlings either had a death wish, or he wanted to push the limits to see how far he could go. As it stands now, I'll bet we can count between ten and twenty suspects who could've had a reason to bump this guy off. But the question keeps coming back to me, 'why was his family taken out too?' That part bothers me. It suggests that the family could have known something about what was going on, or at least the killer thought they did."

Stevens was unsympathetic. "I wouldn't let it bother you too much John. I think who ever decided to take him out figured that anyone around him at the time would have to go too. No witnesses, no conviction. Plain and simple."

"Whoever it was, can't have much of a conscience."

Stevens was quick with his answer. "I'll put my money on Santino. What grinds me is that I can't find the one piece of hard evidence to nail him with."

"Let's call it a day, Frank. My mind is getting too fogged up to do much good here. Maybe tomorrow Boyd Zackery can throw some new light on this fiasco."

The detectives put on their jackets and quickly walked out of the building.

CHAPTER 22

May 19, 1969
9:00 a.m.
State Police Post-Detroit

Boyd Zackery eased his lanky frame into the chair in front of detective Ford's desk. Bushy eyebrows that arched over cold blue eyes, made a common looking face, a little more attractive even with its weathered look. A small scar from the bottom of his left ear lobe that ran for an inch or so down to his jawbone gave the face character.

Stevens began the questioning. "Mr. Zackery, how did you become acquainted with Richard Rawlings?"

Zackery leaned forward, looked directly at Stevens an answered. "The first time I met Richard Rawlings he was with Joe Santino. It was sometime in late May of 1967 at the advertising agency. I was looking to see if Rawlings & Associates might be useful to me, in case I needed to make a change with my advertising dollars. We met several times. Richard was a very intelligent man and we enjoyed discussing politics, business ventures and things like that. "

"Did Mr. Rawlings ever discuss with you a business venture that used the name of Round Table?"

"No. Never heard of it."

"What about a business venture centered around promotional advertising ideas that required large amounts of money?"

"Nope. All I know is that Richard was involved in the advertising business and had a magazine that dealt with Detroit show people. Actors, actresses and people like that."

"Our information shows that you have recently placed your advertising with Mr. Santino. Can you tell us why?" Ford asked.

"Certainly. When Santino took over the business, he made some major adjustments in how the company did business. Richard never asked for my business, but Joe Santino did. And I only made my move after Joe Santino lost the Diamond account. Joe was professional about it. He asked me directly for my account and I told him that I would think it over. After a while, I made the decision to pick Santino. Is there a law against that?"

"No, there's no law against that, Mr. Zackery. About how much will that decision cost you, if I may ask?" Stevens said.

"The account runs between one hundred and fifty-thousand to two-hundred thousand per year."

"That's a lot of money to give to an agency that has just lost it's founder and has a novice like Mr. Santino as it's chief operating officer, isn't it?" Ford asked.

"I don't think so. I wasn't very happy with the agency that I had, especially with the people who handled my account. I believe Joe has the necessary connections to market my products in the right manner. It was all I wanted the other company to do, but they never did it and I believe Joe can."

"Did you sell two Beretta hand guns to Bill Hathaway, who was buying them for Joe Santino?" Ford asked.

"Yes I did. Everything is legit and above board. I have copies of the receipts and purchase orders for the two guns and ammunition that I sold to Bill Hathaway for resale. I didn't know at the time the guns were for Joe Santino." Zackery replied as he handed the copies of the invoices to Stevens.

Stevens handed them to Ford who placed them in an envelope and marked it for reference.

"Do you have anything more to tell us about your relationship with either Rawlings or Santino? Stevens asked.

"Nope."

The interview ended and Zackery left.

Ford and Stevens spent the rest of the day updating and processing correspondence with different people closely related to the case. They filed newspaper clipping from different sources around the state that had published stories about the murders. Phone calls were made to former staff writers for the Rawlings Agency seeking any controversial material that may have been produced but not published.

Finally, Stevens looked over at Ford. "John, we need to set up an interview with Richard McMullen, the head of Diamond Faucet. I think we should discuss this false billings thing with him. It's solid, factual evidence that we might be able to cultivate and develop into something positive. Besides, I'd like to know how he feels down deep about his vice-president in charge of sales, Harry McFarland."

"I'll call him right away Frank." Ford replied, reaching for the telephone.

May 20, 1969
9:00 a.m.
State Police Post-Detroit

Richard McMullen was thirty-two years old and president of Diamond Faucet Company, one of the largest plumbing fixture manufacturers in the world. He looked the part of the young business executive climbing the ladder of success. His dark blue suit was tailored to his average build and he moved about with an air of confidence that would have been attributed to a more seasoned businessman. When he arrived at the Post in Detroit, he was escorted immediately to the detective's office. Richard Mazur, the corporation accountant accompanied him.

Stevens and Ford greeted both men and they sat down to discuss the management habits of Harry McFarland.

The detectives brought the two executives up to date on the investigation and specifically how it pertained to McFarland. Stevens made them aware that they were investigating McFarland's business and personal association with Rawlings and Santino.

Ford asked McMullen and Mazur to keep that information confidential and to avoid any discussions with McFarland that could compromise the investigation.

McMullen guaranteed his cooperation and that of his company staff. He also volunteered any services that he or his company might be able to provide to the State Police in their pursuit of the facts. Mazur was given a verbal directive by McMullen to assist Stevens and Ford in providing any and all company billing and advertising expenditure records relative to the Rawlings' case.

Richard McMullen thought it was the appropriate time to reveal to Stevens and Ford that since the death of Mr. Rawlings, Mr. Mazur had been instructed to do a complete and through audit of the former Rawlings advertising account. And subsequent to the detective's meeting with Mr. Jordan at the company headquarters, the corporation board had decided to do a complete audit and job performance evaluation on McFarland going back the last five years. The company board of directors had also agreed to hire a private investigator and that Mr. Mazur was in the process of evaluating the investigator's preliminary report.

Mazur was able to tell the detectives that at this point, the audit had revealed that Diamond Faucet Company had been overcharged in excess of twenty-eight thousand dollars. That figure only included the first eight months of 1968. They had yet to complete the audit for 1967. Mr. Jordan expected the amount to total more than one hundred thousand dollars before they were through.

Stevens and Ford, realized that if the audits proved successful, the potential embezzlement charges against Santino and McFarland could be another key in trying to open a different door in the investigation. It could be used as leverage in trying to make Santino and McFarland reveal more about their relationship with Rawlings.

Ford suggested that McMullen put his investigation on hold until both he and Stevens had a chance to interrogate McFarland one more time. They wanted one more chance to see if McFarland would break.

McMullen was reluctant to commit to that proposal until he had a chance to talk with his corporation attorney. A phone was made available for McMullen and he called the attorney to discuss the proposal. Ford explained to the attorney the reason for the request to speak with McFarland one more time was to lock McFarland into his story. Ford then handed the phone to Stevens, who provided the attorney with all the information that he was permitted to release regarding their own investigation and its status.

After a complete and exhausting discussion, the corporate attorney was satisfied that McMullen could cooperate without putting the company in jeopardy and gave him the go ahead to work in tandem with the Michigan State Police detectives. The meeting ended with everyone understanding the future course of action by each party.

The puzzle that confronted the detectives was how they would be able to put all these new pieces together in order to extract a confession from either McFarland or Santino for murder or as an accessory to murder.

It was clear to Stevens and Ford, that McFarland and Rawlings had reasons to be suspicious of each other. There was no doubt that both men had been cut from the same bolt of cloth. More questions needed to be answered.

Did Rawlings find out about the new advertising agency for the Diamond account beginning in January 1969?

Did Rawlings threaten McFarland with revealing McFarland's role in the money scam that he and McFarland were a part of in defrauding the Diamond Faucet Company? A sort of "If I go down- you go down," scenario.

Did McFarland have other secrets he thought Rawlings might reveal, and for that reason needed to eliminate him?

Could Rawlings or McFarland have been involved with a Detroit organized crime family?

And, what about Zackery? Why would an arms dealer want to invest over one hundred thousand dollars worth of advertising in basically an arts and entertainment magazine?

Was someone trying to launder money? If so, where was the money coming from?

Stevens and Ford decided to do a more comprehensive background and fingerprint investigation of McFarland. It needed to be done before bringing him in for a second round of questioning.

In the meantime, a formal letter was sent to the U.S. Border Patrol's Main Office requesting them to check their records between June 21st and the 26th, 1968 as to the possibility that a person by the name of a "Mr. Roberts" or "Robiere" may have tried to cross either the Canadian or Mexican borders during that time period.

Ford called the Pellston and Harbor Springs airports to see if they would re-check there records for any private planes that could have landed during the June time period the Rawlings family was murdered. He received an immediate response telling him that the airports only kept records if they had provided fuel or maintenance service to the aircraft. There were no records kept for landings and takeoffs. Both air control supervisors had reviewed the request with the persons assigned that day and none of the staff could recall a Lear aircraft having landed or taken off from either airport.

Other Michigan airport logs were obtained and reviewed. None revealed an aircraft of that type as having been serviced with a registered pilot's name or ownership name of Roberts or Robiere.

Within 24 hours, Stevens received a telegram from the U.S. Border Patrol office informing him that they had no record or information regarding any person by the name of Roberts or Robiere crossing either the Canadian or Mexican borders during the time period in question.

May 22, 1969
11:00 a.m.
Sterling Heights, Michigan

Bonnie Jean Syminski sat quietly in her living room in an old, oversized rocking chair. Sometimes she would unconsciously put both hands on her stomach. She was pregnant and very uncomfortable on this unusually hot and humid day in May. Mrs. Syminski had worked a year as the art director for Rawlings and The Director magazine.

Stevens and Ford were anxious to get their questions answered and move on.

She told the detectives that after three months of working there, Rawlings had made sexual advances toward her but she refused to be intimidated by him. She said that he persisted but she did not have anything to do with him.

It came as no surprise to the detectives to learn from this former secretary, that in late August of 1967, Rawlings left his cottage at Thunder Point, and returned to Detroit on the pretense of finishing an advertising project. He then called the office and requested that Bonnie bring some materials to his house so that he could finish the project.

Mrs. Syminski told detectives that Rawlings told her he did not want to come to the main office because he didn't want to get stuck answering phone calls, and other things like that. He asked her to come to the back door of his house and walk in. She did exactly as she had been instructed. She arrived at the house and entered through the back door. She said that Rawlings was in another room and called out to her to make herself comfortable in the living room and that he would be right out.

"And then what happened?" Stevens asked, his suspicions waiting to be confirmed.

"I placed the packet of materials I'd brought from the office on the dining room table and sat on the living room couch expecting that he had some work for me to take back to the office. I must have waited three or four minutes assuming he was using the bathroom. Just as I was about to call out, he walked into the room, wearing a smoking jacket and only a pair of briefs underneath. Then he started to make advances at me, but I just grabbed my purse and ran out of the house."

"Did he say anything or do anything while you were running out of the house?" Ford asked.

"No. I think he was just surprised that I took off running. I don't think he was prepared for the way I reacted."

"Did you do or say anything to Mr. Rawlings after that?"

"No. But when I got back to the office, he had called another secretary, Corrine Linn to bring him some papers out to the house. She had been gone only a short time and returned to the office crying. She told me the same thing had happened to her, but that the advances by Rawlings were even cruder. We both quit a short time after that."

"Did other secretaries make it known that they had been or were being harassed by Rawlings while they were working there?" Ford asked the young woman as he carefully took notes.

"Yes. All the secretaries that I knew or that ever worked for Rawlings had to watch out for him. It was a bad situation, but all of us had to survive until we could find another job."

The detectives thanked her and left.

"I wonder how many other young women were subjected to that type of abuse by Rawlings, while at the same time he was professing to be a pillar in his church and the business community?" Stevens asked.

" It could be a short jump for a jealous boyfriend or husband to take revenge on Richard Rawlings and his family." Ford replied.

Stevens nodded in agreement.

May 26, 1969
9:00 a.m.
State Police Post-Detroit

A telegram arrived from Richard Mazur, Diamond Faucet's accountant. Mazur confirmed that overcharges in billings had been made by Rawlings and that Harry McFarland had approved the charges. The amount of the overcharges came to more than one hundred thousand dollars.

The telegram also stated that the private detective hired by the firm had turned up activities by McFarland, which revealed other false monetary procedures and potentially major conflicts of interest.

Mazur told the detectives that Mr. McMullen was prepared to file felony charges against his regional manager as soon as the detectives were finished with their work. However, if murder charges were filed against McFarland, then the company would coordinate their information with Michigan authorities in order to assist in prosecuting him. Diamond's information would be beneficial and relevant in any case brought against McFarland.

Stevens immediately called Mazur. He told the accountant, that he and Ford were concerned that filing embezzlement charge against McFarland at this time might cloud the main purpose of their investigation. That purpose was to see if they could uncover a substantial motive or connection between Rawlings, Santino and McFarland that would provide a motive for what happened to the Rawlings family on that rainy June night.

Mazur agreed and would tell McMullen to wait until the detectives had the opportunity to conduct another interview with Harry McFarland.

Stevens dialed the phone and waited for McFarland to answer.

May 27, 1969
9:00 a.m.
State Police Post-Detroit

Harry McFarland knew the routine and felt very comfortable coming down to the State Police Post to meet with the two detectives on this pleasant spring morning. The only thing that agitated him was that he had to pass up a day of hitting golf balls and practicing his swing. He'd guessed wrong on the weather. Based on a previous weather forecast, he had thought it was going to be a day of constant rain. Instead the bright sunshine and blue sky made a picture perfect day. McFarland was about to find out that the dark, gloomy day he'd thought of, was waiting for him inside the police building. The lightning and thunder he had perceived in the skies above him would instead come in his interview with Stevens and Ford.

"How are you this morning, Mr. McFarland?" Stevens asked pleasantly.

"Oh, I'm fine. Damn mad that I guessed wrong about the weather. It's beautiful outside. I should be out on the golf range."

"I know what you mean. It's too nice a day to have to stay inside, but that's the breaks."

"Yes, I guess you're right," McFarland answered.

Ford eased into the questioning. "Mr. McFarland, the last time you were here we had sort of general conversation regarding Richard Rawlings. Today, however, we'd like to get into some specifics regarding your relationship with Mr. Rawlings. Is that okay?"

"Sure. Fire away," McFarland answered confidently.

"How long have you been with the Diamond Faucet Company?"

"I have been with them since they started in 1954 and was with the parent company, Moton Plumbing Fixtures for almost four years before that."

"What did you do from 1950 to 1954 with Moton?"

"I was a regular salesman. I called on accounts."

"And in 1954?"

"In 1954, I was made vice-president in charge of sales and advertising. It was part of the reorganization of Moton merging with Diamond."

"Is that when you met Mr. Rawlings?"

"Yes. When I became the vice-president, Mr. Rawlings called on me at my office. We had a very cordial discussion regarding the advertising business. Richard explained the necessary steps in order to generate business in the Detroit market and he seemed very knowledgeable about the area. A couple of months later, I recommended that the account be given to the Rawlings Agency."

"So they have been your advertising agency since 1954. That would be about fourteen years at the time of Rawlings death," Stevens continued.

"Yes. That would be right," McFarland acknowledged.

"Did you ever think of changing to another agency during that time?" Ford asked.

"No. Under the circumstances, Mr. Rawlings was a prime catch. He was pushy enough to land some very big magazines and newspapers to carry our product line. We met once a week, but not much in the summer because he liked to be up at his cottage."

On cue, Stevens moved in closer to McFarland, until his chair was about a foot away, facing McFarland's.

"Mr. McFarland, do you know what the Miranda Rights are?"

"Yes. Why?" he asked, his body tensing.

"Because we are required to read them to a suspect when we are about to bring charges against that person or arrest them," Ford answered.

"For what?" McFarland asked, feeling agitated and trapped. This was a new approach by the detectives and he didn't like it. "I've only been to the Rawlings house once, and I've never been to his cottage."

"This has nothing to do with the cottage, Mr. McFarland," Stevens replied. "We are dealing with some billing overcharges and potential conspiracy criminal fraud charges."

"I don't know what you're talking about," McFarland protested.

"What we are talking about Mr. McFarland is that you and Mr. Rawlings manipulated the advertising expenditures for the Diamond Faucet account. Would you like to explain your involvement in that before we go any further?"

McFarland leaned back in his chair. He took a deep breath and started to explain. "At the beginning of each year, in January, Rawlings and I would get together and make up the advertising budget for that fiscal year. I would approve the proposed budget, which would contain the ad rates for the upcoming year. Rawlings would send me the billings for each month as outlined in the budget. I would check it over and then send it to the main office in Franklin for payment."

"You did this with every billing?" Ford asked.

"Yes, for the most part. It worked as it was supposed to. Rawlings was doing a good job for Diamond, and if he were alive today, he would still have the account."

" Is that so? Are you positive of that, Mr. McFarland?" Stevens asked.

The detectives knew that the Rawlings Agency was going to be terminated at the end of 1968 and replaced with a new agency because of McFarland's recommendation. They waited for McFarland's answer.

"Yes, I'm sure. There wasn't any action taken to drop Rawlings until after his death. Then in September of 1968, the company made the decision to terminate."

"Are you telling us that you never found any discrepancies in Rawlings billings?" Stevens asked.

"No. I'm not saying that. I did find some double billings several times, but he corrected them when I brought them to his attention. I monitored his billings each month by checking the budget charts and the rate cards I got from the publishing companies."

"So you used a check and balance system with Mr. Rawlings, is that right?" Ford asked.

"That's right. I used the rate cards each month to check the billings and then I would forward them to Mrs. Howe, my secretary."

"Why?" Ford asked.

"I always asked her to double-check the figures and confirm that the ads were placed in the magazines that Rawlings claimed the agency had placed them in."

McFarland was becoming visibly uncomfortable with the questioning and he began to sweat. The sight of perspiration to Stevens and Ford indicated that they were touching a nerve. With each passing minute, the detectives were becoming more convinced that McFarland and Rawlings had been involved in an embezzling scheme to defraud Diamond Faucet. They believed one of the principal architects of that scheme was sitting in front of them. The detectives knew McFarland was aware that he could be charged with a felony and sentenced to a long prison term if convicted. They wanted to see how he would withstand the pressure of the interrogation.

McFarland tried to maintain his composure and continued with his explanation. "Other than the three or four times that I found the double billings, I never found any individual overcharges by Rawlings. It would have been impossible for Rawlings to slip any overcharges past me."

"Why is that?" Stevens asked.

"Why? Because representatives from other advertising agencies call on me on a regular basis and tell me what the current advertising rates are. In September of 1968 I found an overcharge of thirty dollars. I called Joe Santino on it. He told me he was billing the same way that Rawlings had it set up. I told him that he would have to set it up according to the rate cards."

Stevens looked at McFarland with contempt. "Did you ever speak to any of your superiors about this type of overcharging?"

"Well, no. I guess I never did."

"Did you ever audit any of your back invoices or records to see if Rawlings was conducting a pattern of overcharging your company?"

"No."

"Did you ever personally check to verify that Mr. Rawlings had placed the ads in the magazines he claimed he had?"

"No. I never thought it was necessary. Like I said before, I asked Mrs. Howe to do that."

"But you never told Mrs. Howe about some of the billings did you? She couldn't have checked for ads in magazines, if she wasn't told about them, isn't that right Mr. McFarland?" Ford pushed.

McFarland sat still and swallowed hard. "I don't remember."

"Why not?" Ford asked in harsh tone, hoping to push McFarland into a slip up.

"I just don't. I guess I didn't want to make problems for anyone. I did think about it just before Rawlings died and I was getting ready to look into it when all this happened."

"Did you ever think that you had accountability to the people who employed you to keep an eye on these potential problems?" Stevens asked, rising from his chair and walking towards the water cooler. He pulled a paper cup from the dispenser and held it under the spout until it was full. He handed the water to McFarland.

McFarland took the cup and drank its contents quickly. Then he wiped the sweat from his brow with his handkerchief. He loosened his tie and paused for a minute, while Stevens and Ford stood near him. Trying to regain his composure, he continued. "My personal opinion is I believe that the comptroller of the company and some of his assistant accountants should have been more aware of what was going on than I was. They should have made me aware of it. After all I'm not an accountant!" McFarland said, paring the thrust of responsibility back to Stevens.

"So you think it's their fault that Rawlings was overcharging the corporation, is that right?" Ford asked, shaking his head in a disgusted manner.

Stevens moved, standing directly in front of McFarland. He hovered over him like a hawk watching a field mouse in a pasture. His blue eyes stared straight at McFarland's two dark pupils and then he spoke. "I'm going to be very direct Mr. McFarland. I think you had a very strong motive to murder Richard Rawlings and his family."

McFarland froze in his chair and the sweat beaded up again on his forehead as Stevens continued. "And I think you committed Rawlings to overcharging the account for your own benefit. Rawlings, being as greedy as you, saw something in it for himself and agreed to participate in order to make sure he would have the account and a share of the scam. But when he got wind that you were going to dump his agency for a different one, he probably threatened to expose you to your superiors. That's what I think your motive was to kill him. Am I right Mr. McFarland?"

McFarland sat motionless for a long time trying to clear the pounding in his brain. Finally, after wiping his brow for the third time, he responded. "No, that's not right. Rawlings was a son-of-a-bitch to deal with, so I never discussed the possibility of taking the account away from him. I didn't discuss it because he would go berserk if he thought any of his clients would go to another agency. He felt everyone else in the business was stupid or incompetent. I didn't need him. He needed the Diamond account and me. Besides, I was at Cobo Hall attending the convention at the time of the murders and I was home by 6:30 p.m. that evening."

Ford and Stevens knew that McFarland had gained an advantage with his denial and the reasons for his actions, but they felt he was still hiding something about the business dealings.

"Did Rawlings ever give you anything in cash or gifts for the Diamond account?" Stevens asked.

"The only thing I ever did was to buy a 1964 Buick, early in 1965 for around $600 dollars. It was valued at twice that much."

"Did you pay tax on that deal?" Ford asked.

"Yes."

"On which amount, the $600 or the $1200?"

"The $1200."

"You're sure?"

"I think so."

"So you are not sure, are you?"

"Yes, I am sure!"

"Do you have your bill of sale?"

"No."

"Do you have anything that shows what you paid for the car?"

"No. Rawlings wanted cash, and I paid him cash." McFarland was becoming very agitated and edgy.

"Where's the car now?" Ford continued.

"It's in Florida. It has been there since 1965."

McFarland asked for more water. Stevens obliged. McFarland grabbed the paper cup and drank the entire amount in one gulp.

"Would you be willing to take a polygraph test, Mr. McFarland?" Ford asked, deciding not to pursue the car sale any longer.

"If you mean a lie detector test, I guess I wouldn't have any objection, so long as my doctor thinks I'm physically capable of doing it."

"Is there something wrong with your health that you need to consult with your doctor?" Stevens asked.

" No, but I had rheumatic fever when I was a child and I would like to make sure that I'm okay to take such a test."

"That's fine, Mr. McFarland. We'd like you to contact your doctor within the next day or so and tell him that you're being requested to do this procedure. For now, that is all we have to ask you."

McFarland rose quickly from his chair. It was obvious that he wanted to exit the building as fast as he could.

"I will check with my doctor about the test and have him call you. "Goodbye." McFarland said, as he turned quickly and rushed out of the office doorway.

Stevens and Ford looked at one another as a slight smile crossed their faces.

May 28, 1969
1:00 p.m.
State Police Post-Detroit

Detective Ford read the message on his desk from Dr. James North of Southfield. Dr. North had given his permission for Harry McFarland to take the polygraph test. As a follow-up and to close any loopholes, Ford immediately phoned

McFarland's attorney. The attorney had no objection to McFarland taking the test providing he could be present.

June 3, 1969
9:00 a.m.
State Police Post-Detroit

Detective Stevens contacted Harry McFarland in order to set up a time for the polygraph test. McFarland told Stevens that he had discussed the polygraph test with his doctor and also his attorney and that they had advised him, "not to take the test."

No test date was established and no polygraph test was scheduled, but the obvious questions about McFarland's refusal and lying about his doctor and the attorney refusing to allow him to take the test, made Stevens and Ford put McFarland at the top of the list together with Santino.

June 4, 1969
10:00 a.m.
State Police Post-Detroit

Ernest Gladden, the managing editor of The Director magazine called the State Police Post and spoke with Stevens. He told Stevens in no uncertain terms that as far as he was concerned, Richard Rawlings had been a tyrant, a schizophrenic and was paranoid.

He also revealed that he knew that Wanda Hopkins, a former secretary, had told different people in the office of having an affair with Mr. Rawlings. Wanda, he said could supply a lot of information.

As for now, he was going to try and find another job. He told Stevens that if he left the area he would notify the detectives as to where he was going.

June 6, 1969
9:00 a.m.
State Police Post-Detroit

Robert Arnold decided to stop at the Post and inform Stevens and Ford that he had resigned from the advertising agency. He wanted the detectives to know that he and his family were preparing to leave for Naples, Florida on June 18th. He tells them he will be staying with relatives in Naples until he starts his new job with the American Medical Association located in Chicago.

Arnold made it clear to the detectives that he had a great deal of fear for himself and his family, caused by the odd behavior of his new boss, Joseph Santino. He firmly believed that Santino was a liar and a cheat and maybe even mentally unstable.

When Stevens pressed him to be more specific, Arnold told them that Santino had been passing bad checks and that the company was in terrible financial condition. He made the detectives aware that Santino even had to layoff his secretary, Glenda Saunders. As far as he was concerned, Santino must have had something to do with the Rawlings' family deaths, "even though I have no real proof, but just a gut feeling." He told Stevens and Ford that Santino had borrowed more money from Mueller and was looking for financial partners to help him keep the agency. Mr. Zackery cancelled his Gun Sight company account with Santino and went with another advertising agency.

Ford asked Arnold why he thought that had happened.

Arnold responded that his personal opinion was that he never believed Santino had the skills to keep the Zackery account, or any other account for that matter. In his opinion, Zackery had been a fool to believe that Santino knew anything about the advertising business.

Saying goodbye, Stevens and Ford told Arnold they appreciated his candor and cooperation. They warned him to be careful.

From their office window, the detectives watched as Mr. Arnold walk to the new Cadillac Seville, and drive off.

They would never see or hear from him again.

CHAPTER 23

Cleveland Police Department
Intelligence Division
June 10, 1969
1:00 p.m.
Cleveland, Ohio

Stevens and Ford had received information from an anonymous source that initiated a visit to Cleveland, Ohio. They had received confidential information that needed to be verified with the Cleveland Police Department Intelligence Division. The person of interest was another former personal secretary to Richard Rawlings. Her name was Wanda Hopkins.

Miss Hopkins had left her job with Rawlings in the fall of 1967 in order to become Mrs. Ransom Boles. Mr. Boles was a successful Cleveland businessman and married Miss Hopkins in January of 1968. It was her first marriage; it was Mr. Bole's second.

Mr. Boles was a sixty-year old, tall, long-limbed figure in the manner of a Gary Cooper look alike. He was a self-made millionaire in the manufacturing business and a well-known entrepreneur. He and Wanda made their primary residence in Cleveland, but also maintained a second home in Palm Beach, Florida.

The Cleveland press, notably within the society pages, made its readers very aware that Mr. Boles was a deeply jealous and possessive of his younger, beautiful, twenty-five year old, wife.

Stevens and Ford wanted to verify the information with the Cleveland Police Department and obtain an update on Mr. and Mrs. Boles. What they knew of Mr. Boles was that he was an exceptionally wealthy man and liked to invest large sums of money in new companies. He preferred to keep his investments diversified and would buy fifty thousand shares of stock in a startup company if it looked like it could become a flourishing enterprise in the future.

The detectives speculated that Boles could have been a primary money source for Rawlings' new business venture.

Stevens and Ford arrived at the Cleveland Police Department and were directed to the office of Charley Roma, head of the Intelligence Unit for the department. Roma told the detectives that Rawlings was suspected having been using his former secretary, Wanda Hopkins Boles to obtain money or loans from Mr. Boles. The possibility that Rawlings was blackmailing Boles was also high on their list. Roma also confirmed that if his department could make the connection a reality. He believed that it would be a clear motive for Mr. Boles to have had Mr. Rawlings eliminated. Boles certainly had the contacts and resources to have it done. The last thing Roma mentioned was that Mr. Boles had been observed on numerous occasions, in heated arguments with his wife at local nightclubs and restaurants in the summer of 1968, after he found out that she was pregnant.

According to Roma, on one of those occasions, Mr. Boles had been overheard by a Cleveland undercover agent, mentioning the name of Richard Rawlings as the father of the child his wife was then carrying. He provided Stevens and Ford with specific documentation that verified Wanda Boles had been seen talking with Joe Santino at the advertising agency office shortly after attending the Rawlings family funerals. It was not certain what the reason was for her visit with Mr. Santino, but it appeared very suspicious to the agent.

Roma was reluctant to let Stevens and Ford know their confidential sources because the department had been required by a district attorney's agreement to protect the person's identity. It was a Federal case that involved a potential tax evasion and drug-dealing charge against a top Mafia crime figure in Cleveland and Roma was locked into that agreement.

It didn't bother Stevens or Ford. They realized the situation that Roma was in. Roma had given them more information than they had expected.

Stevens called the offices of Mr. Boles at the Industrial Tool & Die Corporation, located in a suburb of Cleveland to arrange an appointment time. The receptionist told Stevens that Mr. Boles was out of town, but she would make sure he received message.

Stevens and Ford thanked Roma for his cooperation and returned to Detroit with renewed confidence. By the time they had arrived at the State Police Post that evening, Ford found a call-in message from Mr. Boles on his desk. The message indicated that Mr. Boles and his wife were going to be in Detroit the following day for a convention of Golf Driving Range owners. Among his many companies, Boles owned a manufacturing group that had the patent on making the rubber grips that covered the end of golf club shafts. Mr. and Mrs. Boles would be staying at the Cadillac Hotel in downtown Detroit.

Cadillac Hotel, Room 502
June 11, 1969
10:00 a.m.
Detroit

Ransom E. Boles appeared tired and distracted as he shook hands with Stevens and Ford when they entered his hotel suite. The prosperous businessman moved slowly toward the woman standing near a large sofa and two matching chairs in the middle of the room. She was holding a drink in her hand.

There was a vast, visual difference between Boles and his wife when the detectives looked at Wanda Boles. Her hourglass figure, striking blue eyes and platinum blond hair attracted the stares of both men and women and she was not reluctant to wear clothing that accentuated her physical attributes.

Today was no exception. She wore a cardinal red dress, cut low at the neckline and tight fitting. She coordinated her dress, with a pair of red, high-heeled pumps.

Mr. Boles appreciated the gazes his wife attracted, but only to a point. His eyes would reflect a deep-seated resentfulness when someone would stare too long at her curvaceous figure. His jealous nature made him suspect his wife was being mentally undressed by her admirer.

Stevens and Ford settled themselves comfortably onto the sofa across from their hosts. Mr. and Mrs. Boles each took one of the leather lounge chairs directly across from the detectives. A rectangular coffee table, with a small floral arrangement, acted as a barrier between them.

The couple waited patiently until Stevens spoke. "Thank you for agreeing to see us this morning on such short notice. As you both know, detective Ford and I are investigating the Rawlings murder case. We've been contacting numerous people who may have known or been associated with either Mr. Rawlings or members of his family. Today, we're here to try and tie up some loose ends if we can."

Wanda Boles responded quickly. "I can assure you detective Stevens, I've discussed all of my previous employment positions with my husband. He knows that I worked for Mr. Rawlings and I have nothing to hide. I will be happy to answer any questions you may have."

Mr. Boles also felt a need at this point to tell the detectives that he was fully aware of Mr. Rawlings and his crude behavior as an employer and the advances he had made on his wife before he and Wanda had been married. "I'm totally aware of my wife's association with the Rawlings firm and her encounters there with Mr. Rawlings. Personally, I think the guy was a bastard. I knew eventually that you'd be trying to reach my wife and that's the reason that I sent you the message yesterday with an invitation to meet with us here. I'd rather have you come to my hotel room here in Detroit rather than meet with you in Cleveland. The media thinks people like Wanda and I are fair game for scandal and would make something more of it than what it deserves. I believe that you both know what I'm talking about."

"We appreciate your frankness Mr. Boles. We're not looking to create turmoil in your private life. On the other hand we have a job to do and the cooperation that you and your wife have shown is very much appreciated," Stevens responded.

A rare smile crossed Mr. Boles' lips.

Looking directly at Mrs. Boles, Stevens continued. "Mrs. Boles, what can you tell us about your relationship with Mr. Rawlings."

Wanda Boles shot a quick glance at her husband and then spoke. "As I have told my husband, when I first went to work for Mr. Rawlings, he began to make advances toward me. He was very awkward in his approach and I never allowed him to carry out his intentions with me. He was a very childish type individual."

"What kind of advances, Mrs. Boles?" Stevens asked.

"Towards the end of the day, he would send the other help home and would call me into his office for his 'special dictation sessions,' as he would call it." A slight smile crossed her lips, but she went on. "He would start to talk about his sex life, then he would ask me about my sex life, saying all the time that he was only trying to see if his desires were normal. Toward the end of our meeting he would try to make some physical advances toward me, but after a couple of times, especially when he got the idea that I wasn't going to get involved in any kind of sexual activity with him, he quit. At least with me."

The detectives had confidential information that contradicted Wanda Boles' statements about her involvement with Mr. Rawlings, but Stevens and Ford remained silent on the issue and allowed her to continue. They were fully aware that her relationship with Mr. Rawlings had resulted in her becoming pregnant but they did not see any benefit in bringing it up at this time.

She confidently continued on with her story. "He would always apologize for his actions afterwards and seemed to be very insecure by trying to prove to me that he was a real man. From what I heard, I think he did this with a lot of the girls who worked for him. After my marriage, I didn't see or hear from Richard for over seven months, until I heard about his death and that of his family."

Sensing that his wife required a break, Mr. Boles interrupted her story. "I've never met the son-of-a-bitch. In fact, Wanda only told me that she had worked for him after we saw the story of the murders in the papers."

Ford made a mental note that Wanda Boles had waited until the Rawlings murders had been made public before informing her husband of her relationship with the deceased Rawlings. He wondered how much else she might be keeping in her mental lock box.

"I was pregnant at the time," Wanda remarked. "It was a difficult pregnancy and I lost the baby due to some complications. Ray and I stayed in Florida most of this year because I needed time to recuperate from the loss of the baby, both physically and emotionally."

"Mrs. Boles" Ford asked. " Did you ever hear the name of a Mr. Roberts or Robiere while you were employed at the ad agency?"

She paused, a slight frown crossing her face before she spoke. "The only Mr. Roberts that I ever heard of is a John Roberts. I believe he lives in Columbus, Ohio. He's a business promoter and is involved with a lot of golf meets around the country. I think he has an apartment in Chicago. I believe that he's probably around Ransom's age."

Mr. Boles winced when he heard his wife's words, but didn't say anything.

"Sorry dear," she said, trying to soften the embarrassing reference. "That's the only Mr. Roberts I know."

"Fine. That'll be all for now, Mrs. Boles. Again I want to thank both of you for your cooperation in this matter, Stevens said. The detectives rose from the sofa as Ford handed Mr. Boles his business card. The detectives said goodbye and left.

As Stevens and Ford walked down the hallway to the elevators, they thought they could hear a heated argument occurring from the room they had just left. As the door to the elevator was closing, the sound of breaking glass could be heard in the distance.

The detectives realized immediately, that for Mr. Boles to have contacted them as soon as he did, he must have had a confidential informant of his own within the Cleveland Police Department who was looking our for Boles' interest. It also alerted them to the possibility that Mr. and Mrs. Boles might have more information about Mr. Rawlings than Wanda's employment record.

Almost a full year had gone by from the time the murders had been committed. The trail of witnesses and suspects were drying up as quickly as the hot summer heat dried up the green grass. The remainder of June, then July, August and September passed, without any new evidence coming to light.

Stevens and Ford felt obligated to give the case their undivided attention, but as the case loads increased for all the detectives on the force, less and less time could be devoted to the Rawlings' murders.

There was even a directive from Colonel Darrens to pay more attention to more recent murder cases that could be concluded quickly, and recommended that the Rawlings case be placed on the back burner, reviewed only when time permitted or new evidence came in.

The full time effort was being downgraded due to personnel requirements. Fate, however, would not let go of this horrible crime that easy. In October, the detectives again had their attention directed toward Joseph Santino.

October 18, 1969
9:00 a.m.
State Police Post-Detroit

Responding to another confidential tip, Stevens and Ford invited Santino to take another polygraph exam. Surprisingly, Joseph Santino agreed to do it.

Detective Sgt. Earl T. Newman of the Second District Headquarters conducted the examination. At the conclusion of the test, Detective Newman stated in his report that the emotional responses of Mr. Santino revealed that he was "not truthful in regards to the shootings of the Rawlings family or being at the Rawlings cottage in June of 1968."

Stevens and Ford knew this information would be red meat for the press, but they also knew that it was inadmissible in a court of law. Still, the two detectives knew that these types of admissions, when obtained through a skillful and professional examiner were usually correct within ninety to ninety-five percent of the time. What they needed was an admission by Santino of the crime or his involvement in it. It didn't look like that would come anytime soon.

A day after Santino had taken the polygraph exam, the detectives sat quietly at their desks as thin streaks of vapor clouds painted the fall sky a brilliant orange outside of their window. Autumn was fading quietly and winter was looming just over the horizon.

"You know Frank," Ford began, breaking the silence. "If we believe the poly exam, Santino is the guy who did it. But if he is, the only way we're going to really know is if he comes in here and admit he killed Rawlings. I don't think he's going to do that. He knows that polygraphs are inadmissible in court and he's just going to sit tight."

"You're right John." Stevens replied. "I'm not sure that he'll break. Then again, you never know."

November 11, 1969
9:30 a.m.
State Police Post-Detroit

A memo from State Police Headquarters in East Lansing advised the detectives that Joseph Santino previously owned two AR-7 Armalite .22-caliber semi-automatic rifles. The rifles were described as Air Force survival weapons.

The State Police crime lab, together with FBI ballistic results verified that this was the type of weapon involved in the Rawlings murders.

Another report from the crime lab indicated that a number of expended .22-caliber casings obtained from a practice target shooting area, at a local gun club, where Joseph Santino was a member, matched the evidence casings found at the scene of the murders.

With this information, Stevens and Ford brought Santino in again for questioning and attempted to make him divulge exactly where those weapons were located. Santino would not cooperate. He maintained his previous story about giving away the rifles. "One of the rifles" he said went to his brother-in-law, and the other to a friend who lived in Chicago.

It was Santino's attitude and uncooperative spirit that made the two detectives determined to concentrate on him as the perpetrator of the Rawlings murders.

December 1, 1969
12:00 noon
State Police Post-Detroit

The bitter cold and winter winds whipped around the outside of the Post building and made the warmth of their office feel good to Stevens and Ford as they reviewed a number of documents, along with some payroll checks allegedly written by Mr. Rawlings.

Detective Hal Osmond, a State Police Document Examiner from the East Lansing Post had driven to Detroit through a brutal snowstorm that morning in order to do his meticulous evaluation of a number of written questions he had regarding the Rawlings murders. Eventually, Osmond found a pattern of discrepancies in the Rawlings company checkbook regarding checks issued to Joseph Santino. The discrepancies occurred during the time period after Mr. Rawlings' death. That information allowed Stevens and Ford to use a different approach in trying to solve the murder case.

December 7, 1969
9:00 a.m.
Richard C. Rawlings & Associates
Main Office-Southfield, Michigan

On the 28th anniversary of the surprise attack on Pearl Harbor by the Japanese, Stevens and Ford arrested Joseph Santino III on complaint # 20 842 69. Santino was charged with "obtaining money under false pretenses."

Stevens and Ford advised Santino of his rights and was arrested. He was taken directly to the State Police Post, fingerprinted and taken to the detective's conference room for questioning.

Stevens began his interrogation by asking Santino about his participation in signing checks to himself at a time following Mr. Rawlings' death. This interrogation was anything but pleasant.

"Joe." Stevens began, "this whole check writing system seems a little odd to John and I. Would you like to explain it?"

Santino had a look of defiance on his face, as he answered. "Sure. It's very simple. But, I think you guys have it in for me and I'm getting a little fed up with this interrogation bullshit every time the case goes cold on you guys. I've told you a thousand times that I didn't have anything to do with Richard's death or that of his family. But you two don't want to believe me. You want me for some reason, but both of you are way off base."

The sudden outburst by Santino at Stevens and Ford caught them by surprise. This was a side they hadn't seen in Santino before. He was beginning to show a little anger and emotion. The coolness and confidence he had shown in previous interviews was wearing off.

"Nevertheless, Joe you haven't answered the question," Ford responded quickly.

Santino shook his head in disgust and then answered. "Richard had a way of sending me checks from the cottage, signed by him for specific reasons. He would send me the checks, then call and tell me how to make them out. Sometimes it went to publishers of different magazines, or newspapers. Sometimes, he would have me make it out to myself so that I could negotiate a rate with some of the magazines by offering cash instead of a check. That usually occurred when we might be past due on a previous invoice or something. It happens all the time in this business. Look, Richard was gone from the office a lot and he trusted me to complete the checks with his input. You guys don't have a thing on me for this. When my lawyer gets here, he's going to raise hell with your supervisors about you two harassing me."

Stevens and Ford knew that they were on thin ice. They didn't have enough to charge Santino with forgery or embezzlement, both of which would be felonies. They had decided to settle for the 'false pretense' misdemeanor charge and hoped that they could make Santino admit to something more serious, like the Rawlings' murders. They had mistaken Santino's nerve. They decided to tone down their accusatory volume and went into a discussion mode.

Stevens was quick to pose the question. " Joe, we understand that you own a couple of Armalite, AR-7's survival rifles, can you tell us about them?"

"Sure, it's no big deal. I bought them from my brother-in-law, Herb Jackson, over in Pontiac. The first rifle I got, I gave to Hal Beckwith, a friend of mine who lives in Chicago. When I gave it to him, he was living here in Birmingham and had his own advertising company."

"And the second one?" Ford asked.

"The second one, I kept for about a year and then gave it back to my brother-in-law, Herb."

"Did you ever fire any of the two weapons?" Ford continued.

"Yeah, the second one. I never used the first one. I went over to Union Lake, on my father-in-law's property and did some target shooting with Herb."

The story sounded very familiar to Stevens and Ford. It was just like the one he gave regarding his purchase of the two-.25- caliber Beretta handguns.

Without warning, Santino stopped, then said. "You two have been hounding me since Richard died. From now on, you can talk to my lawyer. I'm through cooperating with you. Every time I tell you something, you try and tie me to the murders. So screw you and the horse you rode in on."

The detectives stopped talking and left the office. Within a couple of hours, Santino's attorney had posted bond and he was released under his own recognizance. It was going to be a test of wills.

Five-Star Gun Shop
December 10, 1969
10:00 a.m.
Pontiac, Michigan

Ford turned the wheels of the police cruiser into the snow-covered parking spot in front of Herb Jackson's gun store. Joe Santino's brother-in-law was busily stacking boxes of ammunition on the shelf behind the counter as the Stevens and Ford entered the store.

"Be with you gentlemen in a minute." He said.

The detectives nodded. They knew Herb Jackson from photographs of him that were on file as a registered gun dealer.

Herb Jackson, having dealt with a lot of law enforcement people who visited his store had picked out Stevens and Ford immediately as State Police detectives.

Pushing aside the empty cartons that once held boxes of ammunition, he stood behind the counter and looked directly at the two men. "Good afternoon. Can I help you with something?"

The detectives introduced themselves and showed Herb Jackson their badges.

Jackson asked a helper who was stacking some boxes against a wall to watch the store while he went to his office with the two men. He motioned for the detectives to follow him and they made their way through a narrow corridor until they reached Jackson's backroom office.

When all three were seated, Stevens began the questioning. "Mr. Jackson, your brother-in-law, Joe Santino told us he bought a couple of Armalite–AR-7's from you and that you both did some target practice with them. Can you tell us about that?"

Jackson leaned back in his chair and stared at the two detectives across from him. "It was like this." He said, "In late 1966 or early 1967, Joe came over to the shop and bought two Armlite-AR-7's, survival rifles, along with probably ten boxes of ammunition."

"Did he ever say why he wanted the rifles or why he was buying two?" Stevens asked.

"I think he told me that he and his boss wanted to do some target shooting up north."

"Did he ever give the rifles back to you?" Ford asked.

Jackson rose from his chair and walked over to an old, four-drawer filing cabinet and pulled out the third drawer from the top and began looking under the "S's" for Santino.

"Okay. Here we go," He said as he opened the folder. "I sold Joe one rifle, serial #68314 on September 30, 1966 and the second one on November 28, 1966, serial # 75878. There is nothing in this folder that says I ever received them back or that I ever resold either one of them. So the answer is no."

"Can you give us a copy of those records for our files, Mr. Jackson? Stevens asked.

"Sure, no problem. Just give me a minute." Jackson stepped outside his office, made the copies and returned. He handed the copies to the detectives and told them he was always available to cooperate with the law.

In the spirit of the season, they wished each other a "Merry Christmas" and Stevens and Ford left. On the ride back to the office, Stevens remarked about Santino's audacity in trying to tell them that he had given one of the rifles back to his brother-in-law. "Didn't that bastard think we wouldn't check his story? I mean, how dumb can a person be? You'd think he would have enough brains to know that you can't lie to our faces and think were not going to check up on it, can you? I think he must have a screw loose!"

Ford quickly responded. "I'm beginning to think this guy is a pathological liar Frank. He seems to be willing to say or do anything except tell the truth. I can't wait to see what he says when we question him about this." Stevens could only shake his head and wonder.

The sound of Christmas music blared through the outside loudspeakers of the Hudson Department Store building in downtown Detroit as hundreds of people, most with overcoat collars turned up, were fighting against the driving snow and cold wind. Many of these people were trying to do their last minute holiday shopping. Like ants looking for a passageway, the shoppers scurried from store to store, buying presents and gifts for their friends and loved ones. Some shoppers were loaded down with bags of presents, while others appeared to still be seeking the proper gift.

On this second Christmas after the murders, no tree or decorations could be seen at the vacant Rawlings house. A vandalized real estate sign on the lawn seemed out of place in the otherwise well-to-do neighborhood. Snow blanketed the dormant lawn and the house, once filled with life and laughter, looked like an abandoned outpost.

CHAPTER 24

December 27, 1969
9:00 a.m.
State Police Post-Detroit

"That's a hell of a nice looking sweater vest you got their Frank," Ford said as he entered the office and hung up his overcoat.

"Yeah, it is," Stevens replied. "The wife gave it to me. She thought I needed something to keep me warm this winter. Fits good too, covers my .38 special."

" Yeah, mine gave me a couple of shirts and ties, but she always buys them a little too large and now I'm going to have to go and exchange them. Maybe I'll get around to doing it tonight. I just hate doing battle with those women at the counters. They'll kick the hell out of you to get to the cashier. I can't take that crap."

Stevens took a long sip from his coffee cup and let the java warm his insides. "John, headquarters just sent us a memo this morning. It says that Santino has sold The Director Magazine to Sentinel Press over in Kalamazoo. It also says that he will act as some kind of advertising vice-president for the company."

Ford sat down at his desk and looked at the memo. After reading the contents he threw the memo on his desk. Stevens waited, but there was no response from his partner.

"Okay, John. What are you thinking? What's stirring inside that coconut of yours?"

"Just thinking Frank," he answered, "In less than a year after buying the business from the estate of his deceased partner, Santino turns around and sells part of it to a competitor. It doesn't sound like a guy who killed six people to get the goose that lays golden eggs, does it?"

"You made your point John."

"Think about it Frank. If Santino killed Rawlings, what was his motive? Mainly, from what we've heard, it was that he would take over the business. But from what we've been able to uncover, this business was running in the red. It wasn't making money hand over fist, or had a ton of assets that could be sold. There wasn't even expectations of acquiring new business. In fact, Rawlings was about to loose one of his most important accounts, the Diamond Faucet account. Santino must have known that."

"That's two good points," Stevens said with a large grin on his face. "You're on a roll, keep going."

Ford's reasoning made a lot of sense. At that moment, whatever the issue was that resulted in Richard Rawlings and his family being murdered, he did not believe that Joseph Santino pulled the trigger.

"Are you telling me that you believe that Santino was an innocent bystander in all of this John?" Frank asked.

"No, not exactly. But right now, I think Joe Santino knows why Rawlings and his family were taken out, but he's afraid to tell us or anyone else. That's why he's lying every chance he gets. He's hoping he can lie his way out of the mess he's in. I believe he's more scared than he's letting on."

"I don't know John. You think there was some kind of deal that went bad and Rawlings was expendable, along with the family?" Stevens asked.

"I'm not sure. Whatever the deal was, if Rawling's tried something cute to screw somebody, they may have made him pay along with his family. And they may have done it just to show Joe and anyone else, they were not to be messed with. That's why I don't think Santino is ever going to tell us anything because he's probably afraid for himself and his family."

"You thinking Mafia, John?"

"Possible."

"Possible or probable?"

"Possible."

"Why possible and not probable?"

"Possible because Rawlings could've met someone from the Mafia with his contacts in Detroit and entered into some kind of business arrangement, without knowing this person was 'connected.' And not probable because..." Stevens couldn't complete his thought before Ford answered for him.

"...Because Rawlings had enough contacts to keep himself away from those people. And if it were the Mafia, I don't think the plan to take him out would have called for them to drive four or five hours up north and whack an entire family."

"How about Canada?"

"No, I don't think so. Why risk trying to cross the border? Anything could happen there. Besides, if the Mafia wanted him taken out, why not wait until Rawlings came back to Detroit. It's their home turf and they know all the hiding places. Up north, they don't know diddley squat and their people would take a big risk of being noticed as outsiders."

"The polygraphs John, what about the tests? Santino's failed every one." Frank reminded him.

"That's the puzzle that keeps bouncing around in my mind. The best reason that I can think of, is that we're getting those negative reactions because Santino is hiding something illegal that he knows about. I don't think we're getting the negative readings because he did the killings. He's covering for somebody. I think he knows who the people are. Or, it could be something he and Rawlings had been planning to do to someone else and they acted first."

"You think that's why the poly people are getting negative results from Santino?".

"Yes. He lies because he has to. I think he knows how to play the machine, Frank. At least that's my opinion."

Stevens was pondering over Ford's conclusions when the phone rang.

Ford answered. It was Herb Jackson.

"Sure Herb, we'll meet you there," Ford said. "See you in a little while, bye."

Ford turned to Stevens. "Herb Jackson wants us to meet him at his father-in-laws place over at Elizabeth Lake. It's where he and Santino took target practice a couple of years ago with the .22 rifles he sold to him."

The detectives grabbed their overcoats, and headed for the lake property.

When they arrived, Al Ball, Jackson's father-in-law gave them permission to search the grounds to see if they could locate any spent cartridges that may have been left after Santino and Jackson had taken target practice. The detectives, along with Jackson located 21 cartridges with a metal detector.

Stevens identified them with his initials inside the shell casings. They would be sent to the lab in East Lansing for testing. As an after thought, Herb Jackson mentioned that Joe Santino had been spending large sums of money about three months before the murders.

December 29, 1969
11:00 a.m.
State Police Post-Detroit

Stevens and Ford received an inter-office memo from the East Lansing Post inviting them to meet with the Director on January 5th, 1970. The largest contingent of law enforcement officials since the murders happened would be there. It would be a meeting to up-date everyone on the status of the Rawlings' murder case.

12:00 Noon
3181 Delaware Ave.
Livonia, Michigan

A tip coming in through the 'secret witness' program prompted an appointment made with Corine Nelson, a former secretary to Mr. Rawlings who had recently been located living in the suburb of Livonia, near Detroit. Her maiden name at the time of her employment was Linn. Her husband Christopher was a sergeant in the Air Force.

The detectives arrived at the Nelson residence. The small, gray colored bungalow was located on a winding side street in a middle-class neighborhood. Mrs. Nelson told the detectives that she had worked for Rawlings from September 1966 to September 1967. She quit because she was getting married.

"What was your relationship with Mr. Rawlings, Mrs. Nelson?" Stevens asked.

"On the whole it was all right. However, one day, during the summer of 67' Mr. Rawlings called the office and asked me to come over to his house to pick up some materials he had for the next issue of the magazine. He told me to come to the back door and walk in. When I got there I went to the back door, but I knocked on the door instead of going right in as he asked me to do. Mr. Rawlings called for me to enter. When I did, I found him in his under shorts and a smoking jacket. He started to make advances toward me. He asked me to sit next to him on the couch. I refused. He started following me around the house trying to talk me into some sort of sexual activities with him. I told him to stop because I was getting married within a short time and didn't appreciate his conduct. I made up my mind that I was going to quit working for him after I got married. I walked out of the house. For the rest of the time I was employed there, he never made any advances or bothered me again."

"Did he ever mention a 'big business deal' when he was around you, Mrs. Nelson?" Ford asked.

"No. I was hired to do proofreading of materials submitted for the magazine and never was around any talk of business deals."

Satisfied that Corine Nelson had confirmed another episode of attempted sexual misconduct by Richard Rawlings, the detectives thanked her for the information and left.

Stevens pulled the cruiser into the Post parking lot as Ford spoke. "It's a wonder this pervert Rawlings didn't get shot a lot sooner."

"Real nice guy," Stevens mumbled sarcastically.

"Nice my ass. He was a real screwball, in my opinion," Ford responded.

The workday slowly came to a close, just like the end of the year. When Stevens and Ford left the Post that evening, they would be off duty until January 3rd.

The fireworks on New Years Eve showered over the City of Detroit. The brilliant colors lit up the Ambassador Bridge and were reflected in the dark, placid waters of the Detroit River that runs beneath it. The biting, cold air pushed its way through the empty streets, seeking out every corner and crevice. It blew old, dirty newspapers and debris through its asphalt corridors, piling them up in the corners of decaying and empty buildings. Downtown Detroit was in decline.

Stevens and Ford would find out that starting the new decade of the 70's would try most of their patience and that clues would be harder to find than a real white elephant. The New Year, would be less than cooperative, it would be cruel.

January 5, 1970
10:00 a.m.
State Police Headquarters-East Lansing

Colonel Darrens opened the meeting by introducing each one of the eighteen law enforcement individuals seated around the conference table in the large meeting room. When he had concluded his introductions, he made a short statement indicating his concern of the current status of the Rawlings case. Everyone who sat at the table, especially Stevens and Ford realized that the passage of time is always detrimental in solving a murder case.

It was hopeful that this meeting would get the investigation back on track and with a little luck, solved.

Each law enforcement person present was to give their assessment of the case, based on information they had substantiated and passed on to the MSP offices. This group session was designed to determine the standard questions of who, what, when and why they thought the crime occurred.

It became immediately evident that many of those sitting around the table wondered why there had been a lack of specific information forthcoming from the Sands County Sheriff Department. The Sheriff himself was noticeably absent from this meeting.

No one, including Stevens and Ford offered up the name of Joe Santino as the possible prime suspect in the case. The detectives wanted to keep that under the radar until they were confident that whatever evidence they could obtain would hold up in court. They were not going to throw that information out for general consumption.

A few of the detectives felt that the concentration of effort should be with the Petoskey Post where the murders were committed and not in Detroit. There was a lot of give and take in the meeting and some very strong opinions put forth in an attempt to look at the case from numerous perspectives.

In the end, everyone agreed that Stevens and Ford should carry the ball in trying to bring this case to a successful conclusion.

Shortly before noon, as the meeting was winding down, the assistant prosecutor from Oakland County, Mr. Ronald Chapman entered the conference room. He had been delayed in a court hearing in Lansing and apologized for his being absent at the start of the meeting.

Colonel Darrens took a few moments to brief him on the variety of ideas suggested by the people there and politely asked him if he had any information that he thought might be useful in attempting to move the Rawlings case along.

Chapman explained that the Oakland County Prosecutor's office had been cooperating and working in tandem with a number of law enforcement agencies. However, their office had initiated their own private investigation because they had access to certain confidential informants who had some knowledge about the Rawlings murders. Without batting an eye, Mr. Chapman then proceeded to tell everyone present, "In my opinion, we have sufficient reason to issue a warrant for the arrest of Joseph Santino, Mr. Rawlings' business partner for the Rawlings' murders."

Stevens and Ford, along with Colonel Darrens were stunned by the assistant prosecutor's remarks. The look on everyone sitting at the table was one of shock.

The Colonel immediately questioned in his own mind how Chapman's office had obtained the information and who his informants were.

Stevens and Ford, giving a quick glance at the Colonel knew that they had never shared that information with the prosecutor's office because they didn't believe that they had enough evidence at this point to arrest Santino on an embezzlement charge, let alone for murder. They could assume it was Santino all they wanted to, but in a court of law you had to have certain, concrete facts in order to make the charge stick. They began to wonder what else the prosecutor's office knew and why Mr. Chapman decided to reveal it today at this meeting.

Chapman continued, but with a caveat. "However, there are additional meetings scheduled this week to determine, when and how we will deal with Mr. Santino. There's an important discussion scheduled later today with my boss, Prosecutor Brooks Page before anything can be initiated. We need to verify certain allegations by one of our informants, first."

Everyone around the table sat quietly and deferred to the Colonel, whose eyes were directed at Chapman. Those eyes conveyed a different story to those who knew the Colonel. You didn't come into the Colonel's den, drop a bombshell without first having the courtesy to prepare him for it. There would be hell to pay and someone would find out the hard way.

It was obvious that the meeting was finished when Colonel Darrens slapped his hand on the table and certified its end.

As each person rose, they gathered their briefcases or other materials and moved slowly towards the doorway, occasionally stopping to shake hands with an old friend, to say goodbye or to ask directions to the bathroom.

Colonel Darrens stood in one of the doorways, grabbing hands and back patting some of his fellow comrades as they left. When Stevens and Ford approached, he asked them to follow him. They walked through a doorway into the Colonel's private sanctuary behind his normal office. He closed the door behind them.

"Gentlemen." he said as he lit his pipe. "We've been screwed! I suspected all along that son-of-a-bitch Page and his people were conducting their own investigation. I'll call him later and have a nice little chat with him about having his assistant come up here and cutting us off at the knees. This is more political bullshit than police work and that's not going to make the Governor very happy. What do you two think about this announcement?"

The detectives glanced at one another, then Stevens spoke. "I'm not sure what it means Colonel. Obviously, they're going to charge Santino, but on what grounds? Ford and I don't think there's enough evidence out there to do it or we would have told you so. If they have an eyewitness, then more power to them. If they do, why didn't they tell us? I don't think they do. Their people couldn't have been anymore resourceful than we were. I guess we'll have to wait and see."

Darrens waited for a moment, then knocking some ashes from his pipe into a tray; he folded his arms, turned and looked out the window. "You know men, Mr. Page might have done us a favor with this announcement. Let him try and make hay with Santino. Page has let his little ass-kissing gopher, Chapman carry the ball even though he hedged his bet there at the end. All hell might break loose over this, but we'll just sit tight. Right now, I need to talk to you about another problem we have with the case."

Stevens and Ford grabbed a quick glance at each another. They waited patiently for the Colonel to tell them what it was.

They all walked into the main office as the Colonel moved around his desk and dropped into his chair. "I want you to take a look at these two letters I just received this morning," pulling them out of a side drawer of the desk. He gave one to Stevens and one to Ford. As they each read the letters, it felt as if someone had kicked them in the groin.

That morning, Colonel Darrens had received by registered mail, an envelope from the new prosecutor in Sands County, Donald Nevels. The envelope contained two confidential letters, one written by Nevels, the other from John Chilson, a reporter from the Petoskey News Review. Chilson was a colleague of Fred Lowrey, who had been the reporter at the Rawlings crime scene. Chilson had done considerable follow-up work on his own in trying to determine a prime suspect in the case.

After exchanging and reading both letters the detectives gave them back to the Colonel.

Stevens spoke up. "Colonel, these letters are basically accusing, Monty Barr of the murders!"

"Yes they do. You can see what kind of predicament we could be in if this reporter knows something that we don't. We now have Nevels probably trying to make his own political hay, and this reporter from Petoskey coming up with information that says that Monty Barr is our killer. I spoke to Schafer and Rodgers in Petoskey after I got the letters this morning and told them to expect you two by tomorrow. I want both of you to work with them and get this damn thing straightened out immediately! I want a clear and concise report on this as soon as you put all the facts together."

"Yes sir, Colonel," Stevens said quickly.

" I told my secretary to compile a list of things I want both of you to concentrate on. I especially want clarification on these alleged comments made by Barr to a couple of our troopers about,"How much time will I get for this?" The letter suggests that Barr mentioned something about a certain piece of evidence that he couldn't have known about unless he'd been inside that cabin before the bodies were discovered. I definitely want an answer to that question. As you leave, pick up the list and be in Petoskey tomorrow. I want both of you there no later than noon or you can count on being assigned to the Copper Harbor Post. Is that clear?"

Stevens and Ford acknowledged the Colonel's directive. The thought of being stationed at Copper Harbor ran chills up and down their spines. Copper Harbor was Michigan's most northern city, located in the Upper Peninsula, toward the western end of Lake Superior. Some people say it snows twelve months a year up there and nothing ever thaws out there. Ever.

January 06, 1970
State Police Post
12:00 Noon
Petoskey, Michigan

The five-hour trip from Detroit to the State Police Post in Petoskey was much easier than either Stevens or Ford had expected when they left the Motor City early that morning. The bright sunshine and clear blue sky lifted their otherwise depressed moods. Virgin white blankets of snow covered the rolling hills and valleys that surrounded this northern city by the bay. The air was cold and crisp as they pulled into the Post parking lot and entered the building.

They were greeted by a couple of State troopers who where taking down the last remnants of a small Christmas tree and decorations. One of the troopers directed the pair of detectives to where they could find Schafer and Rodgers. The smell of fresh brewed coffee permeated the air as they stepped through the doorway into the office.

Schafer and Rodgers were reading sections of the local newspaper when Rodgers first heard the footsteps on the hardwood floor. He slowly lowered the paper and stared at Stevens and Ford, who were standing side by side in front of him.

"Well, I'll be damned," Rodgers said, lifting his large frame from the chair and reaching out to shake hands.

The sound of Bill's voice made Schafer look around the sport section of the paper to see what the commotion was about. "We'll I see that you two finally made it," He said, offering his hand. "Bill and I made a bet this morning that you two wouldn't make it up here until late afternoon. You sure made good time. You didn't break the speed limit, did you?"

"You're damn straight," Ford said, taking off his overcoat and hanging it up as Stevens did the same.

Stevens and Ford pulled up a couple of chairs and sat down at the table.

Rodgers poured hot coffee into four Styrofoam cups and handed one to each detective.

"There're some donuts over next to the coffee pot. Help yourself. Ray and I are trying to cut back," Rodgers said, sipping slowly on the coffee.

Ford reached over and grabbed a couple of donuts while nodding to Stevens to see if he wanted one. Stevens refused. He was eager to find out about the recent developments that had made the Colonel send them there. "The Colonel threatened us with Copper Harbor if we didn't get things straightened out up here with this new prosecutor and that reporter. We're supposed to work with you guys and report back to him as soon as we've finished."

Schafer explained the situation. "We knew the minute the Colonel called us that he was a little upset about how all this was being handled up here. We're not too happy about it ourselves, but unfortunately, the Prosecutor's office and the Sheriff's Department have jurisdiction and responsibility over this case. The Colonel knows that. I think that he just doesn't want the department to get caught with their pants down and I don't blame him for that. The best we can do is to give you all the information we have."

"And that's the truth," Rodgers added.

"We know that it must be tough on you guys. We've been running through a maze of evidence downstate and every time we think we're close, someone or something pulls the rug out from under us," Ford said.

Schafer and Rodgers walked over to the far corner of the office where file boxes of information and evidence were stacked neatly on a long table against the wall.

"They're numbered from one to fifteen," Schafer said as he pointed to the boxes.

Rodgers pulled some colored photographs from one of the envelopes and handed them to Ford. He took a long drink of his coffee and watched the look on Ford's face.

Ford shuffled the murder scene pictures in his hands. He'd seen them earlier in the investigation in black and white, but still couldn't get over the brutality shown in them. In color, they were more revealing. The photographs gave an apt description of how the bodies had been hid and stacked in the hallway of the cottage. One of them showed a female body, lying face down on the floor, the bottom half of her body uncovered, with her tattered underclothing wrapped around her ankles.

Schafer looked at Ford. "John, in my opinion, whoever killed them was not just content to kill Rawlings and his family. They wanted to humiliate them even in death. Those pictures tell me that the person who did this must have hated that family with a vengeance. Even professional killers don't humiliate their victims like this."

Ford handed the pictures to Stevens as he picked up a folder that held copies of reports about inmates from the prison farm at Pellston. The report stated that all inmates had been accounted for during the time period that the murders had taken place.

"Nothing here," Ford said, placing the folder back into one of the boxes.

Stevens thought it would be best to set an agenda and spoke. "Tomorrow morning we'll meet with Troopers Hyde and Larkin and see what they have to say about their interview with Mr. Barr. Tell them, we'll be here at seven sharp."

Stevens and Ford got their coats, said goodbye and left.

January 07, 1970
7:00 a.m.
State Police Post-Petoskey

The winter wind whipped its way inland off Little Traverse Bay, making the temperature plummet to a minus 20 degrees. Stevens and Ford tried to turn their heads away from the biting wind as they listened to the snow crunch under their feet.

"Jesus, it's cold, " Stevens said as the vapor from his breath left a pale cloud in front of his face.

"It just seems like it's colder. It's because the climate is drier, up here Frank."

"Drier, hell. It's just plain freezing. I need some hot coffee just to thaw out. I can't feel my fingers, for Christ sake."

As they entered the police Post, a couple of young looking State Troopers stood near the entrance desk. They were discussing a local high school basketball game that had been played the night before. The troopers greeted Ford and Stevens and introduced themselves. They were Troopers Hyde and Larkin.

Stevens motioned for the two men to follow him and Ford to one of the empty conference rooms.

All four men grabbed a coffee mug and filled it. Three of them sat down, except Stevens who was fumbling through a box of day old donuts trying to find the freshest one.

"Damn, I knew we should've stopped at the donut shop on the way over, John. I hate coffee first thing in the morning without something to go with it."

"I'll start with you Trooper Larkin," Ford said as he stirred some sugar into his cup.

"This report filed in October of '68, says that you and Trooper Hyde interviewed Monty Barr. During that interview, Barr apparently makes a remark to the effect: 'How much time do you think I'll get?' or 'What will I get for this?' Do you remember him saying something like that?"

Trooper Larkin looked straight at Ford and answered. "Yes Sir. I do."

"Do you recall anything else?" Ford asks.

"As I recall," Larkin continued. "Trooper Hyde and I went out to the Watkins cottage that was under construction by Monty Barr and his helper Steven Lightfoot. We'd received a confidential tip that Lightfoot had made a remark at one of the local pubs that the hammer that had been removed from the Rawlings' cottage belonged to Barr. We were just following up on that information."

Ford turned to Trooper Hyde. "Trooper Hyde, what do you remember about this situation?"

"As best as I can recall, sir, Trooper Larkin and I were given the responsibility to follow up on some of the tips coming into the post regarding the Barr family and the Rawlings' murders. The hammer was one of the things we were directed to clear up." Hyde paused for a few seconds.

"Go on," Ford said.

"When we got there, Monty Barr was working on the cottage with Lightfoot. I asked Mr. Barr to come over to the patrol car and take a seat in the back, which he did. Specifically, I wanted to speak with him about the rumors that had been circulating about his alleged bad relationship with Mr. Rawlings."

"Did he say anything at that time?" Ford asked, as Stevens pulled up a chair and sat close to the two troopers. He listened intently, holding his coffee cup in one hand and a day old donut in the other.

"No. I opened the back door of the patrol car and Barr got in and closed the door."

"Was there anything unusual in his demeanor?" Stevens interjected.

"No sir, nothing unusual. He did seem a little depressed. I gathered that it was mostly because of the loss of his son a few months before and he did complain that he was very frustrated by the people he was building cottages for. They wanted them done right away and didn't understand or care about his craftsmanship. I guess he wanted to do things at his own pace and it made for some confrontational meetings."

"But you were there to check up on the hammer, right?" Ford said.

"Yes sir, that's true. Trooper Larkin and I were reviewing a list of questions that we were going to ask Mr. Barr when Barr, sitting in the back seat of our cruiser just blurted out 'What will I get for this?' or something very close to that."

"Did you say anything to Barr at that point, Trooper Hyde?" Stevens asked.

"To be honest sir, I was reading some information off one of the tip sheets and didn't hear what Barr said. Trooper Larkin made a note about it on his notepad."

Stevens turned to Larkin. "Trooper Larkin, when you wrote this remark down that Barr made in your presence, did you ever think to ask him what he meant by that?"

"Yes sir. I started to ask him about that, but Barr started mumbling something about a note and a wastebasket. I decided to ask him what he was talking about to see if he had been inside the cabin before the Sheriff's department arrived on the scene."

"What did he say, Trooper Larkin?" Ford asked.

"Barr began to mumble, incoherently. I asked him three or four times, but received no definitive answer."

"I'm afraid that some of that is my fault, sir," Hyde said. "I was intent on asking the questions that I had on my list, and I cut Trooper Larkin off, and asked Barr if the hammer at the crime scene belonged to him. He said it didn't."

"So neither one of you pursued the questioning of Barr regarding his mentioning of the note or the wastebasket. Is that correct?" Ford asked.

"That's correct sir," Hyde replied. "It was only when we got back to the Post and we were typing up our notes that we both realized that we had failed to follow-up on the 'what will I get for this?' statement by Barr."

Stevens and Ford glanced at one another.

Stevens spoke up with a tone that was stern, but not harsh. "Gentlemen, your both fine young troopers and have excellent performance records. I'm sure that your intentions were sincere. I'm positive that you felt you were doing your duty in the best interest of the department. However, I hope you both realize that your eagerness to follow a pre-planned course of action, instead of letting the interview follow a natural course, may have cost you the opportunity to obtain valuable information from Mr. Barr. It certainly sounds to me, that at that moment, Barr may have been willing to divulge information that may have been crucial to this case."

Hyde and Larkin were visibly embarrassed over their serious error and it showed. Stevens had made his point.

Hyde was the first to speak up. "I realize now sir how serious a mistake that was. I'm truly sorry about that."

Larkin did his mea culpa with the detectives and sat quietly, hands folded in his lap.

Stevens and Ford hoped that they could piece it back together, but they knew it was a long shot.

"It says in your report that he denied losing any of his tools, especially the hammer. Did you ask to look at his hammer?"

"Yes sir, we did," Larkin replied. "It looked like a hammer that had been used for some time. Of course, there really wasn't anyway for us to know for sure if this was the actual hammer he had in his possession at the time of the murders."

"Yes that's true, but for now we have to go with what we've got. Detective Ford and I will speak with Monty Barr and see what he has to say about those remarks."

"I believe we're finished here, at least to this point," Ford said as he rose from his chair. "We will get back with you later if we need more information."

The two troopers left the conference room.

"You know Frank, even with our experience and training, we might have made the same mistakes. This is a very valuable lesson for them, without really anyone getting hurt."

Stevens looked at his partner for a brief moment. He then turned and looked out the window towards the frozen, white covered bay. "Your right John. Nobody was hurt. I hope that they have learned a valuable lesson from this. The fact still remains that old Monty Barr may know something more than he has been willing to tell us. All of the Barr family members are down in Florida and won't be back until April. I'm sure the department is not going to send us down to Florida to interview him and I sure as hell don't want to do it over the phone. I think it's best to wait until he gets back. I don't want to alert him that we need information in order to clear up some of his statements. We'll wait until April. For now, I think we should make arrangements to visit Steve Lightfoot over in Thunder Point. Let's see what he has to say about this hammer business."

Schafer and Rodgers entered the room to retrieve some files.

Rodgers spoke first. " Gee, what the hell did you two do to Hyde and Larkin? I was thinking about asking the Post commander to take their pistols from them.

Man they look down."

"Damn right. They should too," Stevens responded. He proceeded to tell them what had transpired.

"Well, Frank, you know that's how it goes sometimes. You think everything should be in its right place and then you find out something or someone has screwed it up. They'll learn Frank," Schafer added.

Stevens just shook his head and walked toward the door.

"We need to move on," Ford said. "We're going to go over to Lightfoot's place and talk with him. We want to see what he has to say about the hammer."

It was almost noon as the detectives drove along the snow-covered road to Thunder Point and to the home of Steven Lightfoot.

The Lightfoot residence was a single story, log cabin style bungalow that sat adjacent to the red general store. Steven Lightfoot opened the door as the two officers approached. He held the door as they entered the house. The cold wind swirled outside and the open fireplace heat was a welcome condition for the two detectives.

Lightfoot asked them if they would like to remove their coats, but the detectives decided to keep them on.

The home was neat and tidy with little ceramic teacups placed in cubicles, each cubicle representing some past historical period related to Indian folklore.

Lightfoot was wearing his red and black plaid hunting shirt and blue jeans. He led the way quietly toward the dining room. His wool lined moccasins hardly making a sound on the hardwood floor.

The men sat at the large dining room table while occasionally, the popping of the logs in the fireplace pushed the flames and sparks upward through the chimney opening. The radiant heat spread out from the fireplace and warmed the inside of the cottage evenly.

Lightfoot offered them coffee, but they declined.

"Mr. Lightfoot," Ford began, "Detective Stevens and I wanted to see you about a report that states that on one occasion while you were at the Seagull Tavern in Sturgeon Bay, someone overheard you telling another person that it was Monty Barr's hammer removed from the Rawlings cottage. Do you remember saying that to anyone at the bar?"

The Indian's dark eyes looked directly at Ford. "No. I never said anything like that to anyone."

"Are you telling us that whoever told that to the authorities here, lied?"

"Yes, I'm telling you that."

"Why do you think that someone would make up a thing like that against you, Mr. Lightfoot?" Ford continued.

"I don't know. Some people don't like me or the Barr family."

"And why is that?"

"I don't know. Maybe it's because I'm Indian. Maybe it's because the Barr family owns a lot of land around here, or maybe it's because they started building these cottages, I really don't know and I don't care."

"Are you still working for the Barr family and building cottages?

"Yes. When spring gets here, Mr. Barr and I will begin to build more cottages."

"Mr. Lightfoot, how well did you know the Rawlings family? Did you ever speak with Mr. or Mrs. Rawlings or the children?"

"I only talked with the mister a couple of times."

"Did you like the Rawlings family?".

The big Indian shrugged his shoulders as if to say he didn't know or care about them.

"Is that a yes or a no?"

"The woman was nice, but the others were not good people. The mister was always giving orders to everyone. He acted like a big shot all the time. I didn't like him, but I didn't shoot him."

"We didn't say that you did, Mr. Lightfoot," Stevens said probing deeper.

"Do you think Mr. Barr could shoot Mr. Rawlings?" Ford asked quickly.

The Indian thought for a long time then finally shook his head no.

"You're sure about that?" Ford responded.

"Yes." Lightfoot replied. His voice was not convincing.

"Was that Barr's hammer that was removed from the cottage after the murders, Mr. Lightfoot?"

"I don't know," he said as his eyes looked away towards the little cubicles.

"You don't know or you just don't want to tell us?" Ford pushed.

Lightfoot gave Ford a look of contempt.

"Did you ever see any of the bodies inside the cabin after they had been shot?" Stevens asked.

"I saw the naked, lower half of Mrs. Rawlings sticking out from underneath a rug for just a second, before Mr. Barr closed the door to the cottage. Then he went and called the Sheriff."

"Can you recall anything else?"

"No. That's all I can remember."

The detectives thanked Lightfoot and walked outside to the cold patrol car.

Steve Lightfoot stood in the narrow doorway and waved goodbye as Stevens pulled the cruiser back onto the highway.

The snow was falling harder, making visibility difficult as Stevens guided the car along the icy road. Large, gray clouds hung low over the snow-covered landscape and rolling hills. There was an iridescent hue that lingered in the sky and nightfall was coming fast.

Stevens maneuvered the cruiser over the winding, snakelike road the best he could, but his body felt tired and his eyes began to burn. At the first enlarged berm he pulled the cruiser off to the side of the road.

The snow cover was light and fluffy, but the road was coated with a thin sheet of ice. It made the driving difficult and dangerous.

"Damn cold weather," he said as he put the gearshift into park. "John do you mind taking the wheel, I'm not feeling so good. Must be some type of indigestion."

"Probably those damn stale donuts," Ford replied as he traded places with Stevens. His partner moved quickly outside and around to the passenger side.

The absence of the normal conversation between the two men after an interview made the drive even longer as Ford mentally reminded himself how dangerous the road conditions were. He realized that one mistake and both of them would plunge over the steep slope at the edge of the road and drop a hundred and fifty feet below to the narrow beach and the cold Lake Michigan waters.

Stevens sat quietly, staring at the frozen plateau of the lake and gray horizon in the distance. The barren trees with their spindle like branches stripped by the cold wind moved slowly past the car's side window. He could only think of home and a warm bed.

The normal half-hour to forty-five minute drive had taken two hours for Ford to conquer and reach the Post. Ford completed the necessary reports regarding their meeting with Lightfoot before he and Stevens called it a day.

They decided to stop at a local restaurant that served hot soup and a good roast beef sandwich before returning to their motel. It was a good meal and satisfied their appetites.

The streets were deserted by the time they left the restaurant and the snow was piling up at a steady pace. What they needed was a good nights' sleep before leaving in the morning for Detroit.

Stevens rested comfortably between the sheets and the heavy wool blanket.

His mind recalled the statements made by Mr. and Mrs. William Foresman, who owned the cottage on the bluff above the Rawlings place. Their statement to the investigators echoed again and again in his brain as he drifted off to sleep.

Mr. and Mrs. Foresman repeatedly confirmed the same facts each time they had been interviewed:

"It was June 25ᵗʰ, 1968, shortly before nightfall, when they heard gunshots coming from the south of their cottage toward the location of the Rawlings' place. First, they heard one shot, then a pause, then a burst of shots, four or five fired in rapid succession. Then another slight pause, when Mrs. Foresman heard voices. She was positive that she could distinguish a female voice and two male voices in a high state of anxiety. Then three or four more shots. At the time, they thought someone was just shooting gulls on the beach."

Ford was already asleep as Stevens fell into full slumber.

January 08, 1970
9:00 a.m.
State Police Post-Petoskey

Before Ford and Stevens stopped by the Post to say goodbye to their counterparts, they contacted the Prosecutor and the Petoskey News reporter, and had established that neither of them wanted to disclose information they felt was confidential to their own investigations. The detectives would have to report these facts to the Colonel.

As Stevens and Ford were leaving the Post, Schafer gave them a copy of the June 1968 official weather report from the Pellston airport weather station.

Ford pulled the cruiser onto the main highway and headed for Detroit while Stevens took the weather report out of the manila envelope and began to read its contents. The report was the official document kept on file by the airport weather staff that covered the twenty-four hour period of June 25, 1968. The report stated that:

At 6 p.m. the temperature was 60 degrees, with winds northeast at 8 knots, light rainfall. By 9 p.m., the only thing that had changed was the temperature. It had fallen to 58 degrees. The official sunset was listed at 8:32 p.m.

The drive back to Detroit was long and tedious. The blustering winds and light snow made the roads slick and it was a full time job to keep the cruiser on the road. They would stop from time to time in order to clean off the windshield wipers as the wet snow clung to the rubber strips and froze. When the opportunity arose, they would stop at different State Police Posts along the way to top off their gas tank, refill their thermos with hot coffee, and check the weather conditions ahead.

When they finally arrived back at the Post in Detroit, they were told them they had traveled in one of the worst snowstorms the State had experienced in fifty years. Ford and Stevens looked at one another and shrugged their shoulders. They were back safe and sound.

January 12, 1970
12:00 Noon
State Police Post-Detroit

Nineteen months had passed since the Rawlings family had been found massacred in their summer cottage and the cold biting winds of January matched the cold trail of evidence that had stalled the investigation. The clues were as barren as the trees that stood outside the office windows. Stevens and Ford were fighting a lingering flu bug when a uniformed corporal entered the office and handed Stevens a letter addressed to the detectives.

Stevens opened the letter and read the message from a woman who used to baby-sit for the Rawlings' family. The message told detectives of a small TV and a set of walkie-talkies that Mr. Rawlings had purchased for the children that had been kept at the cottage. According to the woman, she did not see that listed in any of the news stories after the murders and wondered if the detectives knew about them.

Ford looked at the inventory list and could not find any of the articles mentioned in the letter.   Stevens decided to call Mr. Rawlings' sister, Elaine Finney to see if she might know anything about the articles described in the letter.

The phone rang a couple of times before Elaine Finney answered. "Hello. Finney residence."

"Mrs. Finney, this is Detective Stevens. Sorry to bother you, but we've received a message this morning from a lady who used to baby-sit for your brother's children. She claims that your brother kept a small TV set and a pair of walkie-talkies for the children at the cottage. Is that right?"

"Yes, that's right Detective Stevens," She answered. "Those items have been divided up among the family. I hope there's nothing wrong with that."

"No. It's just that they were not listed on our inventory sheet as items that were at the cottage. When we got this message, I decided to call you. I just wanted to make sure that they we weren't missing something because our people may have overlooked it."

"No. They're safe and sound. They weren't at the cottage, they were here at Richard's house in Towne Village."

"Fine. I'll just mark that down on our sheet so if it should come up again we have a record of it. Thank you." Stevens paused for a moment before hanging up the receiver. He had noticed a distinct tone of melancholy in Mrs. Finney's voice while she was speaking with him about the articles. Stevens then asked, "How have you been doing Mrs. Finney?"

Her response was slow in coming. "Oh there are good days and then bad ones. It's all been so dreadful. I can't seem to put it out of my mind since it happened. It was such a horrible thing. I can't believe that Richard and Shirley are gone. Everyday I think about the children. It's so unreal."

"I'm sorry, Mrs. Finney. I really didn't mean to stir up memories about what happened at the cottage. After all, you have your own family and I would certainly think that they would need you at this time too."

"Your absolutely right. It's just that I keep thinking about who could have done such a terrible thing. I don't know how to explain any of it, especially to my children."

"I realize it must be very hard for you, but you must move on for yourself and your family," Stevens replied.

"I know, I know. It's just that I've thought about it ever since it happened and I've tried to think of any little thing that might be important to help find this terrible person."

"Have you thought of anything else?" Stevens asked.

"No. That's what's been so frustrating for me. In fact, when you called I thought you might have something to tell me."

There was another long pause and then she just kind of said it naturally, the words rolling off her lips without hesitation. "You know Detective Stevens, Richard didn't know that he was an adopted child."

For a moment, Stevens didn't think he heard her correctly. "I'm sorry, Mrs. Finney, what did you say?"

"I said that Richard was an adopted child. My mother and father never met the mother. Apparently, she was a young girl, around sixteen years old at the time she gave birth to Richard. It was all handled through an adoption agency. She left town and her whereabouts were never known. No one knew who the father was."

"Your brother was an adopted child? Are you sure he didn't know that?" Stevens asked curiously.

"Yes, he was adopted. And no, he never knew, I'm quite sure of that. I would've known if he had. I probably shouldn't have mentioned it, but it's the only thing out of the ordinary that comes to mind." Elaine Finney was feeling a little embarrassed that she had revealed something that had been a family secret for a long time.

Stevens made a notation on his legal pad before continuing the conversation. "Do you think Richard could have found out, but never said anything to you or your parents?"

"No, I don't think so. Mother would have said something to me if he had. Please, Detective Stevens don't tell anyone that I mentioned this. My mother and father would be terribly upset," Mrs. Finney pleaded.

"Don't worry Mrs. Finney, it will remain confidential."

"Thank you, thank you very much Detective Stevens."

"Thank you Mrs. Finney. Detective Ford and I will stay in touch. Goodbye."

Stevens placed the receiver gently back in its cradle and looked squarely at Ford. "You know John, this is one of the weirdest cases that I've ever worked. I hope we find the person who did this, or I'll never have a peaceful nights sleep."

"What are you talking about?" Ford asked, as he looked up from reviewing some autopsy reports. He hadn't been paying close attention to his partner's conversation with Mrs. Finney.

"Mrs. Finney just told me that Richard Rawlings was an adopted child. She just let it slip out. Can you believe that?"

"Adopted? The guy was adopted? Did she tell you who the parents were?"

"No. She doesn't know and I didn't want to push it. She's still having a rough time with all of it. We can do some checking and find out."

Ford quickly checked a reference card. "Let's see, Rawlings was born on November 30, 1925 according to my card."

"Okay," Stevens interrupted. "What Mrs. Finney said was that the mother was sixteen at the time. If the father had been sixteen or seventeen, he would be fifty-eight or fifty-nine now. We need to look at some birth certificates."

"Yes, even if the father was twenty, it would only make him sixty-two or three. Could still be living Frank. Are you thinking what I'm thinking?"

"It could be that Rawlings found out who his father was and maybe tried to put the squeeze on him. Maybe the father was well to do or holds a high level position somewhere. Doesn't want to be exposed or blackmailed."

"That's exactly what crossed my mind Frank. Just knowing the way Rawlings operated, I don't think he was beyond trying something like that."

"I wouldn't think that a father would kill his own son," Stevens said. "But from what we know about Rawlings' character, it certainly could be possible."

"After all, this is the same guy who ran out on the girl he got pregnant," Ford responded.

"Yeah, that's true. But I can't imagine a father being pushed that far."

"He sure as hell didn't take responsibility for what he did to the girl. And, what if he's now in a position that he can't reveal he made a mistake when he was younger? I'm just saying it could be, that's all."

"We need to check out the birth records over at the County office tomorrow and see what we can find out," Stevens responded.

January 13, 1970
9:00 a.m.
County Clerks Office
Wayne County, Michigan

Stevens and Ford sifted through the files and documents until they came across what they had been looking for. The adoption papers for Richard C. Rawlings showed that Ruth O. Hazleton had been the mother. There was no name listed for the father. It said "Unknown." The adoption had occurred on May 5, 1926 and had been handled by a religious group for unwed mothers in Detroit.

Stevens searched the files for more documentation to see if he could find out where Miss Hazleton may have moved, but was unsuccessful. He did note the last know address as 3503 Sheridan Ave., Detroit.

They hit another dead-end when the records showed that Miss Hazelton's mother; Mary had recently sold the house and left no forwarding address. The detectives hoped that eventually the name of the father would surface, but the odds were very much against that happening unless they could locate either Miss Hazleton or her mother. That would be a trying task, and they didn't have the time to spend on that type of search. They left the Probate Court and headed back to the Post.

When they entered the building, the desk officer informed them that they had a couple of visitors waiting for them outside their office on the second floor.

Mr. and Mrs. Forrest Wood sat patiently on the bench outside their office as they approached. The introductions having been made, all four people entered the conference room.

Mrs. Wood had been a radio personality in Detroit with the stage name of Edith Milton. She also had worked as the fashion editor for The Director magazine.

The detectives were impressed with her warm personality and listened intently to her story. She told Stevens and Ford that she had known Richard Rawlings for many years, but that she had usually dealt with the editor, Ted Schmidt.

Stevens asked her about her relationship with Joe Santino.

She became very agitated and told the detectives that when Santino came to work for the magazine and the ad agency, it appeared that he was making most of the decisions instead of Mr. Rawlings. She believed that Santino had taken Rawlings in on some nefarious scheme and that was the reason that he was killed. She believed that Santino could furnish a lot of information as to what was really going on with the business and told the detectives that she believed Santino was deeply involved in something sinister and that she felt it was her duty to tell the police. She was hopeful that by doing so, she would 'see that justice was done.' She made it a point to explain that her prime reason for coming in to talk with them was to make sure that they concentrated on Santino because she felt he knew a lot about what had happened to the Rawlings family. She had nothing in the way of hard evidence, only her intuition as a woman and co-worker.

The detectives thanked Mrs. Woods and her husband for their cooperation and information. The couple left quickly and quietly.

Stevens poured a couple of cups of coffee, handing one to Ford. He sat down and propped his feet up on his desk. "Well, John, it seems that a lot of people don't think much of Santino and it seems that most of them think he may have something to do with the murders."

"Okay, Frank. You know what I think. We're still going to have to get Santino to confess and he knows that time is on his side."

Stevens glanced outside and watched large, gray clouds move quickly across the sky. Sometimes, there would be a mist of rain mixed with snow. Other times, it would just snow. Occasionally, a slice of sunshine would break through and brighten up their little part of the world. In Michigan, the weather changed every five minutes. You couldn't escape it.

The cold and snow, in varying degrees continued through the months of January, February and March. The Rawlings case by this time had fallen into its own deep freeze. It was buried under a mountain of reports and files. Stevens and Ford were relegated to reading those reports. In the meantime, they waited for a phone call from the Oakland County Prosecutor's office regarding the announcement that Santino would be indicted. So far, nothing had come from the overconfident claims made by Mr. Chapman at the State Police Post meeting held in January.

CHAPTER 25

April 1, 1970
9:00 a.m.
State Police Post-Detroit

Joseph Carlos Santino, at the request of Stevens and Ford, accompanied by his lawyer, appeared again at the State Police Post to take a polygraph examination.

In all of their weapons and ballistics reports, the State Police and FBI confirmed that one of the murder weapons had been an Armalite AR-7, .22-caliber, self-storing rifle. Both agencies emphasized for the record, that this type of weapon was used predominately by military insurgent forces who were dropped behind enemy lines or by pilots who had to eject over hostile territory.

Santino had admitted that he had once owned two Armalite AR-7 rifles, purchased from his brother-in-law, Herb Jackson in Pontiac. He insisted, however, that he had given one the rifles back to his brother-in-law and the other one to a close friend by the name of Hal Beckwith, who lived in Chicago.

Stevens and Ford had checked with the Chicago Police Department and Mr. Beckwith could not be located. Chicago records indicated that he had lived in a brownstone apartment on the north side of Chicago, but according to the landlord, Beckwith left without paying his last month's rent. Mr. Beckwith had disappeared, without leaving a forwarding address.

With his attorney in tow, Santino was directed to the interrogation room and administered the scheduled polygraph exam.

Detective Sergeant Richard North, the polygraph examiner asked Santino the following questions:

1. Do you know who used the AR-7 to shoot the Rawlings family?
2. Before it happened, did you know an AR-7 would be used to shoot the Rawlings family?
3. Do you know where the AR-7 is now?
4. Did you lie to the police about giving that AR-7 to your brother-in-law?

When Santino finished answering the questions, North wrote his evaluation on the official report. North's concluding statements were: 'Mr. Santino has answered all the questions in the negative... It is the opinion of the undersigned examiner, that the emotional responses of the person examined, Mr. Joseph Santino, are sufficient to indicate deception. Therefore, it is the opinion of the examiner that Mr. Santino is not being truthful.'

With his attorney at his side, Joe Santino denied having any knowledge of the murders, or that he had participated in them in any way and stood by his previous statements given to the detectives.

Again, without any hard, physical evidence, Stevens and Ford could not charge their prime suspect with any involvement in the crime. Reluctantly, he was permitted to leave after the polygraph exam.

Through all of April, the case dragged on. A few of the tips that came in were forwarded from one of the Detroit newspapers whose reward money offer continued to provide a source of information, valid or not. All the 'tips' were checked out. Many of these newspapers tips came from former artists, or advertising people who had known Rawlings and did not add anything of importance to the case.

Stevens and Ford were slowly being worn down by the repetitive tasks of false leads and report filings.

A report taken by the Ohio State Police on a Mr. Roberts who was a traveling salesman and lived in Columbus, Ohio, led the two detectives to conclude that this was not the infamous 'Mr. Roberts' associated with Mr. Rawlings.

May 1, 1970
12:00 Noon
Birmingham, Michigan

Stevens and Ford arrived at the home of Karl Osterhouse at noon sharp. A phone call the day before from Mr. Osterhouse suggested that he might have some information regarding the Rawlings case.

The detectives approached the doorway of the large, two-story, brick front and aluminum sided home as Mr. Osterhouse, who had been watching from his living room window, moved to open the front door and greet them.

He was a large man, standing 6', 5" tall and weighing close to three hundred pounds. His pockmarked face made him look older than his thirty years of age, but he was neatly dressed in casual clothes and well groomed. He invited Stevens and Ford inside and introduced them to three other men sitting at a dining room table.

The men were introduced as Werner Barton, twenty-four years old, who was half-brother to Osterhouse, George Barton, twenty-two years old, also a half-brother to Osterhouse, and finally Timothy Dunn, a twenty-one year old friend of George Barton.

The detectives sat themselves at the table waiting for Mr. Osterhouse to begin the conversation. He cleared his throat and then spoke. "I used to live across the street and about five houses west of where Joe Santino lives now. I've known Joe since July of 1966. My wife and I have been social friends of the Santino's since that time and I've also done a lot of trap shooting with Joe."

"What kind of weapon does Mr. Santino use to trap shoot?" Stevens asked.

"He uses a 16-gauge Remington pump. Nice gun."

"Have you seen him with any other weapons while you were shooting?"

"Yes. I've seen him with a .25-caliber Beretta pistol and a .22-caliber rifle."

"Did it look like this?" Ford asked, handing Osterhouse a photo of the AR-7 rifle.

"Yes. In fact, it looked exactly like that."

"Do you remember when you first saw the .25-caliber Beretta?" Stevens asked.

"No. I'm not sure exactly. But I believe that it was sometime in early 1968."

"How did you come to see that pistol, Mr. Osterhouse?" Stevens continued.

"Well, I remember Joe coming over to my house one night. It was very cold outside, but when he came in, he showed me this pistol and it was loaded at the time. Joe asked me if I'd like him to get a Beretta like that one for me."

"And what did you tell him?" Stevens asked.

"I told him that I didn't think I could use something that small, but that I'd think about it. That's when he told me he had bought this one for his boss."

"Did you ever see Mr. Santino fire that pistol?"

"No, I can't recall ever seeing him shoot it at the club. I expected that he knew how to use it because he has all those other guns in his house."

Ford looked directly at Osterhouse and spoke in a clear tone. "Did you ever see Joe Santino use the survival rifle for target practice or at the shooting range?"

"Well, I recall seeing the rifle on several occasions when I would visit Joe at his house, but the rifle was always disassembled with the barrel and trigger mechanism stored in the stock. The entire package is only about twelve to eighteen inches long and he usually kept it on a book shelf in his den."

"This is very important, Mr. Osterhouse," Stevens interjected. "Can you ever recall a time when you saw Joe Santino fire that weapon?"

Osterhouse bowed his head in thought, searching deep into his mind as to if and when he might have seen Joseph Santino fire the AR-7 rifle. "Yes. Now I remember," He answered, slapping his thigh. "There was a time when Joe and I went out to the Multi-Lakes Gun Club near Walled Lake and Joe brought the rifle with him. Both of us fired it. Maybe five shots apiece. I think the clip held ten rounds. You'd have to check on that. But that's the only time I remember seeing Joe use that rifle."

"Do you remember what day, or even the date that you went out to the gun club and fired the rifle?" Stevens pressed.

"I think it was sometime in 1967, after one of the Detroit riots. Most of the time, it was on his shelf at home."

Werner Barton spoke up. "Karl, you remember that time that you went over to Joe's and borrowed that rifle to show me what it looked like?"

"Oh yes, I remember. You told me that you had seen one like it in Germany when you were stationed there. Thought you could get it for less money."

"It was during the time that I was home on leave," Barton continued. "I was surprised that a survival rifle like that was available to the civilian population."

"Do you recall when you were home on leave, Werner?" Stevens asked.

"I came home sometime in March, 1968 just before Easter and left maybe sometime shortly after the holiday. Probably around the middle of April."

Osterhouse spoke again. "One night, sometime in June of '68, maybe around 8 o'clock, Joe called me up and asked me if I wanted to make some money. 'It depends,' I said. 'What do you want me to do?' Then Joe said that he would pay me ten dollars if I would make a phone call for him."

"Santino wanted to pay you for making a phone call?" Ford asked, a note of skepticism in his voice.

"Yes sir, old Joe was always offering me money to do things. It was usually simple stuff and I went along with it. I made some pretty good pocket change that way. Anyway, I went over to Joe's house and he was in his basement. I asked him what he wanted me to do. Well, he tells me that he's been working on this big deal for the company with another employee. He tells me that the other employee had quit and now he needed someone to fill in for him, or pretend to be him, otherwise this big deal wouldn't go through."

Stevens interrupted. "Did he mention what kind of 'big deal' he was talking about?"

"No, but Joe asked me to do him this favor and I said that I would. So, he hands me this small piece of paper that has a bunch of words on it. It's the stuff he wanted me to say."

"What did you do or say then?" Ford asked.

"Joe asked me to read it over a couple of times at first, just to see if I knew what had to be said. I tried, but because of my German accent, I suggested to him that maybe he should let George do it. Joe said Okay. I called George on the phone and asked him to come over. In a few minutes, George arrived, along with his friend, Tim here."

Timothy Dunn, who had been sitting quietly while Mr. Osterhouse had been talking, spoke up. "George's accent was just as bad as Karl's. Because of that, Santino asked me to read it. I read it and Joe Santino said that I should make the call."

"Who did Santino want you to call?" Ford asked.

"As far as I can remember, I believe the call went to Mr. Rawlings. I didn't know who I was supposed to have been pretending to be when I made the call but, Santino dialed the number and handed me the phone."

"Who answered?" Stevens asked.

"I think it must have been a small girl because of the sound of the voice. I asked for Mr. Rawlings. Before I made the call Santino told me not to carry on any conversation with anyone else. If Rawlings asked any questions, I was supposed to tell him that Santino had all the details on the complete package and that if he had any questions, he was to contact Mr. Santino."

"What was the message Santino wanted you to read?" Ford asked.

Karl and George looked at one another as if to say that they couldn't remember any of it.

Dunn however, tried to fill in the blanks. "The best that I can remember is that the note read something like: I'm calling in regards to the deal we have been working on with Mr. Santino and my client has informed me that he will go as much as FIVE, but no more. If you want more details you'll have to contact Mr. Santino as he has all the answers."

"When you called Rawlings, did he ask any questions regarding this deal?" Stevens asked.

"I think he repeated the word FIVE a couple of times, but I'm not sure what he meant when he said it. I just told him what Santino had instructed me to tell him. I repeated the last sentence to him forcefully, that he was to contact Mr. Santino if he had any questions."

"Did Rawlings have any reaction to what you had told him? Stevens asked.

"Yeah, he did." Dunn said. "He seemed pleased with the news. He said goodbye and he hung up the receiver.

Osterhouse quickly spoke up. "After leaving the Santino house, we all began to wonder what five meant. We weren't sure if it meant $500, $5000 or $5 million."

"Did anyone ask Santino why he didn't make the phone call? Ford asked, looking directly at Osterhouse.

"Yeah, I did," Osterhouse answered. "Joe said that in a big deal like this, he didn't want his voice recognized and maybe lose the deal."

"That didn't sound suspicious to you?" Stevens countered.

"Not really. If you knew Joe, he was always coming up with some hair-brained ideas, so we didn't think much of it. We knew he did things different in his advertising business, so we just thought it was crazy Joe trying to make a buck."

Stevens and Ford looked at one another. Both were wondering what could the phony set-up phone call mean? How does it fit in with the other information that was on file?

Ford asked Osterhouse if he had more to tell them.

Osterhouse looked at the others who shrugged their shoulders. "No, I guess not."

The interview was concluded and the detectives left.

When they arrived back at the Post, they checked the telephone records for any calls made from the Santino's home to the Rawlings cottage. One of the records indicated that the only calls made from Santino's house between 7:00 and 9:00 p.m. were two calls on Monday, June 24, 1968. Both calls were made to the Rawlings cottage.

It showed the first call was made at 8:22 p.m. It lasted nine minutes.

The second call was made at 8:42 p.m. and lasted one minute.

Both detectives were positive that the first call was made by one of the people they had just interviewed at the Osterhouse home. The time and date matched the phone log and must have represented the curious conversation.

The weekend was coming and they decided to do more research into the time frames mentioned by Osterhouse and Dunn but would wait until Monday to question Santino.

May 4, 1970
9:00 a.m.
State Police Post-Detroit

Stevens and Ford arrived at the office and reviewed their research done over the weekend and the mysterious phone calls that Santino had requested Osterhouse to make. As they looked over the documents, they specifically tried to find ones that revealed the activities of Santino on the June 24th date.

During this process, Stevens received a call from the Oakland County Prosecuting Attorney's office and spoke with Assistant Prosecutor Chapman.

Chapman was able to confirm that the office was ready to convene a grand jury in the case, subject to additional information, which they believed would be coming from a confidential source regarding Santino.

Stevens told Chapman about potential conversations initiated by Santino to Rawlings on June 24th 1968, using people Santino duped into making the calls.

Chapman said that if the State Police had information that could tie Santino directly with conversations made to Rawlings shortly before he was murdered, then they would delay their proceedings until the State Police finished their investigation surrounding those calls. However, Chapman again emphasized that it was imperative the prosecutor's office protect their confidential source.

Feeling more confident than they had in the last year and a half, Stevens and Ford began to work frantically to gather each piece of relevant evidence they had in the case and index it for easier review.

Stevens called the East Lansing Post Headquarters and spoke with Colonel Darrens. He relayed the conversation he had with Chapman. Colonel Darrens approved of giving current information about the phone calls to the Prosecutor's office, but suggested it would be better to allow the Oakland County Prosecutor do his political thing. "We'll wait until we have a sure thing. We can arrest Santino at the proper time."

For the first time in months they believed the long process they had endured might produce the light at the end of the tunnel. Unfortunately, that light was an oncoming train that would derail them again.

The day progressed quickly as the detectives worked passed their self-imposed deadline of 6:00 p.m. They left the office close to midnight and both men were sure that the next day would produce even more beneficial results and that the prosecutor's office would have their request for a grand jury validated.

They had no way of knowing that tomorrow their enthusiasm and jubilation would turn to dust.

May 5, 1970
4:30 p.m.
State Police Post-Detroit

After a long day of compiling reports and rechecking interview notes, Stevens was stuffing manila folders into a cardboard storage box when the phone on his desk rang. The boxes were full of statements and evidence that he and Ford had been working on most of the day in order to have it organized before delivering it to the prosecutor's office.

He picked up the receiver. "Detective Stevens, can I help you?"

The voice on the other end was serious and direct. "Detective Stevens, this is Detective Herb Wing of the Southfield Police Department. I'm in an office building here in Southfield, along with some people from the county coroners office. What we have right now looks like an apparent suicide. We believe the victim's name is Joseph C. Santino. We have notified the next of kin to establish a positive ID. But we're pretty sure it's him."

Stevens felt a twinge. He held the phone to his ear, but didn't speak. Ford noting the unusual silence by his partner immediately knew that something was wrong.

"What is it Frank?" he asked.

"Santino. Apparent suicide." Stevens answered shaking his head and pointing to Ford to pickup the extension.

Ford stopped what he was doing and picked up the extension and introduced himself.

Wing repeated his introduction to Ford.

"How did you know to call us Detective Wing?" Ford asked.

"He had Stevens' card in his wallet and I thought it was a start." Wing replied.

"Can you tell us, what you have up to this point?" Stevens asked.

"Sure. Right now, I'm calling from Santino's office. It's listed as some kind of marketing firm, but there isn't much furniture here. He just moved in according to the building manager. Apparently, he made an arrangement to rent this office space starting on May 1st, just four days ago. The Standard Leasing Company is the listed Lessor. Santino named his business Diversified Research Incorporated. His name is listed on the building directory as the occupant of this office space."

"Did you find any documents that showed when he had formed this company?" "According to what we found in some files, it appears that it was on April 7th."

"Detective Wing, I know that your people have a lot of preliminary stuff to do. I'm sure you don't need a couple of extra bodies getting in the way. I think we'll pass on coming over until you tell us that it's clear to come down and take a look around. But I would appreciate it, if sometime tomorrow you could stop by our office and fill us in on the details."

"You got it. See you tomorrow. Bye."

May 6, 1970
9:00 a.m.
State Police Post-Detroit

Detective Wing sat comfortably in the wooden chair, sipping hot coffee. Ford and Stevens sat quietly across from him on the other side of the conference table as Wing began to lay out the scenario about Santino's suspected suicide.

"Around 3:30 p.m. yesterday, I was called to the Gold Coast Plaza Building, Suite 121 to investigate the possible suicide of an individual who later turned out to be Joseph Santino. When I first arrived, I found a white male lying on the floor behind a desk with a bullet wound to the right side of the head. I learned that the victim had rented this space and moved in about a week ago. Santino had his name listed on the building directory under the name of Diversified Research Incorporated. The entire office consisted of an outer office area and another office, located right behind that. His secretary and receptionist, Beverly Santino, used the outer office. She's the mother of the deceased."

Stevens and Ford thought that odd, but decided to let Wing finish before interrupting.

Wing continued. "Santino apparently was sitting in a high back chair behind his desk when he put a Colt .32-caliber, snub nosed revolver to his head. He held it in his right hand and put it against his right temple and fired one shot. The shot passed through his head and struck and broke the glass in a picture hanging on the wall behind him."

Ford poured Wing another cup of coffee and topped off his own. "Did the medical examiner find anything unusual?"

"No. He conducted a very thorough crime scene examination and concluded that it was definitely a suicide. They removed the body to the Hamilton Funeral home in Birmingham. The mother objected to an autopsy and there was none conducted. I'll forward a copy of the report to you as soon as it's complete."

"I understand that you also found a written note at the scene," Stevens asked.

"Yes there was. Only it was typewritten, not handwritten. Here's a copy of the note that Santino wrote."

Wing handed the copy to Ford. It read:

Mother…where do I start…I am a liar, a cheat and a phony. Any check that any of the people have with your signature on it isn't any good, because I forged your name to it to get them off my back. I owe everybody you can think of. I have made poor investments, and in some case no investments at all.

Jim Kaiser wasn't trying to get me money, he's already done so, and I owe him money. I love you dearly, but living will only cause you more heartache. I know I am sick, but seeking help isn't going to help the people I've hurt.

I just can't help myself…please understand. Love JOE.

Then in his own handwriting he wrote the following:

I had nothing to do with the Rawlings murders…I am a cheat, but not a murderer. Joe. I'm sick and scared…God and everyone please forgive me. I hope my family will understand. Joe. Call Jim Belloumo…he will help you.

Detective Wing paused for a second, but continued. "There was a note attached to the door of his office. The door was closed when we arrived. It was handwritten on a sheet of paper with a heading that said:

From the Desk of Joe Santino,

Mother…don't you come in…I will already be dead! Please have someone else come in….and you call the police or whatever. Joe.

"Anything else?" Stevens asked as Wing put the paper on the desk.

"Just the usual. We took the opportunity to examine various files and business records that the deceased had in his office. From those records it does appear that he was heavily in debt and was being pressured by various business associates to repay a lot of loans. His mother offered little if any information relative to the victim's business activities."

"Did you have an opportunity to compose a list of items and names that were found at the crime scene? Ford asked.

"Sure. Got it right here in my folder." Detective Wing pulled out a typewritten sheet of paper. "You'll be happy to know that all the physical items have been sent to your State Police Crime Lab for evaluation."

"Thanks, Herb." Stevens said.

"Call me anytime if you need assistance with this thing. Always glad to help." Detective Herb Wing said good-bye and left.

Stevens and Ford spent the rest of the day making phone calls and checking out different leads as a result of Santino's suicide.

The two individuals mentioned in the suicide note, Kaiser and Belluomo were friends of Santino, but were unwitting accomplices to Santino's business transactions. Like everyone else that came in contact with Santino, they had been led astray by his big talk and would lose every penny they had invested.

It was the one thing Stevens and Ford never suspected that Santino would do. It just never occurred to them he would take the suicide route. Now they were frustrated and upset that they hadn't arrested Santino before he had taken this final measure. The detectives sat quietly looking at a stack of boxes filled with statements and evidence that meant nothing to them at this point.

In the days following the suicide, the Rawlings case was like a car low on gas, sputtering and about to stop. Unless the two detectives were able to refill their investigative tank with new evidence the investigation would stop dead in its tracks.

May 13, 1970
3:00 p.m.
State Police Post-Detroit

A phone call from the Ferndale Police Department informed the detectives that a wallet turned into their night desk may be connected to the Rawlings' murder case or the Santino suicide. According to the detective at the Ferndale station, the wallet had papers in it that identified the owner as Paul Jewell, a black male, twenty-seven years old, living in Detroit.

The wallet also contained a newspaper article written by Sam Cohen of the Detroit News about the death of Joe Santino. Also found in the wallet was a promissory note made out to Paul N. Jewett from Joe Santino in the amount of $4,765.00 dated a couple of days before Mr. Santino's untimely death. In addition there was a company check in the amount of $850.00 also signed by Mr. Santino.

Stevens and Ford did a quick history check on the late Joseph Santino and his new company, Diversified Research Inc. What they found was very interesting and fit the modus operandi of Mr. Santino. This new company had been set up to conduct a check-kiting scheme between the Federal Bank and Trust and the National Bank of Detroit.

The check kiting scheme that Santino appeared to be using with each of the banks was to deposit around a thousand dollars in the checking account in each bank, then write checks for substantially higher amounts against both accounts.

As Stevens and Ford dug deeper into the investigation, they found that Paul N. Jewett had a long criminal record and activity that involved drug trafficking. A lot of that drug activity was conducted near the motel area where the wallet was found. Additional records showed that Mr. Jewett was on probation for an embezzlement conviction and was making restitution on thirty-five thousand dollars that had disappeared from his previous place of employment. His current employer, American Motors Corporation had him listed as a laborer working on the assembly line building passenger vehicles in the city of Pontiac.

The detectives thought it would be a good idea to bring Mr. Jewett into the Post and have him take a polygraph test.

May 22, 1970
10:00 a.m.
State Police Post-Detroit

Paul N. Jewett, accompanied by his attorney, walked through the State Police Post doors and was escorted to the detectives' office. Stevens and Ford along with State Police Detective/Sgt. Earl Edwards, the polygraph expert greeted them.

Ted Thurman, Jewett's attorney was a little upset over the fact that his client had been requested to come in for the test. After a short discussion with Stevens and Ford he calmed down and allowed his client to proceed with the polygraph exam. The test was completed within an hour.

The exam showed that, 'due to a lack of emotional responses to the pertinent test questions, it is the opinion of the undersigned examiner, that Paul Jewett is being truthful when he denies participating in the murder of Richard Rawlings or members of his family.'

It was signed and dated by Det./ Sgt. Earl Edwards/MSP

May 27, 1970
11:30 a.m.
State Police Post-Detroit

Stevens and Ford were preparing to leave for lunch when the phone rang. Ford answered.

"Detective Ford. Can I help you?"

A feminine voice on the other end spoke. "Detective, my name is Ruth Glenn and I believe I have some information regarding the Rawlings' murders. Would it be possible to come in and talk with someone who is handling the case?"

"I'm one of the detectives in charge. Would 2:00 o'clock, this afternoon be okay?"

"That would be fine." She answered. "I'll be there at 2:00 this afternoon. Goodbye."

"What the hell was that?" Stevens asked as both detectives walked outside through the main door and headed to their car.

"A woman named Ruth Glenn who thinks she might have some information regarding the Rawlings case."

Stevens shook his head. "They just keep coming out of the woodwork. I hope she has something that will help."

2:00 p.m.
State Police Post-Detroit

Precisely, at 2:00, a short, robust woman, with brown hair and blue eyes appeared at the front desk of the State Police Post where she was shown the way to the detectives' office.

Mrs. Glenn sat quietly, her eyes looking downward as Stevens and Ford listened to her story. "I hope you don't think this is strange, but I will understand if you do," She said politely.

"Let us be the judge of that Mrs. Glenn. Do you mind if we record this conversation?" "Heaven's no. Go right ahead."

"Well, you can begin anytime you like Mrs. Glenn," Stevens pushed down the record button.

"It's like this. I've been having this recurring dream about once every ten days. I visualize the Rawlings murder scene as a two-story frame house in a wooded setting with two vehicles parked side by side in the driveway. I then see two young men. They appear in the doorway of this house. They are recognized by one of the Rawlings children and admitted inside by Mr. Rawlings. Within a few minutes, an argument ensues over a business deal on which Mr. Rawlings reneged. These two men are brothers. The oldest one is short, maybe around 5'-8". He has dark curly hair and appears to have had a harelip, which has been medically repaired. He's about thirty-five to forty years old. He has a very violent temper and mean in nature. The other man is younger, between twenty-five and thirty years old. He is a little taller, close to six feet. He is very slim. He's also very obedient to the instructions given to him by his older brother. I believe that the older one is called Frenchie. I see them flying into upper Michigan in a private plane coming from Florida. Both men came with short barrel type pistols. Anyway, all the individuals are standing in the main room of this house, when Frenchie becomes violent. He has been having a heated argument with Mr. Rawlings. All of a sudden, Frenchie shoots Mrs. Rawlings. I see her body drop to the floor and rests near a big armchair or sofa type piece of furniture. I see blood on Frenchie's lower pant leg and shoes. Then the other brother shoots Mr. Rawlings and the little girl. Both Mr. Rawlings and the little girl fall in the hallway, side by side. Then I see two boys running down a hallway trying to reach a gun that is hidden in the bedroom. I see a lot of gunfire and then the two boys lying dead in the bedroom. This all happens in the late afternoon, during the summer season. There are lots of shadows around the building. I see a stone path leading to the front door. I see in the back pocket of the younger brother, a paperback book, titled, 'How to make a million dollars.' I see this same dream every time."

As Mrs. Glenn concludes her story, her face is flushed and her body looks drained as the detectives look at each other and wonder what they have done to deserve this.

Stevens picks up a legal pad from the table. "Mrs. Glenn, why do you think you're having this dream every ten days or so?"

"I'm not sure. I know that it has become like clockwork. I remember only hearing about the case from people at work. I've never really read anything about it. I have a two-year old daughter and a four-year old son. It doesn't leave me much time to read newspapers or watch television."

"Can you recall any other distinguishing marks or tattoos on these two men you say you see in your dreams?" Ford asks.

"I see a tattoo on the young one, but it is covered by his shirt sleeve. It looks like the figure of a woman, but only the legs and feet can be seen. It's on his left arm."

"Are there any other types of marks on these two brothers' as you call them?" Stevens asks.

"None that I can recall. The harelip and the tattoo are the ones that keep coming back in every dream. I thought someone should know. I hope that it can help."

"Thank you, Mrs. Glenn, we'll put it in the record. At this point we'll need to have our forensic people listen to the tape. For obvious reasons we're not at liberty to discuss any aspects of the case, however what you have told us may have some merit, we just don't know right now." Ford pushed the stop button on the tape recorder. She apologized if she had been a bother to them, but explained that she needed to let the detectives know what was going on in her mind. She politely said goodbye and left the building to return home.

The detectives sat quietly for a time, thinking about what had just happened. Ford broke the silence. "You know Frank, she came mighty close to describing the scene, but she left out a lot of the published facts that were in the newspapers."

" I agree. She left out Randy Rawlings entirely, never even mentioned him. Plus, she failed to include other information and evidence that was at the scene. I think she honestly believes that she's some kind of psychic."

"We should have asked her how many times she watched the movie, In Cold Blood. It sure as hell would be scary if we ran across some guy named Frenchie who fit the description she gave us." Both detectives started to smile, then broke out with a short burst of laughter.

Since Santino's death, their enthusiasm for the case had diminished significantly, but they still kept their eyes and ears open for any clues that came their way.

Most of the public had forgotten about the brutal murders that had been committed in the northern woods of Michigan. The Rawlings' relatives put closure to their grief by avoiding the media as much as possible and sometimes even the police.

It looked as if Frank Stevens and John Ford had spent their time putting together a case that would ultimately die its own death and possibly never be solved. Stevens had put Santino in his cross hairs as the prime suspect, now he was gone. Ford steadfastly kept digging for clues, but was convinced more than ever, that it was going to take a confession or an informer to reveal all that had happened in that cottage in order to solve the case.

What they didn't know was that in the coming month of July, the they would follow a lead that would make chills run up their spines. And thoughts of Mrs.

Glenn, the clairvoyant, would return to them full force.

July 6, 1970
10:00 a.m.
State Police Post-Detroit

On July 2nd, a few days before the start of the holiday weekend, Stevens and Ford received an anonymous phone call informing them that an individual by the name of William Hooper was involved in the Rawlings murders. The informant had told the detectives that Hooper owned a small diner in the town of Omer. The town was a short distance from Bay City, Michigan, just north of Detroit.

The tipster indicated that Mr. Hooper was involved because of fast money and a previous criminal record. The reason: drugs, and lots of them.

Stevens was driving the State Police cruiser along the two-lane highway headed towards Omer while Ford flipped through the pages of his notepad intermittently making notations on a clean page. The traffic was light, but the temperature had hit the 85-degree mark and noon was two hours away.

Within an hour they had reached their destination and pulled into the parking lot of a working man's diner called the Red Spot.

William Hooper, the owner, was fifty-five years old with thinning brown hair that had been dyed to keep away what little gray had crept in. He moved quickly, back and forth behind the diner counter. He was very good at flipping hamburgers, handling the french-fry baskets, cracking eggs and turning onions as the customers moved steadily in and out of the restaurant.

"Billy boy" as his regular customers like to call him was well liked by almost everyone in the town. People who lived in Omer knew "Billy boy" Hooper as an honest, reputable businessman who was always there to help the community when asked to do so. Since arriving in Omer ten years before, he had led a decent and honest life.

The detectives entered the eatery and found themselves an open booth at the back of the restaurant. They sat down as a waitress brought two glasses of water and set them on the table. She handed the detectives a menu.

Stevens ordered a burger basket while Ford ordered the breakfast special. They asked the waitress if she would tell Mr. Hooper they would like to speak to him when he had a chance.

Hooper, looking towards the two detectives between filling orders, had recognized the men as lawmen the moment they walked in. He had already assumed that at some point, he was going to have to talk with them. After the waitress had relayed the message, Hooper handed his spatula to a young man who had been assisting him at the grill and headed over to the detectives' booth. They introduced themselves and told him why they were there.

Hooper told them that he didn't know why anyone would want to point him out as being involved with the Rawlings' case. He had never met Rawlings or even knew who he was until he read about the murders in the paper. He admitted to having been in trouble with authorities before, when he was 22. He explained that he would run a boat out of Bay City over to Canada to buy fifty or a hundred cases of Canadian whiskey. He would bring it back across, warehouse it, and then sell it to whoever wanted to buy it.

Most of the time it would be underage high school kids for their beach parties. However, sometimes his deliveries were to local bars. The owners didn't have to declare it on their taxes and the Liquor Commission had no way of tracing the sale.

It all came to an end, he told detectives, when the Coast Guard caught up with him on a night he had some motor trouble and his illegal contraband was found on the boat. He was sentenced under federal law and did a couple of years at the Federal prison in Milan, Michigan. Emphatically, he told Stevens and Ford that at the time he was released, he made a pledge to himself not to get in trouble again because he never wanted to spend another day behind bars.

Stevens and Ford accepted Hooper's explanation. There wasn't any reason for them to suspect that he wasn't keeping that promise. But, like most ex-cons, their instincts told them that Hooper was holding something back.

Hooper continued to speak with a tone of sincerity about not having anything to do with the Rawlings case, but it was not enough to convince the detectives that he wasn't just a "little involved" in some way. The detectives trusted their source.

Hooper, sensing that he was not convincing the detectives that he didn't have any knowledge of the crime, gave them some information that he hoped would convince them that he was telling the truth. He told them to contact two brothers by the names of Bobby and Jimmy Oliver who lived in Tawas City, Michigan. He told detectives that he had overheard some conversations in his restaurant that these two individuals may know a lot about the Rawlings case. The detectives were satisfied, finished their meal and headed back to Detroit to review their files and make plans to have a meeting with the Oliver brothers.

Sheriff's Department
July 8, 1970
9:00 a.m.
Tawas City, Michigan

Sheriff Ed Sinclair was a short, muscle-bound, jovial type of individual. He had been the sheriff of Alpena County for over fifteen years. He knew almost everyone in the county, the good people and the bad ones. He knew those "outsiders" who liked to temporarily come in and create mischief and he definitely knew the Oliver brothers.

They were outsiders from the City of Dearborn Heights, a suburb of Detroit. He categorized both brothers as extremely mean, unruly and contemptuous of the law. The sheriff didn't like the two brothers one bit. When they were in the county, trouble developed regardless of where they were.

The sheriff was more than pleased when Stevens and Ford asked to visit the two malcontents. He had just arrested the Olivers for car theft. They were locked up in one of the county jail cells. The jail itself was attached to and behind the sheriff's office.

Stevens and Ford sat themselves across from the sheriff and the large wooden desk that separated them.

"I'm very pleased that you're here to talk to these two rascals. They're a real pain in the ass every time they come up here from Detroit," Sheriff Sinclair said as he lit up a stub of an old cigar and leaned back in the swivel chair.

"Well Sheriff, we're just here to follow up on a tip. We can't promise you that it'll lead to anything," Stevens said. "We know from their records that these two have been in trouble with the law a lot, and it's possible they may be involved in the Rawlings' murders over at Thunder Point a couple of years ago."

"Yeah, I remember the murders. Whole family wiped out. I wouldn't put it past either one of them. The Oliver boys are just plain bad. They have the potential to commit any criminal act you could think of. Personally, I think they've gotten away with so much since they were young, that you can forget about rehabilitation. They just need to be locked up permanently so they won't do anymore harm to innocent people."

"What have you arrested them for now Sheriff?"

Sinclair picked up a file folder and opening it, handed it to Ford. "Right now, they're both in jail for stealing their aunt's car. But, as you can see here," the sheriff said pointing to the folder, "Robert Joseph Oliver, white male, six foot,

200 pounds, brown hair, brown eyes, twenty-six years old, is being charged with grand larceny theft, and concealing stolen property, etc., etc."

Then the sheriff picked up a matching folder and handed it to Stevens. "And here we have James Leo Oliver, twenty year old white male, five-ten, 150 pounds with black hair, brown eyes. His record contains about the same kind of stuff as his brother. He likes nighttime break-ins more than stealing cars though."

"It sounds to me like both of them are potential long term residence of 2000 Cooper Street," Stevens said referring to the address of the Michigan State Prison in Jackson, Michigan.

"Believe me, they keep trying to get in," the sheriff replied, chuckling.

"I think it's about time we had a little talk with them. We'll interview them one at a time. You can pick the first one, Sheriff."

"I'll have my jailhouse deputy bring over Bobby Oliver first."

The sheriff called the jailhouse section and told his deputy to escort Bobby Oliver to his office. A few minutes later, the deputy and Bobby Oliver stepped into the sheriff's office. Oliver was handcuffed, wearing the standard issue gray prison jumpsuit. Stenciled on the upper back of the jumpsuit was a large, bold white letter "P" indicating the person was a prisoner. The deputy guided him to any empty chair and sat him down. The office chairs had been rearranged so that Bobby Oliver now sat directly across from the detectives.

Sinclair introduced Oliver to the State Police detectives, but there was no response. Oliver sat motionless and let his dark eyes evaluate the two detectives in front of him. He pursed his lips and then let his eyes drop to the floor. Stevens tried to elicit some conversation with the prisoner, but he refused to talk.

The sheriff was a man who didn't like to waste time. He instructed the deputy to take Oliver back to his cell. As the deputy helped Oliver up from the chair, the short sleeve of his shirt partially covering his left arm raised up. It was like a magnet had grabbed the eyes of the two detectives! Stevens and Ford stared at the tattooed figure of a naked lady on Bobby Oliver's left arm. The hairs on the back of their necks stood up as they watched him being escorted out of the room.

"That's odd as hell," the sheriff said. "Usually he can't stop talking. He's always trying to get off the hook by bullshitting his way out of something. Do you want the deputy to bring in his brother Jimmy?"

Stevens and Ford were still recovering from seeing Bobby Oliver's tattoo and remembering their interview with Mrs. Glenn.

The sheriff had to ask a second time if they would like to interview Jimmy Oliver.

Ford, pushing away the thoughts of Mrs. Glen answered the sheriff. "Yes. Let's see if his brother will cooperate and talk with us."

The sheriff picked up the jail phone a second time and asked his deputy to bring in the younger Oliver.

Jimmy Oliver, his curly black hair accenting his pale chiseled features, moved easily into the room and plunked himself down on the same chair, that only moments before, his brother had sat in.

"How about a smoke sheriff?" he asked politely.

"Depends, Jimmy boy. You can go back to your cell with a full pack if you answer some of the questions these gentlemen have for you."

Jimmy stared at Stevens and Ford for a few moments. "Who the hell are you guys?"

"We're from the State Police, Mr. Oliver." Ford answered formally.

"We'd like to ask you a few questions about a case we're working on."

"I don't know nothin', " Jimmy replied quickly. "And I ain't no squealer. So forget it."

Ford knew the type. It would be a challenge, but he was good at this type of obstinate personality. "Jimmy, we're not going to ask you to squeal on your friends. And we're not here to interrogate you. We only want to see if you can verify or confirm something that we already know. That's all we're asking from you. We'd just like you to tell us if we're right or wrong."

The younger Oliver gave Ford a curious glance, then returned his gaze to the floor.

Ford continued, "Detective Stevens and I know some things about a crime that happened a couple of year ago, and I think you might know if what we have found out is true or not. I don't think that's squealing. Do you?"

Jimmy Oliver was not prepared for this type of approach and casually agreed to participate with Ford in this evaluation process. "No. I guess that wouldn't be squealing."

The sheriff quickly picking up on Ford's technique tossed a pack of cigarettes on the table for Jimmy. The prisoner, with his hands still cuffed, was able to open the pack, and remove a cigarette. With a nod of approval from the sheriff, the deputy provided a lighter and held an open flame for Jimmy Oliver to light his cigarette. Oliver took a long, deep drag and let little rings of smoke drift towards the ceiling.

Ford continued, " Jimmy, have you ever heard of a place called Thunder Point?"

"Yeah, I've heard of it. So what?" Jimmy replied as he leaned back in his chair, taking another puff on his cigarette.

"Jimmy, listen closely to me. In June of 1968, there were some people who lived in a cottage by Lake Michigan and the people in this cottage had a fight with someone. A whole family was killed. Did you ever hear anything about that?"

Jimmy Oliver's eyes widen slightly and he sat upright in his chair. He leaned forward in the chair and looked at the floor for a long time. The only sound was a small fan pushing the hot air around the room.

Small beads of sweat began to accumulate on Jimmy's forehead. He took a quick drag of his cigarette. Finally, he looked up and spoke. "Nope."

"Does that mean you don't know about the case or that you don't know who the people were who were involved in it?" Ford asked.

"Both," Oliver answered quickly.

"Have you ever been up around the Thunder Point area Jimmy?" Ford continued, his voice pleasant and even.

"Nope. I've never been in the area. I stay on this side of the state. The people over there are too snooty and uppity. I don't like 'em."

"Has your brother Bobby ever been over on that side of the state?"

" I don't know. Ask him."

"Are you telling me, the two of you who do a lot of things together, that you wouldn't know if Bobby went over to Thunder Point sometime in the past and pulled a job?"

"Look, we don't pull jobs. We're a lot smarter than that." Jimmy was beginning to become irritated. He now realized the detective had set him up to "squeal," and he was feeling the pressure that he may have already said too much.

"So the rap sheet that Sheriff Sinclair has given us about you two is a big lie, right?"

"Most of it is. Yeah, Bobby and I take things, but most of the time the owners have given us permission, then they change their minds and call the cops on us."

Stevens stepped in. He had been evaluating Jimmy Oliver and knew that he would be the easier of the two brothers to crack for any information about the Rawlings case.

Ford had tried his way, now Stevens came at Jimmy Oliver full force. "Jimmy, I'm going to tell you this just once. We have information that you and Bobby were involved in that mass murder over in the Thunder Point. What your telling detective Ford and I is that you and Bobby have never been over in the Thunder Point area. All right. But if we find out positively that you lied to us today, I'm going to come down so hard on you that you'll have wished you had taken the plunge off the Mackinac Bridge, got that?"

Jimmy Oliver squirmed slightly in his chair, but remained silent.

Stevens continued. "I'll bring the hammer down on you so quickly, they'll have to pry your ass out of the floor with a crowbar. We're not here for some goddamn stolen car heist. Were here because six people got butchered up north and if you know anything about it, you'd better cough it up now."

The threatening tone and coldness in Stevens' voice made Jimmy's insides shutter. Still, he held his ground and denied any involvement or knowledge about the Rawlings murders or that he and his brother had ever been in the area.

The sheriff seeing that the second phase of the interviews was also going nowhere, nodded for his deputy to return Jimmy Oliver to his cell.

When they had left, the sheriff turned to the detectives and said, "I'm not sure how much you got out of him, but I hope it was enough."

"It's never enough Sheriff," Stevens answered. "Thanks again. John and I will be on our way. We need to get back to the Post."

They left the sheriff with his two favorite prisoners and headed back to Detroit to work on some other cases that needed their attention.

For the next few days, the two detectives searched through records and reports about the Rawlings' killings and gave special attention to the backgrounds of Bobby and Jimmy Oliver. Just as the sheriff had told them, the Oliver brothers had been in all kinds of trouble. As it always seems to be, their taste for calamity started in their early teens.

Bobby and Jimmy had spent time in numerous detention homes, then jails throughout the state, but had never been sent to prison. There were always accusations and charges filed, but when it came time to convict, witnesses either disappeared or would not talk. It was peculiar for two fairly young ruffians to have that kind of power or luck.

July 22, 1970
4:30 p.m.
State Police Post-Detroit

Stevens and Ford were standing near the water cooler complaining about the heat and the miserable air conditioning unit that the department had tried to install, only to have it quit just five minutes after the maintenance people had it up and running.

A trooper from the front desk approached them and told them that Corporal Jack Matlin would like them to come over to the garage area. Apparently, a car from the Livonia Auto Salvage Company had been towed to the Post vehicle impound area and there was something he wanted to show them.

The detectives hurried across the scorching blacktop parking lot to the department garage. As they approached the building, numerous signs warned trespassers that this was an area for impounded vehicles and that guards were on duty twenty-four hours and would arrest anyone attempting to enter without proper authority.

Stevens and Ford flashed their badges at one of the security personnel as they entered the building and quickly located Corporal Matlin. He was standing next to a 1965 Chevrolet two-door sedan with 1970 Ohio license plates, holding a small clear plastic bag in his right hand.

"Corporal Matlin, what do you have for us?" Stevens asked as he looked at the bag Matlin was holding in his hand.

"Well sir. I had a call from Livonia Auto Salvage this afternoon about an abandoned car in their storage yard. I went over to run a stolen car check on it. The manager told me that he had a local police call on this car that was on the shoulder of highway M-14, about two miles east of Telegraph Rd. He towed it to his yard and held it the thirty days like he was supposed to but no one came to claim it. That's when he called us. I started my search looking in the glove box. This is what I found."

Matlin handed Stevens the plastic bag. The object inside the bag was a luggage tag. Stevens took the bag but did not open it. He didn't want his prints on the object inside. He held the bag up so that Ford could also look at tag. It was a small leather bound nametag that is commonly used to identify a piece of luggage. The condition of the nametag appeared to be brand new. Hand printed in dark blue ink was:

Shirley L. Rawlings
18790 Delores St.
Towne Village, Michigan

Stevens and Ford looked at each other in disbelief. It was surreal. How could this luggage tag, which was in excellent condition, have survived the past two years without a scratch or some other form of mutilation? From what they could recall, the tag color matched some of the pieces of luggage at the cabin. The tag was as clean as if it had just been made.

Stevens turned back to Matlin. "I want you to call the Forensic Lab people and have them search every square inch of this vehicle for evidence. Give them this tag and have them look for prints and anything else that they can find. When they're finished, have them call us."

"Yes sir." Matlin responded.

"Corporal, did you happen to run a registration check on this vehicle? Ford asked.

"Yes sir, I did that first thing. The owner's name is William M. Hooper, 210 Church St., Bowling Green, Ohio. However, he is living at…" Before he could finish, Ford interrupted, "We know where he lives corporal."

"Thanks corporal." Stevens said as the detectives left the building.

A thousand thoughts crossed their minds as to how the tag could have been left in that glove box. The important fact was that it had remained there without any marks, scars or dirt on it. It also meant that one of the suitcases from the cabin could still be around. If they could find the suitcase or who had possession of it, maybe there would still be a chance they could find the person or persons responsible for the Rawlings murders.

It would be a long shot, but it was the best thing right now they had to go on. The humidity in the office area was so heavy their shirts were full of perspiration and the detectives felt like they needed a shower.

"The son-of-a-bitch, I just knew he was hiding something. I could see it in his eyes," Stevens said, angry with himself for not being more aggressive with Hooper when they first questioned him. "We need to get back and see him right away, before he knows that we found the car Frank." Ford said.

"Let's go. It's too damn hot to hang around here."

In less than an hour, Stevens and Ford had, for the second time, pulled their car into the parking lot of the Red Spot diner in Omer. They entered the building and looked for a place to sit down. The air conditioning alone had made the trip worthwhile. It was dinner hour and there was a crowd of workers from the tool and die plant across the street. They located a corner booth and ordered a couple of burgers with coffee.

Hooper was working the cash register and saw the two detectives come in. He asked one of the waitresses to cover for him as he made his way over to talk to them. "Didn't expect to see you guys back so soon," He said, standing in the aisle next to the booth.

"'The food was so good last time we decided to come back," Stevens said.

"Best in the area. I guarantee it." Hooper replied.

"Really? " Ford asked.

"We have the best chili and the best goulash this side of Mexico and Romania."

"How about joining us for a cup of coffee while we wait for our order, Mr. Hooper. We have a couple of questions we need you to answer for us," Stevens said, his tone more commanding than requesting.

"Sure." Hooper motioned for the waitress that he was going to join the two men at the table.

Ford began, "Mr. Hooper, a few hours ago, our State Police Post in Detroit found a 1965, Chevy abandoned in a junkyard. The vehicle was listed as stolen and was impounded by one of our troopers. The vehicle was registered in your name. What can you tell us about it?"

William Hooper paused for just a second before answering. "I bought it for my son Ronnie last year, I think it was in September or October from a Ford dealership in Toledo."

Stevens pulled a Polaroid photo of the luggage tag from his coat pocket and showed it to Hooper. "You ever see this tag, Mr. Hooper?"

"No, never saw that before."

"Where is your son now?"

"He lives over in Caro. You know, just southeast of Bay City. I can give you his address and phone number." Hooper scribbled out the information on a napkin.

"We'll eat first, then drive over there and talk with your son," Stevens said, placing the photo back in his coat vest pocket.

"Sure. Let me call him first to see if he's there." Hooper responded.

"Fine." Stevens said, stirring more sugar into the coffee.

A few moments later, Hooper returned and told the detectives that his son would be waiting for them when they arrived.

The detectives finished their meal and headed for the small town of Caro, Michigan. It was eight o'clock when they turned their police cruiser into the gravel driveway of the broken down bungalow located on the outskirts of the small city. They knocked on the door and waited.

It didn't take long before a young man, in his early twenties, sporting long blond hair that reached the middle of his back, opened the door. The scent of marijuana filtered in the air, but Stevens and Ford ignored it for the moment.

"My old man said you guys were coming down, so I've been watching for you. Come on in. You guys want to sit down?" The detectives picked a couple of worn chairs placed around a battered dining room table and sat down with Ron Hooper.

Stevens asked him to explain about the stolen car report.

"The car was stolen just after Memorial Day, when I started working down at Cedar Point. You know, the amusement park near Sandusky, Ohio."

"Yes, we know where it is Ron." Ford acknowledged.

"Anyway, I made a report to the Cedar Point police. Sometimes, I would let my friends use the car. Most of them were like me, just trying to groove, you know what I mean?" Ron said, laughing at his own words.

Stevens produced the photo of the luggage tag and handed it to Ron. "You ever see this tag before?"

"No man. Never saw that before. Who's this Rawlings chick, she got a complaint or something?"

Ford ignored Ron's question and moved on to another of his own. "You're telling us that your car was stolen while you were working at Cedar Point, is that right?" Ford asked.

"Yep. I was working one of the rides, but I think I know who took it. At least, I think I know who did it."

"And who do you think took it Ron?" Stevens asked.

"Bobby Oliver."

At first Stevens and Ford thought they had misunderstood the name. Stevens recovered immediately and asked. "Did you say Bobby Oliver?"

"Yeah. We're friends. We both had jobs at Cedar Point. He and his brother are from the Detroit area. When Bobby got fired one day and the next day my car was gone, I just put two and two together and thought that it must've been him."

"If he took your car without your permission, and you filed a stolen car report, then why don't you press charges against Bobby Oliver and have him arrested?" Ford asked.

"No! No! No! I don't want to prosecute or have anybody arrested. Let's just forget about the car, Okay. I don't want to have anybody arrested. Besides, I got an old Mustang that I've been using." Ron Hooper was more than excited, he was scared.

"Okay, Ron, just relax. We understand. But for the record, are you telling us that you never saw this luggage tag while you had the car?" Stevens asked, rising from the table.

"That's right. I never saw it." He said quickly.

"All right." Ford replied. " But tell me one thing. Why are you afraid of the Oliver boys?"

Without the slightest hesitation, Ron Hooper answered Fords' question. "Your damn right I am. They're a couple of mean bastards and I don't want to piss them off. Your not going to tell them I talked with you, are you?"

Stevens paused, then answered. "Don't worry Ron. As long as you play it straight with us, our conversation is confidential. We won't tell the Oliver brothers." Ron Hooper felt a world of fear lift off his shoulders, but Stevens put it right back on.

"As long as you tell us the truth Ron, we're on your side. You've told us that you've never seen this tag before and I believe you. But if you have seen it before or you've let the Oliver brothers use your car for something illegal, you could be in a lot of trouble."

"I don't know what you mean? It's my car and I don't want to press any charges. Isn't that what this is all about?"

The detectives realized that Ron Hooper thought the purpose of their visit was about the stolen vehicle, not the Rawlings murders. Ford made it clear to him. "Ron, this investigation is about a mass murder over in Thunder Point a couple of years ago. The luggage tag in that photograph belonged to the woman that was killed there and it was found in your car, in the glove compartment. We think the Oliver brothers know something about those murders. If you know something that you're not telling us, you'd better come clean now. Otherwise, you may become an accessory to murder, do you understand that?"

The look on young Hooper's' face was pale and drawn. He was in a state of shock. The detectives could tell that none of what they had told him made sense to him. He started shaking his head and mumbling. "No sir, no sir, I wouldn't have anything to do with something like that. If Bobby and Jimmy took my car to do something bad, I didn't know anything about it. I was high most of the time at the Point. Partying all the time. Honest, I never saw that tag, ever. You got to believe me."

"Okay Ron. But if you hear of anything, you better give us a call right away. Got it?" Ford said placing his hand on young Hooper's shoulder.

"Yes sir, yes sir." He said as he fell into the couch, putting his head in his hands.

The detectives left him sitting there and made their way out of the house.

The stars were like scattered diamonds in the black sky, with a half moon punching a hole in the middle of it. Stevens and Ford got in the cruiser and headed back to Detroit.

"We need to speak with Bobby Oliver again, Frank. We should call Sheriff Sinclair and have Oliver transported to our place for an interview."

"Good idea." Stevens replied.

CHAPTER 26

July 23, 1970
10:00 a.m.
State Police Post-Detroit

A title history check was being done on the 1965 Chevy two-door as Stevens and Ford spent most of the morning looking at crime scene pictures. They didn't find anything new.

Earlier that morning they had spoken to Sheriff Sinclair about Bobby Oliver. He agreed to deliver Oliver to the Post before noon for questioning. It was 10:30 a.m. when Bobby Oliver arrived at the Post building. Stevens and Ford were eager to try and obtain any information they could from him.

The deputy sheriff handcuffed Oliver to the chair and left the room. Oliver looked surly and his eyes wandered around the room.

Ford began the questioning and pressed hard to get Oliver to reveal anything that would put him at the scene of the murders. Ford presented a series of tough questions, but Oliver refused to answer. This Oliver was a tough customer.

Then Stevens questioned him about the Hooper car. Oliver admitted to taking it, but insisted that he told Ron about it and was given permission to take it. He said he left the car on M-14, near Telegraph Road, because it broke down and he had to walk. He told Stevens that he didn't feel any responsibility to tell Ron Hooper about it. As far as the luggage nametag was concerned, he said he never saw it at anytime while using the car. He vehemently denied to the detectives that he had any knowledge about the Rawlings murders and repeatedly told the detectives that he had never been to the Thunder Point area in his life.

Stevens and Ford realized that Bobbie Oliver was going to be a tough suspect to question. They released him to the deputy sheriff and watched the pair walk down the corridor and out of the building. A contrast of life, Ford thought.

Bobby Oliver was definitely a hard-nosed criminal and it was apparent that he had no intention of providing any information about his activities or those of his cohorts to any law agency today, tomorrow, or forever.

Their next hope was their request to the Ohio Secretary of State's office that would provide them with a list of vehicle owners for the Chevrolet two-door.

July 28, 1970
9:00 a.m.
State Police Post-Detroit

The morning was cool and pleasant with low humidity and the early morning sun suggested a nice day. The official report from the Ohio Secretary of State's office containing the complete title history of the Chevy two-door had been Tele-typed to the Post.

Stevens and Ford looked at the information.

> *TITLE HISTORY*
> *1965 Chevrolet Coach- VN 164375F255027*
> *The vehicle was originally purchased by Jack Towns Chevrolet in Toledo from the General Motors Corporation on June 9, 1966   Title# 480967146 was assigned to that vehicle by this office.*
> *The vehicle was then sold to Lanny Richmond of 412 Eaton St., Toledo, Ohio. Mr. Richmond than sold the vehicle to Mr. Robert J. Longmier of 1335 Franklin St., Toledo, Ohio on 4-24-68.*
> *Mr. Longmier traded the car in to Ron Champs Ford, 1135 Long Blvd, Toledo, Ohio on 6-1-68*

The Ohio Secretary of State's office concluded by saying that their records showed that from June 1, 1968 until September 15, 1969, the vehicle was listed and claimed within the inventory ledger of Ron Champs Ford of Toledo, Ohio.

When Stevens called the dealership and spoke with it's general manger he informed Stevens that according to their records, they had other dealership associates during that time who took the car on assignment to see if they could sell it. Their list of dealers included two in Ohio, three in Indiana and two in Michigan during that time period. The dealerships in Michigan were located in Flint and Pontiac.

So much for trying to pin down who may have had use of the vehicle during the period the crimes were committed.

Ford reviewed the phone numbers provided in order to follow-up on the information contained in the report and made the phone calls.

First, he contacted Lanny Richmond. Mr. Richman was a foreman for the Castle Glass Company in Toledo. He explained that he had purchased the car for his family, kept it for almost two years. The family needed to purchase a station wagon in the spring of 1968 and he sold it to a fellow worker at the Glass Company. That person was Robert J. Longmier.

Ford then called Mr. Longmier. Mr. Longmier explained that he was really surprised when Richmond wanted to sell the car, but it was a very good deal, so the bought it. Unfortunately, his wife after a couple of months had an accident and the front end had to be redone. They traded that car in for another one at Ron Champs Ford dealership.

It appeared that after a year of the car being transported to different dealerships it was eventually purchased by Ron Hooper Sr., for his son Ron.

Neither of the two previous owners saw a luggage tag in the glove box while they had possession of the car. Both said if they had seen it, they probably would have thrown it out.

Ford thought, "Why should they have seen it? The murders were committed after the car had been sold or traded in by Longmier."

Either Ron Hooper and the Oliver brothers were lying or it had to be someone that had access to the car through seven dealerships in three states.

Stevens and Ford spent the remaining months of 1970 trying to tie the car to the crime dates, by contacting each of the dealerships and having them check their records, but without any success. The year slipped away without any more information or clues coming into the State Police Post regarding the Rawlings murders.

By necessity the detectives became more involved with other cases because of the accumulating backlog of other crimes.

A written memo to Stevens and Ford from the Headquarters in East Lansing instructed them to maintain the file as being "open" but they were not to spend full time on it. They were to monitor the case occasionally, in the event some new evidence came to light, but for the most part the case was to be put in the cold case files.

From the beginning of 1971, through 1974, the Rawlings murder case did not generate one tip, phone call or letter. The media and the public had forgotten about it. Many of the relatives of the Richard Rawlings family had died, moved or disappeared to different parts of the state or the country.

Stevens and Ford were involved in a multitude of different cases and had little time to even think about the Rawlings murders.

Yet, from time to time, they would check to see if any new information had come in, but for the most part the case no longer held out any prospect of being solved.

With each passing day, the June 1968 murders of the Rawlings family faded quietly into the background of everyday police work.

November 06, 1974
10:00 a.m.
Cheboygan, Michigan

Circuit Court Judge, Theodore L. Brown contacted the State Police Post at Cheboygan and advised them that a subject by the name of Armedeo DeRosa of Cheboygan had spoken with him and stated he might have some information on the Rawlings homicides that had occurred in 1968. Mr. DeRosa had asked the court if he could speak with someone from the State Police.

Stevens and Ford were notified and they immediately left for Cheboygan. They arrived at 3:00 p.m. and entered the Cheboygan State Police Post where Mr. DeRosa was being detained.

They were given an interrogation room and Mr. DeRosa was brought in for questioning.

Mr. DeRosa was built somewhat like a fireplug. He was short and stocky and looked like a man in search of a neck. He had coal black hair, slicked straight back with hair cream and dark bushy eyebrows that arched over dark brown eyes. His complexion was ruddy, with a small scar on the right side of his chin. He wore a silk gray suit with a clean, finely knit white shirt and dark tie. He settled his rotund frame into a standard courtroom chair.

Stevens asked Mr. DeRosa to tell them about the information he told the judge he had regarding the Rawlings murders. Ford leaned against the wall and studied the figure in the chair.

DeRosa, in a low, almost muted voice began talking. "In July and August of 1969, I was a partner with a guy by the name of Butch Lundy. We owned the Palomino Bar on Mackinac Island. We had a bartender by the name of Chuckie. I don't remember his last name. He was always talking about the Rawlings murders. One time, he made a remark that he had been a driver for the group that had murdered the Rawlings family and that he was real familiar with the Thunder Point area. In fact, he claimed that he knew exactly where the Rawlings cottage was located and where the rifles were thrown away. Every once in a while he would comment about having to drive this group of people on different jobs. He said it was why he always had cash in his pocket. In some cases, he would get fifty to a hundred dollars to take 'good people' on a short drive or to pick somebody up. He claimed the people that he drove for were from East Detroit."

"Did he ever mention to you who these 'good people' were?" Ford asked.

"No. He never mentioned any names, just jobs that he worked on with them."

"Okay, continue Mr. DeRosa," Stevens said, not wanting to interrupt the flow.

"Once Chuckie told me that he had worked at the Mackinac Island Hotel during the fall of 1967, and because of that, he had connections with several people from Chicago. My ex-partner Lundy, who lives in Pompano Beach, Florida probably can tell you Chuckie's last name."

Stevens broke in. "What did this Chuckie person look like?"

"He was a big fella, probably around six-foot four or five with blond hair, blue eyes. I'd say he weighed around two hundred and fifty pounds. He woulda' made a good German Army Poster boy," DeRosa said, chuckling at his own humor.

"Your ex-partner Lundy, did he have any other friends, maybe a girl friend?" Stevens asked.

"Yeah. He had a girl friend named Dee-Dee Thurman. I think she still works at a Ford dealership here in Cheboygan."

That was the extent of Mr. DeRosa's information.

Stevens and Ford told DeRosa that they would get back to him after they had time to checkout his information. A deputy came in and escorted the prisoner back to his cell.

Ford picked up the phone and called the Detroit Post and told them that he and Stevens had another stop to make before returning to the Post.

Within an hour they had located Dee-Dee Thurman. As DeRosa said, she was still working at the local Ford dealership.

The detectives introduced themselves and explained the reason for the visit. She told them that she still corresponded with Butch Lundy in Florida and that she would obtain whatever information she could and get back with them. They thanked her and left.

November 12, 1974
11:00 a.m.
State Police Post-Detroit

Dee-Dee Thurman arrived at the Post with a small briefcase, as detective Stevens met her at the front desk and escorted her to the office where Ford was waiting.

The trio made their way into the Post conference room. Miss Thurman settled herself into one of the chairs at the conference table and opened the briefcase.

Ford asked her if she would like a cup of coffee and she said "yes, one sugar please."

She began to pull out papers as Ford handed her the coffee and sat down beside her. Stevens sat on the other side of the table.

"It was very hard to reach Butch," She said in a soft voice. "He travels around Florida regularly and he was hard to track down. But here's what he told me. He said that this Chuckie was a bad character and had connections with the syndicate. Chuckie travels around the country a lot, running errands for some of the 'connected guys.' Butch told me that he had run into Chuckie at a Florida airport back in September."

"Did you happen to find out where Chuckie is now?" Stevens asked.

"No. Butch didn't know where he was going either."

"What about his last name, Miss Thurman?" Ford asked.

"I'm sorry. I should have mentioned that first thing. It's VanZant. Charles Leonard VanZant."

Stevens wrote the name down on a sheet of paper and left the room.

Ford continued with the questioning. "Did you ever have contact with this Chuckie person, Miss Thurman?"

"No, I never met him. But I remember seeing him one time, working the Palomino Bar on the Island. He was a good-looking guy, but his eyes were scary looking. I used to do some substitute payroll for Butch and Armedeo when they had the place. The guy gave me the creeps."

"Is there anything else you can remember about him?" Ford continued.

Dee-Dee Thurman thought for a moment and then answered. "Yes. Butch once told me that Chuckie was into the car auction business. Some of Butch's friends had seen Chuckie at the Flint Auto Auction about a year ago and that Chuckie was working as a car salesman for one of the dealers there in Flint."

Miss Thurman gave the detectives some copies of payroll receipts from the Palomino Bar from 1969. The name on the pay stubs verified the last name of Chuckie to be VanZant.

The interview ended and Miss Thurman returned to Cheboygan.

Stevens and Ford began to research the files of both Armedeo DeRosa and Charles "Chuckie" VanZant.

The first file was that of VanZant. It showed that he had been arrested a number of times for different minor crimes like petty theft, drunk and disorderly, and had a string of speeding tickets, but no felony convictions. It appeared to the detectives that Mr. VanZant, if he was tied to syndicate figures, was extremely lucky in whatever larger crimes he may have committed.

The second file was completely different. It belonged to Armedeo DeRosa. His file showed that he had been arrested on a number of felonies in the Cheboygan area and at the time of the interview with Stevens and Ford, he was under investigation for possession of stolen property. Other information showed that both Mr. DeRosa and Butch Lundy themselves each had ties to the syndicate in Detroit.

There was a special notation in the file that showed that Mr. DeRosa had been an informant with the Detroit Police Department vice squad in the late sixties. The notation indicated that Mr. DeRosa had revealed this same information to an unnamed detective with the Detroit Police Department in 1969. The detective, whose name had been omitted from the confidential report, had met with DeRosa on several occasions while vacationing on Mackinac Island in 1969. At that time, DeRosa had told the detective that maybe he should look into VanZant regarding the Rawlings murders. The detective confirmed to DeRosa that he would do that when he returned to Detroit.

Stevens and Ford could not locate any files or documentation to show that the detective had ever checked the information that he was given by DeRosa.

A feeling of apprehension alerted both Stevens and Ford. They sensed that something wasn't square and that normal police procedures were absent from the notations.

"You realize John, we may have a real can of worms here," Stevens said.

"I think your right Frank. We better call Colonel Darrens about it. I don't think we want to stick our necks out on this one."

"Damn right. If they have something going on in the Detroit Police Department, I think this might be something the Attorney General will have to make a decision on, not us. Let's give the Colonel a call and see how he wants to handle this."

November 15, 1974
10:00 a.m.
State Police Headquarters-East Lansing

Christmas decorations were mounted on buildings and lampposts along Michigan Avenue in downtown East Lansing. The first signs of the holiday season were beginning to show as Stevens and Ford drove through the city and turned down Harrison Road toward the State Police headquarters.

The chill of the November wind swirled around in the parking lot blowing snowdrifts into small piles while plunging the temperature to near zero.

The detectives, covering their faces with their coat lapels to avoid the blistering wind, entered the main building and checked in at the front desk.

A uniformed trooper escorted them upstairs to the reception area outside of Colonel Darren's office. A new secretary sat at the desk.

She was a petite brunette, with brown eyes and a rose colored complexion. She offered the detectives some coffee. They took it and let the cups warm their hands while the fluid warmed their insides. She offered them some cookies and they each took one.

When she had finished, she notified the Colonel that Stevens and Ford had arrived. The Colonel asked her to let them into his office through a newly installed electric lock door.

Stevens and Ford set their coffee cups down on the secretary's desk and walked into the Colonel's office.

"Good morning gentleman" the Colonel said, making his way from around his desk to shake their hands. "Please, be seated." He returned to his large chair as the two detectives settled into chairs across from him.

Stevens spoke first. He informed the Colonel about the new information they had received regarding DeRosa and VanZant and the concerns they had after looking into it a little deeper. Stevens drove the point home that it was possible there may have been a cover-up of the investigation by a detective in the Detroit Police Department.

The detectives believed that maybe their investigation had been compromised from the beginning and that the Rawlings murders could have been a "hit" by the Detroit Mafia.

They told the Colonel that at this stage of the investigation they would not proceed with the information at hand unless he directed them to do so.

As far as they were concerned, the case could be left "open" and that all evidence and information that had been collected would be saved in MSP storage.

The Colonel sat quietly, contemplating the information that was being divulged. Periodically he would glance out his large office window. The snow was falling quite heavily and it was slowly covering the rooftops of the assorted buildings that dotted the university's campus. Finally, he spoke. "I think you two did the right thing by coming here first. This is something I think needs to be discussed with the Attorney General before I can give you an answer. It's been a little over six years since the Rawlings family was murdered and we've compiled a lot of evidence, but nothing concrete enough to determine who did it. The Oakland Prosecutor's office had their grand jury probe shot down because of the Santino suicide. And it doesn't appear that any of the current family members are interested any longer. They probably have accepted that Santino did it and have left it at that."

Stevens and Ford sat quietly, nodding their heads in agreement with the Colonel's evaluation.

Standing and moving away from the desk, the Colonel looked directly at Stevens. "Frank, you always believed that Santino did it or knew who did it, what do you think now?"

Stevens hesitated for a moment then answered. "Yes sir. I thought Santino did it or knew who did it and why. Obviously, when he shot himself, the suicide note and his disclaimer that he did not kill them, I've had to rethink my theory."

"In what way?" The Colonel asked.

Stevens answered directly. "Colonel, Santino's suicide note I think said a lot. I think he took his own life in order to save his family. He may have been next on the hit list; we'll never know that. But with the potential of being called before a grand jury, even if he pleaded the fifth, the syndicate guys would always suspect he might be pressured to turn on them. They may have made him an offer he couldn't refuse. I really believe that he did know who was involved but never was going to tell us."

"So now, you're not so sure, is that it?"

"Yes sir. I hate to admit it, but that's how I see it."

The Colonel looked at Ford, his eyes pleading for a response.

"I'm not sure at all sir. This case is like a maze of dead-ends. We've had a bunch of oddball characters, some of which are just plain rotten people. All of them seem to be connected in a strange sort of way. You have Rawlings, who tries to portray himself as a good family man, while at the same time trying to bed down every one of the females that worked in his office. He writes righteous editorials in his magazine, while at the same time he's trying to steal another man's ideas about a promotional advertising business. Then there is all this talk about making big money, with heavy, financial backers, yet no one ever sees or talks to these people except Rawlings. And finally, when this big deal is supposed to happen, the entire family is wiped out like the Valentine's Day massacre. What clues the killer or killers may have left, have been or were destroyed because of the length of time between the murders and the discovery of the bodies. Plus we have a screwed up crime scene investigation by the sheriff's department and the prosecutor's office there in Petoskey."

The frustration in Ford's voice prompted the Colonel to cut in.

"Okay, I think I get the picture. Let me talk with the Attorney General. I hope that I can meet with him before Thanksgiving, if not, I will get back with you as soon as I can. For now, process any information you have, file it confidentially, but do not, and I repeat, do not have any conversations with the Detroit Police Department, or the Oakland County prosecutor's office, is that understood?"

Both detectives acknowledged that they understood the Colonel's instructions and would sit tight.

The meeting ended at noon.

November 29, 1974
9:00 a.m.
State Police Post-Detroit

The ringing phone cut through the silence of the detective's office as Stevens quickly picked up the receiver. "Stevens."

"Frank, this is Colonel Darrens. What I'm about to say is for both you and Ford. Have him listen in on an extension. I'll be sending a written correspondence to the Post shortly, however I did want to get back with you as soon as I could after talking with the Attorney General."

Stevens motioned for Ford to pick up the extension. They patiently listened as the Colonel continued. "The A.G. has made the decision that we are to leave the case in open status, however for all intents and purposes the case is closed. This department and the A.G.'s office don't see a need at this time to waste department resources on a six-year old murder case, especially under these circumstances. Regardless of how terrible the Rawlings crime was, we have too many other cases that need your attention. Based on that necessity, both the A.G. and I have spoken with the Governor about this and have come to the following conclusion. We are ordering both of you to take a thirty-day paid administrative leave so you can wind down and be ready to come back to work after the first of the year. We want you to disassociate yourselves from the Rawlings case and come back fresh and ready to work on other cases. Is that clear?"

Stevens and Ford, looked at one another across the desk. Both men knew this was the end of the line as far as the Rawlings case was concerned.

Stevens answered the Colonels directive. "Colonel sir. I think that I can speak for both John and I and say thank you. We both appreciate the time off. I know our families will too. If I may Colonel, I do have just one question."

"Go ahead," The Colonel answered.

"Can you tell us about that unknown detective in the Detroit Police Department?"

There was a long silence at the other end of the line before the Colonel responded. "Frank, both the A.G. and I discussed that. What I can tell you is this. The A.G.'s office will deal with that situation. It seems that the FBI has been looking into some activities within the Detroit Police Department since the 1967 and 68' riots, and basically it's a federal matter. That's all I can tell you."

"Thank you Colonel. We really appreciate your confidence in us, and your support. We will process all the information we have and send it up to the Records Division in Lansing."

"I want to personally extend my deepest appreciation to the both of you for what you have done in trying to solve this case. It was an excellent job, with many obstacles to overcome. I'm not sure this one will ever be completely solved. Goodbye gentleman and enjoy your vacations."

The click on the other end of the receiver told the detective's all that they needed to know.

Putting the receiver back in its cradle, Stevens spoke. "You know John, We really can use a vacation."

"Yup," Ford answered.

Looking outside their window at the exhaust fumes, the traffic, the overcast sky and the dismal appearance of a once proud city. Stevens and Ford both realized it was time to move on.

Ford took a drink of coffee from his Styrofoam cup, then, turning to Stevens, he said. "Frank, who do you think would have had the best chance to kill the Rawlings family and walk away?"

Stevens turned away from the window and looked directly into his partner's eyes.

"Looking back on everything now John, my guess is that it was either Lightfoot or Barr. Or maybe both of them."

A slight smile crossed Ford's lips. "Me too."

"Of course, I could be wrong," Stevens answered quickly.

"It's a tough call. We may never know." Ford acknowledged.

CHAPTER 27

Stevens Orchard
September 12, 1999
6:30 p.m.
Ottawa County

Ray Randall sat quietly at the kitchen table before asking Stevens. "Frank, whatever happened to your partner, John Ford?"

"Old John? He retired shortly after I did. Moved to Texas, bought a boat and became a salt-water fishing captain along the Gulf Coast. He died a couple of years ago. I went to his funeral and spoke to his wife and family. She told me that he was always happy with his experiences being with the State Police, but that one case never left his mind."

"I'm sorry to hear that he passed on,." Ray said.

"Thank you, I know he would have appreciated that. He was a good man and a loyal partner and I'll miss him. He used to write or call me at least once a week, always complaining about the heat. But that's life, eh?"

Ray was silent for a moment then resumed his questioning. "Frank, do you still think that Lightfoot or Barr killed Rawlings and his family?"

Randall turned the volume up on the tape recorder in order not to miss the answer.

"As I get older and play it over in my mind, I'm not so sure anymore Ray. The Mafia may have played a role in it, but there is nothing to confirm that either. Lightfoot was shot in 1976. Got in an argument outside a bar in Mackinac City. He pulled a knife on some fellow. The other guy had a gun, plugged him."

"And Barr? What about him?"

"I think it was around Christmas time, 1977. The family had him committed to the asylum up there at Traverse City. The same one his mother was in. The story I've heard is that before his family put him in the hospital, he would leave his house in the middle of the night and drive around the cemetery where his son was buried. The neighbors said he was yelling out Indian war chants or something like that. He would raise all kinds of hell in the middle of the night. Some people even claim they heard him yelling, 'I killed them all, I killed them all,' but nothing ever came of it."

"Is he still in the mental hospital?"

"No. I think it was on New Year's Eve of 1978. He walked away from the hospital directly out on the ice in Traverse Bay and fell through. Some beachcombers found his body in the spring. Washed up on shore. Tragic."

"Can you remember what happened to some of the others?"

"No, not too many of them. Many of the people who owned those Barr cottages sold them to people from Chicago, Detroit and other parts. The new people tore down the small cottages and built big summer homes. I'm not sure if there are many of the Barr-style cottages left."

"Anyone else?"

"Yeah, the Oliver brothers. They finally got their wish. Both are in Jackson Prison, serving life for shooting a bank guard in Detroit. They tried robbing the place and screwed it up. There was a big shoot-out. In fact, the Hooper kid was with them. He was the driver of the getaway car. When the shooting started, he took off, left the Oliver boys behind. Too bad he ran a red light. Semi truck broad sided him and killed him instantly."

"What about that VanZant and the DeRosa fellows?"

"Small potatoes. DeRosa is serving time up at Marquette Prison. VanZant is still on the loose somewhere. Funny, after all that time, the state didn't care about tracking him down. He sounded like a prime suspect to me. If he was as bad as that Dee-Dee said he was, he's probably dead by now. Those guys don't last long in that business."

Ray Randall looked straight into Stevens' eyes trying to elicit some deep personal thought about the case from him. Stevens sensed it.

"Look Ray, for a long time I was certain that Santino did it. I just couldn't figure out how. But now, I think my partner was right. If the Mafia wanted Rawlings taken out, I think they would have done it different. They would've roughed up Rawlings a couple of times before whacking him. Dead men don't repay debts. In fact, if they had decided to take him out, why waste an opportunity not to make Rawlings an example. They would've killed him in Detroit and let the police find the body so it would be reported."

There was a pause as Randall replaced a tape in the recorder, then hit the start button.

Stevens continued. "Now, if I owed the Mafia money that would make me think twice about paying up. A residual effect, if you get my drift."

"I guess your right," Ray said, obviously hoping for a more startling revelation.

"Damn right, I am right. Besides, if you take a look at where the cottage was located, who in their right mind would have tried to commit a crime like that. It's too damn dangerous even for the most professional of assassins. No. Whoever killed the Rawlings family knew a lot about the area. They knew the surroundings, the terrain and were able to conceal whatever evidence there was. The murder weapon is probably at the bottom of Lake Michigan."

"That would take us back to Lightfoot or Monty Barr then, right?"

"Most likely, neither one liked Rawlings. I think Monty Barr resented the fact that Rawlings wouldn't let his boys associate with his son. Personally, I think Barr felt threatened by Rawlings. Who knows the reason? John and I were never able to figure it out. Then, that tragic accident that killed Barr's son, Billy, may have been enough to upset Barr or made Lightfoot mad enough to do it for his boss. There were just a lot of things that my partner and I could never piece together. Maybe they'll find out someday."

"You think they can Frank?" Ray asked.

"Sure, with today's technology, murder profiling and all that new forensic science stuff, it might be possible that some of the evidence that's still in storage could be used to trace the murderer."

"Specifically?" Ray asked.

"They found a few pubic hairs on Mrs. Rawlings. Today, with DNA testing, they might be able to match it with Santino, Lightfoot, Barr or some of the others. Alive or dead, they can do so much more today."

" But would the families let it happen?"

"Depends on how forceful and tactful the Attorney General is about it. Personally, I don't think it will happen, but you never know. It's been such a long time. No one likes to dig up old misery."

"Is there one thing about the case Frank that you regret or still wonder about?"

"I think there are a lot of things. Especially when you don't have an arrest or conviction with a case you've been working on. What I regret the most is not getting Santino to come clean. There are a few things I still wonder about. Whatever happened to that Roberts or Robiere fellow that was supposed to pick up the Rawlings family? We never found him. Did he ever show up? Was there ever such a person? Did Barr tell him the Rawlings family left? Was he the one who wiped out the Rawlings family and got away? That I don't think we'll ever find out."

"Anything else?" Ray asked.

"Yes. That nametag that was found in the Hooper car, that one drives me nuts. Could the Oliver brothers have been involved? Did they know Santino or Rawlings? I don't know. And finally, I keep thinking that if someone in that cottage had decided to run out the back door, would there have been someone waiting to kill them, which means more than one person would have been involved. If no one was there, they may have escaped to tell us the rest of the story."

"A real interesting case all the way around." Ray answered.

"Always was and probably always will be Ray. Six people are massacred and no one knows who did it. I can't believe it and I was involved with it for the major part of my career with the State Police."

"That's a very interesting thought Frank. Maybe if my editor will let me write this story in a series format, it might generate enough interest so that the Attorney General will take another look at the case."

"I can tell your mind is working overtime Ray."

"Yes it is. But it will have to wait. Right now, I want to thank you for your cooperation and for allowing me to be able to hear and record the story from your own personal experience. I hope my editor thinks it was worth my time and gives me the opportunity to print it."

"Don't worry Ray. When this big shot editor of yours finishes reading it, he'll put it on the front page," Stevens said with a large smile on his face.

Both men walked back outside to the porch. They shook hands. Stevens gently sat himself into his rocker on the porch as he watched Ray Randall walk to his car.

Ray opened the door and unloaded the numerous tape cassettes from his pockets into a leather bag on the front seat.

Twilight was easing its way across the fall sky as Ray started the motor and rolled down the window of his car. He shouted out to Stevens. "It would make a great mystery novel or movie Frank."

"Yup," Stevens said as he watched the reporter drive slowly along the gravel driveway to the main road. His eyes followed the vehicle as it eased out onto the two-lane blacktop highway and watched until the taillights had faded in the distance.

"Another Sherlock Holmes who thinks he's going to solve this case," Frank Stevens thought. He just shook his head and nodded off to sleep.

29239272R00184